Books by Donna Anders:

THE FLOWER MAN
ANOTHER LIFE
DEAD SILENCE
IN ALL THE WRONG PLACES
NIGHT STALKER

Published by POCKET BOOKS

DONNA ANDERS

AFRAID

OF THE

DARK

POCKET BOOKS
New York   London   Toronto   Sydney

This book is a work of fiction. Names, characters, places and
incidents are products of the author's imagination or are used
fictitiously. Any resemblance to actual events or locales or persons,
living or dead, is entirely coincidental.

An *Original* Publication of POCKET BOOKS

POCKET BOOKS, a division of Simon & Schuster, Inc.
1230 Avenue of the Americas, New York, NY 10020

ISBN: 0-7434-2731-9

First Pocket Books printing December 2004

10 9 8 7 6 5 4 3 2 1

POCKET and colophon are registered trademarks of
Simon & Schuster, Inc.

Front cover background image © Daryl Benson/Masterfile
Running Woman photographed by Michael Frost/Model:
Krista Coyle/Recich New York

Manufactured in the United States of America

For information regarding special discounts for bulk purchases,
please contact Simon & Schuster Special Sales at 1-800-456-6798 or
business@simonandschuster.com

For Ruth, Lisa, Tina, again and always

ACKNOWLEDGMENTS

For their inspiration, encouragement, and professional support during the writing of this book, I am indebted to Ruth and Greg Aeschliman, Lisa and Bryan Pearce, Tina Abeel, Ann Rule, Leslie Rule, Mike Rule, Marnie Campbell, Meg Chittenden, and too many others to list. Special thanks to Lieutenant Denise Glentoli of the Bainbridge Island Police Department for her expert advice, and to her fellow officers who also kindly shared their expertise with me.

And again, a very sincere thanks to Amy Pierpont, my talented editor at Pocket Books, and her assistant, Megan McKeever. Also to Sheree Bykofsky, my agent, and her assistant, Megan Buckley.

PROLOGUE

THE LITTLE GIRL CURLED UP IN THE OVERSTUFFED CHAIR BY the fireplace in her mother's bedroom, her eyelids drooping. She was too sleepy to continue wondering about why she was there and not in her own bed. She tried to be brave.

But she was frightened.

The wind outside blasted across the open water of the Strait of Juan de Fuca to their house on the cliff, rattling the shake shingles on the roof like a clown with a deck of cards, and gusting pine needles against the windows like tapping fingernails. The child shivered, and hoped it would not find a way inside.

Tsonoqua was mad, and that scared her even more. She remembered her grandmother's stories, and she didn't want the Wind Spirit to get her.

Time seemed endless to the girl. She wondered if morning was close. Then she heard the clock in the lower hall strike the hour.

It was only midnight.

The gongs drifted away into the silence, and her mom stood up from the opposite chair. "It's time to go, sweetie." Her mother spoke in a whisper as she helped the girl into a hooded jacket and rubber boots.

"Go?" The child trembled. "Go where, Mom?"

"We're going to have an adventure—but we must be very quiet." Her smile was meant to reassure. "It wouldn't be nice of us to wake up the house just because we're still awake, would it?"

The girl shook her head and an unruly curl slipped over one eye. Her mom smiled and gently tucked it back under the hood she'd just adjusted over the child's hair. The girl felt the tremor in her mom's hand.

Her mother was afraid.

The house around them creaked and shuddered under the onslaught of the late fall storm, and the child started to ask why they were dressed to go outside. Before she could speak her mother motioned her to silence.

"Shh," she whispered, and then remembered to smile. "We must be very quiet—right?"

But her attempt at reassurance only frightened the child more, even though she nodded again. Something was wrong.

But what?

And then her mother took her hand and led her out into the hall to lead her to the wide staircase that divided the house. "Shh," she cautioned again with another smile.

At the bottom they hesitated, as her mother seemed to be listening. An icy cold had settled over the entry hall but outside the storm still raged against the house. The girl squirmed against her mother's grip but in seconds they'd moved forward to the front door. Her mom eased it open, pausing again to listen, as though she feared that someone would stop their flight. Once they stepped onto the wide stone porch and she closed the door softly behind them, she was running again, pulling the child after her, urging the girl to keep up, that they would soon be able to rest.

The rain slashed into the girl's face, blending with her sudden tears, while the wind swooped to nudge them down the driveway. A flash of lightning startled her into a burst of speed, and then she tripped and fell on the inlaid stones. Instantly, her mom stopped to help her.

But the girl's eyes that were turned upward had already fastened on the totem pole at the bottom of the driveway, the carved figure that had significance to her father's Indian heritage.

Tsonoqua.

The mythical being stood where it had always stood, the symbol of the family, the namesake of the house. Tsonoqua, the Indian spirit of the wind, female monster of the forest who stole children.

More lightning danced below the clouds, touching the carved face with a moment of life. The electrified air currents jolted the child's nervous system; it was almost as if the wide O of the mouth had breathed—was about to speak—to urge her to hurry away or—or what?

The girl began to cry in earnest. Her mother stooped to see to her skinned knees under the torn corduroy pants.

"It's okay, sweetie. I know it smarts but I have Band-Aids in the boat. I'll fix up those skinned knees in a jiffy once we get to the boat."

The child looked up through her tears. "Boat?"

"That's part of our adventure, sweetie." In the darkness the girl could still sense her mother's sincerity—her absolute resolve to get to the boat. "And there will be ice cream, your favorite candy and pop, and a wonderful future for both of us."

"F . . . future?"

"Uh-huh. I promise, sweetie. Just be strong now and everything will be just as I say—okay?"

The child nodded and got up.

And then they were running again, headed for the spiral stairs that hung down the cliff to the beach. Once there, the child clung to her mom as they descended the iron structure, realizing a sudden movement could tip their balance and throw them into the black abyss below.

The wind strengthened, then gusted away leaving a lull, as though protecting them, enabling them to move more quickly down the steps. Finally at the bottom, her mom pulled her over the short jetty to the dock where they paused to catch their breath.

The child glanced back, upward to the dark house outlined against the mood of the night, perched on the cliff like an eagle's aerie in a high fir tree.

Suddenly a light snapped on in the tower room, jolting her thoughts back to herself and her mom on the dock. She saw that her mom noticed, too. A figure moved around on the widow's walk, as though searching the grounds and the strait. Had someone realized they were gone?

Abruptly, her mom helped her into the small motorboat that bobbed against the pilings, straining at its moorings. In seconds they were untied from the dock, the engine started and her mom was steering them away from the island, headed out into the turbulent Strait of Juan de Fuca.

Her teeth chattering from fear and the cold, the child was unable to voice her terror. Her mom was afraid of boats, even in summer when the water was flat and serene. Now, in the midst of a storm her mother had taken command of a motorboat, the way the girl's dad always had in the past.

Her dad.

He was dead. He couldn't help them now.

As the motor droned them out to sea, the bow pounding the waves and then dropping into sudden troughs, the child's fear became acceptance, even as she was terrified. She and her mom would drown, too—like her dad.

Another boat suddenly appeared as though it had been spit up from the depths. Frantically, her mother manipulated the waves for a position alongside while the lone occupant of the larger craft secured the connection.

The child glanced at the person under the slicker and hat that glistened from the rain. Mutely, the figure held out its arms for her, as the boats crashed against each other with an alarming gnashing of boards and scraped paint. The wind screamed and whistled, and in the distance she could see the timeworn precipices of the island that loomed like faceless ghosts above the sea.

The child hesitated.

Was it a man or a woman? She couldn't tell. But she was afraid to let the figure take her away from her mom.

"It's all right," her mother said in her ear above the howling wind. "I'm right behind you. You'll be safe."

Before the child had time to question anything, the person on the other boat grabbed her and pulled her aboard. In seconds her mom joined her.

The person in the rain gear let her go to loosen the line to their speedboat. In seconds it was swallowed into the swells that were higher than they were.

The child watched, horrified. "Grandma will think we drowned," she cried.

"No, she'll only know that we're off on our adventure," her mom shouted back. "She'll know that we're okay."

But the child was unconvinced as her mother carried her down to the tiny cabin where there was a berth. Once she'd lain down her mother saw to her skinned knees, dabbing them with antiseptic before covering the wounds with a Band-Aid.

As the boat moved even farther away from the house on the cliff, the little girl finally drifted off toward sleep, lulled by the steady sound of the engine.

But vaguely, almost as though it was a dream, she heard her mother giving thanks for them having gotten away from the House of Tsonoqua.

"We'll start a new life," her mother said, "safe from Tsonoqua and all the others who can harm us. We'll forget."

Tsonoqua? the child wondered sleepily. Who were the others? And what would she forget?

She opened her eyes to the porthole that was suddenly illuminated by the boat's running lights. Beyond the round opening she watched the strange patterns on the water rushing past the boards.

But somehow the girl knew she wouldn't forget, that whatever she needed to remember would not let go of her.

Nor would Tsonoqua or the other Great Spirits who silently reigned over their chosen islands—the place where she'd been born, where her father had lived . . . and died.

And then she slept.

CHAPTER ONE

JESSIE CLINE SLOWED THE PATROL CAR, BRINGING IT TO A stop in front of an early nineteen hundreds row house that was typical to the Sunset area of San Francisco. It was the address where the call for help had originated. She was about to follow her partner, Matt Spence, out of the police cruiser into the foggy late afternoon when the dispatcher's voice crackled over the radio, stopping her.

"Possible gunfire reported at your location."

"Copy that," Jessie said, responding immediately to the transmission. Then she stepped out to the street and unsnapped her holster. Matt's revolver was already in his hand. Another domestic dispute turned deadly? she wondered. Jessie hoped not. But they had to be ready—just in case.

Damn, she thought, glancing at the nearby draped and shuttered houses. She had a bad feeling. It was too quiet, too spooky. Something had scared the neighbors into lying low, out of the line of possible fire. There wasn't a person in sight anywhere, not even the one who'd made the call.

Upon reaching the porch steps, Matt continued up to the door while Jessie headed for the narrow walkway between houses that led to the back. She moved cautiously, her body edging along the side of the building, alert for whatever awaited her in the fenced backyard.

It was an anticlimax. The tiny enclosed patio was an unexpected oasis behind the drab house. It was a miniature paradise of multicolored flowers and overgrown evergreen shrubs, a fountain and a small table with two chairs, all positioned with the perfect balance of an artist about to paint a still life. The drapes on the French doors were closed so that she couldn't see into the residence itself. All was quiet except for the tinkle of water in the fountain.

Surreal, she thought. The brilliant blossoms were subdued by the thickening fog, and the line of cookie-cutter backyards were obscured by high fences. It was like no one existed on the planet, let alone in the Sunset area of San Francisco.

An icy finger seemed to touch her spine.

Jessie quickly checked out the backyard, her senses alert to the shuttered windows. She went to the backdoor and turned the knob. It was unlocked.

And then it suddenly opened to frame Matt in the doorway. "The front door was open but no one is here—except a dead woman," he said, shaking his head. "She's badly beaten and has multiple stab wounds, but death appears to be strangulation. The coroner will make the determination. Backup is on the way."

She nodded, realizing her partner was shaken by what he'd seen. "Everything secure out here," she said.

As in the past she'd wondered why Matt had become a policeman and not a lawyer. His interest was law enforcement but he seemed too sensitive for the grizzly reality of viewing violent death up close and personal.

Like her.

She hated the inhumanity-to-man aspect, the disregard for life. But she knew why Matt wasn't a lawyer and she wasn't an artist, as she'd originally planned. They both needed a steady income. She, like him, had a family to support and monthly bills to pay. And there was never anything left over to pursue dreams that cost money.

He nodded. "Okay. Go on back around to the front and wait for the backup. I'll make sure everything stays secure in the house."

She lifted a hand, acknowledging his request. He closed the door, and the drapes waved in the sudden draft, settling back over the windows. Jessie started toward the corner of the house, the only way out of a backyard that was enclosed by eight-foot fencing.

She'd just entered the narrow corridor between the houses when she caught a sudden movement out of the corner of her eye.

Before she could react it was too late. Someone had an arm around her neck, yanking her backward, someone who must have been hidden in the fog behind an overgrown shrub.

She managed to scream.

"Bitch!"

The man's word was muttered into her ear. Then her air was squeezed off as the arm tightened brutally on her neck. She struggled to raise her gun but a chop to her wrist dropped it from her hand. She was helplessly overcome by a superior strength. Her last thought was of her son, Danny. What would become of him if she weren't there to take care of him?

Jessie felt herself falling as the fog seemed to close in around her, shutting off her mind. She didn't even feel herself hit the sidewalk.

CHAPTER TWO

By the time Jessie went off duty, switched to her own car and headed for the Oakland Bay Bridge on her way home, she almost felt like her old self. Although still shaken from her encounter with the suspected murderer of the woman in the house, she'd revived almost immediately once Matt had pulled the man off her.

She'd been lucky. If her partner had been five seconds later she would be on her way to the morgue now, instead of driving home.

And—dear God! What would have become of Danny if she'd died? Her worst fear was not to be there as her son grew up, not to be the person who influenced his growth in becoming a man. There was no one else to raise him, except her bohemian mother who was in her sixties and could hardly take care of herself.

Her son. She was his only parent, her mother his only grandparent. Danny's own father didn't recognize Danny as his. Old anger surfaced and Jessie forced it back. One day he might change his mind—after it was too late. For now she needed to stay alive, be there for a great kid until he became the terrific adult she knew he could be.

"Father in heaven," she muttered into the quiet of her '98 Saturn Coupe, knowing her thoughts were going in circles, that she was still pretty shook up. "Please keep me alive to raise my child."

Because there is no one else, she added silently. Her own mother was a struggling artist who lived in Mendocino, a town on the rugged northern California coast. Although a loving grandmother and emotionally supportive to Jessie, Clarice lived on Social Security and could ill afford the financial liability of raising a child. Jessie's dad was long dead.

I must stay alive for Danny, Jessie thought again, knowing she was still obsessing about her close call. It was time she pulled herself together, before she got home.

She passed the Berkeley exits, headed toward Oakland where she veered off onto her ramp and waited at a light to make the turn toward home. Jessie realized she had some tough decisions to make. Tonight had only brought them to the top of her mind, not allowing her to procrastinate—again. If she were to be alive long enough to raise Danny, then she needed to reconsider her career, and their home environment in an area where street gangs were claiming territory.

She turned from a main drag of strip malls and fast food restaurants onto her own street, one congested with old model parked cars in front of rundown pre–World War II identical houses. The one in the middle of the block with cut and trimmed grass, and geraniums and petunias in the flowerbeds, was hers. It stood out because all the other yards were overgrown and strewn with debris.

She had been saving, little by little, so they could move to a better location. But what if she died before she could see to her son having a better life? And what if he was sucked into a gang before she could afford their move?

Stay focused, she instructed herself. Just because she'd been accosted while on the job didn't mean the whole world was falling apart. Wasn't dealing with criminals just a part of being in law enforcement?

It was, she reminded herself. But she also needed to consider her own son who was under increasing pressure by gang members to make a stand in a neighborhood inhabited by druggies, thieves and burglars.

His life must not be influenced by such choices.

Not if she had any say in the matter.

But what were her choices? She had to make a living. Where else could she go to do that? It was a dilemma that had reared its ugly head in that tiny backyard.

She drove slowly toward her house, and then stomped on the brakes before turning into the overgrown driveway that led to the carport.

There was a small group of boys blocking her way.

Several of them were pushing against her son and were obviously threatening him. Although Danny was tall for his age, he was no match against the husky boys who were bullying him. And he was outnumbered. She jumped out of her car, shouting at them.

"Police officer! Back off—now!"

The boys saw her uniform and quickly dispersed, running off down the street. The ringleader hesitated a moment longer, giving Danny a final shove as he said something Jessie couldn't hear, and then with a malevolent glance, ran after his gang.

"Fuckin' bitch!" he yelled over his shoulder. "You can't save him or your fuckin' guard dog."

And then the juvenile thugs were gone, leaving her son alone on the front lawn by the time she reached him, his year-old Bernese mountain dog barking furiously behind the front door of their house.

"Thanks, Mom," Danny said, his voice shaking, his body trembling. His clothing was rumpled and torn, and his eyes, bright with tears, darted from her to the street where the gang had disappeared. "You saved me for the moment, but you cemented my fate—and Footer's. They hate my dog 'cause he's so big and they're scared of him."

"Fate?"

"Uh-huh." His voice still wobbled and tears glistened in his eyes, even as he tried to sound brave. "These guys aren't intimated by a badge, Mom." He swallowed hard. "Sticking up for me only made them madder and now they'll really be out to get me." He lowered his dark lashes over the fear in his brown eyes. "They'll wait their chance and if not tomorrow, then next week or next month." He hesitated, trying to control his tears. "I'm glad Footers was inside. They would have hurt him, too."

"I won't let that happen, Danny—to you or Footers." She pulled him into her arms. "I'll contact your school, let them know what's happened, okay?"

He hesitated, looking about to cry in earnest. "That won't help, Mom. School rules can't protect me. They'll get me, sooner or later. I have to be with them—or become their target." He sounded scared to death.

"Target?" She tried to control her concern.

"Uh-huh." His lower lip trembled, and she could see how hard he was trying to compose himself.

She knew what he meant although she downplayed the situation as he explained on their way into the house. They were the kids who ruled the neighborhood, their street. "I'll have to do what they say or they'll come after me," Danny explained. His words chilled her to the bone.

With contrived cheerfulness, Jessie made small talk, trying to allay his fear, although she recognized that what he said was true. Her precious child was in danger—and she needed to address that issue, somehow make sure that he stayed safe. But how could she do that?

Juvenile gangs were lethal. And they'd targeted Danny simply because he lived in their territory. She'd encountered the scenario many times on the job. Her son was in real danger unless she could protect him.

Her thoughts whirled as she saw him to their tiny living room where he sat down to watch television while she went to the kitchen to prepare supper. After taking frozen spaghetti sauce from the freezer to the microwave and putting water on the stove to heat for the pasta, Jessie checked on Danny again. Seeing that he was absorbed in a sitcom rerun, she went out to their front porch for the mail. Among the bills was a legal-looking letter from an attorney's office in Seattle, Washington.

Curious, she nevertheless went back to the kitchen before opening the envelope. As she read the covering letter, Jessie sagged against the counter behind her. Was this an answer to her prayers? An unexpected intervention?

The letter stated that she'd inherited a house—on the island where she'd been born—where her mother had fled with her after her father's death when she was a child.

Her mother. She needed to call her mother. Her mom would know what the letter meant. Her mom could explain.

She made sure that Danny was still watching his show, and then, unable to contain herself, Jessie picked up the phone and called her mother in Mendocino, waiting as it rang on the other end, hoping her mom was home.

"Hello." Her mother's melodious voice came over the wire.

"Mom, can you talk?" Jessie could hear oldies music and a low hum of voices in the background.

"Course I can for you, sweetie."

Jessie shifted position, bracing herself. It was her mother's "back to basics" night. She'd forgotten her mom's one-night-a-week class for fledgling artists, part of her monthly income aside from Social Security and the occasional sale of a painting.

"I forgot it was your class," Jessie began.

"No, that's okay." A pause. "What's up? I can tell something is wrong, Jessie."

"I had a letter from a lawyer up in Seattle. Seems I just inherited a house up in the San Juan Islands. My father's uncle died and I'm the only living descendant."

Jessie's words were met by a brief silence.

"Oh, my God!" Her mother's indrawn breath came over the line before her next words. "Look Jessie, I can't talk now. Let me call you back after my students leave, okay?"

"Of course. In fact, I'll call you back after Danny's in bed. There's another issue I want to discuss with you and I don't want him to hear."

"I'll wait for your call, Jessie."

"Love you, Mom."

"Love you, too."

The dial tone sounded in Jessie's ear, but not before she'd heard the fear in her mother's voice.

What did it mean? Why had her news upset her mother? She'd have to wait to find out.

She went back to preparing their meal, and despite her mother's negative reaction, couldn't help but feel uplifted. A house meant money. She could either sell it or live in it. Either way, it meant a way out of their neighborhood.

Nothing her mother would say could cloud the issue. One way or the other she and Danny were moving.

CHAPTER THREE

"MOM?" JESSIE SAID INTO THE RECEIVER.

"Yeah, it's me, Honey. I was waiting for your call."

"I'm sorry it got so late. I wanted Danny to be asleep when we talked."

"You didn't want him to overhear?"

"No, I didn't."

"Good. He shouldn't get his hopes up about an impossible situation."

"Impossible?"

There was a silence.

"Uh-huh." Her mother's sigh came over the wires. "Of course I know you would never consider moving up to that remote island, even if you have inherited a house." Another pause. "You can sell it and move to a better location in San Francisco."

This time Jessie hesitated. She'd reread the letter many times, and had decided to defer any course of action until she'd spoken to the lawyer handling the estate. The attorney, Leonard Wills, had asked her to call as soon as possible, that he'd been unable to get her unlisted number.

"That is what you'll do, isn't it Jessie?"

"I don't know, Mom." Jessie shifted the phone to her other ear so that she would hear if Danny got up. "While Danny was doing his homework, I checked out this Cliff

Island up in Washington State on the Internet." She hesitated. "Seems there's a vacancy for assistant police chief, and they're taking applications." She gave a laugh. "The pay isn't great, it's only a three-person force, but the added benefits of no house payments, a cheaper lifestyle away from druggies and gangs, and a good school system are enticing."

Clarice's gasp sounded in Jessie's ear. "Surely you aren't thinking of—of moving up there?"

"I'm only saying that I'm looking into my options at the moment."

"That's not an option, Jessie."

"Why not?" Before her mother could answer Jessie explained what had happened earlier, that she could have been killed, that Danny was in danger from the gangs that had moved into their neighborhood. The letter concerning her inheritance seemed like an answer to her prayers.

"But like I said, Jessie, you can sell the Cliff Island house, and then use the proceeds to buy another place in a safer neighborhood."

"I know that, Mom." A pause. "But that still doesn't change the danger of my job."

A long silence stretched over the miles between them. Clarice was the first to break it.

"I have a better plan," she said with contrived calm. "Sell the island house you've inherited, quit that damned job that I've hated from the beginning, move up here and stay with me until you get settled. You could get a part-time job, Danny would be safe and you could take up your brushes again." A pause. "You do have a little equity in your Oakland house, don't you?"

"Yeah, if I get a decent price."

"The sale of the island house would give you the

means to relocate up here. Then you could put the Oakland equity into a college fund for Danny."

Jessie's thoughts spun. Her mother's suggestion was good, so long as she could sell both places, and if she could really generate enough income from her art to support them. Otherwise there would be no college fund; they'd have to use that money to live on because she no longer had a profession. Her mom was a dreamer who believed the future would take care of itself. While she was a realist who knew nothing happened without a lot of planning and hard work. Jessie also knew that she was too independent to live with her mom for long. Besides, Clarice was allergic to dogs and an attack of asthma could send her to the hospital. And Danny wasn't about to give up Footers.

"Tell you what," she said finally. "I'll call you as soon as I talk to the lawyer in the morning, find out exactly how much the place is worth and how long it takes to sell a house on a remote island."

"Please do, Jessie." Her sigh came over the line. "I'll be on pins and needles until I hear."

"I promise." Jessie hesitated. "Tell me, Mom, why are you so emphatic about me not moving to Cliff Island? You once lived there with Dad and I thought you were happily married, that you loved the rugged beauty of the cliffs and beaches, that you called it paradise. Were you lying?"

"No, I did love it, until your father died." A pause. "After that everything changed."

"How so? You've never explained and I've often wondered."

Clarice's reply was a long quivering sigh.

"Mom, are you there?"

"Of course I am Sweetheart. I don't want you to go back to that island. It may not be safe for you."

"Why, Mom? As I just said, you've never really explained why we left after Dad died."

"I will, after you talk to that lawyer fellow." She drew a sharp breath. "You will call me after you do?"

"Certainly. I said I would." Jessie tried to keep an irritated note out of her tone. Her mother was being dramatic again, a typical artistic temperament, she thought. As she hung up she wondered if that was why she'd never made much headway with her own art. Maybe she was too much of a realist and not enough of a dreamer.

She looked in on Danny who was sound asleep, dropped a light kiss on his forehead, and then headed for her own room across the hall. Once in bed Jessie stared at the leaf patterns on her ceiling, her thoughts swirling with possibilities. At least now she had an option to change their lives. That was the first positive thing that had happened to her in a long time.

She thought about her mother's reservations, and realized again that she had no clue as to where those fears came from. Her mother had always been closemouthed about the past, even as she'd always praised her husband, a man who'd been a quarter Native American and grown up on Cliff Island. Her father's ancestors had been part of the Pacific Rim totem tribes, their culture far advanced from the early explorers who'd once conquered them. The one thing Jessie did know was that the family house, the oldest on the island, was guarded by the family totem pole of Tsonoqua, the spirit of the wind.

She was suddenly chilled under the top sheet and pulled up her down quilt. I won't think about the negatives, she thought. Only the positive. Tomorrow she'd find out which was which.

*   *   *

Jessie waited until Danny had caught his ride to the youth basketball session a couple of miles away at the YMCA gym. Then she placed her call to Leonard Wills in Cliffside, the town on Cliff Island in the San Juan Islands. The lawyer himself picked up the phone, surprising her.

"This is Jessica Cline," she told him. "You sent me a letter concerning—"

"Yes, I know who you are, Ms. Cline," he said crisply. "You're responding to my letter about the property you've inherited."

"That's correct," she said, her tone going from friendly to businesslike. He was obviously not responsive to idle chatter. "I have some questions. Needless to say, your letter took me by surprise."

"How so?"

She was taken aback. "I had no idea I was in line to inherit the family house."

"Hmm, I expected you knew that, Ms. Cline." He paused. "But there are several conditions attached to the will."

"Such as?"

"You must occupy the house for a full year before it officially becomes yours. Although your great uncle passed away after your grandmother, Caroline McGregor's will still takes precedence on that issue." He cleared his throat. "It was her way of making sure her lineage continued in the house she loved."

Jessie was momentarily silent. She'd realized her grandmother's will had changed after her father's death, and the death of her great uncle's son, and that the estate had reverted to her great uncle. The one thing she didn't expect was to be the one to inherit the property.

"Are you still on the line, Ms. Cline?"

"Yes, I'm here, just thinking about the terms. You're

saying that I must live there for one year before the house is mine? After that I could sell it if I wished to?"

"That's it in a nutshell. If you don't live there, it will be tantamount to relinquishing all rights to the property, and it will revert to charity."

"And do properties sell very fast on the island, Mr. Wills?"

"Yes, I'm afraid that they do."

"Afraid?"

"Uh-huh. We locals don't like the California people who come up here looking to buy up choice land for peanuts—and unfortunately, that's what usually happens."

She looked out of her kitchen window to the tiny backyard where a hummingbird was sucking from the feeder Danny had filled only that morning. What the lawyer's words meant to her was that she couldn't sell the island house for one year, which meant if she stayed put and turned down the inheritance, she and Danny had no real hope for changing their future prospects.

"Tell me about the will," she asked. "I need to know everything that's involved here."

The lawyer filled in a few minor points and then they hung up after agreeing to talk again in the near future.

But she already knew what she had to do. There was no real choice, not if Danny was to have the future she'd always intended him to have.

A short time later, facts in hand, she switched on her computer, going again to the Cliff Island page that advertised for an assistant police chief. As she downloaded the information, Jessie knew her mother was waiting for her call.

She braced herself. Her mom would not like what she was about to tell her.

* * *

"Jessica Cline, please." The male voice was low, deep and professional sounding.

"May I ask who's calling?" Jessie shifted the receiver to her left hand, because her right one was caked with dirt from weeding the front flowerbed. She'd barely caught the phone before it went to voice mail.

"Hank Shepherd, Chief of Police for Cliff Island."

She plopped down on a kitchen stool, taken aback that she'd have gotten a reply from her faxed application a day after she'd sent it. "This is Jessica Cline," she said, grateful that her response reflected her own professional tone.

"You applied for the assistant chief's job here on Cliff Island in Washington State?"

"Yes, I did. Yesterday in fact."

"But you work for the San Francisco Police Department at this time?" His expelled breath sounded in her ear. "Why would you quit that job for this one?"

"I explained that in my faxed resume."

"Explain again, if you don't mind."

Jessie started with her positive feelings about her current job, how much she cared about the people she worked with, that she'd been dedicated for all the years she'd been with the department, but that she had concerns about her son and their living environment.

"Could you explain that?" Hank Shepherd asked.

She decided to be completely honest. If they were to live and work in a small community there would be no place for evading questions.

"As you probably know, I inherited a house on your island. But my main reason for moving there is my son." She briefly explained their situation and her concerns. "I want my son to have a future beyond being a latchkey kid in a marginal neighborhood where gangs are demanding allegiance, or else." Jessie drew in a breath. "Sadly, our neighborhood is all I can afford on my salary and I see a better life for Danny on your island."

"Thank you for being candid, Ms. Cline. I've spoken to the people on your reference list and they all speak highly of you." She heard a low chuckle. "I think your superior hopes you'll reconsider and stay in San Francisco."

"You work fast, Chief Shepherd, considering you've had my application for less than a day."

"That's true. Guess we don't get many applicants with your credentials way up here." A pause. "So do you think there's a chance you'll reconsider?"

"What? You mean stay in my present position?"

"Uh-huh."

"I can't do that, regardless of whether or not I get the job on your island."

"How so?"

"I have to place my son's security above career advancement." She took a deep breath and went on. "But if you can't understand that Chief Shepherd, I understand. I'll say right up front that my child is my first priority. My job is second."

"My feelings exactly," was his surprising response.

She hesitated, uncertain of how to respond.

"Your job references are impeccable. You're almost too good to be true, Ms. Cline."

"Jessica," she corrected him.

He cleared his throat. "Uh, yes, Jessica. The job is yours if you agree to our requirements, and I think you'll fit all of them if you're planning to live on the island."

"I have the job?"

"Yeah, that's about it."

"I accept."

They discussed the job description further, the date when she'd be able to start, and then went on to talking about her move to the island.

"I look forward to meeting you," Hank Shepherd said.

"And I you," Jessie replied.

And then they hung up.

As he'd learned when he'd checked her work references, she'd already resigned from her position, and here she was accepting another one that could change her life completely. Was she ready for that?

She had to be. But she suddenly felt shaky, as though she'd just run a marathon. Then her mind flashed to her reasons behind such a drastic decision: almost being murdered on the job, fear of leaving Danny an orphan, then coming home to him in danger from street thugs. The realization that they were locked in a hopeless future had been the last straw.

The letter was fate, their way out of a desperate lifestyle.

It meant her future and that of her son. Jessie knew there was no other choice.

CHAPTER FOUR

"I HAVE A BAD FEELING ABOUT THIS, JESSIE. I WISH I COULD change your mind about going, inheritance or not."

Her mother's final words stayed in Jessie's thoughts as she drove up the California coast from Mendocino, and then headed for Portland, Oregon, and on to Seattle on Puget Sound. Hoping to calm her mom's apprehension, she and Danny had stopped for a short visit on their way north to Cliff Island in the Strait of Juan de Fuca. But her mom had stayed adamant. Jessie was making a mistake.

Now, as she drove into the ferry line at Anacortes after a ninety-minute ride north from Seattle, she had a sudden jolt of fear. What if her mother was right? Everything had happened so fast once she'd applied for the assistant chief position on the island. There'd been no time for hesitation. One decision seemed to depend on another: decide if she could accept the island house, and when she did she needed a job after resigning her San Francisco position, and when it was offered and she took it, she needed to withdraw Danny from his school and list her Oakland house with a realtor.

No, she reminded herself. Inheriting a house was an answer to her worries. Then getting the island job ce-

mented her belief that she'd done the right thing. Danny
would grow up in a wonderful environment and the proceeds from their Oakland house would guarantee him a
college education. Even Footers was better off away from
the city.

Waiting their turn at the toll booth to buy their ferry
passage to Cliff Island, Jessie sensed Danny watching her.
He'd shared in her excitement about the move, and she'd
realized how unsettled he'd become in the neighborhood
where he felt threatened on a daily basis. The last thing
she wanted to do was burst his bubble with her own
belated misgivings. Even her mom had been careful not
to mention her own fears about their move in front of her
grandson.

"Nervous, Mom?"

She glanced and managed a smile. "No, Danny. Just remembering bits and pieces of when I was a little girl and
lived out in those islands you're about to see on our ferry
ride." She hesitated. "Guess I was being a little nostalgic."

"You remember much?"

Jessie inched the car forward toward the toll booth,
and realized that the amount of traffic using the ferries
was one thing that had changed in over three decades.
The islands were obviously no longer as remote as they'd
once been.

"I remember some stories my grandmother used to
tell about her people, the totem Indians."

"People call them Native Americans now, Mom," he
corrected her gently.

She grinned. "I know that, Danny, but I guess since
I'm descended from that culture I can repeat what my
grandmother said."

He grinned back. "And I am, too."

"What?"

"Descended."

"Yeah, that's true, although since my grandmother was just half Native American, the other half being Norwegian, my father was only a quarter and I'm an eighth."

"And I'm a sixteenth—and that counts," Danny replied at once.

Jessie suppressed a grin. Her son, like her, was proud of his ethnic heritage. "Of course it does," she agreed.

"Would you tell me one of your grandmother's stories?" Danny asked.

"Well, she once told me that her ancient descendants said that all of the islands in the Strait of Juan de Fuca, and those farther north in Canadian waters, were thought to be stepping stones of the giants." Jessie moved the car forward again, just one away from the toll booth now.

"Who were the giants?"

Jessie shrugged. "I probably don't remember the whole story, and I suspect my grandmother didn't either. In any case it was just a myth I think."

A few minutes later they'd driven onto the huge ferry and were parked in a line of cars headed for Cliff Island. There would be two stops before theirs, which was the end of the line before the ship made its return trip to Anacortes.

"Shall we explore?" Jessie asked. "We'll be on board for over an hour and a half."

"Yeah!" Danny was already getting out of the Saturn, and then hesitated. "What about Footers? Will he be okay by himself down here?"

"Course he will," Jessie said. "Just look at him. He's sleeping like a baby on the backseat." She lowered her window a couple of inches. "He'll have plenty of air and no one will bother him." She laughed. "His bark would scare them away if they did."

Danny nodded, convinced. They headed toward the stairs to the upper levels, weaving through the parked cars on the lower deck. "Would you like a pop?" Jessie asked as they reached the top of the steps. She indicated the dining area where people were already lining up to buy something to eat or drink.

He sniffed the air. "Mom! Can I have a cheeseburger?"

She grinned. "We'll both have one. Fries, too."

They placed their orders, took a number and found a window table and sat down to wait for their food. She could see the excitement in Danny's eyes, and she had to admit that she felt it, too.

"This is a—a real adventure," Danny told her, grinning, his dark hair mussed and flyaway from the wind.

"Yes, an adventure," she repeated. But as their food number was called and she went to get their cheeseburgers, the word adventure stuck in her mind. She'd had a sense of déjà vu, as though someone had said those words to her before, as though she'd once been in a similar circumstance. But when?—and where?

The moment passed.

They took fresh water back down for Footers after they'd watched the cars unload at first one island and then another. Cliff Island was next, and although it would still be another twenty minutes until docking, Jessie's Saturn suddenly felt like their haven.

Although she hid her unsettled feeling from Danny, Jessie felt as though she was bracing herself for something. What? Had she caught her mother's apprehension about returning to the island after all these years? Her mom had never clarified why she'd left in the first place, although Jessie had always believed it was because of her dad's death. Her mom no longer had a reason to stay after that, her own roots having been in California.

"You know, Danny, I think I'll go topside again so I can watch the ship approach Cliff Island. You up for a little wind on the outside deck?"

"Ah, Mom." His dark eyes met hers. "I think I'll stay here with Footers. He seems a little upset, didn't even want any water."

"You don't mind if I'm gone for just a few minutes then?"

"Gosh, Mom, who do you think's gonna get me on this boat? It's almost empty now, and besides, Footers is a great watchdog, as you said earlier."

"True." She grinned. "I'll be back before we're docked, okay?"

He nodded, for once looking the wiser.

She headed to the bow, watching as the ship sliced through the water, creating elongated patterns of shiny dark color. The sky had lowered and a light mist of rain had started to fall, infusing the approaching shoreline with the impressionism of a Monet painting. Jessie lifted the hood of her windbreaker over her hair, her eyes glued to the small island looming in the distance. White rock cliffs marked part of the shoreline, above which dense evergreen foliage made a vivid contrast. For a second time she was struck with a feeling a déjà vu.

And a sense of danger.

Ridiculous, she told herself. She was alone on the deck aside from one other person leaning against the opposite railing. It was her mother's warnings again. She'd been programmed, that's all.

But what was it?

The wind strengthened and she turned away to head back inside the ship. By the time she went down to the car deck she had herself in hand. She and Danny were about to begin a new adventure, a better life.

She meant to make it so.

The other person, a woman, watched her go, and then turned back into the wind, exhilarated. It had been a long wait.

It would soon be over.

Tsonoqua was pleased.

CHAPTER FIVE

THE RAIN CAME DOWN IN EARNEST AS THEY DROVE FROM
the shelter of the ferry onto the ramp that led to the road.
A gust of wind blasted off the water, momentarily jolting
their car.

"It's a typical squall," Jessie announced, smiling reassuringly at her son's startled expression.

"Jeez, I wondered, Mom. I'm glad we weren't standing outside. We'd of been blown away."

"Yeah, it was strong all right, but not that strong." She
pointed to the deckhand who was directing traffic off the
ferry. "See, his rain slicker is whipping around his knees
but he didn't lose his balance—or his hat."

Danny nodded, even as his gaze darted from the man
to the tiny ticket terminal where the ramp met the shore,
and then on to a tiny drive-in restaurant across the road
from the ferry building. A few island vehicles waited in
line for the unloading so they could drive on board for
the return trip to Anacortes. The setting was almost surreal to Jessie; she didn't remember any of it from when
she'd once lived on Cliff Island.

But I wouldn't, she reminded herself. She'd been too
little and over thirty years had passed. She tried to quell
the unexpected sense of uneasiness that had settled over
her. Her mother's words of caution surfaced yet again

and she made an effort to push them aside. Now was not the time for second thoughts. She'd inherited a house, had a new job and she and Danny were about to start a new life.

"Do you know how to get to the house, Mom?"

"Not really, but I have the island map, and I know we're to follow Island Highway to the north end of the island, exactly opposite from where we are now on the south end. The island isn't very big, Danny."

"I know." He glanced. "I looked it up on the Internet before we left Oakland." She could hear the excitement in his tone. "Everyone knows everyone on the island. The Web page said people look out for each other here." A pause. "It's gonna be a lot different from my school and our old neighborhood."

A silence went by as they approached the town.

"Are you worried about the change, Danny?"

He shook his head. "I'm looking forward to living here." Another pause. "You are, too—aren't you, Mom?"

"Yup, sure am." She gave a laugh. "For me being here is an answer to my prayers."

"Me, too." Danny's tone hardened. "I hated where we used to live. I never want to go back."

Jessie slowed the car through town, slightly taken aback by her son's words. The last few months in California must have been even worse for him than she'd imagined. Her own apprehension slipped away. Their move was life altering for Danny, if not for her as well. He now had a future. They both did.

"Look!" Danny leaned forward on the seat, pointing out the car window. "There's a movie theater."

Jessie grinned. "Yeah, I see that."

She liked the look of the town, its wide main street lined with evergreen trees and hanging flower baskets that no longer bloomed with summer flowers. The clapboard storefronts, although early nineteen hundreds, were well preserved and the front windows were colorful with displays, whether clothing, hardware or video posters. Altogether, the town was quaint, modern, yet a step behind the world beyond its gravelly beaches.

"Oh, Mom. I love it!" Danny cried after they'd passed the police station at the edge of town and were approaching the island schools. A square two-story grade school was surrounded by playfields complete with swings, slides and monkey bars. Separated by a chain-link fence were the grounds to the high school, its gym and ball fields.

Even Footers seemed to have caught the excitement, his front paws resting on the seat behind Danny's shoulders so he could look out the window. As they passed the town and Island Highway headed into the trees, he subsided back down onto the seat.

"The directions say to go five miles beyond the town limits," Danny said, peering at the map and directions he'd propped on his lap.

"What's the name of that road again, the one we're to turn off on?" Jessie asked, her eyes on the blacktop, grateful that the traffic was almost nonexistent so that she could concentrate on directions.

"North Point Road." Danny squinted harder at the map. "It seems the next turn after that must be the driveway. It's like a circle, looping off the main road and then back again." He glanced at her. "Are you sure that's right?"

Jessie nodded, making the turn onto North Point Road. "It's basically a private road that goes to Cliff House." She hesitated. "The property it crosses is ours now."

He inclined his head, and then went back to studying the map, but Jessie could see that he was in awe of the magnitude of it all. Why wouldn't he be? she thought. Even she as the adult was becoming more impressed by their good fortune with each passing mile. And he was only a kid.

"There!" Danny cried. "That road on the right."

She slammed on the brakes, coming to a stop beyond the tiny wooden sign that read Wind House. She glanced in the rearview mirror, then slowly backed up until she could make the turn onto the narrow lane that appeared overgrown and unused. The afternoon had eased into evening and now, as the woods seemed to enfold their car, Jessie realized that night was not far behind. She was just glad that it had stopped raining and they'd gotten there before dark.

"Gosh, Mom. I don't think anyone's been on this road for ages." His voice sounded unsure. "It's kinda spooky."

"Naw, just a bit overgrown." She managed a laugh, suppressing her own uneasiness. "But that'll soon change once we begin using the road. We might have to hire someone to cut back the brush, that's all."

The trees thinned as they drove closer to the house. Jessie caught a glimpse of pointed roofs and stone chimneys before they left the woods to circle up a driveway to the front steps of the house.

"Wow!

Danny's breathed word captured Jessie's feelings exactly. Behind the house, which was obviously perched at the top of a cliff overlooking the Strait of Juan de Fuca, the sun was setting behind dark storm clouds on the distant western horizon. The streaming red and yellow rays were spectacular, stretching all the way to the front courtyard of the house. The spectacle was suddenly gone as the sun sank out of sight, and dusk was immediately apparent by the creeping approach of night.

"C'mon," Jessie said as she brought the Saturn to a stop and put on the emergency brake. "Let's get our bearings and turn on some lights before it gets dark, okay?" She opened the car door, her eyes meeting Danny's.

"Yeah, I agree. I don't want to be out here in the dark." He climbed out of the car and Footers bounded out after him, sniffing the shrubs and rockery that lined the driveway.

"Where did the banker say the key would be, Mom?"

"Under the flower pot on the porch."

He ran ahead, Footers loping at his heels, and retrieved the key from under the pot. About to follow him, Jessie's eyes were suddenly on the totem pole that stood as a sentinel a few yards away at the foot of the driveway. Tsonoqua, the female spirit of the wind, was the namesake of the house. The ten-foot wooden carving seemed to watch them with round eyes and a mouth opened in a huge circle, as though her scream had been frozen into silence.

For a second Jessie couldn't move, her own limbs paralyzed by a jolt of fear. Silly woman, she chided herself, knowing the totem, a symbol of her grandmother's Indian heritage, was only made of wood and not a living, breathing entity. With resolve, she moved forward over the inlaid stones and joined Danny at the door.

She took the key he handed her and fitted it into the lock. A moment later the massive front door swung open and they stepped into the entry. Danny felt for the light switch, turning on the rustic chandelier above them. Instantly, the lower floor was illuminated and Jessie closed the door behind them.

Danny darted forward to explore, stopping in the archway to the living room, reaching to flip on more lights. Behind him Jessie could see that the room was furnished with exquisite antiques, and was surprised. She had no idea that the house would be so elegant.

"Mom? Where did you get that costume?"

Danny's question brought her eyes back to him, and she followed his stare to the life-size painting that hung over the huge stone fireplace across the room. The woman in the low-cut emerald green gown, her long chestnut hair soft against her pale face, seemed to be staring right at Jessie, her large brown eyes questioning.

"That's not me," she managed finally.

"But she looks just like you."

Danny was right. The woman in the painting was an exact double of her, period clothing aside.

At that moment the front door blew open, caught by a sudden draft. The both jumped, startled by the sound and the rush of cool air. She ran to close it again, and this time she locked it.

Outside the night had crept closer, and the chill on her flesh was almost as though something had touched her.

Oh dear God. What had she done in coming here? What hadn't her mother told her?

CHAPTER SIX

HER MOMENT OF PANIC PASSED QUICKLY ONCE JESSIE'S reason reasserted itself. Her mother hadn't been back to the island in over thirty years. She wouldn't have remembered exactly how Jessie's grandmother had looked, other than that her own daughter resembled her. She could not have realized that grandmother and granddaughter were carbon copies of each other.

Jessie moved forward into the room, controlling her first reaction to the painting. "I believe it's my grandmother, painted decades before I was born." She glanced at Danny. "Isn't it amazing how genetics influence future generations? My mother told me I resembled my father's mother." She gave a laugh. "I didn't believe it until now."

"More than resemble, Mom." Danny squinted up at the painting. "She could be you."

The front door which she'd just locked suddenly shook itself against the bolt, startling them again.

"Just the wind," she reassured. "The door isn't fitting right. It's probably been warped by time and the salt air." But as she went to check the door she hid her uneasiness, her vague flashes of memory concerning Tsonoqua. The wind wasn't a magical force, she reminded herself. It was just a current of air that had created a draft. She remembered her mother saying the cliffs at the north end of the island always got the worst of the weather.

She turned from the front door after she'd secured a second lock, and saw that Danny was still anxious. She shot him a reassuring smile. "Don't forget this house is perched on a cliff that juts out into the strait and gets the brunt of the wind. We need to get used to it."

"Yeah, before fall turns into winter." Danny grinned back. "I bet this house rocks and rolls in the winter."

"Hopefully not that bad," she said, and dropped an arm around his shoulders. "How about we unload the car, at least get our overnight bags."

They walked to the kitchen in the back of the house as they talked and used the side entrance that opened onto an inlaid stone veranda. That door was closer to the car. Jessie forced herself to avoid even a glance at the totem of Tsonoqua. Fraidy cat, she admonished herself, unsure of why it scared her so much. It was only a wooden carving.

They retrieved their bags, as Footers ran all over the front driveway, sniffing and snorting at the new smells. It didn't help Jessie's state of mind when he stopped at the foot of the totem, whimpered and then ran back to Danny. She stifled a moment of foreboding and led her son and dog back into the house. Her hand was on the knob to close the door when another draft caught it so that it seemed to swing shut of its own volition.

Danny didn't notice, already following Footers through the kitchen to the back of the front hall and on to the main staircase. She tagged along, her expression masking the nervousness that had intensified within her. A draft must have caused the second door to close as well as opening the first one. Where had it come from? Was there something open at the back of the house? They'd soon see. Danny and Footers were off on a tour of the place. She followed, turning on lights.

They explored the whole house, from the kitchen and pantry to the dining and living room on the main floor. The bedrooms were at the top of the wide staircase on the second floor. Another flight of steps went to the third floor which housed the widow's walk and attic. A glance upward told her the door to the third floor was padlocked, which suited her just fine for the time being. She felt more secure knowing they were separate from the top of the house, until she could check it out tomorrow.

Jessie chose the large bedroom that overlooked the strait, feeling somehow enfolded by the old-fashioned room that had once been her grandmother's and seemed familiar to her. Danny chose the bedroom that was connected to hers by a huge bathroom. Both had the same view, being on the exposed side of the house. But as night came down, and the house timbers creaked and groaned from the change in temperature, Danny was reluctant to leave her.

"You hungry?" she asked him.

He nodded.

"So, how about we look in our cooler chest and see what snacks we have left from the trip?" she suggested. "There's wood and kindling to build a fire in the fireplace right here, and once we have it going, we could have a picnic—of sorts," she added.

"Yeah, that'd be fun."

"Good." She tousled his black hair. "And then, because it's our first night in a strange house—even if it is our house now—why don't we camp out here together?"

He brightened and she could tell that he'd been apprehensive about spending the night in his own room, however close it was to hers. And, she admitted, she felt the same way.

They went downstairs for the cooler and Jessie reminded herself to thank the lawyer for having the utilities turned on. They hadn't tried the television set yet. She still couldn't believe that the house came fully furnished. They would have a lot to explore tomorrow, not to mention enrolling Danny in school.

And don't forget your appointment with Hank Shepherd, she reminded herself. Her heart seemed to skip a beat in her chest. His voice had been deep, confident but businesslike over the phone. She imagined an attractive man behind the words, but she could be wrong. She just hoped the job worked out. But if not, she'd find a way to make it, maybe find another job, even borrow from the college fund after the Oakland house sold. Once the island house was legally hers in a year, she'd have more options. That was the decision she'd come to before she'd ever taken the job and left California.

And then she followed a jabbering Danny and a bounding big dog back to the bedroom where she set about building the fire while Danny poked in the cooler for food.

"This is fun, Mom!"

She nodded, grinning. She hoped his words were a precursor to good times ahead for both of them.

CHAPTER SEVEN

THEY SETTLED INTO THE HUGE BED, FOOTERS STRETCHED out between them. Danny and the dog were soon asleep, but Jessie lay awake, staring out through the undraped windows at the moon-silvered sky behind high flying clouds. Here she was, in her grandmother's bed, wondering if she'd done the right thing in bringing her son back to the place her own mother had fled from with her when she was a child.

She knew she was obsessing on her decision, because her mother had been so against the move, and because of her own sense of apprehension once she'd driven onto the island.

Why was that? she wondered, her eyes still on the windows, and the turbulent weather that raged beyond the walls of the house. Because she'd bought into the legend of Tsonoqua? Because that very totem in the courtyard had scared her? Jessie had never heard the whole story from her mother, only vague fears of the place. But she was convinced that if the place had been truly dangerous her mother would have stopped her from coming. She suspected her mom may only have been frightened by her overactive imagination once her father died.

She plumped the pillow under her head, careful not to disturb Danny. Of course that was it, she thought. Weren't her own feelings too emotional right now, too influenced by irrational thoughts?—because of the circumstances and the remote location of the house? It was time she got a grip.

Jessie lay there trying to find sleep. She attempted to visualize a peaceful place but found her concentration was fragmented by her problems. She remembered reading that reciting poetry made the insomniac sleepy, but the lines that surfaced were dark and foreboding: . . . *in a kingdom by the sea . . . the wind came . . . chilling and killing my Annabel Lee.*

Poe's words seemed like a warning in the quiet of the night. Where had they come from? she wondered. She hadn't thought of Poe's writings in years. Why not "Daffodils" by Wordsworth or something else that was soothing and peaceful?

She slipped out from under the covers and padded barefoot to the bay windows that overlooked the strait. She knew why. Her thoughts were clouded by dark thoughts; sunny scenes like a field of daffodils were beyond her capability right now.

No, she thought. Not dark thoughts, only anxiety about their drastic move, her mom's warnings and her change of jobs. Didn't some national statistic claim that the biggest stressors in anyone's life were coping with death, changing jobs, moving and divorce? All of those elements were present in her decision to alter their lives, even if some of them had occurred in the past, and now affected her current choice for the future.

Shit, she thought. Did life ever get easier?

She stepped into the arch of the bay windows and sat down on the window seat, her eyes on the incoming tide beneath the cliff. "Yes," she whispered into the silent room, answering her own question. It would get better.

Wasn't she already ensconced in a completely furnished house that would become hers, without condition, in a year? Didn't she have a job, a godsend given the limitations of the small island? And didn't her son have a chance for a happy life devoid of city gangs and drugs?

She shook her head, as though to shake away her doubts. She'd been given a second chance on a golden platter. The least she could do was to act grateful.

As she was about to get up, her eyes fastened on a tiny light that seemed to bob in the water off the north point of the island. She strained her eyes, wondering if it was a boat.

Dumbbell, she chided herself. Of course the light was a boat. Lights didn't float on water all by themselves.

But as she strained her eyes on the spot, the light suddenly disappeared, as though someone had flipped a switch. She sat for minutes longer, her gaze fastened on the place but the turbulent water remained black and inscrutable. Finally she got up and tiptoed back to the bed and slipped under the sheets. Her last thought was one of gratitude for the lawyer who had taken care of everything: telephone, lights and clean linens for the beds.

She snuggled deeper into the bed. Tomorrow would be a busy day. She needed her sleep. And then she did just that . . . slept.

Jessie awoke to sunshine streaming through the bay windows. She sat up and the covers fell into her lap. A glance told her Danny and Footers were no longer in the bed, nor were they in the room. Instantly, she flung the bedding aside and got up, grabbing her robe before heading for the door, which was now ajar. She met Danny in the hall.

"Footers needed to go outside," he said, grinning.

Jessie smiled back, and realized her apprehension

wasn't shared by her son. He seemed refreshed and upbeat and ready to face their first day on the island. In fact,
she hadn't seen him look so—so little boyish in a long
time. Jessie's stress level took an instant plunge to zero.

"Mom, you won't believe what a great place this is."
He gulped a breath, and jabbered on as they went to the
open staircase and started down to the first floor. "I don't
know why you and grandma ever left here. It's—it's—"
he groped for words. "A dream come true, as you said
after we got the letter from the lawyer."

She laughed and rumpled his hair, catching his upbeat
mood. "I'm glad," she said, glancing around the big entry
hall. Off to the side she could see through the arched
doorway to the living room, a straight route to the fireplace and the painting that hung above it. A ray of sunlight angled in through the windows and touched her
grandmother's face, lighting up the features with a sense
of approval.

Rubbish, she thought, even as she recognized the skill
of the artist who'd painted the portrait so that light and
angle influenced the viewer's perception. She felt a
twinge of regret for her own artistic talent which had
fallen prey to the need for a steady income. But maybe
now she'd find time to paint again, Jessie told herself.

"C'mon, Mom." Danny took her hand and led her to
the back of the hall where another doorway opened into
the kitchen and a breakfast room she hadn't inspected
last night. "This place is like something out of a fairy
tale," he said, as they went into a brightly lit room of windows and sunshine. It was obviously the place where her
grandmother had taken her meals. By contrast, the dining
room across the hall from the living room was big and
formal, while this room was cozy and well lived in.

They stepped across a shaft of sunlight to the French

doors, beyond which was the inlaid stone terrace that was surrounded by a low, matching wall. "C'mon," Danny said again, tugging her hand toward the doors. "I want to show you something cool."

They went outside and Footers ran in though an opening in the wall from the front of the house, seeming as excited about the place as Danny. Crossing the stones to the wall, Danny leaned over it. "Look, Mom. This side of the house is right on the cliff."

Jessie leaned forward and peered over the wall. Her stomach gave a sudden heave and she jumped backward. "My God!" she cried. "Only these few stones protect us from falling into the strait."

"Oh, Mom. It's not that bad." He leaned against the stone wall, and the air went out of Jessie's chest. "It's solid," he said. "Besides, I'm not scared of heights, but I know you are." His grin was lopsided and for a second he sounded like the adult warning the child. "Just don't look over the wall and you'll be okay."

She managed a nod.

"See," he said, pointing to the opening in the wall where Footers had entered the patio. "There's a path beyond that that leads to another one to the beach."

"Danny!" Jessie found her voice. "Promise you won't use that path until I say you can."

"But everyone who ever lived here must have used it, Mom. There's a dock down there and a little boathouse. I want to see if we have a boat."

She took a deep breath, trying to calm herself. Things were racing ahead faster than she'd expected. "We'll go down and have a look, but later, okay?"

"When, Mom?" He hesitated. "I was thinking Footers and I could go down the path this morning, before we head into town. It wouldn't take long."

"No, I want to go with you the first time, so that I know it's safe."

"But—"

"No buts."

"Can we do it this morning then?"

She dropped an arm around him, directing him back toward the French doors. "No, but maybe tomorrow morning. We'll see how things go." Knowing how exciting the place must be to an eleven-year-old boy she didn't want to squash his enthusiasm. Besides, she was relieved that he liked their new home so much.

So, what's wrong with you? she asked herself as they went into the huge kitchen to fix some breakfast.

She and Danny were pleased to find a fresh supply of food in the refrigerator and in the pantry. They hadn't thought to look there last night. As Jessie started coffee she again made a mental note to thank the lawyer for all of the details he'd seen to. She figured the estate had been charged but she didn't care. It was so nice to have such service.

And then she started breakfast after she and Danny had rummaged in the cupboards for dishes and taken a frying pan from the rack above the stove. It was almost too good to be true.

She hoped that wouldn't be the case.

The woman was hidden in the trees when Jessie and her son climbed into the car. She stood perfectly still, barely breathing, willing the dog not to pick up her scent.

She needn't have worried.

The car doors slammed, closing all three inside. And then they were driving away and she assumed they were headed to town.

She smiled, for the moment forgetting her own afflictions and cares. The boy must register for school and Jessie probably should get together with the police chief or Leonard Wills, or both.

It was too soon to make her presence known, she decided. She needed to be careful. Too much was at stake. A false move could destroy everything.

When the time was right she'd know.

Patience, she reminded herself.

CHAPTER EIGHT

THE DRIVE INTO TOWN DIDN'T TAKE LONG, AND AS SHE
drove, Jessie's thoughts focused on meeting Hank Shepherd, her new boss—after she'd registered Danny in
school and met with the estate lawyer. Beside her, Danny
stared out the window, excited by the sights of their new
island home. Behind them, Footers sat on the backseat
with his front paws and head resting on the top of
Danny's seat next to his head. It was as if their dog was
also checking out the island.

She drove into the school parking lot, bringing the
Saturn to a stop next to a yellow school bus. Then she
turned to Danny who'd unclipped his seat belt but was
hesitating to open the car door.

"It's okay, Danny."

"But Mom, what if the kids don't like me?"

His old fears were surfacing, the gang mentality that
he'd learned in the urban neighborhood. She reached to
cover his hands with her own.

"This is a new place, sweetie, and the only problem
you're going to encounter is that the kids might think
you're a big city guy and feel intimidated, okay?"

"But, I'm not."

"I know that, but they're mostly small town kids
who've never lived anywhere else and will wonder if

you're looking down on them because you lived in a city."

"I wouldn't do that!"

She opened her door and stepped out onto the blacktop, hiding her smile. Her son would be okay. Give him a week or two in the school and he'd be an islander, accepted by everyone, she just knew it.

Danny got out and as they headed toward the school's front doors, Footers slipped down onto the seat to nap until they returned.

Jessie went back to the Saturn alone, the principal having taken Danny under his wing to introduce him to his classes, teachers and other kids. She would return to pick him up in two hours, after she'd met with Leonard Wills and Chief Hank Shepherd.

Driving toward the business district, Jessie pulled into an empty spot on the street, then got out and checked the sign. There were no parking meters and she had two hours free parking. Good, she thought. The attorney's office should be a few doors down while the police station was a block away.

She found the doorway with the attorney's name and street number emblazoned in gold letters on a plaque next to it. Jessie opened the door and started up the steps to the second floor, her thoughts on her inheritance and what additional information she might learn about it.

A receptionist who was dressed in gray slacks and a black turtleneck sweater looked up and smiled as Jessie entered the room and introduced herself.

"I've been looking forward to meeting you, Mrs. Cline," the receptionist said. "You've inherited an island landmark and we all hope you're going to love living here. Wind House has a lot of history."

Jessie nodded. "I know we will," she said, grinning as she amended her words. "When I say we I'm including my son Danny."

"Of course." The woman stood up and then came around her desk, offering her hand. "I'm Violet West, everyone calls me Vi."

Jessie took her hand. "As you know, I'm Jessie. So nice to meet you Vi."

"Same here." Her smile broadened. "Everyone knows everyone on the island. My husband, Tommy, runs the arts and craft store for his mom who had a stroke last year." She shrugged. "He and I are both struggling artists, so living out here is beneficial for all three of us."

About to explain that she was also an artist, albeit not a practicing one, she was interrupted when the door to an inner room opened to reveal a heavyset man around sixty whose brown eyes were instantly on her. He smiled, stepped forward and extended his hand to hers. As they shook, he introduced himself as Leonard Wills and indicated she should follow him into his office.

With a final grin at Vi she complied, and he closed the door behind them.

"Please, sit down, Jessie." He hesitated. "I hope you don't mind me calling you Jessie. I almost feel that I know you, especially since you have such a strong resemblance to your grandmother."

Jessie shook her head and sat in the chair opposite him, his desk between them. "Of course you knew my grandmother."

"Uh-huh, but not well until her later years when I was seeing to her affairs." He leaned back in the chair, and the buttons on his shirt strained over his stomach. "But I know the painting. You and she could have been twins— if you'd both been young at the same time."

She nodded. Unable to think of an immediate response, she thanked him for preparing the house, declared that she and Danny both appreciated his efforts on their behalf.

"You're quite welcome. Glad to do it." He shuffled some papers into a tidy pile as he spoke. "I knew your great-uncle's son and your father—went to school with them." He indicated the coffee pot near the window. "Can I offer you a cup?"

"No thanks." She gave a quick smile. "I think I've already had my quota for today."

"Yeah, I probably drink too much of the stuff myself." He paused, and before she could pursue the topic of her family, he abruptly changed the subject. "I have a few papers for you to sign," he said, sliding the pages he'd been fidgeting with toward her. "Mainly it's just routine procedure for the transfer of the estate, except for the top document which simply states that you've moved into the house." He glanced up. "Remember I told you that a clause in your grandmother's will requires that you live on the property for a year? After that the place becomes legally yours."

She nodded.

His brief laugh sounded forced. "So your signature starts the countdown from yesterday when you arrived. Even though all the paperwork will be signed today, it will be null and void if you don't last the year. In other words, the estate will pass out of your hands, the property will be liquidated and the funds given to your grandmother's favorite charities." His gaze was suddenly direct. "But she hoped that you'd stay, thus her clause. She often said that you'd inherit one day and she didn't want you to sell your birthright without ever knowing the place. She believed that if you lived on the island for a year you'd want to stay."

"I intend to, Mr. Wills."

Something flickered in his eyes and was gone before she could identify what she'd seen. "Good," he said, and then began passing the documents to her, explaining each one before she signed it. A few minutes later they'd completed the task and she stood to go.

"Thank you for everything," she told him as he handed her a list with the names of the utilities she needed to call, and then led her back to the waiting room. "And I'm especially thankful for the food in the fridge and fresh linen on our beds. You made our move much easier."

"Glad to help," the lawyer said. "And I'm happy the police job worked out. Cost of living might be less for you on the island but a steady income is needed here like everywhere else."

She knew what he meant. The cash value of the estate remained moot until her year was up.

"You met Hank yet?" Leonard Wills asked.

"Only on the phone, but I'm going there next. I see that the police station is just a block away."

"You'll like Hank," Vi said, having overheard the conversation. "He's big, good-looking and best of all single."

"Vi, don't you have work to do?" Leonard Wills sounded pleasant but the look he shot his receptionist was annoyed.

Vi shrugged, winked at Jessie when the lawyer wasn't looking, and then went back to her computer.

After shaking hands with the man, Jessie went outside, and then stood buttoning her coat against the wind that was blowing in off the water. The air was fragrant with the smell of saltwater, and a glance at the sky told her it was about to rain. She turned toward the police station.

I like Vi, she thought as she hurried along the sidewalk, passing quaint little shops. The arts and crafts store was across the street and she made a mental note to stop in there soon, maybe buy a few tubes of oil for herself, in case she actually had time to paint one of these days.

But for now she braced herself to meet her new boss, and prayed that they'd hit it off, that her new job would turn out to be as perfect as she'd been reassuring herself it would be ever since she accepted it. She hesitated once she reached the station, then took several deep breaths and pushed open the door to step inside.

After giving her name to an elderly woman behind a windowed barrier that separated the front of the building from the back, the woman grinned. "The chief's been expecting you, Mrs. Cline. He said for you to go on back." She waved a hand toward the small hall. "His office is behind that closed door at the very end."

"Thanks, uh, I don't think I caught your name."

The woman pointed to a badge that was pinned to her blouse. "I'm Rose, part-time receptionist, file clerk and bookkeeper." Her face crinkled when she laughed. "But I'm not a cop."

Another nice person, Jessie decided as she made her way down the hall. Her knock was followed by a gruff "Come in."

She opened the door as a uniformed man looked up from his desk. And then she knew what Vi meant. For a moment her mind went blank.

She did something she hadn't done in years—blushed like a schoolgirl.

CHAPTER NINE

THE MAN JESSIE ASSUMED WAS HANK SHEPHERD STOOD UP and came around his desk to greet her, his blue eyes piercing and steady, holding hers in an electrifying gaze that didn't allow her to look away, pink cheeks or not.

"Jessie Cline?" he raised his eyebrows in a question.

She nodded. "Chief Shepherd?"

"Guilty."

She held out her hand. "I'm pleased to meet you." She managed a smile, relieved that her tone sounded professional, if not her unexpected reaction to him.

"Believe me, not half as pleased as I am. We've been a person short for several weeks now, ever since Guy, your predecessor, took a position down south in the Seattle area."

"And that means you've been pulling extra shifts?"

"Exactly. Along with Max DeForio, our part-time officer who has been picking up some of the slack even though he's semi-retired. And of course we have a few trained and state-certified volunteers."

"Well, I'm reporting for work now," she said, even as she fished for words to lower her sudden anxiety about working for such an attractive man. She hesitated. "And I'm hoping to start soon."

"How soon? I figured you'd want a week or so to get settled on the island before hitting the time clock."

She shrugged. "Us working folks can't afford that kind of time off."

"But most folks aren't in your shoes, Officer Cline." His tone had gone dry. "You just inherited a valuable property."

A silence went by while she considered her answer, wondering what his comment really meant. She decided to ignore the implications and stick to facts.

"Maybe so," she said finally. "But the place isn't mine until I've lived in the house for a whole year." She paused. "The local scuttlebutt may not reflect the complete terms of the will," she added, hiding her annoyance.

"Whatever, Officer Cline. Good to meet you and I'm glad you can start right away. I can use your help." His grin was sudden, brightening his expression. "If you're even half as good as your impressive resume and the recommendations from your department, our small community is fortunate to have you." He shook her hand again and she was suddenly aware that he was a tall man, lean, broad shouldered and in top shape. "Welcome to our island."

She lowered her gaze, dropped her hand and took the chair he indicated as he went back around the desk and sat down. His eyes were suddenly direct.

"So, when *can* you start?" he asked.

"Today is Thursday. How about Monday?"

"Will that give you enough time to settle in?"

"The movers will arrive with our belongings tomorrow, and then Danny and I will have the weekend to get ourselves organized."

"Danny?"

"My eleven-year-old son."

"Oh yeah, that's right." He grinned. "We talked about your boy. You told me he was the main reason for moving to the island, right?"

She hesitated and then wondered how he could have forgotten that, even momentarily. "I believe I also said my child comes first. If that makes a difference in starting this job, then I need to know now, Chief." She managed a smile and waited for his reply.

"Good God, no."

Jessie hadn't realized she was holding her breath, waiting for his answer, until he'd spoken. "Good," she said. "Because job or not I intend to stay on the island, even if we have to live on unemployment insurance and I take up my brushes and try to sell my paintings for the year."

"You're an artist?"

"Was," she replied, "before I had to support myself and my child."

There was a pause.

"And that was before you went into law enforcement?"

His softly spoken words set off an alarm in her brain. She chose her words carefully, wondering if her response would influence her new position as assistant chief.

"Yes it was," she answered truthfully. "But my second love was to be in law enforcement, and I decided long ago to take up that career and place my art in a hobby position."

"I see."

"You see what, Chief Shepherd?" she asked, again deciding to be direct. The tone of their conversation was confusing. "That I'm not who you want as assistant chief after all?—that an artist is not a proper policeman?"

"Hell, no. Let's not get off on the wrong foot here, Officer Cline. I was only thinking that it was too bad that you had to give up your art." He spread his hands. "I have a very talented son who wants to be an artist. But unfortunately he's taken up with the wrong group to accomplish that I'm afraid."

She didn't know what to say. "Wrong group?" she repeated.

"Yeah." His gaze seemed to drift inward, beyond their conversation momentarily. "Once you're on the job you'll know about our local commune slash religious cult," he said, refocusing on her. "They're an assortment of musicians, artists and writers, and although they don't appear to be involved with subversive groups, they're damned odd and clannish. Aside from shopping in our stores and an annual summer fest where they sell their arts and crafts and perform for money, they keep to themselves. Their two-day event brings lots of people to the island, is good for business and so no one complains."

"Your son is a member?"

"Uh-huh. He and the others live in yurt huts on the property while the leader of the group resides in a large modern house." He shook his head. "It all seems strange, but like I said, they're legal as far as we know."

She could only nod, sensing disappointment rather than anger in his tone. His son's lifestyle was obviously on his mind. She could identify. She'd feel the same way if Danny grew up a throwback to a sixties hippie. Her first impression of Hank Shepherd was suddenly altered. There was more to the man than his good looks and an impeccable police career. He seemed as damaged, if not more so, than she was by past events.

Typical, she thought. How many people in law enforcement had a personal cross to bear away from the job? Too many. Was that a by-product of the commitment needed to be a successful cop? she wondered, as she had on many occasions in the past. Or was it the reason a person chose law enforcement in the first place? She had no answers.

"So, Officer Cline." He came back around his desk to

tower above her, once again the chief. "I'm going to see you at 9:00 AM on Monday morning, at which time we'll go over what'll be expected of you here on the island."

"I'll be here."

"Good. We'll make a great team, I'm sure of it." He tilted his head. "Agreed?"

She resisted a grin and sensed that he did the same. "Sounds good to me."

He walked her to the door. "You'll be assigned a patrol car which you'll park at your residence when you're off duty, okay?"

"That'll be great. I won't have to check a car out each day as I did in California."

They'd reached the door and he opened it, just as her comment made him smile. "You'll find a lot of differences between our little island and the San Francisco Police Department, Officer Cline."

"I can see that already, Chief." And then she walked under his arm that held the door and stepped into the hall where she faced him again. "And I also think I'm going to like it far better than my last job."

He raised his eyebrow in a question.

"I don't think this job is half as dangerous, for starters," she said, finally allowing a slight grin in return. "And I don't believe your crime stats are anything like those of my previous job."

"You're probably right on that score," he agreed. "I'll give you an overview on everything Monday morning."

"Sounds good."

And then she was moving away from him toward the front door, aware that he was still in his doorway watching her go. She didn't breathe normally again until she was on the sidewalk headed for the Saturn. A glance at her watch told her to hurry. Danny would be waiting.

* * *

"Mom, you won't believe it! I've got new friends already. And the basketball coach says I'm a natural to try out for the team."

Jessie shot Danny a grin. Even Footers, who'd slept their appointment times away in the car, roused himself to slide his head onto the back of the front seat next to Danny, his tail wagging a tattoo.

"I'm so glad you like your new school."

"I love it! It's the best. And like Coach Tigard said, we're gonna take the B league championship this year!" He gulped a breath. "It's perfect that we moved here just in time for me to be on the team."

She could only smile and nod at his excitement. And her mind kept telling her how right she'd been to come to the island, for both of their sakes.

She drove up the driveway to the house, past the totem and into the curve by the entrance where she stopped. They both got out of the car, Footers bounding ahead of them to the door. Jessie had her key in her hand but Danny was ahead of her and had his hand on the knob.

The door moved open.

"Mom." He faced her. "You forgot to lock the door!"

But she hadn't.

So who'd unlocked it?

CHAPTER TEN

"YOU DON'T THINK SOMEONE IS IN THE HOUSE, DO YOU, MOM?"

"Course not." She applied her best professional tone to her words. "But since I'm a cop I guess you'll have to wait outside until I check everything out." She shot him a grin. "But I suspect the lock didn't engage when I turned the key as we left. The lock is old and may not always work, even when the key turns. I'm going to call a locksmith to change all the door locks."

He nodded, and she ignored his anxious expression.

"You wait here and I'll be right back."

"Okay, I'll give you a couple of minutes, and then I'll follow you if you don't come back out."

She grinned reassuringly, and then stepped into the main hallway. Her senses were immediately assaulted by a sense of danger—the uneasy feeling she and her San Francisco co-officers often talked about when something didn't seem right. Once Danny was on the other side of the door and couldn't see her, Jessie grabbed a walking stick from an umbrella stand in the corner, wishing she'd already been issued a police pistol. Her improvised weapon in hand, she moved forward through the house, first the lower floor and then the second floor. All was as they'd left it so she didn't continue on to the third floor which was still padlocked anyway. Her sense of danger had dissipated as she moved upward through the house.

Imagination? she wondered. Was she being overcautious?

It's the fear syndrome when you move into a new place, she thought, rationalizing. Nothing was wrong. It was just an old house with uneven door frames and floors caused by decades of weather and settling.

There were no intruders in the house.

Jessie replaced the walking stick next to the umbrellas, and then went to the front door where she motioned Danny inside. "Everything safe here," she told him, grinning.

He came inside followed by Footers who seemed oblivious to any threat. Another good sign, Jessie told herself. Their dog would know if something was amiss.

Wouldn't he?

She hoped so.

The balance of the day passed quickly, and by suppertime they'd made a lot of progress in settling in. As they'd decided the night before, Jessie kept the main bedroom, and Danny and Footers took the smaller room on the other side of the connecting bathroom. She and Danny did a complete tour of the house, while he chatted excitedly about everything, but they still skipped the basement. Jessie felt too new to the house—too vulnerable—to explore the cavernous dark place under the kitchen that would smell of age and dampness. They'd save that for another day, and in the meantime, she made sure the door stayed bolted.

The high point of their tour had been the widow's walk above the tower room. Once she'd found the key to the padlock and opened the third floor door, they were surprised to find the tower room empty. But the view was incredible.

"You can see forever up here," Danny had said. "I bet all the way to Canada on a clear day!"

She'd grinned at his excitement and assured him that they could, that Canada was really only the landmass on the northern horizon. They went back downstairs and she padlocked the door behind them.

Later, as she'd tucked Danny into his bed, Jessie was relieved that he didn't share her apprehension about the house. Talk about her mother's imagination; she was just as bad. The thought had even crossed her mind that the house could have a secret passage. Damn silly thinking, Jessie told herself, and wondered where such feelings came from—her childhood in the house? Even though she hardly remembered even being there?

Go to bed, she instructed herself. A good night's sleep will calm your nerves. Wasn't it true that sleep deprivation could conjure up all manner of mental images and fears?—monsters and phantoms in the night?

Jessie kept reminding herself of those thoughts as she got ready for bed, then left the doors open from the bathroom to both her bedroom and Danny's. She climbed into bed, switched off the bedside lamp, and stared out at the night sky. Everything was quiet. She relaxed.

And then she slept.

Jessie sat straight up in the bed, her breath coming in ragged gulps. Fragments of mental images flashed in her mind—the remnants of a nightmare? she wondered.

All was silent around her.

Then what had awakened her?

She forced herself to calm down, even as her eyes

darted about the room which was slightly illuminated by a half moon that flickered in and out of the night sky. She strained to hear, and realized she wouldn't know what was normal or not. It was only her second night in the house.

After a few minutes her breathing had slowed and she smiled to herself. Once she'd been called out to a disturbance in a downtown San Francisco flophouse because of a 220, someone believed to be crazy. The man in question had been experiencing night terrors and was convinced monsters were after him. In his case the condition had been alcohol induced.

Not my circumstances, Jessie told herself and slid out of the bed. Even though she knew that all the doors were locked, that she was being irrational, she had to check on her son—because something had awakened her.

What? she wondered again.

She slipped across the carpet on tiptoes, crossed the cold tiles of the bathroom floor, and stepped into Danny's room. Footers lay at the bottom of his bed, and as she moved into the room, his tail wagged against the quilt.

Of course he'd known she was there. Berners were excellent watchdogs. So if there'd been something in the house wouldn't he have barked?

Of course, Jessie reassured herself. Nothing had awakened her but her own nervousness in adjusting to their new home. She patted Footers gently, pulled the quilt up over Danny's shoulders, careful not to disturb his sleep, and then headed back to her own room. Tomorrow the movers would arrive with their things and it would be a busy day. She needed her sleep.

But she was wide awake. Snuggled back under the down comforter, she couldn't seem to get comfortable and found herself tossing and turning.

Finally she got up again and went to the bay windows to look out over the strait. It seemed infinite and she couldn't tell where the shoreline met the water, or where the water met the sky. It was a dark night and the moon was obscured by a low cloud cover.

Then her eyes fastened on the light that seemed to bob offshore. The same one she'd seen last night? she wondered. It seemed to hover in one spot and again she realized it had to be a boat.

Fishermen?

But surely it wasn't fishing season. But then how would she know that? She made a mental note to ask someone tomorrow.

The light was suddenly gone, just like the last time she'd seen it. A little mystery, she thought, grinning as she went back to bed. It gave her something safe to think about.

Her eyelids drooped and then she knew no more until morning.

CHAPTER ELEVEN

HANK SHEPHERD ADJUSTED HIS REARVIEW MIRROR AS HE turned off the main road onto the driveway that led to Wind House. The overgrown foliage obstructed everything but the narrow lane leading to the house.

Caroline McGregor, his new employee's grandmother, had been a virtual recluse and Hank had never met her in the short time he'd been on the island before her death. She'd been an enigma, just as much as old Nita who'd been her friend was still an enigma, and an elusive presence who lived on a rusting tugboat offshore. He'd even wondered if Jessie's grandmother had been a myth, until she died of natural causes and he'd been called out to determine that her death had not been the result of foul play.

And then he'd hired Jessie Cline, the granddaughter, to be his assistant chief. He smiled ironically. Although she had impeccable credentials, and had not been on the island since she was a child, the whole scenario seemed unreal. Especially once he'd heard the legends of the house.

He slowed the patrol car to save his paint job from the long arms of branches, and reminded himself that, credentials or not, she'd been the only applicant for the job. Not many law enforcement professionals would ever consider a move to a remote island with little or no prospects to advance their career. He was lucky to have someone like Jessie Cline, Wind House superstitions or not. He didn't allow himself a question on his own motives for being there. He no longer worried about career advancement. His only concern was for the future of his son now that his wife was gone. No easy task, he thought. His son no longer listened to anything he had to say.

The trees thinned and Hank was suddenly out in the open, headed up the curve of the driveway, past the totem pole and namesake of the house. He scarcely glanced at it; the Wind Spirit gave him the creeps. He pulled up behind an Atlas Van Lines truck and stopped. Two men were unloading furniture and boxes and they glanced up, nodding. Jessie and her son were nowhere in sight.

"The owner's inside," the heavyset mover told Hank as he got out of the patrol car.

"Yeah, with Footers, the Berner," the smaller man added.

"Footers? The Berner?" Hank raised his eyebrow.

"Uh-huh. Footers is the name of their Berner, a huge Bernese mountain dog," the wiry man explained. "That goddamned dog didn't like us going in and out of the house and made that known right away. He scared the shit out of us until Mrs. Cline locked him in an upstairs bedroom."

Hank suppressed a grin. He hadn't known about Jessie's dog but he approved. A big dog was a must on a remote estate as big as this one, even though the breed was basically gentle, the bark being worse than the bite, as the old cliché stated.

"Yeah, some of those big dogs can take a fellow down," Hank said, agreeing. It didn't hurt to let them think the worst, given they must have realized Jessie and her son would be living here alone.

You're becoming a typical islander who suspects all outsiders, he told himself. He was grinning as Jessie answered his knock.

"What's so funny, Chief?"

He shook his head, sobering. "Sorry, my mind was on something your movers said." He cocked his head at her as he shoved his cap back. He'd forgotten how attractive she was behind her professional exterior, and wondered why she was in law enforcement in the first place. Even in Levis and a sweatshirt she was a sexy woman. And it was obvious that she'd come from a wealthy family, yet he had a sense that she'd never had financial security.

"Come in," she said, quickly, as though suddenly aware that she was talking to her boss. "I must say I'm surprised to see you." She hesitated. "Was there something more that you needed to tell me?"

He spread his hands, looking her straight in the eye. "Nothing that can't wait until Monday. This is Cliff Island, Officer Cline. Not the city." A pause. "I was just checking in on your progress. The island drums said your movers had arrived and I wondered if you needed any help."

"Island drums?" She grinned up at him, and her relaxed smile took years from her usually serious expression. "I thought that type of communication only existed on primitive jungle islands."

Hank laughed as he stepped into the huge entry hall. "Island is the operant word here," he said. "Some things hold true for all remote islands."

She shrugged, and led the way into the room Hank had been told was the salon on his only visit to the house after the owner had died. "Please find a comfortable chair," Jessie told him.

But he'd hesitated halfway into the room, his gaze on

the painting above the fireplace. Slowly his eyes went to Jessie, then back to the young woman who'd been immortalized on canvas.

"She's not you—or is she?"

"My grandmother," Jessie said behind him. "I hadn't realized we looked so much alike until I saw that painting after we arrived." A hesitation. "I hadn't seen her since I was a toddler, so I didn't know."

"But my mom isn't her," a voice said from the doorway. "My grandmother was old-fashioned—and my mom isn't."

He turned to see a slim, dark-haired boy who'd moved to stand next to Jessie. They didn't look alike—where Jessie was green-eyed and had chestnut-colored hair, her son had dark eyes and hair. But the child was obviously protective of his mother. His dog sat down next to him, a huge black, brown and white animal whose whole demeanor was one of protective attention to his owners.

Hank saw what the movers had meant. This was a watchdog. Although Footers, as the movers had called him, was a gentle dog he would be a force to be reckoned with if there was a threat.

Good, he thought again. They needed that kind of dog out here on the northern point of the island.

He stepped forward. "Hello, Son." He stretched out his right hand. "I'll be working with your mother on the island police force."

"I'm Danny," the boy said, shaking Hank's hand. "I know you're the chief and I'm honored to meet you, sir."

"No sirs here, Danny. You can just call me Hank. We don't have to stand on formalities when we're going to become friends." Hank grinned at the boy, liking his sincerity and manly bearing. "I have a son who is a little older than you. I'm sure if he gets to know your mother he'd call her Jessie," Hank explained, hoping to put the boy at ease.

"Does he live on the island, too?" Danny asked.

"Yes, he does."

"Does he go to school?"

Hank shook his head. "He's older, graduated from high school several years ago."

Jessie stepped forward, as though she'd sensed his awkwardness about his son and wanted to change the subject before Danny's questions became too personal. "So what brought you out here aside from checking on our progress?"

His admiration for her went up several notches. Not only was she more beautiful than he'd first perceived, she was sensitive and astute to another person's suffering.

Because she'd suffered?

The thought came of its own volition. Hank knew virtually nothing of Jessie's background other than her professional credentials and her family connection to the island. But the perception was intriguing.

"So what's up, Chief?" Jessie asked again as he moved farther into the room.

"Hank," he corrected her.

"Okay." She grinned as she dropped her arm around Danny's shoulders. "Hank then."

"As I said, just checking on the progress of your move. And—"

"And?" Jessie stepped farther into the room. "I figure you have a job for me, right?"

"You're astute, Officer Cline." He flashed a smile to dilute his professional address. "I'd like you to attend an island professional women's group luncheon on Wednesday." He shrugged. "As you women would agree, it's not my cup of tea."

"Why do we need a police presence, uh, Hank?" A luncheon? It was the last thing she'd expected to hear. "Do I need to protect someone?"

The movers came into the house with another piece of furniture and Footers went wild, held in rein by the short leash Danny held. The distraction gave Hank time for a reply.

"The speaker's husband is a political cartoonist, they live here on the island for part of the year and there have been threats to this man because of the vicious potshots he's taking at a senator who is seeking reelection. The newspaper cartoons are suggesting dishonesty, bribes and all sorts of bad PR for the politician."

"Obviously the senator is important."

"Yeah, and he's fighting back. The whole thing is pretty nasty."

"And you think the cartoonist's wife is in danger?"

"I hope not. But we have to protect her nevertheless. She's not his first wife, is much younger than her husband, and I think innocent of the current allegations. And she's pregnant with their first child."

"He sounds a little ruthless." She hesitated, as though her mind flashed on her own past experiences. "Of course I'll be there—with bells on. I hate the thought of a devoted wife who might be in jeopardy because of her husband."

Hank was momentarily taken aback. "Whoa, Jessie. This isn't about marital life, only the status of a wife who believes in her husband and is talking about his professional life, from her viewpoint, to a group of his adoring female fans."

"Touché."

"What?"

She grinned. "Nothing. I'll be there on Wednesday." A pause. "Of course that'll be after I've been updated on the job as planned this Monday morning. I promise to adhere to procedure, Chief. Your speaker will be protected according to police protocol."

Her green eyes sparkled with—with what? he wondered. Humor? Was she teasing him? He wasn't sure so he nodded solemnly. "In that case I'll depend on you, and look forward to seeing you on Monday."

"I'll be there."

He gave a mock salute, but his mind was elsewhere. His gaze had dropped to her mouth as she'd spoken, and he'd had a sudden impulse to kiss her. The thought brought a smile. After making friends with Footers and saying good-bye to Danny he strode back to his cruiser. A final glance at the porch told him Jessie watched him go, an odd expression on her face that gave him a sense of satisfaction.

Why? Because she may have guessed his thoughts?

And then he left, driving back past the totem that seemed to mock him.

CHAPTER TWELVE

THE MOVERS WERE GONE IN TIME TO CATCH THE 3:10 FERRY, leaving Jessie and Danny with only their personal things that needed to be placed in the rooms that were already furnished. In the end she'd stored her boxes of dishes, pots and pans, and her furniture in a back room. She needed time to figure out what she'd do with them, how to integrate those items into the house, should they really stay there for the whole year.

And if they didn't? Then their things were already packed and ready to move.

Don't play mind games on yourself, she'd thought, as she instructed the movers to the storage room. You're going to stay.

You have to stay.

She saw the movers through the whole unloading process and was relieved when they were finally finished. They'd raced through their last half hour of work, conscious of when the ferry left the island. Once they were finished and she'd signed off that she'd received everything, they closed up the truck and were soon on their way back along the lane to the road that led to the ferry.

She'd sighed with relief. She and her son were there to stay. But now as she walked from the driveway to the front entrance she was suddenly assailed with doubts. A glance behind her seemed to be caught by the totem that guarded the house—by the eyes above the round O of the mouth—and Jessie quickly turned away, as a shiver suddenly gave her goose bumps.

Another fall storm was imminent, she thought, and quickly went inside the house, closing and locking the heavy door behind her.

The trauma of moving, she told herself. Everyone felt that way when they moved to a strange place.

Didn't they?

Jessie pulled out of her driveway on Wednesday morning, still trying to get used to the patrol car that had been assigned to her on Monday. It was a four-door Chevy with an oversized engine and bar lights on the roof, and although it had the dash switch for the wigwags in the headlights, and the blue flashing lights on top of the passenger windshield, it wasn't computerized, as her vehicle had been in San Francisco.

She turned into the high school parking lot in front of the auditorium and pulled into the spot reserved for emergency vehicles. Jessie adjusted her belt and holster as she got out of the patrol car, smiling as she headed for the main doors where people were already lined up to enter. Her new black uniform with the yellow accents had been ordered last Friday after she'd met with Chief Shepherd and it had come over on a Monday afternoon ferry. Hank had made the order, guessed at her size and been right, although the size eight was a little big around the waist.

She realized he wasn't oblivious to female body proportions. A reasonable assumption, she reminded herself as she headed for the entrance, nodding and smiling at the people in line, mostly women who would become familiar to her over time, as they were island residents. He'd once been married. And she had no idea how many other women had been in his life since, he being such an attractive man.

She went past the head of the line and into the building, where a huge number of people were looking for their tables in the auditorium. There was a platform with the head table at the front of the room, and a woman was adjusting the floral bouquet under the speaker's podium while another person was testing the PA system. Banquets were the same everywhere, Jessie thought, as she stepped forward to introduce herself to the anxious sponsors.

The president of the women's professional group came forward when she saw Jessie. She smiled and motioned Jessie aside.

"We don't expect problems, of course," the woman who introduced herself as Edie Morse said. "I'm only concerned that we have protection if an unexpected heckler turns up." She laughed nervously. "You know our speaker's husband has savaged a Washington State senator who has been accused of sexually harassing female interns—among a host of other things?"

Jessie shook her head, smiling encouragement. "As you know, because I'm sure you've heard about the latest person hired by the island police department, I'm new to the island." Jessie stepped closer. "I'm here to do whatever is required but I'm not yet up to speed on island, uh, situations," she ended, lamely, although she hoped her sincere expression communicated her dedication to her new job.

Edie smiled. "As I said, we don't expect trouble. But we love Lynda, who is a supporter of our underprivileged children's program. She's donated thousands of dollars."

"She and her husband?" Jessie knew that Lynda had never worked but for a few months as a starlet in Hollywood before marrying her husband, and assumed any donation would be from both of them.

"Uh-huh," Edie said, nodding her plump head so hard that her pageboy hairdo whipped her shoulders, giving Jessie a momentary impression that the overweight Edie had no neck at all. "Although Lynda's husband is rarely home, he's behind her donation of time and money one hundred percent." She looked knowingly at Jessie. "He travels a lot, giving speeches and such. He's in heavy demand." She hesitated. "They have a penthouse in New York City and he stays there for his work while Lynda holds down their home here."

Jessie's smile felt frozen. "I see."

The woman's wide face seemed suddenly to be sliced in half when she smiled. "Lynda is going to talk to our group about her life as the wife of a world famous cartoonist."

Jessie could only nod. She moved away to the side of the room which would be her station until the end of the talk. She realized she wasn't into the rhythm of the island, that women here might not be as reality based as the women she'd been used to in San Francisco. No one that she'd known had been so focused on her husband.

But then you only knew career women, she reminded herself as she watched the tables fill up with chattering ladies, excited to hear about another woman's life with a famous man.

So they could live vicariously? she wondered. Yet she knew these women were all normal. Maybe she was cynical? Yeah, that's it, she thought. Her own experience as a woman and as a law enforcement officer had jaded her. She needed to be aware of that now that she worked in a community where people rarely left the security of a small island—and still believed what they were told in the media.

And then, in the hubbub of the room, everyone was seated. A few minutes later the people at the main table filed onto the dais. The speaker was apparent for her youthful beauty and obvious pregnancy, and was followed by a man who was evidently her husband, the famous cartoonist. As he turned toward the cheering audience, Jessie froze.

Her breath caught in her throat, and she found herself taking deep gulps of air, trying to regain her equilibrium.

It couldn't be.

But it was.

Oh, dear God, give me strength to see this through. Don't let me fail now. The future of my son depends on my being strong.

And then she threw back her shoulders and stood straight against the wall. She could face it.

And process the ramifications later.

Keep your priorities straight, she instructed herself. Don't forget what your actions will mean to your son.

And she did.

Even though her emotions were on a roller-coaster ride and she could hardly keep from crying.

CHAPTER THIRTEEN

JESSIE MANAGED TO KEEP HER MIND OFF HER OWN FEELINGS about the man on the dais, concentrating instead on his wife, Lynda, who obviously adored her husband.

The famous Ben Thrasher.

Infamous was more like it, she told herself. She knew all anyone ever needed to know about Ben Thrasher. She wasn't surprised that he was trashing a well-known politician in his cartoons. Success had gone to Ben's head long ago, and he actually believed that he was above the masses, that there were two rules for living, the one that applied to him, and the one that applied to everyone else.

A sociopath, she thought, knowing she was biased, but believing her evaluation nonetheless. He was oblivious to the suffering of others, and had no empathy for another person's feelings.

Get a grip, she commanded herself, aware that her feelings must not register on her face.

She scarcely noted what was served at the luncheon, not being seated herself as she moved around the room of tables, making sure that everything was secure. When Lynda was introduced, a hush fell over the several hundred people in the auditorium, and all eyes went to the young woman who got up slowly from her seat and stepped up to the lectern.

Even at eight months pregnant, Lynda was a feminine woman who exuded her future motherhood. As she began to speak about how much she and her husband loved the island, how his career was second to his family and how they planned to live there for years to come, Jessie knew that Lynda was sincere in believing what she said. She wondered if Ben had changed after all these years, and doubted it.

By the time Lynda sat down, her husband's position was secure on Cliff Island. In glancing over the crowd, Jessie could see that the young woman's words had won the affirmation of everyone present. Her husband was above reproach because Lynda said he was. And they believed Lynda—that the politician was the liar, not Ben. It didn't seem to occur to the audience that both Ben and his adversary might be in the wrong—that Ben might be capitalizing on the senator's scandal.

Not my problem, Jessie reminded herself. Her job was to make sure everyone was safe, and that seemed to be the case as the crowd began to disburse.

And then she turned around to find Edie Morse approaching her with Lynda and Ben in tow. Edie, the ever gracious hostess, was trying to get the Thrashers through the crowd to their car.

"Can you clear the way? she asked Jessie. "Lynda is feeling a little unsteady and needs to get home."

"Of course," Jessie said. Her eyes flickered over Ben who appeared concerned about his wife. Lynda definitely looked like she needed air. Ben only glanced, acknowledging his need for her help with a nod.

Jessie moved as if by rote, clearing a passageway for them to the door, then over the concrete walk to the driveway where their car was waiting. Two minutes later

Ben had helped his wife into the backseat before climbing in beside her and slamming the door shut. A moment later their driver was taking them down the lane away from the auditorium and their adoring fans.

She watched them go, taking deep breaths. It was inconceivable that Ben hadn't recognized her, but he hadn't. She wondered why. Because she'd grown older?—or because he'd had so many women that he didn't recognize any woman from his past?—or because a face had never registered with him in the first place, only how that female could service him for the moment?

Although she'd never expected to see him again, she'd never considered that he wouldn't remember who she was. She felt unsettled, if relieved. He was everything she'd known him to be—a self-serving, emotionally detached man who purported to be a human being. She just hoped she never had to see him again.

But she felt sorry for Lynda, and wished her the best. The woman was vulnerable, not only because she was pregnant, but because she loved Ben Thrasher.

The woman watched the situation, ending with Jessie getting into her own car and leaving as well. She knew the whole story, had heard it from a very good source. She meant to make sure that history didn't repeat itself.

As the patrol car disappeared the woman's attention moved to the other person she'd been watching in the crowd, a person who blended in well, who didn't give any reason for a second glance. But that person concerned the woman. She'd been watching for weeks now and knew something bad could happen.

But not to her people. She would make sure of that. Nothing bad must ever happen to them again.

* * *

Jessie finished out the day, relieved when her patrol was over. Aside from the luncheon, nothing else of any significance had happened on the island. She got home just ahead of Danny, who'd ridden his bike to school, stayed after for basketball practice and then pedaled home just before dark. It was her agreement with Hank that she have the day shift so that she was home for her son. She knew she was on call any night if there was an emergency, and she figured by then that she'd have a backup plan for someone seeing to Danny.

"Hey Mom," he told her as he came into the house. "I met the greatest person on my way home."

"Who?"

"Some old lady who was walking along the road." He opened the fridge for a Coke. "She was really cool, said she knew my great-grandmother, that she also knew you."

She frowned. "I don't know anyone on the island yet. What was her name?"

"Didn't say." He took a gulp of Coke. "All she said was that the Wind Woman would take care of us."

There was a silence.

"Wind Woman?"

"Uh-huh. Said we were going to love it here." He pursed his lips. "Then she added, 'ultimately.'"

" 'Ultimately'? What does that mean?"

"Darned if I know, Mom." He moved toward the doorway to the hall, on his way upstairs to wash his hands and get ready for supper. "I'd stopped to talk with her and at that point I got back on my bike and started for home again. When I glanced back she was gone."

"Strange."

He shrugged. "Didn't seem so. She seemed nice."

And then he went upstairs and she continued her preparations for supper. But his encounter lingered in her thoughts. Maybe he shouldn't ride his bike to school, until he really knew the lay of the land. Although the old lady seemed harmless, she revealed some startling statements—like she'd known Jessie's grandmother—and her. How was that so?

I'm driving Danny to school tomorrow, she decided. And she'd ask Hank if he knew who the woman on the road was. She wasn't taking chances with her son. He was her whole life and the reason for everything she did. Without him . . .

She stopped short in the kitchen. Dumb thought. He was safe. And she'd make sure he stayed that way.

CHAPTER FOURTEEN

THE NEXT AFTERNOON IT BEGAN TO RAIN. BY THE TIME SCHOOL was out a light drizzle had turned into a torrential down-pour and Jessie swung by the school to pick up Danny and his bike. Her son would be soaked if he attempted to pedal home, not to mention it being an unsafe thing to do.

"Mom, I could have ridden home myself. I was gonna watch the high school basketball practice and by then the rain would have stopped."

"I don't think so. And by then it would have been getting dark."

"Aw, Mom. I'm not a baby."

She shot him a grin. "I should hope not," she said, joking. "You don't look like one." She put the cruiser into gear and started it moving away from the school entrance. "And don't forget that I let you ride to school this morning after you talked me out of driving you. Besides, lots of the kids are being picked up because of the weather."

He glanced around the busy parking area. "But not in a police car. They're gonna wonder what I did to get in trouble."

Jessie gave a laugh. "Remember Danny? This isn't San Francisco. I'd wager that everyone on the island knows that your mother is the assistant police chief, and that's who's picking you up."

"I guess so."

Jessie reached to pat his hand. "Footers will be glad to see you. He seemed lonesome when I stopped by the house earlier to let him out for a quick run."

Danny nodded.

"And, I'm off duty a little early today, although I'll still be on call if there's an emergency. We'll have time to set up your Xbox and the other computer games on the television set in your room."

"Yeah!" He perked up instantly. Danny, like most eleven-year-olds, was addicted to his computerized games. "I have a couple of new friends I'd like to invite over to play one of these weekends." He glanced at her as she turned onto the main road out of town. "Can you imagine, Mom? These guys don't have an Xbox."

"Well, then you can teach them how to play when they come over."

He nodded, digesting her words, his thoughts already on that visit. She was pleased, but it didn't surprise her that some kids didn't have all the high-tech options here on the island. As Hank had told her at the job orientation on Monday, there were many families in the jurisdiction living below poverty level. The lavish summer homes of people who lived elsewhere were a stark reminder of the chasm between the island residents and the vacationers.

The haves and the have-nots, she thought. That social condition was always more apparent in a small community.

Jessie slowed for their turnoff, peering through the rain-streaked windshield that the flying wipers couldn't clear, and steered off the highway onto their side road. She and Danny both watched for their driveway.

"Boy, this is awful!" Danny cried. "I can hardly see through the rain let alone the rain on the windshield."

"I know."

But she found and made the turn onto the lane that led through the woods to their house. The sounds changed around them as they entered a virtual tunnel of foliage, from the steady drumming of rain on the vehicle and the fast swishing sound of the wipers, to a muted sense of drips and wipers suddenly gone dry. When the lane opened again to the half-moon driveway to the house, the noise was again deafening.

But Jessie's eyes were drawn to a flash of red as she brought the cruiser to a stop by the front entrance.

"Mom!" Danny cried. "The woodshed's on fire!"

They jumped out of the car, Jessie dragging her radio phone with her. As she punched in her call to Dispatch, she tossed her keys to Danny and told him to let Footers out of the house.

Their eyes met momentarily over the car and through the cascading rain.

"But the house isn't on fire, Mom." He looked puzzled—and scared.

"Just do it!" she screamed over the din of wind and rain, her professional training taking precedence over her personal emotions. "Get Footers out and then get right back to the car."

He nodded, his eyes frightened, and ran to the front door and opened it. From the corner of her eye, Jessie saw their dog rush outside, as if he knew that something bad was happening. She made sure Danny and Footers were running back to her car before she moved forward, her call for help to Central Communications already sent. She'd unsnapped her holster and was ready to grab her gun at an instant's notice.

A glance behind her and she knew Danny was at the car.

"Get inside!" she yelled. "And lock the doors so Footers

can't escape." Then, to make sure she didn't terrify him, she added. "I need you to mind the radio in case the fire department needs directions." She knew that wasn't true, but was relieved when he climbed into the car with Footers. She assumed he locked the doors.

And then she moved forward, pulling her pistol from the holster when she knew Danny couldn't see. There was no way in hell that her woodshed had caught fire—unless someone had started it.

She moved forward carefully, keeping to the line of the garage wall, and the shrubs and trees that decorated the property. As Jessie drew closer, careful to stay in the shadows, an acrid smell assaulted her nostrils. Accelerant, she thought.

Someone had started the fire on purpose. Who? Why?

She pressed herself against the wall of the garage, her arms outstretched with her pistol fully cocked, ready to fire. Someone had done this. Was that someone still out there, watching? Waiting for her to step into a clear target?

Oh God. Why was she projecting this into a personal arena? Couldn't this be about local island defacement of property by the so-called have-nots?—random events that had nothing to do with her and the imagined perception of her wealth, because she was heir to this property?

But that was second in Jessie's thoughts as she moved forward toward the door of the woodshed, hoping that she might put out the fire before everything was engulfed. The sudden figure that loomed up and moved toward her, deflecting her as she was about to approach, shoved her sideways, causing her to stumble to her knees.

"No! Do not go in there!"

And then with a sudden swoosh, the whole structure collapsed in flames.

As Jessie struggled back to her feet, gun in hand, there was no one in sight. She was left with the warning that had been given in a female voice, one she'd never heard before.

In the distance she could hear approaching sirens. In minutes, Hank's patrol car careened onto the circle of the driveway, coming to stop behind her own cruiser. As he got out, Danny, followed by Footers, exited her car. And then the fire truck popped out of the lane onto the driveway. It circled to the closest point to the fire and stopped. A second emergency vehicle was right behind it. The men were soon unwinding hoses to extinguish the flames.

It took a half hour before the department felt the fire was under control, and another hour to make sure everything was out.

"I'm afraid it might be arson, Jessie," Hank told her after Danny and Footers had gone into the house.

"Yeah."

"You know?"

"I got a whiff of accelerant when I first approached the woodshed."

"Jeez, I'm glad something stopped you from going into that building as it was about to collapse."

"That wasn't it."

"What was?"

"The woman who pushed me aside before I went in."

"Woman? Someone was there?"

"Uh-huh."

"Who?"

"I don't know. I didn't see her face, only heard her voice."

"My God."

"Yeah, I know. She saved my life."

"You think she started the fire?"

"I have no way of knowing." She hesitated. "But my gut says no."

"And—"

"She—whoever she is—as I said, saved my life."

There was a silence.

"Whatever, Jessie." He led her toward the house and opened the door. "But if you remember anything else, mark it down. This is probably some kind of a ritual by kids or some weird group." He paused, and his tone hardened. "But when we catch them we'll prosecute to the max, be assured of that. Thank God it was raining or the fire might have spread to the garage."

She nodded, and hoped his son's group had nothing to do with it. He must be thinking the same thing.

But she only smiled, watched as he went back to his police car, and then closed the door.

Jessie needed to sleep, forget her fears—about the fire, about who had set it—and who had saved her. But first she had to calm her son, help him with his computer games, and then see him to bed with a positive outlook for tomorrow.

She prayed her own outlook would be as positive. Because she had her doubts. Something was going on just beyond her understanding.

But somehow she'd find out what that was. She had to. So much depended on doing just that.

The future of her little family.

Surely that didn't mean their lives?

But she wondered, because they'd come back to her beginnings, a situation she didn't understand. But her vague memories were disconcerting.

She vowed to call her mother in the morning and demand answers. It was time her mom stepped up to the plate.

She just hoped that she would.

CHAPTER FIFTEEN

"MOM, YOU NEED TO TELL ME EVERYTHING ABOUT THE ISLAND and this house that you know."

The heavy rainfall had continued throughout the night and Jessie had driven Danny to school in the morning, not allowing him to ride his bike as he'd wanted. She'd come back to the house to call her mother, her work shift not starting until 10:00 AM. She waited now as a silence stretched through the lines from Mendocino, California, to her remote island.

"Mom? Are you there?"

A sigh came over the wires. "I'm here." A pause. "Before I say anything, tell me what's happened?"

Jessie explained.

"Oh, my God!"

Jessie heard her mother suck in her breath but she didn't give her time for histrionics, so her mom could avoid a direct answer. Jessie needed honesty now.

"Mom?" she said again. "I'm your daughter, Danny is your only grandson, and I need your help."

"I know, Jessie. I'll help you any way that I can." Her voice wobbled. "I just never believed there'd still be a threat, since your great-uncle and his son were both dead, and there are no other descendants." She drew in another breath. "I would have stopped you from moving up there if I'd thought there was danger for you and Danny."

"A threat?"

"Uh-huh." Clarice's voice was stronger. "I once believed, way back when you were a toddler and we still lived on the island, after your father drowned, that our lives were in danger."

Jessie controlled her reaction, maintaining a calm manner. "Please explain."

"I believed that your father's death was not an accident." Her mother gulped, composing herself, and Jessie waited, sensing her mother's upset. "Maybe I was influenced by the shock of him dying, or maybe I was right. I didn't know so I left with you, because I was afraid for us." Her words drifted off into another silence.

"That's it?"

"Basically. But now that you know why we left I'll fill in all the blanks when I come up to visit the two of you."

"When is that, Mom?"

"Over the holidays?" Clarice asked. "I was thinking that would be a good time to come. And—" She hesitated. "Jessie, I don't think old family history has anything to do with your fire, there's hardly anyone left of the family now, no one would have anything to gain." Another pause. "I think it could have something to do with the island and your new job."

"That's an odd thing to say, Mom." She didn't dare mention who also lived on the island—Ben Thrasher. That was a whole different type of threat that was unrelated to fires or family history.

"Not so odd once you've lived on the island for a while, Jessie."

"What do you mean?"

"Only that remote places have always attracted strange people who have opted out of real life. There are people who gravitate to places like Cliff Island where they can feel invisible. A new police officer like you Jessie, who comes from the Bay area might pose a threat to one of them and they go after you before you get them."

"That's a real left-field assumption, Mom. Besides, I only started my job."

"Jessie, you'll soon learn that anything happening on the island is grist for the gossip mill. Believe me, the islanders knew all about you before you ever set foot on their soil."

"What does all this mean in the context of our conversation?"

"I guess I want to reaffirm that you're safe in the house, there's no one left with an agenda to harm you and Danny." A sigh came over the line. "But promise me Jessie, that you'll look elsewhere for the person who started the fire. And take precautions. Wind House is out there by itself, away from other dwellings. I want you and Danny to be safe."

"Don't worry, Mom, we will be. And I look forward to our talk when you come up here during the holidays. You know we'd love to have you anytime. In fact we'd love you to move up here permanently."

"It's kind of an artistic desert, Jessie, but thanks for the invite."

"You might be surprised," Jessie said, and then went on to explain about the art galleries in town, how there were many thriving artists on the island, and ended with the flourishing tourist trade who bought the art. "And don't forget that artists are on-line nowadays." Jessie paused. "People know your art, Mom. You could still sell your work if you moved to Paris, New York or this island."

"We'll talk about it when I visit," Clarice replied. "But in the meantime, keep me posted about everything. And stay safe, Jessie."

She heard the anxious note in her mother's voice. "Of course I will."

After promises and lingering good-byes they finally hung up. As Jessie went out to her patrol car to start her day she was thoughtful. Her mom had a story to tell and she looked forward to hearing it. But she also knew her mom couldn't be pressured, would only reveal past events when she was ready, especially since she no longer believed her daughter was in danger.

Her mom was probably right; she had nothing to fear from old family history. And then Jessie remembered something. Her mother had said *almost* all of her relatives were dead. What did that mean? That there was still someone else?

She headed down the overgrown driveway, making a mental note to hire someone to cut back the foliage. But for now she needed to start her day.

Jungle drums. How apt of the chief to label the local gossip as such, Jessie thought as she drove through town. Everyone she'd come in contact with today knew about her woodshed fire, and had an opinion about what had happened—from spontaneous combustion, to suggestions that some people didn't like a female assistant chief, to a local boater who might have come up the cliff path to borrow one of the gas cans everyone knew were stored in the woodshed, and accidentally started a fire. She hadn't known about the stored gas cans. No one had told her.

"Yeah, it's true, odd as it seems," Hank said when she asked him later, substantiating the common knowledge of stored gas in the shed. "It was once a fairly common practice for islanders to store gas for their boats, the habit going back to the early days when there was no place to buy it here."

"So you lean toward someone coming up the path from the beach to get it?"

"It's a distinct possibility, Jessie."

"But how would that cause a fire?"

"God only knows," he replied. "An accident probably." A pause. "But we're investigating further, as you know."

"Okay, well, thanks." She hesitated. "Anymore on the woman who probably saved my life?"

"Not a word but I'm still checking it out. I'll keep you posted."

They ended the conversation and Jessie went back to work, but she wondered if he was making light of the incident.

In San Francisco the investigation would have followed a different course. But you're no longer a member of the SFPD she reminded herself. You're on a remote island that is behind the times.

At least Leonard Wills, the lawyer for the estate, had assured her that he'd take care of the insurance issues concerning the fire, that there would be compensation.

But that didn't make her feel any better. She wanted to know that the fire was accidental, not deliberate.

She'd just have to wait and see.

Jessie was still on duty when she picked up Danny at school. Although the rain had slowed it hadn't stopped. He was a little upset that he had to go home rather than to the gym to watch practice.

"Don't forget that your computer games have all been

installed," she reminded him. "And I'll put supper in the oven to be ready when I'm off duty, around six."

"Yeah, but I'll be there alone until then."

"You'll have Footers."

"I know, but I get lonesome."

"Goodness, Danny, you've hardly been alone since we got here." She glanced at him, trying to read his expression. "You aren't scared to stay alone for two hours, are you?"

"Nope."

"Then what?"

"Dunno."

She steered the car off the highway onto North Point Road which led to their driveway. "Do you want me to make arrangements so that you can stay somewhere in town until I get off work and we can both come home together?"

"No way! What about Footers? He'd wonder what had happened to me."

"Then what, Danny?"

She glanced and he was staring straight out the window, as though he were considering his answer. "I know there is nothing weird going on at home. It's just that I feel like I'm being watched."

"At our house?"

"No, everywhere."

She slammed on the brakes, bringing the cruiser to a stop in the middle of the road before the turnoff to their driveway. Then she turned to him. "What are you saying, Danny? That someone is following you?" She leaned toward him. "Is it that old woman—Nita?"

"Oh, no. She wouldn't hurt me—or anyone."

"But you said she is often on the road when you ride your bicycle home."

He nodded. "But she's not a mean person, Mom. She's only old."

Despite her concern, Jessie almost smiled. "Honey," she said instead. "I'm not going to drop you off until we sort out your concerns. You can ride with me until it's time to go home. And tomorrow I'll figure out another plan so you don't have to be in the house alone, especially after it gets dark."

"Mom! I'm not scared." He turned to her. "Besides, as you said, I have Footers."

"But we have things to talk about, Danny, and I understand that."

"Like what?"

"Uh, different things that might scare us in a big house." She gave a laugh. "I even thought I saw a light bobbing off the north point of the island, and realized it had to be a boat, not a ghost."

"Oh, Mom. What you saw was Nita's tugboat."

She straightened. His words were unexpected. "Old Nita?"

"Yup. She lives on it, has for thirty years."

"The same Nita you've seen on the road?"

He nodded.

"But that's not a normal place to live," she said, inanely.

He shrugged. "It's normal for her." His expression brightened. "She's a great person. I'd love to have her for a grandmother any day."

Jessie sat stunned by his words. She hadn't known her son had become attached to such a strange person. She wondered what it meant.

She shifted into drive, pressed the accelerator and allowed the car to move forward, make the turn and headed up to the curve past the totem to the door. It was still daylight, although it wouldn't be in another month. They needed an electrician to put in automatic lights out there that came on at dusk. The place needed to be illuminated, especially if her son had to be home alone at times.

She brought the cruiser to a stop. "So go get Footers and you can both ride with me until the end of my shift."

And he did.

CHAPTER SIXTEEN

JESSIE WATCHED THE LAST OF THE FERRY TRAFFIC MOVE UP from the boat onto the island and disappear in the direction of the main street of town. Then the few cars heading off the island drove onto the ferry, and a few minutes later the ship was headed out of the slip, back toward the other island stops and ultimately the mainland where the highway led south to Seattle.

"That's it. I'm minutes away from being off duty for the night."

Danny sat up straighter on the passenger seat and Footers raised his head from between paws on the backseat. "Can we go home then, Mom?"

"Yep, right after I stop by the station."

"How come?"

"I need to get my schedule for the next week." Jessie pulled up in front of the police station. "Only take a few minutes, and then we'll go home." She got out of the cruiser, then stuck her head back inside. "Remember, the Xbox is connected now." She grinned. "You can play it, after your homework, of course."

He smiled back. "If I'd stayed home in the first place I'd already be playing with it."

"I know, but then your mom would have had to finish her patrol alone. Instead I had company to make the time pass more quickly." She lifted her hand in a salute, glad the past couple of hours had been uneventful. "Be right back," she called over her shoulder.

He nodded and she went into the police station, waving to Rose at the front desk before heading down the hall toward Hank's office where he'd have posted the schedule. Glancing at the wall clock, Jessie realized that the woman's shift was almost over, too.

"Wait, Jessie," Rose called after her. "You've got some mail."

Jessie turned back. "Mail?"

"Yep." She gave a laugh. "It's addressed to you but it came through the after-hours message chute on the front door and not through the post office."

Jessie raised her eyebrows. "Is that typical of receiving mail?"

"Nope, but then Cliff Island isn't typical either." She shrugged. "I expect someone didn't know your address."

Jessie smiled as she took the sealed envelope. "So they simply dropped it off themselves?"

"Uh-huh."

"Thanks, Rose," she said, and continued down the hall.

"Hey, Cline," Max DeForio, the part-time officer said from another office as she passed. "You lookin' for Hank?"

She paused, backing up so she could see him through the open doorway. She shot him a grin, having liked him on the spot when she first met him several days ago. A former homicide detective from upstate New York, he'd retired with his wife to the island. Although he seemed low-key now, she sensed that he'd been very effective at his job. Max had taken the part-time position to supplement his retirement income, having moved to the island in the first place because their only daughter and family lived in Anacortes. Hank had told her that Max and his wife had no other relatives still living on the East Coast.

"Well, yes and no," Jessie said, finally. "I'm really only looking for my work schedule for next week."

He got up and stepped from behind the desk where he'd been writing. "The chief's gone for the day but I know where the schedule is posted." He moved toward her, smiling, his balding head shining under the fluorescent ceiling lights. "Just follow me."

He was a big man in his late fifties with an expanding waistline. Jessie trailed him down the hall to the bulletin board on the wall just inside Hank's private office.

"You've got pretty good hours," he said glancing, his brown eyes candid. "Hank's a good guy. He understands needing to be home for your kid."

She scanned the schedule, her eyes verifying his words. Hank had again made sure her hours were mostly during the day, although she was on call for nights.

"I'm looking forward to meeting your wife," she told Max as they walked back toward the front entrance. She noticed that Rose had left for the day. "Rose told me all about Signe's Swedish traditions."

"Signe wants to meet you, too," Max replied, "especially since she's so into totem mythology and knows about the story behind Wind House."

Jessie paused and then dropped the envelope. Max immediately stooped to pick it up.

"What's this?" He turned it over in his hand, seeing that it was addressed to Jessie at the police station but didn't have a stamp or postmark.

She explained.

"You haven't opened it?" His expression tightened and she glimpsed the New York homicide detective in his expression.

He handed it back. "Go ahead. I'm as curious as you are," he said, assuming.

"It's probably nothing," she said. But she realized she'd been avoiding her own sense of apprehension. Before her thoughts went to the next conclusion, he expressed them for her.

"C'mon, Cline. We're former homicide detectives. We both know that kind of feeling when we get it."

A silence went by.

"Yeah, you're right."

They stood just inside the door as she carefully opened the envelope and withdrew the one standard $8 \frac{1}{2} \times 11$ paper sheet.

"You are not welcome. A woman in a man's job is not acceptable here. You will be eliminated," she read aloud, and then looked up. "It's signed with a swastika symbol."

"Son of a bitch!"

"That's what I say."

"No, it's a threat and we have to get to the bottom of it." Max's features were fixed. "There's a group on the island who seem peaceful but may be subversive under their veneer." He hesitated, and then held out his hand. "How about giving me this—this piece of shit. Hank will be checking in later and he and I can discuss it."

She hesitated. Then, as she realized there were island issues she was not yet aware of, she handed it over.

He opened the door for her. "And as I was saying before, Signe is into totem mythology. She, like you, was born out here in these islands."

Surprised, Jessie hesitated, facing him. "Your wife is not a New Yorker?"

He shook his head. "Yes and no."

She raised an eyebrow, waiting.

"Her people were Swedish immigrants and she was an

only child. They both died young and she was sent east to live with an aunt in Albany, grew up there and then met me. The rest, as they say, is history." He laughed, exposing a full set of teeth. "When our daughter married and moved out here, we followed. My wife thinks it was fate that we retired to the area where she was born."

"Who knows?" Jessie moved through the doorway to step into a misty rain. "It could be fate at that."

His booming laugh followed her out to the cruiser. She gave a final wave before stepping inside. And then she started the engine and headed for the local supermarket for a few items. As they drove she filled Danny in on the former New York homicide detective.

"He sounds like a nice guy," Danny said. "But a tough character."

"That about sums it up, Danny." And it did. That was her exact take on Max DeForio.

Shit! The driveway was even more horrible at night.

It had been dark for over an hour, and as Jessie drove up the overgrown lane to the house, she reminded herself to find a handyman to put in automatic lights with sensors and to cut back the foliage.

As she drove out of the woods into the half-moon to the front door, the house lights she'd left on illuminated the way. She brought the cruiser to a stop, leaving it available to be on call, unlike her Saturn in the garage at the far end of the property. Danny jumped out, followed by Footers.

"I have my key!" he called back to Jessie.

Once on the inlaid stone porch Danny turned back to Jessie who'd followed him with the bag of groceries, thinking they should get used to using the kitchen door on the side of the house.

"Mom, I must have forgotten to lock the door when I got Footers." To demonstrate, he pushed it open, and then turned back to her, his expression questioning.

"Yeah, you must have because no one else has a key, Danny. Or the locks aren't catching again." She made a mental note to call the locksmith as well as the electrician. The locks were definitely faulty.

They went inside and, unbeknownst to Danny, Jessie checked out the whole house, even as she told herself there was no intruder. Again, she bypassed the locked door to the basement, still too fearful to go down there alone, even though she realized it was perfectly secure, if dark and scary.

While she cooked dinner Danny did homework and then logged onto the computer in the morning room off the kitchen where she'd also started a fire in the fireplace. They ate watching television in the same room that opened onto the patio that overlooked the strait, the place where Danny had first shown her the sheer drop to the beach.

The cliff had scared Jessie at first, but now it gave a strange sense of security. No one could approach them from beyond the stone wall—unless they had wings.

Later still, after their dinner had been cleared away, she and Danny went upstairs to their bedrooms for an early night, Footers opting to be with Danny, just as Jessie preferred.

She was in bed, the television off, when the phone rang on her nightstand. She grabbed the receiver.

"Hello?"

"It's Hank, Jessie."

She sat up in bed. Oh God. Don't tell me there's an emergency and I have to go, she thought.

"Hank. What's up?"

"No emergency," he said at once. "Max just told me about the envelope you received at the station."

"Yeah."

"I'm sorry about that and just wanted you to know that I'm going to get to the bottom of this right away. Okay?"

"Thanks, Hank. I appreciate that."

"We'll talk about it tomorrow, make sure we cover all bases."

"Sounds good."

"Everything else all right?"

"Yeah, just about."

"What do you mean."

"The front door was unlocked when we got home." She took a breath. "But Danny may have forgotten to lock it earlier, or at times it seems the lock doesn't catch." She managed a laugh. "I need a locksmith I think."

"Good idea." Hank sounded concerned. "But everything is secure?"

"Oh yes, we're in bed, the house locked up, and Footers is on duty."

"Sounds like you're set for the night."

"Thanks for checking on us, Hank. I really appreciate it."

"Welcome Jessie. Just doing my job."

Somehow she felt deflated by his final comment as she hung up and lay back on the pillow. The night sky was turbulent and ever-changing as she stared out though the windows.

And then she forgot her worries as her lashes fluttered and then were still.

CHAPTER SEVENTEEN

"SOMETHING IS SO GODDAMN WRONG WITH THIS SETUP," Hank muttered as he stepped out of his police car in front of the large Northwest-style cedar house. The commune founder of God's Love Enterprises owned everything on his property, including all the yurt huts where his followers lived without indoor plumbing. Patrick Sweers, a former Texan and C.E.O., had dropped out of the corporative world to pursue the meaning of his existence and his own brand of separatist religion. In the process he'd established a place for kindred souls.

Including my son, Bruce, Hank thought, grimly. He hated visiting the place, and wouldn't have today but for the maple burl he was delivering to Bruce.

Glancing around the lighted driveway that was lined with a half-dozen aging cars, and then to the adjoining garage that held the owner's four late model vehicles, Hank's gut recoiled. Son of a bitch, he thought. Would he ever get over that reaction when he was about to face Patrick Sweers?

Hank restrained himself from slamming his car door, mentally acknowledging that his anger was rooted in his doubt of the man's sincerity. Although Sweers preached the simple life to his disciples, he and his own family lived in a lavish, five thousand square foot log home. His followers lived in the rent-free yurt huts that were modeled after the dwellings of nomadic tribes in Siberia. The huts were scattered in the woods within the twenty-five acres that Pat owned. In Hank's book the guy was a con artist who'd sold his bill of goods to needy souls who were emotionally rootless. And it was all a financial write-off for him under his corporation guidelines.

I'd love to see his income tax return, Hank thought. He wasn't doing gullible people like Hank's son any favors. The whole setup was self-serving; Hank would bet his life on that.

In one way Hank wouldn't have cared about how Sweers and his followers lived in their commune environment where many of the residents were rumored to have signed over their meager assets to the betterment of the whole—as long as they didn't hurt anyone or break the law.

But that way of thinking was before his son, Bruce, had become a member.

Before Bruce had become totally estranged from his own father.

Before he'd been brainwashed.

A mist of rain enveloped Hank as he walked to the front door. Inside the house he could hear singing, a droning sound of voices without instrumentation. He waited until the music stopped, then lifted the door knocker.

There was no answer.

After long seconds, Hank thumped the knocker again, this time harder.

Again, there was no sound on the other side of the door. About to try again, he saw a movement at the window down the side of the house. Someone had checked out the porch to see who was there. They couldn't have missed the police cruiser in the driveway, or the uniformed person on the porch for that matter. Abruptly the door opened to reveal Patrick Sweers.

"Chief Shepherd." His tone was calm and noncommittal, as always. "What can I do for you?" He lifted his arm to indicate the room behind him. "As you can see we're having an evening prayer meeting here." His smile seemed insincere to Hank. "You're welcome to join us."

"Uh, no, but thanks anyway." Hank managed to produce his own insincere smile. "I just needed to talk to my son, Bruce. He wasn't at his place, so I tried yours." A pause. "Is he here?"

A silence went by as Patrick Sweers adjusted his expression from a set politeness to contrived concern. "Uh-huh, he's here. If you'll hang on, I'll see if he's available to talk to you."

Hank resisted an impulse to kick the shit out of the bastard. Instead he nodded.

Sweers' eyes glinted, momentarily holding Hank's gaze. A big man with a graying beard, a self-described peace-loving environmentalist, he was the first to lower his eyes, as though he sensed that Hank had never trusted him.

Hank, as hard as he'd tried, could not shake his suspicions about the guy. He couldn't get past the idea that Patrick Sweers wasn't the saintly leader he presented to his followers. His distrust of Sweers had motivated Hank to run him through NCIC computers, the National Crime Information Center that tracked criminals. He'd also checked him out through other tracking systems in Texas. Patrick Sweers had come up clean, with no prior arrests.

It had been a dead end.

Now as Sweers gave a nod, then turned, closed the door to a crack, and went back to his flock, Hank waited.

If his son was in the congregation he figured Patrick Sweers would direct him outside. Sweers didn't want a police problem.

The door opened suddenly.

"Dad, you were looking for me?"

"Yeah, I wanted to talk to you."

"About what?" Bruce shook his head. His long dark hair swished around his face, then settled back on his neck as he went silent.

"About police business, father and son stuff—and I brought a gift," Hank said, trying to sound official and congenial at the same time.

Again, as always, his son's calm manner and steady gaze reminded him of his wife, the woman who'd suffered quietly with cancer while he was often absent, doing his job as a homicide detective with the Seattle Police Department. He didn't think he'd ever get over the guilt for not realizing how sick she'd been, for not putting her above his job. At the time he'd thought he was, as they needed his income and his medical insurance. Bruce had let him know that he blamed his dad, that Hank was somehow responsible for his mom's death. After that Bruce stopped communicating with Hank about anything other than what was necessary. At eighteen he'd left home for good.

Bruce's sober expression didn't alter as he prompted his dad to explain. "So how can I help your police business, and how does that relate to me being your son?"

There was a silence as Hank considered.

Shit, he thought. How did he come right out and ask his own son, a member of God's Love Enterprises, if someone in his group, some of whom were practicing bigots who didn't believe in equality between the sexes, had stooped to leave a swastika-signed note to his second in command, a woman?

"Well, the son stuff means I brought you a maple burl that Tommy at the arts and craft shop thought you might like for your work."

"A maple burl? Like part of a tree?"

"Yeah. Tommy's brother is a logger and he found it in the woods and gave it to Tommy." Hank spread his hands, grinning. "Tommy thought of you and your woodworking and asked me if I thought you'd want it. Do you?"

"Darn right." Pete's sober expression had been replaced by one of pleasure. "That's a real find."

"That's exactly what Tommy said." Hank hesitated. "It's pretty big but it fit in my car trunk. I stopped by your place, and when you weren't home, I figured I'd see if you were here, so I could give it to you."

"Uh, I don't know, Dad." Bruce's expression clouded with sudden disappointment. "I can't afford to pay anything for it." He paused. "Unless Tommy can work a deal with me. I was planning on asking him if he'd take some of my carvings on consignment."

"That's a good idea, the consignment thing, but as far as the burl goes, Tommy wanted you to have it for free."

"You're kidding."

"Uh-uh. Tommy mentioned that the widest end would make a beautiful coffee table top, and the smaller part could be cut to make at least two wall clocks, one bigger than the other as the burl narrows." Hank had walked to the back of the patrol car as he talked. After opening the trunk he stepped aside for Bruce to see the burl.

"It's beautiful." Bruce ran his hand over the rough knot of wood, as though anticipating how his artistic skill could turn it into beautiful pieces of art, already feeling the texture that, under his fingers, would become as smooth as polished stone. "Tommy's right," he said finally. "The wide end could be a table top, the next width a big wall clock and then a smaller wall clock." He glanced up, grinning. "The end piece is big enough for one or two small carvings."

Hank nodded, pleased. It wasn't often that he and his son saw eye-to-eye. Although Bruce was almost a carbon copy of his father in build and looks, aside from the black hair he'd inherited from his mother, he and his son were quite different in temperament. His son was the artist; he was the pragmatic cop.

Don't go there, Hank instructed himself. The water was too deep and he could drown in guilt. The woman they'd both loved was dead, and his son blamed him.

"Can I take it back to your place then?" Hank asked.

"Yeah. I'd appreciate that."

"You don't have to go back inside?"

"No, they'll understand." Bruce's response was clipped, as though he didn't welcome questions, or explanations.

They rode in silence as Hank maneuvered the overgrown track that served as a road on the Sweers property. He pulled into a small clearing in front of Bruce's yurt hut, a circular, domed, tent-like structure constructed of long thin strips of wood. A fire trap, Hank thought. The very look of the dwelling reminded him of how boy scouts constructed a campfire, before they struck the match and set it ablaze.

They unloaded the burl, took it inside the one-room hut and placed it on the floor by Bruce's workbench. The circular room was divided into four sections; the kitchen area, the sleeping place, the work space and a small section for an overstuffed chair near a crude fireplace where Bruce relaxed to watch the nineteen-inch television set Hank had given him before he left home. It was a primi-

tive setup but at least the fireplace kept the room warm
and it was wired for lights.

But a firetrap nonetheless, Hank thought as he glanced
over Bruce's carvings of animals, boats and human fig-
ures. He was indeed a talented carver, just as Hank's own
father had been.

"My inventory for Tommy," Bruce said, noticing his
father's interest.

Hank nodded. "Beautiful work, Son." He bit back his
other thoughts before they became words that his son
would find offensive. *How much of any profit will you keep?
Will it all be donated to God's Love Enterprises?*

They went back outside to the cruiser. Hank was
dropping Bruce off at Sweer's house on his way back to
town. Driving along the overgrown track, Hank tried to
hide his frustration. How had they come to this?—his son
in a commune, he running the police department on a
remote island?

He knew why. He wanted to save his son.

Hank pulled up in front of the log house and Bruce
jumped out. "Thanks, Dad. I appreciate your delivery."
About to close the door he bent down again, facing his
father.

"What was the other thing?"

"Other thing?"

"Yeah, you said you'd come to see me on personal and
police business." He gave a brief smile. "The burl was the
personal issue, but you didn't say what the police stuff
was."

Hank had momentarily forgotten his main reason for
coming. Now he hesitated, trying to form his words so as
not to offend his son about his commune friends.

"I have a new assistant chief, as you may have heard,"
he began. "My officer is a woman."

"Yeah, I know, from San Francisco. I've seen her son riding his bike on the road." A hesitation. "So what does your new assistant have to do with me?"

"I'm sure nothing, but I wanted to ask you a question, sort of between father and son."

Bruce's expression didn't change but Hank sensed that he'd tensed, that he was bracing himself for—what? His son had nothing to hide, did he?

"Someone has been harassing her, left a threatening note in fact, about not liking a woman in a man's job. It was signed with a swastika."

A silence went by.

"And you think it was me who sent this note?"

"God, no. I just thought you may have, uh, heard something about it."

"So you think someone here is threatening your female officer, is that it? And you think I might know who?"

Hank answered out of sudden annoyance, losing his diplomacy. "Do you?"

A long sigh was Hank's answer. His son turned to go.

"You didn't answer my question, Bruce."

"Because it doesn't deserve an answer."

"You're saying no one here would send such a threat, that no one here is prejudiced about a woman's role in the world."

"I'm saying nothing, Dad." Bruce had taken several steps away from the cruiser and now he turned back to face Hank. "I'm just sorry that you had a need to ask me that in the first place." He lifted his hand in a farewell salute. "But thanks for delivering the burl. I do appreciate that."

And then he continued onto the porch, opened the door and disappeared into the house, leaving Hank staring after him.

You blew it again, man, he told himself. Face it. You and your son will never get things right, never have a meeting of the minds—*never get over the loss.*

He drove away feeling depressed. But beneath his depression was something else. Had his son deliberately turned the conversation into their own personal dilemma? If so, why?

Was he hiding something?

CHAPTER EIGHTEEN

JESSIE CAME AWAKE SLOWLY, ROLLING ONTO HER SIDE before scooting up the pillows to a sitting position. A glance at the clock told her it was almost five in the morning. Outside the night was still and black, and she was reminded of the old saying that the darkest part of the night was just before dawn.

But dawn was still a good two hours away. She sighed, relieved that it wasn't time to get up yet. The bed was warm and cozy; the quiet house felt cold and damp and she didn't relish the shock to her nightgown-clad body.

She sat on in the silence, her mind going over all the events since arriving on the island, then moving forward to an inventory of tomorrow's work schedule. Not a good way to get back to sleep, she reminded herself, and smiled into the shadowy room. An active mind was not conducive to a peaceful rest.

But she couldn't turn off her thoughts and decided that a cup of sleep-inducing tea might do the trick. Slipping out from under the quilts, she grabbed her robe from the foot of the bed and put it on quickly, then slid her feet into slippers and moved to the door.

Gliding though the dimly lit house via the backstairs to the kitchen, Julia was suddenly aware that it was even darker in the house than usual, at least since she and

Danny had occupied it. The front lights were out, as were the outdoor lights beyond the kitchen.

She was suddenly rooted to the cold tiles of the kitchen floor. All the exterior lights couldn't be burned out.

What was she hearing?

It sounded like a ticking clock.

Impossible. There was no clock on the patio outside the morning room. But the steady tick of a clock sounded in her ears, even though she stood in the middle of the kitchen. Slowly she tiptoed forward, until she was through the doorway to the morning room where she and Danny ate their meals. The sound was stronger, right outside the French doors to the patio.

All of her police training surfaced. The sound was ominous and out of place; it could be a timing device to start another fire.

Her reflexes took hold. She whirled around and ran toward the front hall and door. Instantly, she saw that the porch lights were also dark. Turning back to the hall table and the phone, she yanked up the receiver. It was dead.

Suddenly terrified, Jessie knew someone was out there, someone who'd made sure the lights were out, the phone wires disconnected. Someone who knew she and Danny were isolated without communication to the outside world. Someone with an ulterior motive.

There was no time for fear. Jessie flew up the steps, her footsteps silent, realizing that the person out there might not have realized that she'd awakened and come downstairs.

Once in her room Jessie grabbed her cell phone that she always kept next to her bed, a practice from her San Francisco days, and punched in 911.

An operator responded and Jessie quickly gave her name, police position, and address before her message for help, knowing that location was most important. In seconds the operator answered that help would be on its way. Jessie knew that the island call for help had been relayed through Central Communications in the county, and then back to the police station on the island, probably to Hank.

In the meantime, she needed to be ready. Grabbing her police-issued pistol, she checked the chamber to make sure it was fully loaded, then headed back to the hall. She needed to make sure Danny and Footers were safe. As she moved forward she wondered why their dog hadn't alerted them to the danger. But she also realized that Danny's room was on the side of the house overlooking the strait, as was hers, and that Footers was probably too far away from the part of the house where the clock was ticking.

Oh God, she thought. Surely the attached clock wasn't a device to set off another fire.

She needed to get to her son.

And then what? Where would they go that was safe? The car?—the woods?—maybe the cliff path to the beach? Dear God, she didn't know if the tide was in or out. And outside the arsonist might be awaiting their flight? To shoot them, like fake ducks in an arcade?

Think calmly, she reminded herself. You're a professionally trained policewoman, not a just a terrified mother who fears for her son.

She burst into Danny's room and Footers woofed softly from the foot of the bed. Recognizing her, he stood up, rocking the bed, arousing Danny who sat up, rubbing his eyes.

"Mom, what's going on? It's not time to get up yet, is it?"

"Yeah, Son, it is." She rushed to his bed, helping him to his feet. "I'm so sorry, but we've got to get out of here."

"But, Mom—"

"Right now."

He caught her sense of urgency and was suddenly wide awake. "What's happened?—why?—"

"Shh," she whispered. "I'll explain later. We just have to leave."

They'd still not turned on any lights, alerting anyone who might be out there watching. And they'd not made a sound, not even a major bark out of Footers. She sensed her son's fear, although he was trying hard to be brave.

As they went down the main staircase, Jessie wondered what to do next, although her gun was in the pocket of her robe, her right hand holding it, finger on the trigger. Should they head out the front door to the cruiser, or wait for help.

Then they heard the sound of a siren moving closer. She knew Hank was on his way. They reached the front entry hall just as the police cruiser pulled up below the steps to the porch, its blue and red lights revolving in through the front windows.

When the knock came on the door she opened it at once. Hank stood in the doorway, gun drawn.

"We're okay," she said, meeting his eyes. "The problem is in the back of the house, the morning room next to the kitchen."

He nodded and stepped into the entry and she closed the door behind him.

"Stay here," he told Danny, "and keep the dog with you."

Danny nodded, looking subdued.

Hank moved forward, gun drawn, and Jessie followed, drawing her own gun after she was out of Danny's vision. They entered the dark kitchen, then moved slowly toward the connecting morning room, where she and Danny, and generations before them, had eaten breakfast and lunch and enjoyed the view of the strait.

Silence met them.

There was no ticking sound anywhere.

Hank moved forward and shone a high-powered flashlight all over the patio. Everything was as Jessie remembered. Nothing was out of place.

"But there was a ticking clock out there," she said, trying not to feel foolish. "And as you can see, the patio light is out."

Hank inclined his head, then went to the wall switch and flipped it. Instant light illuminated the patio.

"But it didn't work before. I swear it was out."

Hank was inscrutable; she couldn't read his thoughts from his expression.

"Something was about to happen, Hank, I know it. Maybe it was your siren that aborted it."

"Possibly," he said, his gaze direct. "You say you heard a ticking sound on the patio." He hesitated. "Do you think it was a timing device?"

Her anger was instant. He didn't believe her. "Yes, I fuckin' think it was some sort of detonation device, Chief Shepherd. And no, I don't know why it was out there. But it was. It's not now. But please, don't forget, I'm not a novice. I've been trained and I know what I'm talking about."

"I wouldn't forget your California background, Officer Cline."

"Just as I respect your background, Chief Shepherd."

They stared at each other, at a stalemate. Hank was the first to glance away. "Okay then, I'll check out the grounds, make sure your house is secure."

"Thanks, I'd appreciate that."

"C'mon, Jessica, were on the same side here," he said. "Let's not get carried away."

"We won't, if you believe my story."

There was a long hesitation.

"Of course, I do."

"Then?"

"Then we need to prove who's responsible for these acts of vandalism."

"Vandalism?"

"Yeah, what else could it be?"

She had no answers. But somehow she knew it was more than vandalism.

He stepped forward.

"We'll get to the bottom of this, okay?"

She nodded.

And then she watched him go outside to check out the property. But she knew he wouldn't find anything. Whatever had been about to happen was long gone. Postponed?

She hoped not.

CHAPTER NINETEEN

JESSICA FELT THE HOUSE WAS SECURE AFTER HANK LEFT, BUT in some strange way, she knew it wasn't. Something was wrong that wasn't apparent. Fortunately, it would soon be daylight. Everything always seemed better after the sun came up. She hoped it would today.

She was still in the kitchen when the phone rang, startling her. She grabbed the receiver from its wall mount, her one thought, not scaring Danny again. He'd gone back to bed and she hoped he was already asleep.

"Hello?"

She realized her voice was too faint. "Hello," she said again.

"Jessie?"

"Yeah, what's up Hank?"

"Nothing's new." A pause. "I wanted to reassure you that what's going on isn't life threatening. I believe one person is behind all of the vandalism, because you're new on the island and in a position of authority."

"Why would you come to that conclusion?"

"I know about a group that has a sexist, bigoted philosophy on life." A pause. "They may have a weirdo or two in the mix."

"And you think one of these people is responsible for my problems?"

"I think it's a strong possibility. And I'm going to check them out."

"Thanks, Hank. I appreciate the call and the fact that you're taking my incidents seriously. But in the meantime, I'm going to institute a few changes here as well."

"Like what?"

"Changing the door locks, having an electrician put in exterior automatic sensor lights and having the wiring checked." She took a deep breath. "It was very strange that the patio light was out until you arrived."

"I'm guessing that someone unscrewed the bulb."

"And then screwed it back after you arrived?"

"It's a possibility, Jessie."

"You're right about one thing, Hank."

"What's that?"

"There have to be weirdoes on this island to do such a thing."

His indrawn breath sounded in her ear. "Yeah, well let's see what happens. For now, you and Danny are all right?"

"Uh-huh."

"Then get some sleep, Jessie. I'll see you in the office in a few hours, okay?"

"Yeah, see you."

They hung up and for long seconds she stared at the receiver in her hand before returning it to the wall phone. What had he meant about the island weirdoes? Did he suspect the commune where his son lived?

"So you say that the wiring in the house seems fine?"

Jessie had made the appointment with the only electrical company listed in the island phone book as soon as she'd come into her office that morning. He'd agreed to meet her at noon during her lunch break.

"Umm, yeah." The skinny man shifted his weight. "Course I've only taken a superficial glance at things, although I know your grandmother had everything updated a few years before her death." He scratched at his skimpy beard. "But I think the house is electrically sound." He hesitated. "You said you wanted some exterior lights installed?"

"I want sensor lights along the driveway and on the porches to come on automatically at dusk."

"I can work up a price estimate this afternoon, and if you approve it, we can start the work tomorrow."

"The sooner the better," she said, hiding her surprise and her reservations. In the Bay Area anyone who would agree to do the work that fast would raise red flags about their credibility.

"You wanna stop by our office after four?"

"Okay, I can do that."

He inclined his head, and then strode to his aging pickup truck. As he climbed behind the wheel he unrolled his window. "We're reasonably priced, as you'll see. We like having all the local work." And with those final words he started his vehicle and headed down the driveway to the road.

She climbed into the police cruiser, gave him a minute and then followed him to the road. It was a relief to know that her dark property would soon be illuminated.

And that reminded her that Skip, the aging hippie locksmith was coming by the house the next morning at eight to change the door locks.

Later in the afternoon she wrote a check for two hundred fifty dollars to seal the electrician's agreement, and then strode out of the tiny office which was close to Tommy's arts and craft shop. On impulse, she headed down several storefronts to Tommy's entrance, hesitating when her eyes caught the headlines of a Seattle daily newspaper in a vending machine next to the door.

BEN THRASHER'S CARTOON STRIKES AGAIN!

Jessie bent closer to read the details. She'd heard rumors in the past, and recently at Lynda's talk, of how Ben had built his career on political controversy, and that his nationally syndicated cartoons focused on the flaws of elected officials. As she read, Jessie realized that he was still savaging the Washington State senator who had been accused of sexually harassing female interns.

The article was cut off by the newspaper's fold and, without hesitation, she rummaged in her purse for the needed coins to buy a copy. As she fed the machine and then pulled open the glass door to grab a paper, she smiled wryly. How like Ben's personal ethics; he was being so pious when he'd been guilty of the same faults of which he'd accused the senator: lying, cheating and dishonesty.

She stepped into the shop and a faint smell of oil and turpentine brought back other memories: her mom's studio, her own years of painting, her university years—a time when she'd lived and breathed for her own art. She gave herself a mental shake. That was then, this was now, but she could still enjoy the work of other artists.

Moving deeper into the shop, Jessie let herself become absorbed in the paintings hanging on the walls, seeing that Tommy was in conversation with another young man. Jessie read the placard under each work that gave the local artist's name and price of the painting. She realized quickly that there was nothing in the shop as good as her own personal inventory, canvases she'd never offered for sale.

Then, as she browsed, her eyes fell on some carvings of rowboats, fish and other sea life, pieces that another woman in the shop was also interested in. As the customer moved down the display shelf to blown glass lamps, she glanced at Jessie and nodded, her brown eyes oddly intense in an angular face that was not quite pretty. Jessie smiled back, then leaned forward to examine the carved rowboat, complete with tiny oars and seats. It was exquisite. And then she saw the name of the artist: Bruce Shepherd.

As in Chief Shepherd? she wondered. "Umm," she said aloud.

"The chief is my dad," a voice said behind her, as though reading her thoughts, if not her uniform. She turned to see the young man who'd been talking to Tommy. "These are my carvings," he said. "Newly for sale today."

She quickly regained her equanimity. "I can see the resemblance to your father," she said, referring to his first statement. "And your carvings are magnificent." She met his eyes, so like his father's. "I'm happy to meet you, Bruce." She held out her hand. "I heard that my new boss had a grown son."

He hesitated, and then took it. "Thanks for your kind words about my work."

Jessie grinned. "Believe me, Bruce, my words aren't necessarily kind, only a realistic evaluation from one artist to another. Your work is special."

"You're an artist?"

"I paint, or did when I was much younger," she said. "Painting was my passion, until I needed to earn a living." She gave a smile and wondered why she was sharing her dreams and disappointments with a strange young man, even if he was the chief's son.

But her intuition told her why. She sensed in Bruce the same quality she'd once had, a feeling of the infinite, a belief that one had a calling to one's art, an irrational understanding of something beyond one's self, that intangible quality an artist always strived to portray in his or her work. She'd always thought of it as one's unique window on the world.

Jessie reined in her thoughts, smiling again. She hoped he would succeed. He certainly had the talent. She suspected that all he needed was funding and a few lucky breaks.

He returned her smile then, and his expression transformed his face. "Thank you for everything," he said. "And I hope now that you live on the island you'll find time to paint." He nodded, as though silently evaluating her. "Because my guess is that you're pretty good yourself."

"Thanks, Bruce."

"You're welcome, Officer Cline, isn't it?"

"Jessie."

"Jessie, then."

"I'll be looking for your work, Bruce."

"And I, yours."

And then he left the shop, just as the other female customer stepped closer to examine Bruce's work. "The young man is very talented," she said.

Jessie nodded. "That's my opinion."

"You're the new assistant police chief, aren't you?" The woman's brown eyes were unwavering.

Jessie smiled. "That's right."

"I'm pretty new to the island myself, haven't been here a year yet. My name's Sarah."

She was saved from more talk by Tommy who'd overheard the conversation and joined them. After he'd helped Sarah with her purchase he turned to her. "Hey Jessie, if you ever want to place some of your paintings on consignment I'd love to hang them."

"Thanks, Tommy, but you don't even know if I'm any good."

"I know your mom is."

"You know my mother's work?"

"Uh-huh. She lives down in Mendocino, right?"

She nodded and they talked for a few more minutes and then Jessie left the shop for home. But she felt uplifted. She'd met Hank's son, a young man she'd liked on the spot, despite his standoffish way. And she had a new reason to get back to her own brushes.

Overall the island seemed a positive place after all. She hoped it stayed that way.

CHAPTER TWENTY

THE OLD WOMAN HAD WATCHED THE CONVERSATION between the new policewoman and the chief's son with interest. Nita also noticed the other woman in the shop who had taken note of the interchange, although neither Jessie nor Bruce had realized that they were being watched, or overheard.

Nita stood protected from the wind that snaked up the street from the ferry landing below the hill, huddling under the overhang outside the arts and craft shop. But her gaze through the huge-paned window didn't waver from the woman who drove the late model Volkswagen Bug that was parked down the street, one of her two vehicles.

The newcomer, a person who'd lived on the island less than a year, had positioned herself in the shop, pretending interest in wooden carvings, then in painted rocks depicting beach snails, clams and crabs, so she could stay close to Jessie. Nita had already observed the woman's fixation on another woman, and now Jessie, and wondered about her motivation.

Nita didn't like the feeling she got from the woman. It was as though the Old Spirits were warning her: *evil*.

And then she watched as Jessie spoke with Tommy, moved back through the shop to the entrance, past the mystery woman and out the door where she turned in the opposite direction from Nita. Nita watched her go, feeling proud. Tsonoqua would be pleased. Jessie was one of them, even if she didn't know that—yet.

Before Nita could amble off, another woman drove up in a Mercedes sports car and got out. Nita settled back, an unobtrusive figure sheltering herself from the wind to scan the sales items in the front window. She watched as the young woman, heavy with child, entered the shop, spoke to the clerk, and was led to an expensive display of paintings that depicted the island, both inland and seashore.

The young woman chose two seascapes, and she and the clerk walked back to the cash register. The owner of the Bug was still in the store, and Nita observed her following the young woman and the clerk—listening?

And then Nita knew.

The woman who'd driven the Volkswagen, who was as new to the island as the woman who'd bought the paintings, was barren, both of a man and of children.

Nita shivered.

She watched as first the young woman walked back to her Mercedes and drove away, then as the listener who went back to her Bug and left for the main highway. Nita was troubled. She knew from family history who Jessie was, and from newspaper accounts who the young woman was. But who was the watcher, the listener?

She didn't know that . . . yet. But she would find out. Nita knew she must. Danger was near, closing in on the last descendant of a powerful clan. A clan that must not die.

CHAPTER TWENTY-ONE

JESSIE MADE IT HOME JUST BEFORE DARK TO FIND DANNY surfing the Internet in the breakfast room, the place where they'd installed their main computer because it had the best electrical access. Danny's upstairs computer didn't have an Internet connection.

"I'm e-mailing my friends in Oakland," he told her, grinning. "They all wish they lived up here and not there."

She smiled back, understanding, and then went upstairs to change quickly out of her uniform into sweats. His friends probably thought he'd died and gone to heaven compared to their lives. None of the families of his friends could afford Danny's circumstances now. Nor could she have done so had she not inherited the house and been lucky enough to get a job in her chosen field.

They were so fortunate.

But some things were not completely perfect. However, those unexplained incidents were about to change—tomorrow lighting would be extended to include driveway lights and automatic porch sensors. And the locksmith would change all the exterior door locks to preclude any-one who'd previously had a key to the house from snooping—and make sure that the new locks engaged.

Jessie felt confident that their house and property would soon be secure. She left her weapon and purse on the bureau, and her cell phone charging in its cradle on the nightstand. Taking her handheld radio with her, she went back to the kitchen.

She and Danny had supper after he logged off the computer. They watched television as they ate, sitting on the small sofa they'd brought from California, trays on their laps, Footers sleeping peacefully at their feet. She was in the process of making the morning room into a family room, and intended to have its small fireplace chimney examined by an expert. The last thing she needed was another fire. She'd already gathered from local residents that the power often went out during winter storms. In such an emergency, the new family room and connecting kitchen could be closed off from the house and heated by the fireplace.

That would be cozy, she thought as she loaded the dishwasher and straightened the kitchen. They watched the end of a movie and then she switched off the television before Danny got engrossed in the next program.

"But it's only an hour long," he protested, as he let Footers outside for a final run around the yard before bed. "And I finished all my homework."

"I know, Son." She raised her eyebrow. "But it's a school night, and tomorrow I have a busy workday and need to get up earlier than usual."

"Okay," he said, begrudgingly, and let his dog back into the house. "I'll be glad for the weekend when I can stay up later."

"But I thought you liked your new school."

"I do, Mom, better than any school." He glanced at her as they went upstairs to his room. "It's the best. Can you believe that I may get to be a starter on my class basketball team? All of us guys are gonna sell candy for the athletic equipment fund." He hesitated. "You will let me, won't you Mom?"

"Probably, if I know just what's involved." They had reached his room and Danny explained as he changed into pajamas and brushed his teeth. "We'll set up a booth at games, hit up all the shopkeepers in town and canvas our own neighborhood."

"It sounds fine, except for the neighborhood part."

He climbed into bed. "Whattaya mean?"

"We don't live in a neighborhood, Danny. The closest neighbor is a half mile down the road."

"I can ride my bike, like I do to school when the weather is okay." He looked hopeful. "And old Nita only lives a short distance away. I know she'll buy some candy."

"How do you know that? She lives out on that rusting tugboat off the point."

Danny nodded, and as he plumped his pillows, Footers jumped onto the end of the bed. For once, Jessie wasn't worried about the dog on the quilt where he always ended up anyway after she'd left the room. "Nita told me she liked candy, even gave me a Snickers bar the other day."

"The other day?" Jessie was suddenly horrified by a frightening thought. "Where did you see her? Surely you haven't been out to that old woman's boat?"

He seemed oblivious to her concern. "Naw, I saw her on the road. She has a bike, too. Only hers has a little cart connected to the back fender, so she can get her groceries home from the store in town."

A silence went by.

"Mom you aren't upset about Nita, are you? She's really a nice person." He paused. "She's my friend."

Jessie managed a smile. "You go to sleep now, Danny." She tucked the quilt under his chin, heard his prayers and then kissed him goodnight. "We'll talk about basketball, candy sales and Nita in the morning, okay?"

"Yep. Thanks, Mom."

She nodded, made sure the nightlight was on in the connecting bathroom and left his room, closing the door behind her. But she felt unsettled and decided to ask Hank about Nita tomorrow, although she knew that he, like everyone else on the island, considered the old woman harmless. But was she?

Jessie went back downstairs to make a cup of tea, get her radio, and secure everything for the night before turning in herself. After her usual ritual of making sure the exterior house lights were on, the doors locked, including the one to the basement, she picked up the newspaper she'd bought in town. She'd held her curiosity in abeyance but now she could hardly wait to get to her room, snuggle into bed with her tea and read about her old nemesis, the island celebrity in residence.

With the newspaper tucked under her arm, her hand-held radio in one hand and the mug in the other, she started toward the back stairs. A sound behind her stopped her cold. She turned, facing the shadowy room where only the light shining in from outside kept it from being totally black.

What had she heard?

She knew what it sounded like. *A doorknob turning.*

Impossible. She'd just checked all of the locks.

But someone could have tried the knob, she reminded herself. She stared at the only two closed doors in the kitchen: the outside door and the basement door.

The hairs on her arms felt like they'd gone stiff with the sudden chill overwhelming her. With all the instinct she'd developed over the years as a policewoman she sensed a presence, something evil—and nearby.

Shit! Her revolver was upstairs with her cell phone.

But you have your radio, she told herself. Slowly Jessie set the mug, radio and newspaper on the table, her mind on the knife drawer that also held a few tools including a small hammer, knowing she had to make sure the doors were secure.

Then she slipped through the silence to the cupboard and quietly retrieved a butcher knife and the hammer. With one in each fist, and sticking to the edge of the room, she moved on to the back door and tested the knob. It was as she'd left it. Still controlling her breathing for sound, Jessie peeked from behind the shade, her gaze seeking the dark places beyond the circle of light. No one was in sight. Carefully, she adjusted the shade before facing the basement door.

You're a cop, she instructed herself. Act like one. Cops don't let unknown sounds terrify them. They don't imagine monsters in the basement.

But she admitted it. She was scared.

Forcing herself forward, Jessie took hold of the knob and held it. Momentarily she had a mental flash of another hand on the other side of the door, waiting.

Her imagination was out of control. The chain lock was still connected, the bolt still in place. For long seconds Jessie almost convinced herself to face her fear, undo the safety devices and fling the door open, so she'd know that no one was on the other side.

The thought of reading the article no longer appealed to her. She didn't need any reminders of Ben Thrasher on top of having been momentarily terrified.

She'd still have her tea in bed. But her gun would be loaded and ready under her pillow.

Because, as irrational as she knew it to be, she was still scared.

CHAPTER TWENTY-TWO

Restless, Jessie found herself unable to sleep. She looked in on Danny several times during the night, satisfied that he slept soundly, protected by Footers who acknowledged her presence with a slight wag of his tail.

Barefooted, she made the rounds of the dark house almost hourly, padding silently over the carpeted upstairs and the hardwood of the lower floor. Everything was peaceful and she knew she was being neurotic as hell, worried about an intruder when even their dog, whose hearing was sharper than hers and would bark instantly, heard nothing.

Each time she entered the kitchen her gaze went to the basement door to make sure it was still locked. That was irrational, she reminded herself, even as she felt reassured. But something about the fact that the house was on a cliff above the sea and had a musty cavern under it unnerved her. Hiring someone to inspect it would help, she thought. She'd make sure that every corner was illuminated by the flick of a light switch.

Finally Jessie grabbed a quilt from her bed, dragging it to the cushioned window seat where she wrapped it around herself and sat down. There was no use in trying to sleep when she was wide awake. Besides, the wind had come up, rattling the downspouts and fingering the loose roof shakes, sounds that weren't conducive to relaxing after her earlier apprehension. A half-moon floated in and out of ghostly cloud wings that stretched all the way to the horizon. Even the tall firs swayed and stretched their branches skyward, like feather dusters that seemed guided by an invisible hand to sweep the night around them.

Tsonoqua?

The image of the totem came unbidden. Jessie shivered, pulling the quilt tighter, as fragments of almost forgotten incidents from her childhood surfaced in her mind. Repressed memories? she wondered. Triggered by the turbulent weather—the house—and her fear?

She realized that the legend of the mythical wind spirit must have frightened her back then, because even now it unnerved her on some primal level she couldn't explain. She vaguely remembered how the air currents had blown in off the strait to claw at the house, as though seeking a way inside. In her mind's eye she saw the small child she was then hide under the covers, hoping it wouldn't find her. The wind blew then just as it did right now.

She shook her head, as if to dispel her childhood fear of the dark, that a mythical spirit who stole toddlers was looking for her. She was no longer a child.

But Danny was.

Jessie jerked her shoulders back. "For God's sake, get a grip," she murmured aloud. Although her grandmother had believed in the imaginary beings, she didn't. It was ridiculous, silly. But now she recalled how her grandmother would calm her on stormy nights. "Don't be afraid of the wind woman, child. She won't harm you because you're part of our family." Years later her mother had explained that the early Native Americans belonged

to clans and that the mythical symbol of that clan protected them. The symbol of her grandmother's clan was
Tsonoqua.

Danny also descended from that clan, she reminded
herself. So if the old ways had any credence at all then
both of them were safe—at least from the wind.

She gave a laugh at her own rationalization, but just
as her grandmother's words from the past had calmed
her back then, she felt less anxious now. She moved back
to her bed. Maybe she'd be able at least to doze until it
was time to get up. It was worth a try.

Jessie came down the back stairs to the kitchen and went
directly to the sink for water to start coffee. She was
woolly-headed from lack of sleep and needed a caffeine
hit. It had just started to drip and she was about to wake
Danny for school, when the phone rang. She grabbed the
receiver and glanced at the wall clock, knowing it was
early for a phone call—unless she was being called to
work. Please God, not today, she prayed silently. Her day
was already too busy, and her shift didn't start until ten,
after the locksmith had changed the locks.

"Hello?"

"Jessie?"

"Yep. It's me all right, Mom."

"Whew. I'm relieved."

"Relieved to hear my voice?"

"Yeah, I guess I had a bad night but I didn't want to
call earlier and wake you up."

"Mom, what's wrong? Are you okay?" Jessie adjusted
her hair away from the receiver to hear more clearly. "You
aren't sick, are you?"

"Oh, no. I'm fine. I was just worried about you and
Danny."

There was a silence.

"And that worry gave you a bad night?"

"Yeah." Clarice hesitated. "But you and Danny are both safe and everything is okay, right?"

"Uh-huh. We're doing fine." She watched Danny come down the steps, his expression questioning. She mouthed that she was talking to his grandmother. He nodded and indicated that he was going back upstairs to get Footers.

"C'mon, Mom. You didn't answer my question," Jessie said once Danny was out of earshot.

"I feel silly now," Clarice began. "I guess I can attribute it to the stormy weather that woke me up in the wee hours." She gave a laugh. "I guess my imagination got out of hand and I had a case of night terrors."

"How so?"

"You won't laugh or be upset, will you, Jessie?"

"You know better than that. I'm just concerned about you."

"Well, I just had this terrible premonition that something was wrong up there, and that you two might even be in danger."

"As you can hear, we're just fine." Jessie managed to keep her tone normal. That her mother had experienced fear in the night when Jessie had also been scared and sleepless was a little unnerving. "I hope I'm able to reassure you, put your mind at rest."

"You did, sweetie. I guess I just got upset after I heard about the ticking clock incident."

Jessie plunked down on the stool under the phone. "For heaven's sake, how did you know about that?"

Clarice's sucked in breath came over the wires.

"Oh my God! I guess I was so disconcerted that I broke my promise to Danny."

"Danny told you?"

"Well, he e-mailed me. Actually we had an instant message correspondence yesterday and he made a slip and then I made him explain." Another hesitation. "Jessie, I promised I wouldn't mention it because he was so concerned that you'd be mad at him for telling me."

Jessie digested the information. If it weren't so upsetting it would be funny. She, Danny and her mother had never been good at keeping secrets from each other. She heard Danny and Footers coming and instead of going deeper into the ticking clock issue, promised not to confront Danny, saying she'd explain later when there was more time, that the incident was nothing. Her mom sounded relieved and changed the subject to her upcoming visit over the holidays. When they hung up Jessie knew her mother's fears had been calmed, even as her own stress level felt elevated. Jessie went to pour herself a much needed cup of coffee.

About to take her first sip, two things happened at once: Danny and Footers bounded into the kitchen and a knock sounded at the back door. A glance through its window told her that the locksmith had arrived early.

Damn. Jessie put down her coffee. Oh well, she thought, grabbing the knob. Skip being early meant she wouldn't be late for duty. About to flip the deadbolt open, she froze, her gaze darting to Skip on the other side of the glass.

It was unlocked.

Slowly she opened the door and stood facing the elderly man in overalls whose expression had suddenly sobered. "You okay, Officer Cline? I know I'm early but I can come back a little later." He shook his head. "I—"

"No, early is fine, Skip." She managed to sound normal, but her mind was racing. Who'd unlocked the door?

"Anything wrong, Mom?" Danny had come up behind her to let his dog outside.

She shook her head. "Skip just arrived to change our locks. He might even have the job done before you have to leave for school."

Skip stepped into the kitchen and accepted a cup of coffee. He sat down while Jessie fixed Danny's breakfast, entertaining them both with stories about the island. By the time he went out to his van for tools and Danny had gone upstairs to get ready for school, Jessie was finally able to think about what had happened. It was definitely time for the locks to be changed because she could no longer deny that an intruder had a key.

As she loaded the dishwasher Jessie wondered if she'd have to start carrying her pistol on her person in her own house, even when she was off duty. She hoped it wouldn't come to that.

And then she went upstairs to put on her uniform and get ready for her day.

CHAPTER TWENTY-THREE

SURPRISINGLY, THE DAY PASSED SMOOTHLY, AND BY THE TIME Jessie headed home around six she felt tired in a way that meant she'd sleep tonight. Skip had managed to change the back and front door locks before she drove Danny to school that morning. His old van had rattled down the driveway behind them as they headed to the main highway.

She'd gone to the precinct to do some paperwork, and then headed back to her cruiser to patrol the island. Despite her sleeplessness, she felt herself relaxing. The island was relatively crime-free, aside from speeders, the occasional domestic dispute and intoxicated drivers when the several taverns closed after midnight. The biggest police event of the month had been her own woodshed fire, which was still being investigated by Hank. She suspected that no one would ever be charged.

Jessie smiled wryly as she slowed down for the turn into her driveway. She just hoped the insurance would pay for the loss; she couldn't rebuild the shed unless they did.

She forgot insurance claims as she steered into the lane leading to her house which was usually black. Phil, the electrician who worked for Island Electrical, had done his job. The driveway was now lit by a line of six garden lights evenly spaced along its edge. He was still loading tools into his truck when she pulled up behind him.

"Hey Phil," she cried through her lowered window. "The lighting is great, even better than I expected."

"Terrific!" he said. "I think it'll make all the difference for you." He paused. "Although this is a safe island I understand your need for lights out here on the northern point where there aren't many houses. A single woman can't feel too safe."

Her smile suddenly felt fixed. She could have done without his condescending comment but knew that he meant well. He was the opposite of Skip who was and looked like an aging hippie; Phil was professional, articulate, and wore a clean shirt and trousers instead of stained overalls. She nodded and smiled, giving him the response he expected.

"Yes, it's a huge improvement. The lights will make us feel safer."

He inclined his head, then explained in a slightly patronizing tone that the sensor was on the exterior of the garage and controlled all of the exterior lights, that there was an interior switch to the right of the door that could turn off the system if needed. "Do you think you understand how it works?"

"Yeah, got it. Thanks." Jessie reminded herself that she was no longer in San Francisco, that this was a remote island in the most northern part of the United States. She must not react to her perceived sexist attitude on his part. He meant well.

She quickly changed the subject to her next electrical project. "So you're coming back to wire parts of my basement on Saturday?"

"That's right. The boss says you're willing to pay time and a half for me to do that."

She nodded.

"I'll be here then, although we could do it before the weekend."

"I know. But I'll be on duty and unavailable, and I need to be here for that job."

She'd been pleased by how the day had worked out. She'd met him there at noon, explained what she wanted, and then gone back on duty. When she'd brought Danny home after school he was still working, and it had given her a secure feeling to know someone was with her son.

"See you on Saturday," he said.

She raised her hand in a salute as he got into his truck and started down the driveway away from the house. And then she went to join Danny in the house.

By Saturday morning Jessie was feeling confident. There had been no unsettling incidents since the new locks and exterior lights had been installed. Except for last night when something had rolled down the front roof and momentarily startled her, she'd begun to relax. She'd realized it was only a fir bough, not pebbles thrown by some imaginary presence.

As she'd settled into the rhythm of the house it had started to feel like the place really belonged to her. The painting of her grandmother over the living room fireplace seemed pleased, although Jessie recognized that when she felt the eyes following her movements she was allowing her imagination free rein. She knew that the phenomenon was only because of the skill of the artist who'd painted the picture in the first place. Whatever, an inner voice told her. You *do* belong here.

A self-proclaimed prophesy, she thought with a smile as she stared at her grandmother's likeness from the doorway of the front hall. She'd been on her way down the front staircase because she'd thought she'd heard the electrician's van outside, but the driveway was empty of vehicles. I'm hearing things again, she thought wryly, knowing he was expected any minute.

Jessie stepped into the room, still transfixed by her grandmother portrait. Caroline McGregor looked so much like her that she wondered if the resemblance went further, that their personalities were also alike.

She moved to the fireplace, her eyes meeting those in the painting, and Jessie had a sudden feeling of sadness. Memories of how her grandmother had doted upon her as a small child flashed in her mind, fragments of scenes she'd forgotten. She remembered that her father had died suddenly, drowned. Then her mental screen fast-forwarded to her mother fleeing from the island, taking her into a stormy night, down the cliff path to a boat.

Jessie's breath accelerated, as though she were going through the event again. But there were many things she couldn't remember. Only the terror.

Why? Her mother had never explained.

Jessie turned away and headed for the kitchen. She'd have a final cup of coffee before the electrician arrived and they headed into the basement.

"That's about it," Phil said. "I've extended the wiring to three more lights around the basement." He glanced into the damp area that was only under a third of the house.

Jessie nodded. She'd been present for the whole operation which had taken four hours. Phil had strung new wires from the old connections so that when she flipped on the light switch at the top of the steps the entire basement was illuminated.

"You've done great," she told him. "I don't think I'll ever be afraid of coming down here again."

"You were scared of the basement?"

"Uh-huh." She hesitated. "It represented a black hole before your work, Phil."

He smiled, satisfied that he'd done a good job. "I'm happy to be of help." Even as he spoke the wall of old canning jar shelves he'd been leaning against moved away from his shoulder, causing him to stumble. He fell to his knees as he tried to regain his balance.

"Oh, my God!" Jessie cried, seeing that there was a space behind the shelves. "There's a secret room!"

Phil regained his balance and stood up, his gaze on the area beyond the shelves. "Yeah, that's what it looks like, a secret room."

"Where someone could hide?" Jessie's words sounded on the edge of hysteria even to her own ears.

Phil stepped forward, entering the small space behind the shelves. "Maybe a hundred years ago," he said with a laugh. "But I don't know from what. Unless it was a spurned beau."

"What do you mean?"

"Only that no one has opened this space for decades."

"How do you know that?"

He shrugged and stepped out of the tiny closet-sized room. "Course I can't say for sure considering that the floor is stone, but I'd guess that this was the place where a family hid valuables if they felt the need."

"And no one would do that today?"

"Can't see why they would." He swung the wall of shelves back into place. "But you might like to know it's here, especially if you take a vacation and want to hide your jewelry while you're gone." He shrugged. "Or whatever it is you own that's valuable."

Jessie laughed despite her apprehension. "I don't have valuable jewelry, nor anything else of monetary worth." She swept back her hair, eyes on the shelves that were now back in place. "My first reaction is to be frightened by secret places."

"Don't be," Phil said. "Believe me, these old houses of a hundred years or more all have secret panels or rooms, because back then that was the way they protected their valuables."

She only nodded and followed him upstairs, watched him turn off the light switch that now controlled the basement, and then waited as he prepared his bill. When he was finished and handed it to her, Jessie glanced at the total, saw that it was in line with his price quote, and agreed. Phil headed outside. "You can stop by the office with the check," he told her.

Danny, with Footers sleeping at his feet, had been on the computer during the whole time Phil worked in the basement. "You done, Mom?" he asked.

"Yeah, we are. The basement now has lights." She decided not to tell him about the secret room.

"And now we're safe from the demons of the dark?"

"We are."

Jessie didn't want to say otherwise, or comment on his characterization of "demons" because it was all too scary for her. After the electrician was gone, the door to the basement chained and locked, she wondered why she still felt so vulnerable.

Maybe because she had unresolved issues from the past.

Or because she was too sensitive to her surroundings.

Or—because there was a secret place behind the jar shelves in the basement.

And there could be other secret places in the house.

CHAPTER TWENTY-FOUR

"HEY, I HEARD ABOUT YOUR SECRET ROOM," HANK SAID, AS Jessie came into his office on Monday morning.

"What?" His statement took her off guard. "How could you know that?" Then she realized he must have been talking to Phil, the electrician.

He watched her changing expression, grinning. "No, it wasn't Phil, but his wife who told Rose who I'm surprised didn't mention it to you when you came in."

"Rose was away from her desk and didn't see me arrive," she said, referring to the front desk receptionist. Jessie hesitated. "Oh my God. It's the infamous gossip mill, the island jungle drums. I just hope Danny doesn't hear about it at school. I hadn't wanted to scare him."

Hank got up and came around his desk to take her arm and guide her out to the hall. "If he does hear about it I don't think it'll scare him. He'll just be intrigued by a secret room. It's only us adults who worry about such things."

His gaze softened, as though he was giving advice to an old friend, not a new employee. Gently, Jessie pulled free of his grasp, uncertain about how to react, and again realizing that professional protocol was different on Cliff Island. She wondered what was behind his sudden action, steering her down the hall toward the holding cell.

"Am I going to jail?"

He laughed. "You haven't heard about our temporary guest?"

She shook her head, puzzled.

"We've arrested and incarcerated a reporter, but probably not for long, once his newspaper's lawyer gets off the next ferry."

"Why in God's name would you arrest a reporter?"

"Because he was trespassing, motivated by a malicious intent."

Surprised, she met Hank's eyes. "Trespassing? Where?"

"Ben and Lynda Thrasher's place. He was trying to get close to the house, using a listening device at Ben's studio window to hear phone conversations. He was caught by a groundskeeper Ben had hired to patrol his property, and then they called me."

"Good God. What in the hell prompted his trespassing?"

"The current controversy between Ben Thrasher and the senator, the one who allegedly compromises female interns."

"So the reporter was trying to get a scoop."

"Yeah, that's my guess. In my opinion I think the whole situation has gotten out of hand. Thrasher is like a dog with a bone—he can't seem to let go of the sensationalized uproar his political cartoons are causing, and so he keeps digging up more dirt." Hank shook his head. "The guy's getting his name on the front pages all over America, propelling his career into superstardom."

"And ruining the senator's political future."

"Without a doubt."

"And Ben Thrasher is above reproach himself?" Her tone had gone flat. The Ben she'd once known had probably done ten time worse. But he was good at keeping his professional image separate from his personal life.

Hank glanced, his pale eyes penetrating, as though trying to read what she hadn't said in her expression. "So it seems." He hesitated. "Do you know anything different about him, Cline? I know he lived in California."

She lowered her eyes, not wanting him to see what might be revealed there. "He taught at Berkley while I was there, that's all," she answered stiffly, and then shifted the conversation back to the present. "But that was years ago."

A silence went by.

"Just asking, Officer Cline. For a moment I had the feeling you might have something to add to the controversy." His eyes crinkled at the corners and she had a sense that he was amused. "Aside from you knowing him from your college days."

She nodded, not risking a response. Her boss was not a backward, small town cop, but a big city homicide officer. It would be hard to fool Hank if she began to explain.

And what would Jessie explain, that she'd first heard of Ben when he'd taught art classes at night—after she'd graduated? That her mother had encouraged her to attend because she was so worried about the toll Jessie's floundering marriage was having on her? That she'd acquiesced to her mom and her ensuing friendship with Ben had saved her sanity—for a while? Ben had raved about her talent, the opposite of her husband, Ted, who'd been highly critical. Could it be because Ben had hinted that Ted was jealous of her artistic ability, because he'd also judged Ted's efforts on canvas as mediocre?

By then Jessie's year-old marriage to Ted had already gone from first love to disaster, and at twenty-three, freshly graduated from Berkeley and hoping for a career in commercial art to support her "real art," Ben's words had gone to her head. She'd believed she had a future as an artist. In truth, she'd believed everything Ben had ever told her.

I'm a naïve nincompoop, she thought. But she hadn't been that dim-witted since and didn't expect to be again.

"This reporter is pretty hot under the collar, so get ready for a little profanity," Hank said, interrupting her thoughts. "Sorry to take you away from your work but I wanted a second officer present when the lawyer gets here. It never hurts to have a witness to the procedure these days."

She nodded, bringing her thoughts back to the room they'd just entered, beyond which was a small hall where the two holding cells were located.

"How long has he been here?"

"Several hours."

"And how long does the law say we can hold him at this facility?"

"Up to eight hours. After that he has to be taken to a regular jail on the mainland." Hank's forehead lines deepened with his frown as he glanced at his watch. "The ferry's due so his lawyer should be here any minute. I'm sure he'll have seen to posting bond."

"Yeah, and then I'm outta here!" The male voice came from the nearest holding cell.

Jessie stepped into the small hall where she faced a thin young man behind the barred door. She could tell that his bravado was only a façade. The kid looked scared.

"Didn't you know that you were trespassing?" she asked.

"I wasn't deliberately trespassing. I was going to knock on the door and ask for a statement from Mr. Thrasher." He hesitated. "It's my job."

"The window where you were found was some distance from the front door, Son." Hank had come up behind Jessie. "Your paper must have told you the rules concerning illegal listening devices."

"Don't answer any more questions," a man said behind them.

Jessie and Hank turned to face the speaker who'd been led to the holding area by Max.

"His lawyer has all the paperwork in order, Chief, so I brought him back to see his client."

A few minutes later, the release protocol completed, Jessie followed Hank back toward his office. "Looks like the kid and his lawyer will be on the next ferry."

"Uh-huh. The bond has been posted so there's no way to hold him here." Hank hesitated at his doorway. "I kind of sympathize with the guy. He's obviously a novice at his job."

"Me, too. But I'm sure his paper will take care of his legal issues, even though the listening device points to premeditation."

Hank nodded and Jessie was again aware of the brilliance of his eyes. She gave a laugh, hoping that she didn't sound as nervous as she suddenly felt. "In any case it's no longer our problem once he's gone," she added.

"Probably not, unless Thrasher presses charges. But I suspect that he won't, considering he'd be going up against a Seattle newspaper."

As he talked, Jessie had stepped back, knowing it was time for her patrol. She said as much and he agreed.

Jessie lifted her hand in a farewell salute. "I'll swing by later in the afternoon." She went out the side entrance to avoid a conversation with Rose about her secret room. That could wait. She didn't feel up to it, just as she wasn't up to evaluating her reaction to Hank. The last thing she needed was to fall for her boss. She must stay focused. She was in no position to compromise her job.

Or she could lose her inheritance, too.

CHAPTER TWENTY-FIVE

THE NEXT FEW HOURS WERE PEACEFUL AS JESSIE CRUISED the island. She'd watched the next ferry arrive to unload cars and passengers, and then saw it leave again, presumably with the reporter and his lawyer aboard. The dispatcher's voice on the radio was a sudden disruption.

"Car in the ditch on View Crest Road near the intersection of Nelson place. Copy?"

"Copy that," Jessie responded. "I'm on my way."

"Affirmative. Let me know if you need backup."

Jessie reached for the switch on the bottom of the dash and the siren and wigwags, along with the bubble lights on the roof, flashed on. Then she accelerated, made a U-turn and headed for the scene of the accident.

A few minutes later she pulled up behind a Lexus SUV that was obviously the disabled car. As she got out and headed for the driver's window, Jessie could see that there was little damage, if any to the vehicle, although the back tires had slid into the shallow ditch and were stuck in the mud.

The driver was a woman who huddled over the wheel. When Jessie knocked on the window she jumped, jerking upright, looking terrified.

"Police," Jessie said. "Unlock the door."

The woman's long hair hung over her face as she scrambled to open her door. "Thank God!"

"It's okay," Jessie said, trying to calm her, recognizing that the frightened woman was Lynda Thrasher who was eight months pregnant. "Did you bump the steering wheel? Are you hurt anywhere?"

Lynda shook her head, gulping air. "I don't think so." She took deep breaths to calm herself. "I tried to stay on the road, braking, but the passenger side of the SUV went onto the shoulder and the back end sort of fishtailed into the mud." She brushed her hair away from her eyes. "I'd almost stopped by then or I might have gone all the way into the ditch. I was lucky."

"Yeah, you're Lynda Thrasher aren't you?"

"How did you know?"

Jessie managed a smile. "I heard you speak at the luncheon. I enjoyed it."

"Thanks, Officer Cline." She'd glanced at Jessie's name badge over her pocket. "I'm so glad you got here. I was afraid that the person who tried to run me off the road would come back."

"Someone attempted to cause this accident?"

"Yes, the driver came up beside me and then veered so close that I thought I'd be hit. I tried to swing over and the other car fell back and then did the same thing again. It all happened so fast that I overreacted and that's when my right wheels left the blacktop and got into the loose gravel on the shoulder."

"Did the other driver come back again?"

"The car stopped and I saw the backup lights come on and I thought it would. I was so scared I dumped out the contents of my purse looking for my cell phone." She gestured to the mess of items that were scattered all over her front seat. "I figured the driver saw me calling for help and took off."

"So it was you who called 911?"

"Uh-huh, and I must have sounded hysterical."

"And it was a car? And it didn't actually hit you."

"I called it a car but it was a small, late model SUV."

"What color was it?"

"White."

"Man or woman driver?"

Lynda pursed her lips, looking upset. "I honestly don't know. It was raining and the windows were a little steamed up."

"Did you catch the make or notice the license plate?"

"Afraid not." Lynda sighed, her trembling chin giving away her upset. "Guess I'm not a very good witness."

"It's okay. The important thing is that you weren't hurt." Jessie noticed a pickup truck pulling up behind her police car and recognized Elmer, one of the island's civilian police volunteers. She felt relief. Lynda's car would have to be towed, either home or to the nearest garage. In the meantime she wanted to drive Lynda into the medical clinic in town. They needed to know for sure that she really hadn't been hurt.

Explaining the plan to Lynda as she dumped her things back into her purse and stepped down from her SUV, Jessie helped the woman into the backseat of the cruiser.

"I'm fine to sit in front, really I'm not hurt."

"I know you're probably fine," Jessie replied. "But let's just be sure. I want you to stretch out, try to relax until we get you to the clinic." Jessie closed the back door, and then, after a few words to Elmer, climbed behind the wheel and radioed Dispatch to inform the clinic that she was bringing a pregnant woman in for a checkup.

"Copy that."

"Affirmative, and thanks."

Before she started the engine, Jessie twisted around to face Lynda. "We'll be there in a jiffy."

"Thanks Officer Cline."

"Why don't you call me Jessie? All the locals call the chief by his first name." She gave a laugh. "No one stands on formality in such a small community, unlike California where I came from."

"That's one of the things I like about Cliff Island. Everyone is friendly, and the people respect the law."

"Yeah, everyone but the driver you encountered."

"I thought of that, too." A pause. "I just hope it wasn't someone trying to get back at my husband."

"Probably not, Lynda. But we'll investigate the incident, you can be sure of that." Jessie had already had that same thought, especially in light of Ben's latest cartoon campaign, and the reporter this morning. She decided it best not to pursue that subject until she and Hank could talk.

"I appreciate your concern." A pause. "And I feel much better now. I'll try calling my husband again after we get there. The ferry should have arrived by then."

Jessie glanced at her watch. "It's not scheduled for another half hour."

When they reached town Jessie turned into the clinic parking area and shortly thereafter they were inside and Lynda was being led off to an examining room. Jessie sat down to wait, placing her handheld radio beside her while she scribbled notes regarding what had happened on a pad. Fifteen minutes later a nurse came out to explain that Lynda was fine, that her husband had been contacted and was on his way to get her.

"She asked me to thank you for your help," the nurse said, smiling.

"Tell her I'm happy to help and extremely relieved that she's fine." Jessie nodded and then got up to go. She headed back to the station with her notes, sure that Hank had heard about what had happened and was waiting for her report. It would help to discuss the incident because something just didn't feel right. The accident had been deliberate. But why would anyone want to hurt Lynda, unless there was a bigger picture here, like someone with a vendetta against Ben.

A scary thought.

Jessie left the police station for home an hour later after her meeting with Hank; they'd gone over her report and agreed about the seriousness of the situation, that they would talk about their course of action in the morning. She'd called Danny around four to make sure he'd gotten home okay. After Lynda's accident she'd been nervous about Danny riding his bike from school, and regretted giving in to his begging that morning. But he'd been fine and was doing his homework when she'd reached him.

"I'm just fine, Mom," he'd said. "Footers is asleep and guess what?"

"What?" she'd answered, playing his game.

"The doors were still locked when I got home. Thought you'd be glad to know that since you paid that guy to change the locks." His laugh came over the line. "Know what me and my friends think?"

"I don't," she said, trying to sound normal. "Tell me."

"That our house is so weathered and warped by the salt spray that the locks weren't lined up anymore. Get it? We thought we'd locked the doors and the locks didn't catch."

"You know, you may have solved the mystery, Danny." She didn't add that the possibility had crossed her mind more than once. Skip had explained that he'd had to remodel the doorjamb to fit the new locks.

Now, as she drove home Jessie couldn't help grinning. From out of the mouths of babes, she thought, and made the turn onto the side road leading to her driveway. The next moment a woman was in the road and she was slamming on the brakes. The tires slid on the damp blacktop, as the car swerved around the person dressed in a black wind slicker and hat, and came to a stop.

Shaken, Jessie jumped from the car, whirling to face the woman she'd almost hit. But the woman was already disappearing into the woods.

"Nita!" she called, guessing.

The woman was gone into the blackness of the trees. Jessie got back into her car and slowly started down the road. By the time she reached the house she had herself under control. It had been a strange day. Thank God she hadn't ended it by running over a person in black who was stupid enough to walk along a dark road.

And then she went inside to make supper.

CHAPTER TWENTY-SIX

SHE AND DANNY BOTH OVERSLEPT. IT WAS THE UNACCUS-
tomed sunlight streaming in through the long windows
that finally awakened Jessie. She glanced at the clock and
jumped out of bed. Danny needed to get up right now if
he hoped to make it to school on time. Not to mention her
getting to work.

But she felt refreshed from nine hours of sleep, and
even though yesterday had been upsetting, it had also
made her feel better about her personal life. Danny's take
on the locks had been right on target, and she was feeling
a lot safer in the house, secret room or not.

As she got dressed, Jessie vowed to overlook the
unexplainable peculiarities of the house; a foundation
compromised by ground settling, walls out of square,
and the roof altered by moisture and warping. She'd get
used to the creaks and groans and odd sounds of the
hundred-year-old house after a while. In the meantime
she would try not to fear it as a living entity.

"Hey, Mom, don't forget I'm selling candy this weekend,"
Danny said after breakfast as he was leaving for school.

"I know that, Danny. What I don't know is if you'll
make it in time for school without me driving you."

Danny glanced at the wall clock. "I'm fine, Mom.
School doesn't start for twenty-five minutes and it takes

me less than twenty to get there." He kissed her cheek. "But I have to leave right now."

"I'd better drive you."

"No, Mom. You have to get to work and I have to get to school."

Jessie hesitated. "Okay then, Danny. Get going."

He grinned, gave her a thumbs up, and then jumped on his bike and headed down the driveway. "Tell Footers I'll be home right after school!" he called over his shoulder.

"Will do," she called back. Jessie watched him go and put another item on her to-do list for the day: get Danny a cell phone. If he were riding to and from school on his bike along unpopulated roads he needed a way to communicate if he got into trouble.

And for you to keep tabs, a voice inside her head said. Yeah, it's true, she thought. Her son was her whole world and he was definitely worth the cost of a cell phone.

She went back into the house, cleaned up the kitchen and then went out the back door, locking it behind her with her new key. She'd thought about an alarm system but had immediately dismissed the idea. In the first place there were no close neighbors to hear the alarm siren, and in the second place it might seem inappropriate because she was the assistant chief on the island, part of the police protection for its citizens.

After all of her rushing Jessie drove into town fifteen minutes early, before her next meeting with Hank. She stopped at Starbucks and bought a latté, taking it back to her car to sip, allowing herself five minutes to relax before giving the chief her evaluation of the Thrasher situation. Ben Thrasher, she thought in the quietness of her vehicle as she sipped the coffee. Once she'd cared about him, before she'd seen the real man behind his charming façade. She hoped never to have to deal with him again.

When it was time she went into the police station. Hank was already there by the front desk, precluding any small talk from Rose as he led her back to his office. She sat down as he went around his desk and took his seat.

"Officer Cline, we might have a real problem here. The national media is aware that Ben Thrasher and his wife live here. We could be in for a media blitz if this situation intensifies." He drummed his fingers on the desk. "The account of her accident has hit the morning newspapers already, including the whole rundown of Thrasher's campaign against the senator. I'm sure it'll be fodder for the television networks as well."

"Do you think Lynda's accident is connected to her husband's work?"

He shrugged. "Whether it is or not I think that will be the focus of the media." His gaze was suddenly direct. "What do you think after yesterday?"

"I think it's quite possible that you're right unless—" She broke off, unwilling to speculate.

"Unless what, Cline."

"Forget it."

"Not on your life. If you have something, I need to hear it."

"Okay, Chief, but bear in mind it's only a left-field possibility, probably not valid."

"Shoot."

"What if Lynda staged the accident herself?"

"Shit! Why in hell would she do that? She's pregnant for God's sake."

"But she wasn't hurt, only upset." Jessie hesitated. "She's having her first child soon, her husband is gone a lot and maybe she was trying to get his attention."

There was a silence as he considered her words.

"I suppose we do have to look at that option, and the

possibility that she might have been momentarily distracted and swerved onto the shoulder and got stuck in the mud."

"And the fact that she was afraid to tell her husband in case he got mad, so she made up the story."

"That doesn't make sense, Cline. What husband would be mad when he should be counting his blessings that his wife and unborn baby were safe?"

She glanced away. "Maybe a husband like Ben Thrasher."

"Why in hell would you suggest that, Cline? The Thrashers seem like a devoted couple."

"Two things, Chief Shepherd," she replied. "First, I'd appreciate it if you'd stop calling me Cline. I think I told you to call me Jessie some time ago."

For a second he seemed about to grin but then quickly controlled his expression. "Agreed—Jessie, as long as you stop calling me chief and say Hank."

She nodded. "I agree."

"So what's your second point, something to do with my question?"

"Uh-huh. I think I told you I knew Ben Thrasher years ago, and unless he's changed completely, he might not be as devoted as you think he is."

He leaned forward. "You told me he taught at Berkley, you didn't say you *knew* him personally." A pause. "Did you?"

"I took a class from him," she said, and realized she might have given away too much. As she'd noted before, Hank was perceptive.

"I see. And?"

"And I think I got a pretty good fix on his character."

"Which was?"

"He could be caring and complimentary or he could be harsh, insensitive and cold. To his students of course, but knowing human nature, he might be just as unpredictable in his personal life." she added.

"I see," he said, and she wondered what he did see. Hopefully he wouldn't conclude that her relationship had been more personal, even though it *had* been for a brief time when she'd believed he was divorced. Later, she hadn't been able to walk away from her feelings for him, until she'd had no other choice.

Abruptly, he stood up, as though choosing to change the subject. "We'll check out everything, including the tire marks on the blacktop. At first glance it does look like there were two sets of tires braking at the scene, which would mean she's telling the truth."

"Good idea, and don't forget Lynda said the other vehicle was white, possibly a small SUV. If there was another driver, and if that person lives on the island, it shouldn't be hard to run a check through the Department of Licenses in Olympia."

"I've already got that going. Course if it wasn't a local they could be long gone on the first ferry after the incident."

"Yeah, but couldn't we notify the ferry people to let us know if a white SUV, station wagon, or anything similar drives onto Cliff Island? There aren't that many cars that get off here."

"Done that, too, Cline. Uh, Jessie."

She grinned. "You're way ahead of me, Chief, uh, I mean Hank."

They both laughed and it broke the strange tension that had sprung up between them.

"We'll do everything we can to investigate Lynda's accident. I've got a couple of other requests out there, just in case," Hank said.

"And what are they, and in case of what?"

"I alerted a couple of neighboring county jurisdictions for possible support from the county, just in case Lynda's accident was part of a bigger picture. We can't forget that Thrasher is a celebrity and the senator is a well-known figure in the national political arena." He spread his hands. "Who knows what lengths people will go to protect their position. All we can do is hope it was a random incident, but if not, we'll be prepared as best we can."

"In the meantime, we have to protect the Thrashers, right?"

"Yeah, that's right, although not noticeably so."

"So off the record, Hank, do you think Ben's political enemies could be after him?"

"Yeah, I think it's a possibility. They could be warning him to back off, or else." Hank wiped his hand over his face. "Jeez, I hope it's not that. Our island isn't prepared for such high drama."

"I need to do more than subscribe to the newspaper, Hank," she said forgetting the chief. "I'm not up to speed on what's been going on with the Thrashers. I'll need to get myself updated if I'm to do my job properly. I can't operate blind."

"Yeah, you're right." And then he explained, regarding Ben Thrasher's cartoons, the ongoing threats from anonymous phone calls and letters. "I even had a thinly veiled threat of losing my job if our little department didn't stop Ben from undermining the jobs of prominent people."

"So what have you done about all this?"

"Not much we can do, as you know, Jessie. Without a suspect we have no one to question let alone arrest. It's a crazy situation."

"Yeah, but how about what happened to Lynda?"

"Like I said, someone could be out to intimidate Ben

about giving up his need to nail people to his personal cross in his cartoons."

"Just so innocent people don't get hurt instead."

He saw her to the office doorway where she faced him again. "What about this old woman who lives on that rusting tugboat. Is she dangerous?"

"Naw, just eccentric. Most islanders give her a wide berth though." A pause. "Why do you ask?"

She explained about almost hitting a woman dressed in black who was walking down the dark road last night. "She ran into the woods and I wondered if it was Nita."

"Yeah, it could have been although she's usually on that bike of hers." He dropped an arm around her shoulders and gave her a squeeze. "You had an eventful day yesterday, but don't worry about Nita. Even though she's scary looking with her long stringy hair and skinny figure, Nita is harmless."

"That's what Danny says."

"Danny's met her?"

"Uh-huh, had several conversations with her. He likes her, says she's really a nice lady."

"Hmmm. As I said, she's harmless."

But as Jessie went out to her police cruiser she wondered. Her uneasy feeling seemed to be getting stronger by the day. What she didn't know was why. Because of Ben or Nita?

Or Who?

CHAPTER TWENTY-SEVEN

NITA STOOD ON THE DECK OF HER TUGBOAT AND STARED down the shoreline to the cliff that jutted out into the Strait. The house had stood on the top of the rock for all the years that she could remember. Her mind flashed on scenes from when she was a child, when she and her cousin played in the shallows, looking for sea life on the beach, careful never to step on any living creature.

She smiled. Those were the happy times, before all the bad things began. But she didn't want to think about the good things until the island was safe again. She needed to concentrate on what was happening now, on what had angered the Wind Woman.

Nita turned away from the view, grabbed her black slicker from just inside the cabin, and then closed and latched the door behind her. Storm clouds were building on the western horizon, and when it hit she didn't want wind-driven rain to soak her living space. Seconds later she'd untied her motorboat, climbed into it and was heading for shore and the tiny cove where she tied up her boat while she was on the island.

Once on the beach, Nita started up the path through the trees to the abandoned shed on the top of the bluff where she kept her bicycle.

The wind had come up and a glance westward told

her she'd barely have time to ride into town, buy her sup-
plies and get back to the tug before the storm. She
stepped into the tiny hut and pulled her bike out from
under what was left of the roof, and quickly disconnected
the cart. The basket on the handlebars would be big
enough for her groceries today.

Outside again, Nita tightened her head scarf and was
about to peddle down the path to the road when a movement caught her eye. Her gaze darted everywhere,
searching for another glimpse of—of what? An animal or
a person? It was definitely something more than the air
currents that ebbed and flowed through the evergreen
boughs. And it had been some distance away, under the
trees out near the road.

But maybe I was mistaken, she thought. Maybe it was
the Wind Woman.

But she won't hurt me, Nina reminded herself. She
climbed onto the bike and pedaled fast, heading for the
road. About to burst out of the trees, she suddenly
braked, stopping before she left the shelter of the woods.

The vehicle had already accelerated and was quickly
disappearing, its red tail lights a vivid contrast to the
white paint of the car. She stayed hidden until she felt
safe enough to move forward.

She'd been mistaken. It hadn't been the Wind Woman
after all. It had been someone far worse.

The evil one.

CHAPTER TWENTY-EIGHT

JESSIE OPENED HER EYES ON SATURDAY MORNING AND knew it was the beginning of a glorious day of blue skies and clear air. She got out of bed and headed for the shower, knowing that rain and wind had been predicted by evening. In the meantime she had her work to do and Danny would have good weather for riding his bike to houses along the road to sell candy for the athletic equipment fund.

I'll make sure to track him, she told herself. If the weatherman's forecast of an approaching storm front came true early, she'd find Danny and bring him home.

An hour later after breakfast came a call from Clarice to check on them, then all of Jessie's instructions to her son on what he could or couldn't do to sell candy, and they were ready to leave the house. Once outside, she went over her main concerns again.

"Remember, Danny, you are not to go into anyone's house, even if you think it's safe because they live on the island. And watch out for speeding cars when you're on the road."

"Gosh, Mom. I'm not a baby."

Jessie nodded, but continued her instructions. "And when you've sold all your candy" (she indicated his full basket and the small box he'd anchored to the fender behind his seat), "you're to come home immediately and give me a call."

He held up the new cell phone she'd given him the previous night. "And I'll call you right away if I have a problem, right?"

She raised her eyebrow. "Are you making fun of me, Danny?"

He shook his head but his grin said otherwise. "I love you Mom, you know that." He climbed on his bike, ready to peddle off down the driveway. "But sometimes you do treat me like I'm still in kindergarten." He took off. "But don't forget you can always call me now that I have a cell phone." He gave a final wave. "Yippee! Wait tell the guys know I have my own phone."

Watching him go, Jessie grinned. He was right on two counts: she was overprotective and the cell phone meant that she could know his whereabouts at all times.

She went back into the house to make sure everything was turned off that should be, that the house was secure. Then she locked up and went out to her police car. She had the Saturday patrol, along with several volunteers in their own vehicles. A glance at the western horizon told her the weatherman had been right.

By noon she'd heard from Danny twice, both times excited about his sales. "I only have a couple of boxes left," he told her proudly, sounding more like a corporate executive than an eleven-year-old boy selling candy. "I'll be home by one, one-thirty at the latest," he said before ending their call.

Jessie glanced at her watch, and then swung the patrol car around to head back into town. She wouldn't be off until five when Max took over for the next shift. In the meantime she could stand a cup of coffee. Later she'd swing past home to make sure Danny was there.

She parked in front on the arts and crafts store, and then walked to Starbucks. A few minutes later, coffee in hand, she started back to her car, pausing to look at the art pieces in Tommy's store window, wooden carvings by Bruce Shepherd. Momentarily hooked by the exquisite works, she went inside for a closer look.

"Hey, Jessie!" a woman said from behind the counter. "Welcome."

Jessie's gaze flew to the woman, and she immediately grinned. "What are you doing here, Violet? I thought your work week in the law office of Leonard Wills ended with a forty-hour week."

"Hmmm, you know how it is when you're married. You've gotta be flexible, especially if you have a kid who has to be at basketball practice on a Saturday, and your husband is the volunteer assistant to the coach."

"I understand." Jessie tilted her head. "So you're manning the store for Tommy today."

"You got it," she said, grinning. "I see you were admiring Bruce Shepherd's work."

Jessie nodded. "I think Bruce is extremely talented. His carvings are exquisite, so true to life."

"We, that is Tommy and I, agree. His work sells really well. His dad is terribly proud of him even though they—" She broke off, shrugging.

"Even though they what?" Jessie asked, not letting Violet's unfinished sentence stand.

A pause.

"Well, I don't really know what's wrong between them. I only know something is."

Jessie set down her coffee and picked up a carving of a deer, examining all the details of the piece. "What's your guess?"

"Don't really have one."

"I see." Jessie still held Bruce's carving, seeing that it was only priced at twenty dollars. "I want to buy this, Violet. One day it'll be worth ten times the price."

Violet took the figure and Jessie followed her to the counter with the cash register. She reached into her pocket for her wallet and pulled out her credit card which she handed to Violet.

In seconds their transaction was complete and Jessie had her purchase in one hand and the coffee in the other. Turning back toward the door she was stopped by Violet's next words.

"I heard you found out about your secret room?" she said.

Jessie faced her, brows raised. "You already knew about it?"

"Uh-huh."

"How?"

She hesitated, looking uncomfortable. "I thought you knew that your uncle had tried to sell the house before he died." Another pause. "Until he realized he couldn't according your grandmother's will, because it was to revert to you after he passed away."

Jessie could only shake her head.

"Oh God, Jessie. If my boss knew I'd told you something you didn't know, even though it was common knowledge on the island, I'd probably lose my job."

"I won't say anything, Violet. But I find it a little sneaky on the part of your boss. Why on earth couldn't Mr. Wills tell me the place had been for sale?"

She looked uncomfortable. "It wasn't for sale for long. When Mr. Wills heard what was happening he put a stop to it fast. Scuttlebutt says that your great-uncle hated your father and didn't want the property to go to you."

"Hated? But he kept in contact with me. I thought he left the place to me because I was his only living heir. I grieved for him when he lost his son." Jessie felt as though she'd been kicked in the gut.

"I'm so sorry, Jessie. You inherited because of your grandmother's will, because you were the last of the family descendants." Violet came out from behind the counter and grabbed her hand. "I've spoken out of turn." She looked stricken. "I shouldn't have told you that your great-uncle had tried to sell the place and had shown it to several people."

"Who?" Jessie asked, managing to keep her composure.

Violet was even more distressed, as though she wished she'd kept her mouth shut. "There was one person who wanted the place."

"Who?" Jessie asked again. "Anyone I know?"

"I don't think so."

"But these possible buyers all went through the house, knew the layout?"

Violet nodded. "Several did."

"Did anyone have access to a key?"

"I don't know. We figured your great-uncle was a little senile near the end."

"But through this process is how you knew about the secret room in the basement, right? My uncle had revealed it to one or more of his potential buyers?—as a come-on?"

"Yeah, at least to one person," Violet said, agreeing.

"Someone who lives on the island?"

Violet nodded again. "A woman named Sarah—can't remember her last name offhand. She was a serious buyer, thought the secret room would be a great wine cellar."

A silence went by as Jessie took a sip of coffee, and tried to organize her emotions. So her uncle had tried to sell the place, get the money and keep her from inheriting. Why? Again she thought of her mother leaving with her long ago. Her mother hadn't come clean about what had happened back then. It was time that she did.

"Besides," Violet continued. "As I said, your great-uncle would not have been able to go through with a sale anyway. Your grandmother's will stipulated that the house had to stay in the family and couldn't be sold unless there were no descendants left." A pause. "He was pretty upset when my boss explained, but the will was as binding in that part as it is for you having to live there for a year before it's yours."

"Yeah, my grandmother marched to her own drummer," Jessie said finally, bothered that she was being told her family secrets by a stranger. "And I'll last out the year, secret room be damned."

And then she marched as well, straight outside, pausing only to buy a newspaper at the paper stand because there was a front page feature about Ben Thrasher.

She was hardly settled in her car when her personal cell phone rang. It was Danny who was already home and wanted to go over to a friend's house. Since Jessie had met her son's friend, Steve, and his mother, she said he could go. Steve's mom would pick him up and bring him back by six.

Arriving home shortly after five, Jessie put chicken breasts, potatoes and a vegetable into the oven to bake. Still waiting for Danny to get home, she went into the adjoining room where they had their computer and logged on. She'd just read the latest article about the Thrashers, Lynda's accident and the fact that the senator had denied all knowledge of the incident. It was a rehash of everything Jessie already knew. But it started her thinking about what she'd known of Ben in the past, after she was no longer involved with him.

But other women had been, many of them from Internet chat rooms where people talked about art. She logged on an old forum where she'd found him while surfing on her computer a couple of years ago, pontificating and cutting down rivals with a different opinion. She'd realized immediately that success hadn't changed him.

Jessie stared at the screen. Oh God, no. Not again.

CHAPTER TWENTY-NINE

HE STILL HAD THE SAME ON-LINE TAG: TRUE2U. HE'D HAD IT for twelve years at least, posting on several artists' forums where he exchanged witty flirtatious comments with women under various topics. His ultimate goal was seducing them.

Jessie sat back on the chair. What an egotistical bastard, still up to the same old crap. Success hadn't changed him and he was still out there conning women, and evidently none had exposed him, including her.

She scrolled down to the topics where Ben had taken part as True2U, keeping his real identity a secret, pausing on his first post to QueenB.

"And don't forget the limo, corner of Fifth and Stewart." Jessie knew he meant that was the corner where they would meet. She had no idea what city they were talking about or the date. Those posts had already dropped off.

"That street corner is gonna get old if I have to make enough for a limo," the obvious female tagged QueenB had responded.

"$500 isn't too much," he'd written back, and Jessie knew that meant five o'clock. "Just make sure the limo has a wet bar." Translating, Ben had told QueenB to bring the booze.

Jessie sat staring at the screen, remembering when

she'd first stumbled upon Ben on an artists forum two years ago. She couldn't believe that he still had the same tag that he'd used ten years earlier. She'd wondered if it was still him and had posted a brief e-mail, using a tag he wouldn't recognize. She'd praised something he'd said, saying that he sounded like a real artist, unlike some fakes like Ben Thrasher who could only draw cartoons.

Her post had generated an immediate response, and all the viciousness she remembered. Although he never admitted to being Ben, his attack on her, defending Ben Thrasher, had been all she needed to know that it was indeed him. All she could figure was that he was so pious and self-righteous that he couldn't drop his tag, that the women he seduced on-line and then discarded were so intimidated by him that he'd never been exposed for the womanizing bastard that he was.

Jessie stood up, leaving herself on-line and strode outside, where darkness had already fallen, although the automatic patio lights had already come on. Unaware of the wind that blew gusts in off the strait, she went to the stone wall and leaned over it, gazing at the water below the cliff that dropped away from the other side of the barrier.

She stared at the dark churning water crashing against the rocks below, giving in to her musing of the past. Ben Thrasher had been her nemesis, her stumbling block to a better life for too many years. That time was past.

She was no longer the young woman vulnerable to a man who wanted everything but promised nothing but self-serving words: "We could do one of three things, Jessie: devastate my wife (his second back then) and my kids with a divorce, have a European-type relationship (meaning she'd be his mistress) or we could leave now and never see each other again."

She'd been blinded by her feelings, not realizing that the words were a repeat of what he'd said to the many other women before her. She hadn't been special even though he'd made her feel like the love of his life. He'd been a fraud back then and he still was, according to what she was seeing on the Internet.

But what about Lynda? She had to be special to him; he'd married her.

It started to rain and still Jessie stood outside, knowing Danny wouldn't be home for another half hour. Her memories wouldn't let go of her. Oh God, she thought. I believed I'd let go of this shit years ago. Why do I have to face it again?

There was no answer except for the strengthening force of wind that suddenly hammered her and the house.

She ran back inside, slamming the door behind her, heading to the computer so she could shut it down. She no longer needed to be reminded about how Ben, the celebrity, had played on her vulnerability and sense of decency, that he hadn't cared about what she had to lose, that his only concern was himself. The policewoman she was now would never be taken in by the sweet talk and transparent lies of that earlier time.

Once she'd turned off the computer, Jessie went back to the kitchen, checking on the chicken in the oven. Glancing at the wall clock, she acknowledged that Danny was still a few minutes away from arriving home.

Going to the refrigerator for salad greens, Jessie went back to the sink to wash them, but couldn't turn off the images in her mind. Ben had lacked personal integrity back then, he'd had no sense of fidelity, guilt or empathy for another person's pain. She'd come to realize that he was a textbook sociopath. Her only surprise was that he lived on Cliff Island, hadn't moved back to the East Coast where he'd grown up. He'd once told her that the West Coast was "provincial—beneath [his] intellect."

Jessie set the table, her thoughts on Danny's arrival at any time. She tried not to think of Ben and his old patterns of on-line seduction, the codes he set up for his assignation, innocent-seeming messages to the casual observer, but not to the woman he was secretly arranging to meet. She smiled, bitterly. Ben was still flouting his superior intelligence in the face of people he believed were beneath him. Like other antisocial personality types before him, he believed he was too smart to ever be caught, that he was above the rules of society. Although his M.O. was subtle it was obvious to Jessie. She had once loved him and played his code games.

But now she was seasoned, an experienced policewoman, and knew that Ben was playing with fire. She'd read the answers from lonely women whose lives were lived through their computers. *They were hoping for a man. Especially a famous man.* The Ben she remembered wouldn't care about their feelings. But he never seemed to realize how those women would take his word for gospel.

That he was their salvation.

Once she'd gone off-line, a silence settled over the kitchen and the connecting room that housed their computer. Jessie slammed the oven door shut after rechecking the chicken. And then the silence was suddenly pulsating with an unseen presence.

You're projecting the past into now, Jessie told herself. You're over this shit.

She wanted to believe that she was. So why had she gone on-line to the forums? Was she trying to pretend a sociopath creep who lived on her island didn't exist?

No, she was only hoping he never connected the new assistant police chief to someone he'd once known.

Again she glanced at the clock. Danny was due at any time now. Jessie calmed her natural instinct to worry.

And then she heard a soft thump.

Startled, she spun around from the sink. But there was only silence in the room. What had caused the sound?

There was no reason she could see.

She added napkins to the place settings on the table, moving back to check the oven. And another sound stopped her.

A scratch?—a knob being turned, without the door opening?

She faced the basement door that remained locked and bolted. But that was where the sound seemed to originate.

Impossible.

The door was locked on the kitchen side, and there was no way there could be anyone beyond it.

Jessie moved to the door, standing with her hand on the locks, ready to open the door. But still she hesitated, remembering her fears, other sounds she'd heard behind that locked door, the times when she'd felt a presence.

Don't be silly, she thought. There's no one down there—*there couldn't be.*

Before she lost her nerve, Jessie grabbed her pistol and unlocked the door with a quick motion, swinging open the wooden panel between her and the basement.

No one was there.

She flicked on the light switch that illuminated the whole basement, and then, after taking a deep breath, went down the wooden steps. Pausing at the bottom, Jessie took more deep breaths as she circled the lower floor, making sure that no one was there. She came to a stop in front of the shelves that made a wall separating her from the secret room. Without hesitation, she pushed the wall to reveal the empty space beyond it, letting the shelves fall back into place.

No one was in the secret room.

No one was in the basement.

Jessie felt good that she'd had the courage to check it out. But somehow she didn't feel secure and headed for the stairs.

Paranoid, she told herself.

Because she still felt as though someone was watching her? But that was impossible. There was no place to hide.

Or was there?

CHAPTER THIRTY

OVER THE NEXT FEW DAYS JESSIE'S THOUGHTS OFTEN FLASHED on Ben Thrasher and their brief relationship over a decade ago. Although she'd crossed paths with him since living on the island, she'd had no sense of his having recognized her as the young woman he'd known in the past.

Jessie almost wished she hadn't checked the art forum, that she'd left well enough alone and hadn't discovered that Ben was still up to his old tricks. On the other hand, the information could help in the ongoing investigation concerning his wife's accident. Her knowledge of Ben might be useful if the situation accelerated, if there were accusations directed at the senator that Ben continued to trash in his nationally syndicated cartoons.

Sighing, Jessie watched the ferry traffic start up the hill from the landing and head into town. She only had another hour to go until the end of her shift. And then her radio crackled to life, interrupting her musing. "Bicyclist run off North Point Road. Vehicle left the scene. Officer, please respond."

"Copy that. I'm on my way."

"Affirmative," the dispatcher from Central Communications responded.

But Jessie's thoughts were whirling, even as she maneuvered the highway, passing cars and heading north as fast as traffic and the road allowed.

Danny rode his bike on that road.

She grabbed her cell phone and punched in her home number. Danny should be home, even if he'd stayed after school for basketball practice.

But he'd said he was going right home, she reminded herself as the phone rang and rang without an answer. He wasn't there.

Shit! The one day when she hadn't checked—because he had the cell phone to stay in touch. And now he wasn't there.

His new cell phone.

She punched in that number next—and a recorded voice said the number was either out of range or out of service.

Oh God. Where was he? Still at the gym?—on the road?—or almost home? Had he forgotten to make sure his phone was on?

She turned off Inland Highway onto North Point Road, and increased her speed, siren blaring. She had a bad premonition. The blue flashing lights up ahead told her that she was right.

She slid to a stop behind Hank's vehicle; he'd obviously responded to the call as well. Jumping out of her car, Jessie saw the twisted bicycle in the ditch. It looked like Danny's bike.

And then she saw Danny sitting on the backseat of Hank's car. At that moment, Hank got out of his vehicle, facing her.

"Danny's okay," he said. "His bicycle is totaled but he isn't hurt." He hesitated. "The person who ran him off the road didn't stop."

She opened Hank's car door and embraced her son. "What happened, Danny?" Jessie was aware that Hank was listening, too.

"The car was coming right for me," Danny replied shakily. "I figured it would swerve away but when it didn't I jumped off my bike and rolled into the ditch at the last second."

"You did the right thing, Danny." She wiped his hair out of his eyes, noting that his hands and knees were skinned.

"Yeah, that's right, Danny," Hank agreed. "But I still think a visit to the clinic is in order."

"But I'm not hurt," Danny said, protesting. "I just wanna go home."

Jessie smiled, trying to reassure him. "It's just procedure and then we'll go home."

"C'mon, Danny." Hank helped him out of his cruiser and back to his mother's car. Then he turned to Jessie. "I'll take a look at the road, see if there are brake marks on the blacktop, though I doubt I'll see much since it's gotten dark. I'll probably have to come back in daylight."

"But we have Danny's bike. There may be paint from the car on it."

"Yeah, looks like some white paint on what's left." He hesitated. "Unless it was there from before."

She shook her head. "The bike was like new."

"Well then, we may have some evidence this time."

"This time?"

"Uh-huh. Remember? This is our second hit-and-run incident within a week."

"Oh yeah, Lynda Thrasher." Her gaze intensified. "You don't think what happened to Danny is connected to her accident?

"Don't know." He walked to the bike, picked it up and

carried it to his car trunk. "The one thing we do know is the Thrasher accident involved a white vehicle, too."

"Oh my God. That's right."

"Go on now, Jessie. Get Danny to the doc and I'll clean up here."

She did as he directed, and all the way back into town her thoughts spun with questions, even as her words to Danny were soothing and calm.

"I was shaking so hard I kept punching in your number wrong," he explained when she asked him why he hadn't called her directly instead of going through 911. "My new cell phone saved me, that and hiding in the woods when the car came back."

"It came back?" Jessie managed to sound normal.

"Yeah, it went past slowly but didn't stop. Chief Thrasher got here so fast that I didn't have to hide long. He told me he hadn't been far away, lucky for me."

"Did you see the car?"

"Sort of. It was starting to get dark and I didn't want the driver to see me so I stayed hidden." He hesitated. "I think it was an older white van, but I'm not sure."

"Could you see who was driving?" She glanced at him. "I mean whether it was a man or a woman?"

He shook his head. "I couldn't tell. It all happened so fast and—and I was really scared."

A silence ensued as she digested his words that had filled her with fear and anger. He could have been killed.

"You aren't mad at me, are you, Mom?"

"Of course not. I'm only thanking God that you weren't hurt."

Danny sank back against the seat, relieved. They rode in silence to the medical center, where the doctor checked him over. A short time later they were on their way home.

*   *   *

"Prowler at Wind House, north end of the island." The dispatcher's call came at the end of the next day as Jessie returned to her car from writing a traffic ticket.

"Oh my God!" she cried aloud. "My house."

She hit the roof and wigwag lights, the siren and then floor-boarded the accelerator. As she headed out of town she grabbed her cell phone, noticed she'd missed a call while outside—from Danny?—and punched in her number. She could picture the phone in the kitchen ringing. No answer but she let it ring.

And felt the bottom dropping out of her stomach. What had happened now? Only yesterday Danny could have been killed on his way home. Today she'd driven him to school, then picked him up and saw him safely in the house with Footers. She'd left him on the computer with strict instructions to stay inside, doors locked, until she returned after her shift.

God, she prayed. Keep Danny safe.

And then she called for backup, flipped down the visor on the passenger side and switched on those emergency lights, too. Her cruiser, ablaze with illumination and siren screaming, scattered cars to the side of the road as she headed north on the highway.

The radio crackled to life and she heard Hank's voice above the din.

"I'm almost there," he said. "Copy that, Officer Cline?"

"Affirmative. I'm two minutes behind you."

"Copy that," he said again.

And then she swung onto North Point Road, her back wheels fishtailing from side to side on the wet blacktop. She managed to control them before accelerating again.

"Please, please keep Danny safe," she prayed over and over. Why in hell had she ever left him alone after what had happened?

She'd never do it again.

CHAPTER THIRTY-ONE

HANK BROUGHT HIS PATROL CAR TIRES TO A SKIDDING HALT IN the driveway of Wind House and turned off the siren. He leapt out before coming to a complete stop, before taking the moment to switch off the engine and bubble lights. With drawn gun, he ran to the back door, and finding it ajar, shoved it open and ran into the kitchen—to find no one.

Then he saw the broken window.

And the huge stone that had landed in the middle of the kitchen floor. But where was Danny?

Quickly, Hank checked out the adjoining room where Danny had obviously been on the computer. There was an unfinished e-mail that he'd been writing still up on the screen. The boy had obviously run out of the room in a hurry.

"My God!" Jessie said behind him. "Where's Danny?— and Footers?"

"Shhh," he said, and motioned that he would check out the house while she waited in the kitchen. He hadn't heard her arrive but he was glad she was there. It would be easier for her to be on scene than to be told about what happened later.

She nodded and pulled her gun, and he saw that she'd been able to maintain a professional manner, despite her fear for Danny.

Silently, he moved through the house, knowing Jessie was an armed backup. It only took a few minutes before he'd gone through the whole place, upstairs and down-stairs. There was no intruder—and no Danny or the dog.

"Nothing," he told her, coming back into the kitchen. "Where would they have gone?"

She shook her head and he saw that she was fighting panic. "I have no idea. Unless, someone was here and—"

She broke off as he grabbed her around the shoulder, pulling her against him. "We'll find Danny, Jessie."

She stiffened against him, pulling away. "Oh shit."

He stepped back, and then followed her gaze to the basement door. "What's wrong?"

"It's unlocked." Her words were hardly above a whisper.

For a moment he was puzzled. Then he remembered the story of the secret room. About to dismiss her fear, he restrained himself. The thought of it was a little spooky under the circumstances, although he doubted Danny would have ventured into that dark cavern under the house.

"I'm going down," she said in a low tone.

Her hand was on the knob when he stopped her. "No, you're waiting up here while I check it out." He inclined his head toward the doors off the kitchen, as though to say she was to watch his back.

For long moments it was a standoff. Then she nodded, stepped back and allowed him to go instead.

Hank opened the door. Her hand went to the light switch, and hesitated until he indicated she could flip it on. The area below them was instantly illuminated.

Hank descended the steps fast, his revolver ready, oblivious of the clatter in his desire to get off the steps as quickly as possible. Once at the bottom he ducked behind a stack of old boxes.

There was silence.

No one was in the basement. But his eyes went to the shelves on the far wall that held the canning jars, and covered the entry to the secret room. He moved forward on the tips of his toes, careful to stay completely silent.

He nudged the shelving with his free hand and it swung backward. Instantly, a blur of motion propelled forward from the exposed room, even before the basement light penetrated the space. Hank braced himself, as Footers rushed against him, barking.

"You can't get me!" Danny cried. "I won't let you!"

Quickly, Hank holstered his weapon and grabbed him. "Danny, it's me, Hank." Still the boy struggled and Hank could see he was terrified, that he hadn't comprehended what he was being told, even as the dog had stopped barking to wag his tail.

"Danny, no one is going to hurt you." Hank's tone deepened to a command. "It's okay. You're safe."

Hank's words finally got through to him. "I've never been so glad to see a cop in my life," Danny said, his voice quivering. "Did you see who was after me?"

"No one is here but me and your mom, who is upstairs."

Hank could feel the boy's body slow down, his trembling subside. He finally let him go and Danny turned to run up the steps to his mother, Footers at his heels.

"Mom!" he cried. "I'm okay. That person didn't find us! We hid in the secret room!"

Hank made sure the shelves were back in place, and then he followed Danny up to the kitchen. While Jessie soothed and reassured her son, he saw to turning out the basement lights and then bolting the door. Then he left them to go outside and turn off his car engine and emergency lights before walking the grounds. He flashed a strong cellular beam everywhere but nothing seemed to be disturbed. He went back inside to hear what Danny had to say about what had happened.

"I don't really know anything more than you guys do," Danny said, calmed by their presence. "When the window broke I was at the computer and I ran to another window and looked out. All I saw was a black shape." He gulped air, upset again from remembering. "So I knew someone was out there."

"And what did you do then?" Hank asked.

Danny hesitated, staring straight ahead. "I got awfully scared, because whoever was out there hadn't gone away and I figured locked doors or not, they could get in here if they wanted to." A pause. "That's when I called my mom's cell phone but she didn't pick up."

"So you called 911 next?" Jessie felt terrible about missing the call. She'd explain later.

"Uh-huh. There was no time to keep trying to call you because I had to hide immediately, before the person out there found a way in—like breaking the door window next."

A silence went by.

"So you knew about the secret room," Jessie said, her words a comment, not a question.

"Yep, the kids at school told me."

Jessie lowered her lashes. "Guess I'm living in the dark ages, before the experience of island drums." She hesitated, and then pulled her son into her arms. "I'm sorry, Danny. I didn't tell you about that room because I didn't want to scare you."

He pulled back to look his mother in the face. "Thanks for that, Mom. But you gotta remember that I'm not a baby, that I need to know what's going on. We're in this together."

Hank turned away from their emotional confrontation, pretending that he hadn't seen the tears welling in Jessie's eyes. A few minutes later he turned back and offered to board up the broken window.

"Thanks Hank. That would be great," Jessie said, her voice wobbling.

And then Hank went back outside where he found a sheet of plywood in the garage. After grabbing a hammer and nails from the toolbox in the corner, he went to secure the broken window. Once finished, he headed back to the kitchen.

"Thanks Hank," Jessie told him. "I can't tell you how much I appreciate your support."

"Isn't that my job?"

She held his eyes before responding. "Yes, but I feel your support is extra special, maybe because we're coworkers and you're my boss. So—just thanks."

He nodded, gave the proper response, and then left after giving her all the appropriate safety instructions under the circumstances. Hank hoped she didn't see how deeply concerned he really was.

"Dad, I just told you. Someone stole my van."

"When Bruce? I've been trying to get a hold of you for the past twenty-four hours since the bicycle accident." Hank hated to confront his son about his white vehicle but it was one of only a few on the island and he had to rule out that it wasn't dented on the front with traces of Danny's bike paint.

"Two days ago."

"Why didn't you report the theft?" Hank tried to keep a normal tone of voice.

"Because I wasn't here, as I just told you. I was over in Anacortes on the mainland, bringing some of my art works to a gallery that has agreed to take my pieces on consignment."

Hank moved closer to the doorway of the Yurt where Bruce stood. "You say that your van was driven away by an unknown person.

"Yeah, Dad, that's what I'm saying."

"And that you'd left the keys in the ignition?"

"That's right. This commune is a safe place. No one ever steals anything."

"But you're saying someone stole your van?"

"For God's sake, Dad, I told you that I didn't know it was gone until I got home today. This is a first. No one has ever stolen anything from the Sweers property."

"Until now."

Hank felt like he was up against a stone wall. His son wasn't giving an inch, but was he hiding something?

"Okay, I'll put out a stolen vehicle report?"

His son held his gaze. "That's okay with me, Dad. I'm telling the truth."

But was he? Hank wondered as he drove away. He could only hope so.

CHAPTER THIRTY-TWO

"HEY, OLD WOMAN!" A BOY'S VOICE CALLED. "ARE YOU AN artist?"

Nita turned from the street display window where she had been viewing the wooden carvings, portrayals of her Native American history. She'd been taken by the talent that spoke of the old ways of her people, an ability given to only a privileged few. She surveyed the two boys who'd gotten out of a Ford Explorer on the curb, both of whom she recognized, one a lifelong resident, the other a newcomer.

"No, only a critic of the art that depicts my ancestors," she replied calmly.

The newcomer caught the other boy's arm. "Steve! You're being disrespectful!"

"Naw, she's just a crazy old woman who doesn't care," Steve replied. "She even lives on an old sinking tugboat."

"C'mon, Steve, that doesn't mean she's nuts."

"Yeah it does, Danny. She's downright scary."

"No she isn't!" Danny retorted. "She's only an old lady who takes care of herself however she can."

Steve hesitated. "You don't understand, Danny. Your mom inherited Wind House, so you're part Indian, too."

Nita watched, proud of Danny who'd stood up for her, waiting for his response to such challenging words.

Danny straightened, an unlikely Native American Indian with his light skin, even though his eyes and hair were dark. "Yeah, that's right. We have Indian blood—and we're proud of it."

They faced off, oblivious to Nita.

Steve backed down first. "Sorry for spouting off."

A silence passed between them.

"Okay, I accept that. Just don't do it again, okay?"

"Yeah, agreed."

They turned toward her, but Nita had disappeared into the next doorway. She watched as they glanced around, unaware that she still observed them.

Danny was special, she acknowledged. He was a throwback, even if he didn't look like a Native American. But he was, in the best sense of the word.

He was genuine.

He was a combination of all people. He was the future of her people, and of the world, not just of the island.

And he needed to be protected.

She would see to that.

CHAPTER THIRTY-THREE

JESSIE MADE HER ARRANGEMENTS FOR DANNY'S SAFETY when he wasn't present, not wanting him to worry any more than was necessary. She called Gail Ames, his friend Steve's mom, a woman who was looking for extra income. Jessie explained that she hated leaving Danny alone while she was on shift and wondered if Gail would be interested in keeping an eye on Danny while she worked.

They agreed that Danny would come home from school with Steve on days Jessie worked, and would also spend weekend days with the Ames family when she was scheduled for work. Then they agreed on the pay.

"Please, Gail, I'd appreciate it if you wouldn't tell Danny that we have a financial arrangement," Jessie said. "If he thought I was paying he'd believe I'd hired a babysitter."

"I understand, Jessie. The boys think they're almost adults and able to take care of themselves." She gave a laugh. "They won't know what us parents go through until they're parents themselves."

"Yeah, that's so true."

After hanging up, Jessie went about the rest of her day feeling better about Danny's safety. He would never be home alone; they would always return to their house together.

Now, as Jessie went into the station through the back door to avoid Rose's chitchat, she was thoughtful. She wondered what Hank had come up with concerning his son's stolen van. She'd sensed his upset, but trusted that he would never sweep evidence under the rug.

She hesitated in the doorway to his office. He was on the phone but motioned her to the chair on the other side of his desk. He quickly ended his conversation and hung up.

"That was the result of my forensic request for a paint match of the accident."

"And?"

"The paint from Danny's red bike matched the paint on my son's van, which we found abandoned on an old logging road." He looked stressed and Jessie felt sorry for him. He was not only involved in a criminal investigation; he was involved in a personal dilemma: the guilt or innocence of his only son.

"But your son left his van in his yard when he took the ferry to Anacortes, right?"

Hank nodded. "That's what he said. He also said he'd left his key in the ignition, as he, and everyone on the Sweers property does, in case someone needed the vehicle." He hesitated. "That's how they do things; everyone shares."

She nodded, feeling his pain. She'd asked around the island, and found that his evaluation of the commune was accurate. So what did that mean? Someone had known his son was leaving for two days, knew the philosophy of the commune, and had then stolen his van? It was logical—and it wasn't.

And why did any of that have to do with her and Danny? She had no answers.

"I've had the van dusted, in case there's something more than the fingerprints of my son and his friends." He hesitated. "It's a long shot, Jessie. The van is covered with prints since it wasn't cleaned or washed very often—from gas station attendants to repair shop workers." Another pause. "Like I said, it's a long shot."

"I understand." She hesitated. "So, where do we go next?"

He shrugged.

"It's my life, Hank. And the life of my son." Her gaze intensified. "So, where do we go next?" she repeated.

He stood up. "I understand your concern, Jessie. But all I can say is that I'll be here as backup, for whatever you need."

"Thanks, Hank. I guess that means I need to protect me and mine." She backed up to the doorway. "And that's what I plan to do."

She fled down the hall to her own office, and wasn't surprised that he didn't follow. Hank had his own concerns, such as his son's allegation that his van was stolen while he was on the mainland.

How did anyone, police or not, determine that?

She didn't know. It was a gray area.

And that still left her and Danny in jeopardy.

The next day Jessie learned that Hank had checked in with Lynda Thrasher concerning her accident with a white vehicle. Although Lynda couldn't identify the van, she still maintained the person who tried to run her off the road drove a white SUV or car.

The one thing that didn't surprise Jessie was that Lynda's husband had just arrived on the island. That fit with what she'd seen on the Internet art forum; he'd said good-bye to his current on-line tryst—before he headed home.

The bastard, she thought. He seduced and set up the meetings on-line and then everything thereafter was private e-mail—after he was sure his latest conquest was safe enough for him to write to, knowing e-mail could be tracked, even if he used a fictitious tag.

But he wasn't the person threatening his wife—or her and Danny for that matter. But were the people who hated Ben, like the senator he was trying to destroy with his cartoons, trying to get back at him through Lynda?

She left her office to start her patrol of the island. At the moment, the only thing she felt good about was that Danny was safe with the Ames family. As planned, she would pick Danny up after her shift around six o'clock.

The ferry traffic came and went and then everything was quiet in town and out on the island roads. Time seemed to stretch longer than usual, and when it was finally time to pick up Danny, she was relieved. They would have a nice supper, check their e-mail and then watch TV, and finally go to bed.

Jessie felt tired as she swung down a short road from town to the southern tip of the island where Danny's friend lived, the complete opposite direction from Wind House. She pulled up in the driveway, impressed by the size and location of the place with its magnificent view of the water and its low bank waterfront. Striding up to the front door, she lifted the knocker and dropped it against the wooden barrier, hearing it reverberate inside the house.

Gail answered the door, looking surprised to see her. "Jessie, did Danny forget something?"

Jessie felt her smile freeze. "Not that I know of, Gail. I came to get Danny."

She seemed even more startled. "What do you mean, Jessie? You called earlier and asked me to drop Danny off at the school gym, that you would pick him up there."

"What are you saying? I never called you, Gail."

"Yes, you did. The boys heard when I answered the phone."

"No I didn't." Jessie felt frustration, and fear. Where was Danny?

"Holy cow!" Gail cried. "Are you saying that wasn't you who called me a half hour ago? Shit! It sounded just like you—I believed it was you."

"For God's sake, Gail, where did you say you took Danny? The gym?" There was no time for small talk. She needed to know what had happened—the details, now.

Gail repeated that she'd had the phone call, had taken Danny to the gym. "I didn't know it wasn't you—"

Her words drifted off as Jessie ran back to her police cruiser, got in and turned it toward the main road. Then she switched on the roof lights, wigwags and siren, floor-boarding the accelerator once she hit the main road.

As she headed toward the school gym she called for backup—that Danny was missing.

She hoped she was wrong.

CHAPTER THIRTY-FOUR

JESSIE WAS JUST MAKING THE TURN INTO THE SCHOOL GYM parking lot when her cell phone rang. She yanked it up and slammed it to her ear, still heading for the pickup area in the front of the building. Her heart sank when she saw that there were no other cars in the lot, that everyone had already left for the day.

"Hello, Danny?"

"I'm sorry, Jessie. This is Gail."

"Gail?"

"Yeah, but I'm calling about Danny."

"You've heard from him? I tried calling him but his phone was off."

"I know. I have his phone. Steve just found it in his bedroom. It must have fallen out of Danny's jacket pocket and he forgot it."

"Damn." Jessie was trying not to panic.

"I feel terrible, Jessie. I'm about to call the homes of Steve's friends, find out if they know where Danny is."

"I'd appreciate that."

"Please call me if there's anything else we can do to help, okay?"

Jessie agreed and then disconnected. She felt like saying the woman had done enough already by losing her son.

Parking, she grabbed her handheld radio and ran up the front steps to try the door. It was locked. Running to the back of the building she checked that entrance. She'd been right in the first place; there was no one on the premises, unless it was the custodian who'd be in the school itself if he was even still there. She saw no vehicles anywhere.

Back in her car again, she forced herself to stay calm. As she headed toward the main road Jessie called the station's main number and Rose answered.

"We know Danny is missing," Rose said. "Hank was at an accident over on the Westside but he's on his way back to town. We've called Max in as well."

"Thanks, Rose. Will you tell Hank I'm on my way home? Maybe it's all a misunderstanding and Danny got a ride with a friend's mother."

"Yeah, I'm sure it's something like that, Jessie. Disappearing kids don't happen on our island."

Neither do hit-and-run accidents, Jessie thought as she turned north. She tried not to think negative thoughts. Danny could be at home right now.

Then why hadn't he called her from their home phone?

And then her cell phone rang again. Full of hope, she grabbed it, her heart sinking when she heard it was Rose, and not Danny, or even Gail with a report that she'd found Danny. She braced herself.

"Jessie, I just heard from one of the moms Gail contacted who said she'd dropped Danny off at his driveway. He'd told her that you must have been delayed in picking him up, and he couldn't call you because he'd left his cell phone at Steve's house. The woman took him home so that he wouldn't be left alone after everyone was gone."

"Did she know if he got into the house?"

"I don't know." A pause. "Hank is still on the way, probably ten minutes behind you."

"Thanks Rose. I'll stay in touch. I'm almost there."

They hung up for the second time and she turned off Island Highway onto North Point Road, slowing for her driveway. She switched off the siren and blue lights, figuring she no longer needed them. The muscle aspect of her heart tightened as the house came into view. The exterior lights had all come on as expected. But the interior of the house was dark.

Something was wrong.

The locked kitchen door with Footers right behind it added to her apprehension. Danny had never made it to the house. If the person who'd manipulated him to the gym had been waiting for Danny to be left there after everyone was gone, she'd been disappointed. But had that person followed him home, where he'd been vulnerable on the driveway between the road and house?

She unsnapped her holster so that her pistol was free to grab, made sure her cell phone was in her pocket, and with her handheld radio in her left hand, moved up to the backdoor and unlocked it. Instantly Footers flew through the doorway, wagged his tail in acknowledgment of her, then continued into the yard, sniffing and turning in all directions, as if he knew that Danny had been there and was trying to get his scent.

Even their dog knew something was wrong.

When Footers took off toward the cliff path, Jessie followed, glad she'd had the extra lights installed, although they didn't add any illumination once she'd reached the top of the path.

She hesitated. Was she wasting her time in following Footers, who'd arrived at the first lower landing and seemed to be waiting for her? Or should she get back into her police car and try to find Danny somewhere on the island?

Don't be stupid, she told herself. You have no starting point to find your son. *This* is your only starting point and Footers might be your guide.

Her decision was instant. Crazy or not, she would follow Footers down the cliff path to the beach.

But the path was harrowing, dangerous, even in daylight, she reminded herself. In the dark it could be suicide.

She didn't hesitate, just as their dog hadn't, even though Footers had never gone to the beach without them. She moved down the path, feeling her way when she was uncertain of her footing. Footers seemed to wait for her at each switchback, until she'd cleared the next level down. Jessie wondered how their big dog could be so surefooted, never stumbling or hesitating on the downward thrust of the trail.

Footers was special, she decided. He loved them.

Momentarily, she used her penlight at precarious places, knowing she didn't want to identify her location should anyone be watching. Finally they reached the beach. A few feet away were the steps to the dock and the boathouse. Even in the dark she could see that their motorboat, the one they had yet to use, was still secured to its moorings, and that the tide was still coming in, that there were only a few feet left of the beach. Pinpricks of icy water hit her face with each surging wave.

But where was Danny?

The sound of breaking waves, wind and its echo off the cliffs was almost deafening. She spun around, surveying the space she could see, realizing that she was vulnerable out in the open on the beach, like a charcoal cutout against a black night. But again she felt strangely invincible; Footers had run up the narrow beach toward the cliff below the house, again waiting for her.

She followed, the rocks and broken shells crunching under her feet. Footer's nose and his allegiance to Danny were all she had right now. She had to keep her fear in abeyance or she'd collapse. Danny had to be okay. If he was hidden, Footers might know where. And so she kept following their dog.

They continued on, until they were at the point of the cliff under their house. Beyond that place they were trapped by the rising water. But Footers had veered away toward the base of the precipice. And then she saw the sliver of an opening in the solid rock, an upward slope off the beach.

"Footers! Oh thank goodness. Up here, Boy!"

"Danny!" she called, moving forward, seeing nothing but the huge rocks at the base of the cliff. "Are you there?" She could no longer see Footers.

"Mom?"

"It's me, Danny! Where are you?"

"I'm here, under the cliff."

And then she saw Footers poke his head out from between two rocks that she would have mistaken for one large outcropping. She picked her way forward over the rough terrain. It was obvious that they had to get out of there right away. The tide had almost cut her off from her route along the beach.

And then Danny jumped down to the beach. "Mom, that person in black was at the gym parking lot, waiting for all the cars to go. And then the person was in front of me, before I could get into the house." He gulped air, hugging her. "I had to run, and the only place I could go was the cliff path. I heard someone behind me—there was no time to get to the boat. All I could do was run up the beach and hide in the rocks. If it hadn't gotten dark I wouldn't have escaped."

"You're safe now that I'm here. We'll get out of this place right away, okay?"

She felt him nod against her chest. But she'd come to full alert. Was the person in black still close by, waiting to take them unaware?

In seconds they were on their way back to the cliff path, and in minutes they had reached the top, just as Hank arrived to guide them back to the house. Once inside, she thanked him, expecting him to turn and go now that they were safe.

"I'm staying tonight," he said, and then grinned. "I just need a pillow and some blankets for the sofa." He indicated the morning room that she and Danny had made into a family room.

She nodded, too relieved and exhausted to argue, and then supplied him with his wishes. After seeing Danny and Footers to their room, she went to hers and slept like a baby until morning.

Hank's presence had made the difference. She felt safe.

CHAPTER THIRTY-FIVE

JESSIE WAS UP AT DAWN THE NEXT MORNING AND HAD brewed the coffee before Hank woke up when his radio, its volume on high, had come to life with a call for a neighboring island. They sat at the kitchen counter, in silence at first. He was the first to talk about the night before.

"Jeez." He shook his head. "I don't get it."

"Someone has targeted my son. First he was run off the road, then the broken window, and now this." She got up, unable to sit still. All of her fears had surfaced and she felt on the verge of a panic attack. "Why, Hank? No one knows us here, we haven't hurt anyone and we hardly know people yet."

"Son of a bitch, Jessie. I haven't a clue. It just doesn't make any sense at all."

"Do you think it has anything to do with us moving into Wind House? Someone who might resent the history of my family?"

"Hell, no. Why would they? No one has anything to gain by harassing you and Danny. Your house was the first one built on this island. If anything, island residents are happy that there are descendants to live here and keep the place going." He hesitated. "I didn't live here for long while your grandmother was alive but I understand that everyone loved her. She was a kind woman who always stepped in to help in one way or another when an island family was in need."

She smiled. "Thanks for telling me that, Hank. I don't know much about my grandmother, except for a few childhood memories from when I was a very little girl." She pursed her lips, remembering. "But I know I loved my grandmother and her stories and grieved having to leave her. I believe she was a kind and loving person."

"You lived here back then?"

"I was born here, Hank, and my mom took me away after my father drowned." She swallowed her coffee. "But I don't remember a lot, and my mother is reticent about discussing those years." She looked him straight in the eyes. "My mother was horrified when she heard Danny and I were moving to Wind House."

He raised his eyebrows and said nothing, listening as she talked. "And now my son is being threatened.

"And so are you."

Briefly, she glanced away. Abruptly, her eyes were direct. "I know. But who? And why?"

"I don't know, Jessie. It's always possible that this is a random situation, that it has nothing to do with either your heritage or you being a female police officer."

"That's the other thing, Hank. Maybe there are people here who hate the thought of a female police officer."

"I wouldn't be able to even guess who they might be."

"What about the commune? Aren't the women expected to take a secondary place to the men? Would they be opposed to a woman cop in a community such as this island?"

A silence went past as he seemed to study his coffee cup. "The commune is patriarchal, but probably harmless," he said, finally. "They hearken to that belief, but take care of and protect their women and children, even if it seems to the rest of us that they repress them." A pause. "It's not my way and I have my own personal issues with the commune, but I don't believe that they are dangerous."

"They wouldn't be upset because I'm a woman in a power position on the island?"

He shook his head. "I don't think so but I can't stake my life on it." His brilliant blue gaze intensified as he reached to cover her hand with his. "Don't worry, Jessie." His voice had lowered to a—a what? Seductive tone? "Believe me, it's my priority to make sure you and Danny are safe."

His words, as well as how he'd said them, caught her off guard. She groped for a reply, unwilling to be the first to look away. Finally, she managed a smile and a simple thank you.

Seconds later he stood to go and she walked him to the door. What had he really meant? she wondered, watching him stride off to his car. That he was attracted to her—as a woman and not just a fellow cop?—feelings she'd also had for him?

Don't go there, she told herself, shutting the door. You don't need another problem.

Jessie knew it was time to wake Danny for school. Hank had left a half hour ago and she'd logged onto the Internet to read her e-mail, and had then talked to her mother for five minutes on the phone.

"Just checking to make sure everything is okay," Clarice had said. "I'm feeling better about coming up for a visit now that things seem to have settled down a bit."

"What do you mean, Mom?" She hadn't kept her mother posted about the current events, not wanting to worry her.

"Nothing. All is well, right?"

"That's right, Mom. And Danny and I look forward to seeing you."

They hung up and Jessie went to the window overlooking the strait. She hadn't explained what happened, knowing her mother couldn't come up with an explanation either, and would only worry. No need for that, Jessie thought, and went to the front hall to call Danny for breakfast. Her eyes shifted to the door, which was always locked, since they chose to use the side kitchen door instead. They'd had no real visitors since moving in, people who would go to the main entrance.

An envelope had been slipped under the door and lay on the hardwood entry floor. She moved forward, bent and grabbed it.

Straightening up Jessie stared at the sealed white envelope, a cheap nondescript container for a letter, something you could buy in volume at any discount store in America. She leaned against the banister, and opened the envelope to remove a sheet of tablet paper with a typed message.

"Move away, or you and your son will die."

Jessie's limbs reacted of their own volition: shaking uncontrollably. She backed up to sink onto a chair next to the hall table.

For long seconds a terror with a life all its own took hold of her body. Then, as reason reasserted itself, she stood up and strode back to the kitchen. Danny could sleep for a few more minutes.

She went to the phone and called Hank on his cell phone.

"Yeah," he said.

"It's me, Jessie," she said. "I just had a death threat."

A silence came over the connection.

"What do you mean?"

She told him.

"I'm on my way back," he said at once. "Stay put. Don't unlock the doors or go outside. Okay?"

"Got it. I won't."

They hung up and she went back to the kitchen. But she felt as though someone was watching.

Paranoid? she wondered. She doubted it.

The message was real.

CHAPTER THIRTY-SIX

HANK WALKED THE GROUNDS AND AGAIN THERE WAS NO sign of anyone hiding on the property. But Jessie sensed that someone was out there in the woods, watching, waiting for the next opportunity to strike.

Why? She and Danny didn't have an enemy in the world—until now. Hank had been right; no one cared that she'd inherited the family house. But someone did care that the assistant chief was a woman. She'd already gotten that message at work.

She watched Hank tweezer the envelope and sheet into a plastic baggie, then leave for the second time, heading to his apartment in town to shower and get ready for his shift. Then she went upstairs to awaken Danny. She braced herself for his questions. She needed enough of an answer to quiet his fear, but not enough so that he didn't stay alert. A catch-22. A mother's dilemma.

As Jessie got ready to drive Danny to school she wondered about the message, if the person who'd left it might have left a fingerprint. She doubted it. The note that had been left for her at the police station had been clean. It stood to reason that both had been left by the same person.

Or group?

A short time later she dropped Danny off at school, and then watched until he disappeared inside the building. He'd had strict instructions not to leave until she got there, that she'd be waiting by the front door at dismissal time. Steve was bringing Danny's cell phone back to him.

Now, as she headed to the station Jessie felt unsettled. What was happening? Was someone trying to prevent her from lasting the year as designated in order for her to take legal possession of Wind House?

She pulled into her parking space near the rear entrance and then strode into the station. With only a glance at her office, Jessie moved on down the hall to Hank's. He sat behind his desk, obviously concentrating on the paperwork in front of him. He glanced up as she came into the room.

"Sit down, Jessie. We need to talk."

She stared at him for long seconds, and then did as he said. "What's up, Hank?"

He got right to the point. "I found another message in your mailbox by the road." A pause. "The red flag was up when I left and hadn't been when I arrived. So I looked because the mailman doesn't come by until afternoon."

"What did it say?"

He indicated the open sheet in front of him that was exactly like the earlier one. When she went to grab it, he stopped her hand. "Just read it, don't touch it. I'm sending it in for a print analysis."

"The Wind Woman can't save you or your son."

She glanced up, meeting his eyes. "Nita?"

"I doubt that. She's odd, but harmless."

"But she's referred to the Wind Woman before. And she's part Native American. Maybe she has a grudge against my family."

He shook his head. "She's the last of her family, a distant relative to yours, and I don't think she's either vindictive or dangerous."

"A distant relative?"

He spread his hands. "That's what I've heard but I don't know for sure. You'd have to ask her."

"You know her, Hank?"

"Only in a casual way. But the old timers on the island have nothing bad to say about her, except that she went round the bend after all her family and friends died."

"I see." She stood, and then changed the subject. "So you're having the notes tested, right?"

"Uh-huh. We'll know the results in a couple of days." He hesitated. "In the meantime I don't have to tell you to be careful, Jessie."

"No, you don't." She gave an ironic smile. "And I'll be doing a little checking around as well, see what I can find out."

"Just watch your back." He stood then. "Maybe you should get someone to stay in the house with you and Danny."

"Who? I'm a newcomer, remember?"

She left before he could respond. But she didn't want him to at that moment, since he'd obviously left out the one direction she'd wanted to investigate—the people in the commune, including his son.

Jessie wasn't about to forget about them. Her life, and Danny's might depend on what she uncovered—and stopped.

She hoped she was wrong.

The situation was more than unsettling; it was critical to Jessie. She needed to get to the bottom of the threat, or if the incidents progressed, they might be forced off the island. That recourse was unacceptable. They had nowhere else to go, and she would be precluding a decent future for her son.

But if moving became their only option because her son's life was truly in danger, then she'd have no other choice. She'd leave it all and make it somehow. One thing she knew: she'd never take them back to their old neighborhood where Danny had to face street violence and gangs. They'd stay in the Northwest, the land of her ancestors.

Once out on patrol, her radio was silent, the roads were peaceful, and there was no threat from any direction. Knowing that all of the county roads were in their jurisdiction, Jessie impulsively turned down the one to the Sweers property where Hank's son lived in a yurt hut. Everyone on the island stayed away, but was it a dangerous place? Time I found out, she told herself.

No one answered the door of the main house, and although Jessie felt the hairs on the back of her neck prickle as she went back to her car, she remained in control. No one would dare take a potshot at a uniformed officer who was driving a police car. She got back in the cruiser and swung around the driveway, braking when she saw the dirt road that headed into the woods. Without hesitation she turned down it, remembering that Hank had said his son lived in the second dwelling. Several minutes later Jessie stopped at the one she assumed belonged to Bruce, and then realized she was deep in the forest, that no one knew she was there. Giving in to common sense, she called in, giving her location, knowing that if Hank heard it he would be upset. She had no reason for visiting his son.

But she did, she thought, smiling. She was about to ask his advice about the arts and crafts shop, and how lucrative it was to place artwork on consignment, so she could report that information to her mother.

A completely innocent request, she reminded herself,

and got out of the car. A moment later Bruce stepped out of his door and she knew she'd found the right hut.

"Mrs. Cline," he said. "We met in Tommy's store. What brings you to my humble residence?"

She smiled. "Your art, Bruce."

He raised his eyebrows in a question, an expression exactly like his father's.

"Am I interrupting your work?"

"Hardly," he said, grinning. "I'm on island time, which means I'm not in a hurry."

She moved forward. "I won't delay you for long and I appreciate your graciousness. I only have one question."

"Shoot."

He slouched against the door frame, his posture for listening another way that he was like his dad. She wondered about genetics. He looked and acted as his father did, but their mindsets seemed so different. What went wrong in the relationship? she wondered.

"I'd like my mother, who is an artist, to consider relocating here from California," she said. "I was hoping you could tell me that it was feasible, that you had a good launching pad on the island to sell your work."

"You must know I've only started to show my work in Tommy's shop."

"I know that, but I figure you did your research about where to show your art. Also, you've lived here longer than I have, and you must have had some feedback about the feasibility of placing your art on consignment before you actually did it." She stepped even closer. "I was hoping you'd share your knowledge of that with me."

He stared at her for long seconds, as though gauging her sincerity. "Yeah, that's true, Officer Cline."

"Jessie," she said, smiling even wider. "I'll feel like a truant officer or something if you call me officer."

"But I'm not a kid."

"Course you're not. And I'm not here on official business."

He relaxed then, and she wondered if he associated her with his father, because they were the island police force. She soon forgot that notion after he invited her into his hut, showed her his work in progress and the finished carvings.

"You are super talented," she told him, truly impressed.

"In a different way from your mother. Her paintings are exquisite."

"You know my mother's work?"

He nodded. "Many people do, especially those of us on the West Coast."

She shook her head, thinking of her mother's modest income. "Too bad her talent doesn't translate into dollars."

"So true. The plight of many gifted people. They never make the money equal to their talent."

His eyes were suddenly direct, another of his father's traits. "So how exactly can I help you, Mrs.—uh, Jessie?"

"Like I said, Bruce, I'm only here in search of information about the consignment issue."

"I'll have to let you know on that."

"Great. I can't wait to pass on anything positive to my mom. I'd love her to move up here."

"That would be wonderful, especially for your son."

"You know my son?"

Bruce shook his head. "Only heard that you had one, and I've seen him from a distance." He suddenly dropped an arm around her shoulder. "But I'd guess he's a good kid, because I'd also guess that you're a super mom."

His words took her aback. Bruce seemed genuine.

As he walked her back to her car she found it hard to believe he would have anything to do with the threatening events surrounding her and Danny. He appeared concerned about the environment and the structure of a family. And she liked him.

Jessie drove away feeling good that Hank's son seemed clean, but insecure about the Sweers commune. She still didn't know about that.

They could be beyond what they seemed.

CHAPTER THIRTY-SEVEN

"So did you satisfy yourself that my son and the commune were safe?"

Jessie was sitting in her police cruiser outside the school, her window open waiting for the dismissal bell. She hadn't seen Hank come up behind her until he'd spoken. Some policewoman, she thought, knowing her mind had been elsewhere, going over her options to keep Danny safe.

"I think your son seems genuine, if that's what you're asking, Hank."

"And the commune?"

"I don't know, Hank. No one came to the door when I knocked at the main house."

"Typical." He shifted position. "They claim to be against violence, to respect the environment, to reject materialism and the waste of natural resources. They also raise their own food, because they are opposed to genetically engineered food." He hesitated. "It's a total patriarchal structure; women have no rights to make decisions." He shook his head. "And they have their own brand of religion that dictates keeping their distance from people like us."

"Isn't that somewhat of a contradiction?" Jessie asked, curious for his response.

"Uh-huh, and the fact that Sweers lives in affluence while his flock are housed in yurt huts."

"I noticed that." Jessie glanced away from the sudden worry she read on his face. "As I said, it seems like a contradiction."

"Yeah, that's my take on it, especially since they drive cars, have electricity, and take advantage of high tech, like computers and the Internet."

"And Sweers has expensive new cars while his followers drive old clunks?"

"Uh-huh. That's the picture I see."

There was a pause between them.

"But Bruce was uh, receptive?" Hank asked, continuing the conversation, and Jessie suddenly felt sorry for him. "The people in the commune, and my son, aren't practical and that's probably why they're out here on this island at the end of the continent, under the control of a fanatic."

She was momentarily silent. "Yeah, he answered all my questions. We had a nice conversation."

"About the commune?"

"No, about art, the reason I went to talk to him."

He looked surprised. "You didn't question him about what happened to Danny?—his white van?"

She shook her head. "Bruce seemed sincere about what happened to his van." She paused. "We'll see."

He rested his hand on the ledge of the open window, his body bent so that he could talk to her. "So what did you hope to gain by going to the commune, Cline?" he asked, reverting to his professional name for her.

"An opinion about selling art on the island, Chief," she replied, following his lead.

"I see," he said and she wondered what he saw.

Their gazes locked, neither willing to express their real feelings. He was the first to break the silence.

"I find it interesting that you would go to the commune on your work time, to ask about"—he hesitated—"art."

They both knew her reason was bogus, but she wasn't about to admit that. Bruce was his son and his son belonged to the commune. She needed to protect her own son. Where was Hank's position in that scenario—if it was her son versus his son? That was another thing that she'd been trying to determine.

She had no definitive answers. She liked Bruce, but had no fix on his stability, except that he seemed sincere and likable. Her gut feeling was that the guy was okay.

Jessie explained about her mother, that Bruce knew of her art, that she, as the daughter, was gathering information to influence her mom to move to the island.

He straightened. "I understand, Jessie." He gave a salute with his hand and then headed back to his own car, leaving her to wonder what it was that he understood.

And then the bell rang and the kids poured out of the building. In minutes Danny was in the car and she was headed for their house.

She braced herself to give him the new rules, after he was locked into the house. Gail Ames had begged out of their earlier arrangement; Jessie figured she'd been scared off by what had happened. And she wondered about Hank's visit to her in the school parking lot. He'd obviously heard her giving a location on the radio before seeing Bruce. Was he protecting his ass? she wondered. Or his son's? Or neither.

She didn't know.

All she knew was that she had to protect her son—and find out who was out to get them in any way that she could, legal or not.

* * *

A few minutes later she pulled into their driveway, and brought her cruiser to a stop in front of the house. She was about to get out when she hesitated as another car stopped behind them. And then the driver got out and she recognized Max.

"Hey, Jessie," he said, grinning. "You ever met my wife?" He indicated the smiling woman who'd stepped out of Max's car on the passenger side.

"No, I've heard all about Signe but we've never met." Her gaze shifted from Max to his buxom wife, a woman who appeared as physically strong as the outgoing personality she couldn't hide. "I'm happy to meet you now, Signe."

"Same here, Officer Cline. I heard about you, too." Her blue eyes crinkled into a smile. "We're here to help out."

Danny left the cruiser to stand beside his mother, looking expectantly between the adults. Jessie quickly introduced him, wondering what the unexpected visit meant.

Then Signe moved forward to shake Danny's hand. "And I've heard all about you as well, Son." She smiled wider. "I'm looking forward to introducing you to my grandson when he comes to visit for the holidays. He's about your age and lives over on the mainland."

"Cool." Danny grinned. "I'd love to meet him."

"Good," Signe said. "But in the meantime we need to keep you safe."

"What do you mean?" Danny looked unsure.

"Well, my husband here, Max who works with your mom, suggested a way for all of us to feel better about you being alone."

"I don't understand, Signe." Jessie dropped her arm around Danny's shoulders. "We're taking precautions."

"Of course you are, Jessie," Max said. "What my wife is saying in her roundabout way is that she's offering her services, that is until we get to the bottom of who has been threatening you two."

"How so?"

"I'll be the adult in residence when you can't be," Signe said. "I can be here after school and when you have to work weekends, Danny can be at our house. We only live a few minutes away."

"But I can't," Danny protested. "I have Footers."

"Footers?" Max asked.

"My dog. I can't leave him alone that long. He's already here by himself when Mom and I are gone."

Signe laughed outright. "Footers can come to our house anytime. We love animals."

Danny nodded. "Footers is part of our family."

Jessie glanced between them. "I can't thank you enough, Signe, Max. What can I say? You can't imagine what this means—"

"Shhh," Signe interrupted. "Enough said. What are neighbors for anyway? Besides, this is only a temporary situation, until you guys catch that coward."

A short time later Jessie had made sure Danny was safely inside the house with Signe and Footers and was on her way back to town to finish her shift. Max had followed her for a short time before veering off toward his own house. His eight hours started when she completed hers.

She was almost to the station when she got the call to the post office. She made the next turn and headed past Tommy's arts and crafts store, then Starbucks and finally pulled into a parking space next to a mail truck. Getting out of the cruiser she grabbed her handheld radio and went inside, past the people waiting for service and directly to the closed door that led to the backroom. She knocked and the heavyset postmaster let her in to the privacy of his office.

"We gotta problem," Val Howard told her as he stepped behind his desk and motioned her to the adjoining chair. "Someone is sending threatening letters to Ben Thrasher's pregnant wife."

"What? Please explain."

Val's plump chin and neck jiggled as he talked. "Of course I've reported this to the Postal Inspection Department and they're looking into it, but the island police need to do an investigation on site."

"Of course. Just give me the details." She'd pulled out her pad and pen to take a report. "We'll follow up."

He nodded. "There have been a number of letters to Mrs. Thrasher that have gone through this post office and were delivered to their mail box." He opened a file folder on his desk, and then shoved it across the desk to her. "These are copies of the letters she received. The originals have been submitted to the Post Office General's Office for analysis."

"Fingerprinting?"

"Of course." He spread his hands. "And now Mrs. Thrasher seems to be receiving letters that don't go through the postal system. Someone is putting threatening letters in her mailbox."

Jessie was silent for long seconds. *Someone had placed a letter under her door and in her mailbox.*

Was it the same person?

She noted all the information Val could offer, then put her pad and pen away and left the post office. She knew what she had to do next—and dreaded the thought.

She had to pay a call on the Thrashers.

CHAPTER THIRTY-EIGHT

SHE SHOULD HAVE KNOWN. THE PLACE WASN'T JUST A NICE house on the island; it was an elegant estate. Jessie drove slowly up the tree-lined lane to where it arced around a huge water fountain to the front entry of the new Tudor style house. The lawn and trimmed shrubbery stretched all the way to the cliffs, beyond which the water view overlooked the ferry lane and the horizon.

Affluence, she thought, and brought the cruiser to a stop just past the entrance. A glance at the open three-car garage told her that all bays were occupied by expensive vehicles, indicating that the Thrashers were at home.

Jessie turned off the ignition, then sat for seconds longer, bracing herself to face Ben and Lynda, not knowing what to expect when she spoke to them face-to-face in their own house. Would Ben remember her then?

Don't ask for trouble, she instructed herself. One step at a time. Isn't that what she was always advising Danny?

Resisting an urge to glance in the mirror, Jessie got out of the car. She already knew she looked okay, even if her hair was pinned into a roll. She chided herself.

Why did she care?

I *don't* care about him, she thought, as she walked up the inlaid brick steps to the porch. I only care that I never really had closure on the issue of my life being altered forever.

And then she lifted the knocker and let it fall. She could hear it resonating inside the house. There was a long silence but she sensed she was being viewed through the peek hole. Abruptly, the door opened and an elderly woman dressed in a black dress with a white apron stood looking at her.

"Yes?" she said, and her glasses slid down her nose.

Jessie resisted an urge to laugh. How typical of the nouveau riche. They needed all the trappings to feel important.

Jessie flashed her badge. "I need to talk to Mr. and Mrs. Thrasher concerning recent threatening mail."

The woman pushed her glasses back up her nose and read her name off the badge. "Please come in Officer Cline. I'll tell them that you're here."

Jessie followed her into the huge entry hall, and then waited while the woman disappeared into the back of the house. She couldn't help her grin when she knew she was alone. *The Thrashers* already knew she was there; it was all staged to bolster their sense of self-importance.

Don't let your prejudice show, she told herself. You're only the police officer stepping in to help in a legitimate complaint. It's your job.

"Officer Cline?"

Jessie turned, recognizing Ben's voice. Nodding, she looked for even a flicker of recognition, but there was none. He'd stepped into the entry hall, a tall, bearded man with an immense presence, his arm around his wife, Lynda, who was so pregnant that she almost wobbled.

She looked him straight in the eyes, her professional persona in place, not allowing herself to feel diminished because he didn't even recall her name. "I'm here in answer to the mail your wife is receiving, Mr. Thrasher. I'd hoped to take her statement about what's been happening?"

"Oh, of course." His dark eyes seemed to nail her to the wall behind her. "Please, let's go into the living room where my wife can sit down."

She followed them into the room off the hall, aware of his scrutiny, and yet, totally committed to not being influenced by his overwhelming ability to control.

"Thank you for coming, Officer Cline. I appreciate your response. I'm really scared." Lynda's words seemed to freeze Ben in place. He disapproved.

Jessie ignored him, concentrating on Lynda who seemed to adore her husband despite his manner, snuggling next to him on the sofa. She was glad that Lynda had expressed her feelings. It made her job easier; Ben could not stonewall her on this issue. Jessie took the chair facing them.

Ben, the stranger. He obviously didn't remember her from a dozen years ago. She wondered how many affairs he'd had, and how many at the same time. Dozens, she thought—too many faces and names for him to remember. She hoped those women had moved past this womanizer—as she had.

But she admitted that a man forgetting a woman who'd loved him could be a devastating event in the life of that woman. Unless the woman recognized that the man was a psychopath who cared for no one but himself. She felt for Lynda, his current wife and the possible target of his powerful enemies. Lynda seemed oblivious to Ben's flaws.

Being the professional, Jessie placed her handheld radio beside her and took out her pad and pen. Then she looked up, avoiding Ben to concentrate on Lynda, the reason she was there.

"Could you give me the chronology of what's happened, Lynda?" She smiled reassuringly.

Lynda nodded, started to smile back and then hesitated. "I'm scared because I think someone out there wants to hurt me and the baby." Her voice broke. "I don't know what to do to protect us."

Jessie saw Ben stiffen as Lynda spoke, and knew he didn't like what she'd said, even as he pulled her closer. "C'mon Sweetheart. Isn't that overstating the facts a little?" He shook his head at Jessie as if to say his wife was overly concerned because of raging hormones.

Jessie felt herself go cold. If she hadn't disliked him before, she would have at that moment. His passive-aggressive words were insensitive to his wife, even though Lynda didn't seem to notice. Jessie's expression didn't reveal her feelings as she posed her next question.

"Can you start at the beginning, Lynda?" she asked, gently. "As a mother, I understand your concern."

She didn't care what in the hell the man on the sofa thought. How dare he dismiss his wife's fear. Lynda wasn't his media prop for an established family; she was a young woman expecting their first child.

"It started with a couple of phone calls." Lynda's words trailed off.

"Was that before the hit-and-run incident?"

Lynda nodded.

"What did the caller say?"

"Just brief threats. Stupid things I didn't understand."

"Like what?"

Lynda kept her gaze fixed. "'You aren't going to win,' 'Your baby isn't yours' and 'I'm going to win.'"

"Win?" Jessie was taken aback. Her gaze shifted to Ben. "Do you think this has anything to do with you, Mr. Thrasher?"

"Of course not," he retorted at once. "How in hell could it? It sounds like gibberish."

"A lawsuit perhaps?" Jessie added, pushing. "I refer to the senator who has not had good things to say about you in the media."

He bristled. "There are no lawsuits, but off the record, yeah, he could be taking his version of revenge—from a distance. On the record, I can't say anything except that he should be questioned."

"I'll make a note of that, Mr. Thrasher," she said, jotting down his response.

"Yeah, you do that," he responded, sarcastically.

"Ben," Lynda said gently. "The officer is only doing her job."

"Uh-huh, I get it." He moved forward to the edge of the sofa. "I just don't want to be misquoted. The senator is already hinting he'll sue me for slander if I accuse him directly."

Jessie controlled her response, but her words were clipped. "The island police department is not the national media, Mr. Thrasher. We only deal with the facts, not speculation."

A silence heavy with Ben's disapproval ensued.

"I'm sure," he said finally. Then, after Lynda added more details that Jessie also recorded in her notes, Ben stood, pulling his wife up with him. "Lynda only wanted this on record because she's unnerved by these letters." A pause. "What else do you need, Officer?"

She stood, too, facing them. "That's probably it then if your wife has nothing else to add." She shifted her gaze from Ben to Lynda. "Do you, Lynda?"

The young woman seemed disconcerted, aware of her husband's disapproval. "I don't think so. I just want to know I'm safe." She shot an uncertain glance to her husband. "Especially when my husband is gone. I'm soon due to have a baby."

Another silence.

Jessie realized Lynda was really talking to her husband who seemed oblivious to her fear. He kept his gaze on Jessie, as though willing her to leave.

Jessie headed toward the entryway. "The only other thing I would have needed are the original letters, but I understand that you've already given them to the local postmaster and he's forwarded them to the post office general who'll investigate," she told them.

"What?" Ben's question was like a bullet being shot out of his mouth. "He'll what?"

"Investigate," Jessie repeated softly, trying not to feel pleased by his upset. "For fingerprints, handwriting analysis, where the letters were mailed from, even to determine the type of paper and ink used."

Lynda stepped forward then, grabbing Jessie's hand. "Thank you," she said. "I remember you from before and I feel secure that you're on my case."

Jessie smiled back, pleased, and realized that she really liked Lynda. Not only was she young and beautiful but she seemed genuine. "I'll do the best I can, Lynda. And believe me, we'll get to the bottom of what's happening." She stepped through the doorway onto the porch. "Wherever the cards fall."

And then she turned away and headed for her car, but not before she caught the expression on Ben's face.

He was furious.

Jessie drove up behind Hank's police car that was parked in her driveway. Startled, she was about to run into the house when he suddenly appeared, coming down the side of the house from the kitchen. "Hey, Jessie, you finally got here."

"Finally? I'm just now off shift." She hesitated. "What's happened, Hank?"

He tilted his head. "Does something always have to be wrong when I appear?"

She shook her head, puzzled.

He grinned. "I just came by to ask you something."

"What?"

He stepped closer, tall and lean in his uniform, and she couldn't help but notice how attractive he was. But she kept her professional bearing.

He paused in front of her. For a second he seemed to hesitate, but then he blurted out his next sentence.

"I'm a Seattle Sonics fan and have season tickets." Another pause. "I was thinking you could use an evening away from the island so—"

"So?" she prompted when he seemed at a loss of words.

"How about going with me? I have the tickets, Max will take over here and we could both use some time away, even for only a few hours."

His offer took her aback. She hadn't expected his request for a date. But she was intrigued.

And she was suddenly tongue-tied.

"Thank you, Hank. Although I love basketball, I really can't leave Danny here alone."

"He won't be alone, Jessie, he'll be with Signe and Max. Danny will be well protected while you're gone."

"But there's Footers and—"

"Footers will be fine too." He grabbed her shoulders. "You need a break, Jessie." A pause. "We both do."

Jessie was silent for long seconds, her eyes locked to his. When she finally spoke she surprised herself. "Okay, if I can, Hank. Danny has some events at school and I promised to be there and—"

He just grinned. "I'll take that as a yes, Jessie, since it's a Saturday night and the school functions are over for the weekend."

She had no other excuses and finally nodded. He looked pleased, gave a salute and told her he'd pick her up on Saturday afternoon in time for the three o'clock ferry. "We'll catch the last ferry back," he told her, as he climbed into his car.

And then Jessie wondered what she'd done. She had always believed it was wrong to mix business with pleasure. And wasn't that what she was about to do?

CHAPTER THIRTY-NINE

THE LAST DAYS OF THE WEEK PASSED UNEVENTFULLY AND Jessie was grateful to Signe and Max who had stepped in to help. She insisted on paying Signe, who resisted but finally agreed to some extra "pin money" as she put it. Although Jessie could never repay her kindness she needed to compensate the woman. She hoped the arrangement could go on for awhile, until they felt safe again, and by paying Signe, it made it worthwhile for everyone.

There had been no new anonymous letters sent to the Thrashers in the past two days and no news about possible suspects. They were still waiting on the fingerprint results. Jessie wasn't holding her breath. The threatening notes sent to her had turned up clean.

Now as she finished up her paperwork and filed it, she was thoughtful. She was missing something. Both Lynda and Danny had been run off the road. The hit-and-run driver had intended harm to both of them. Then the notes and letters had happened, to her and to Lynda. There had been no other incidents to anyone else on the island. The focus of a phantom predator appeared to be the Thrashers and the Clines.

Why, she wondered, and grabbed her jacket. Was there a connection? Or were the threats only random?

She waved at Rose as she left the station and then

headed out to her police cruiser, pausing to buy the *Seattle Times* from the newspaper machine. A few seconds later she got into the car and headed for the school gym. Danny had stayed after for junior high practice and she was picking him up today. After they went home, ate and changed clothes, they would return to the gym for a high school basketball game. Going to the games with Danny was a treat for her and she had looked forward to going all week.

She drove up and parked behind the line of other mothers waiting for their kids. Jessie grinned. The parking lot was always a madhouse after school—for a while until all the cars had gone, and then it was deserted.

Which is why you must always be on time, she told herself, getting out of the car. She waved at several women she recognized as she walked toward the entrance. She figured Danny was loitering with his new friends or maybe still in the shower room. Whatever, he needed a prod, so they could get home, eat and be back in time for the game.

"Hey, Mom!" Danny ran up behind her.

She turned, grinning. "Who else?"

He gave her a quick hug, and then stepped back, hoisting his backpack off his shoulder. His friend Steve and two other boys came up behind them as they walked back toward her police car. Danny was excited, explaining how well he did in practice.

"He was awesome, Mrs. Cline," Steve chimed in. "Our coach says Danny is probably next year's star forward."

"Super!" she said, pleased. For all of the trauma of his last school in California and her angst over the move, seeing her son so excited made it all worthwhile.

"But Mom?"

They'd reached the car, and he'd hesitated after opening the door and throwing his backpack onto the seat. "Steve's mom is having pizza for a few of us guys and then she'll take us to the game." He hesitated. "Can I go? I could meet you at the game?"

"I don't know, Danny. Didn't we have plans?"

"Yeah, I know but this is special, Mom."

She nodded. "Okay, but I need to talk to Steve's mom first."

"Super!" he cried, and Steve gave his a slap on the back. "I'll meet you at the gym when you get there for the game, Mom."

Jessie followed him to where Steve's mother waited in her SUV. "Hi Gail," she said. "I hear you're hosting a pizza party for these guys."

"Uh-huh, Jessie." Her gaze was suddenly direct. "And I promise to see these guys to my house and back to the gym. No stops. They'll be completely safe."

"I said yes, Gail. But under the circumstances of what's just happened I'm sure you identify with a mother's concern."

"Of course."

Jessie watched them go, and then got back into her cruiser, wheeling around the other waiting cars to head toward home. It still wasn't quite dark but she turned on her headlights, and hoped to get to her house before it was.

Turning off Island Highway onto North Point Road, she slowed for her driveway. Abruptly, there was a movement on the road ahead of her and she slammed on the brakes.

She'd almost hit a person in a scarf and parka.

She turned on the emergency lights and then jumped out of the car and ran to help. It was Nita on the edge of the road, adjusting the groceries in her bike basket. She looked startled from her sudden swerve onto the gravelly shoulder. Her braking had jarred the contents she'd been transporting but somehow she'd managed to keep the bicycle from going into the ditch.

"I'm terribly sorry. Are you all right?" Jessie bent to help pick up a bag of potatoes that had fallen to the ground. "I'm Officer Cline and I can radio for help."

For a moment Nita just stared and Jessie wondered if she was too shocked by almost being hit that she couldn't speak. Then the old woman nodded.

"I'm fine. No need to radio anyone." A pause. "There's no mistake but that you are Jessie Cline," she said in perfect English, although there was a slight accent Jessie couldn't identify. Her tribal language?

"Why do you say that?" She met Nita's dark gaze.

Nita finished picking up the potatoes and then placed the bag back into the basket. "You look exactly like your grandmother when she was your age."

"You knew my grandmother?" And then she remembered Hank mentioning that.

There was a brief silence.

"We were distant cousins. We grew up together on this island."

"So you knew her very well."

Nita nodded.

"And my father?"

"Yes, and I knew your mother, too." A pause. "And your grandmother's brother and his son."

"My great-uncle's son who was with my father when he drowned?"

She nodded again, but didn't elaborate.

"And I knew you, Jessie, when you were a child."

This time the silence between them was longer.

"I would love to hear all about the family, Nita. Would you be willing to come and visit Danny and me?"

"I've met your son."

"He told me."

Nita inclined her head, and then retied her scarf that had slipped off her head. "I must go. It gets dark and I have to get down to my boat."

"You sure you're okay?"

"I need to go," she repeated, and getting on her bike proceeded down the road.

The wind had picked up with the approach of night, and Jessie felt the chill. But she stood watching until the woman had disappeared into the gathering shadows. Abruptly, Nita glanced back.

"Granddaughter of my friend, beware of an evil wind. She wants her justice."

Her words seemed to ebb and flow with the strength of the air currents. For long seconds Jessie felt rooted to the blacktop. *Evil wind?*—not Wind Woman as Danny had said she'd called The Spirit of the Wind? Did Nita mean the mythical Tsonoqua? Or something else? Had her words been a threat?

Jessie had already turned into her driveway before she remembered that Nita hadn't answered when asked to come for a visit. She'd changed the subject to Danny. Jessie shook her head. Nita had seemed so normal at first, until she started in about the evil wind. Maybe she really was a little nuts.

As she approached the house she made a mental list of people to question: her mother, Nita and Hank.

Hank. Oh God.

She'd almost forgotten her date with him tomorrow afternoon, and admitted to herself that she was nervous. She hadn't been out on a date for a long time. And then there was her concern for Danny. Even though she knew her son was safe with Signe and Max, Jessie couldn't let go of her worry. Nor her uncertainty about dating her boss.

Don't think of that now, she told herself, and pulled up in front of the house. Cautious as always when coming home, Jessie was glad the exterior lights had all come on at dusk. She felt more settled after being greeted by Footers. And when she let him outside while she changed her clothes and freshened up, he didn't bark. She let him back inside after she'd given him food and she'd had a quick sandwich.

"I promise we'll take you for a long walk tomorrow, Boy," she told him. Then she locked the house and went back to her car.

A twinge of apprehension hit her again as she drove down the driveway to the road. But that's only normal, she thought. She was concerned about her date tomorrow . . . and Nita's warning.

Mostly Nita's warning.

CHAPTER FORTY

NITA WATCHED FROM THE TREES, THE DARKNESS HIDING HER presence, as Jessie stared after her. She could almost guess what was going through the young woman's mind: *Nita is already gone, on her way to the beach.* She smiled. The little girl Jessica had grown into a good woman; her grandmother would have been proud.

But her grandmother could not protect her now, and maybe *she* couldn't either. The evil was too secret; even she hadn't been able to figure it out. All she knew was that she had to take action. Death hovered again above the family.

She waited until the taillights had disappeared, and then continued to the shed where she'd leave her bike. Placing her groceries into a backpack, Nita hoisted it up, hoping to traverse the cliff path to the beach before it became completely dark. The last thing she wanted to do was switch on a flashlight. There'd been another presence in the woods in recent weeks and Nita sensed that exposing herself could be dangerous.

Once on the beach she retrieved her boat from its hidden mooring within a cleft in the cliff. She was soon out in the open water, motoring back to her tugboat. As always her gaze went to the house on the cliff.

She watched as lights came on, first in the kitchen and then in the upstairs bedroom, the one that once belonged to Jessie's grandmother. Nita smiled again. The room obviously belonged to Jessie now.

Her gaze swept down the house to the cliff beneath it, then downward even farther to the waves crashing against the rocks. It was almost high tide and the beach was disappearing under the rising water. Like the other night when Danny's dog led Jessie to the beach.

Nita sobered, her eyes narrowed on the huge rocks where the seawater crashed into the crevices and caves. In her mind she remembered the years when she and the other children had played there, and explored the mysteries of the cliff. She could almost hear their cries of joy on the edge of the wind, see again their innocent days of play in the foamy mist that rose from sea spray.

But all of that could disappear into the past if there was no longer anyone left to remember, no person to carry on the will of the Great Spirits.

She raised her hands to the sky, as if in supplication. It was up to her now. She knew what she had to do. Time was short. She must fulfill the destiny of the family.

Because there was no one else who could.

CHAPTER FORTY-ONE

DANNY WAS IN HIGH SPIRITS WHEN JESSIE MET HIM AT THE gym. While she was seated with Gail and her husband and other adults, Danny sat with his friends on the bottom bench of the bleachers. Jessie found her gaze going to the group of boys as often as she followed the high school basketball team on the court. It pleased her immensely that her son fit in so well with his new friends. *I did the right thing in coming here, anonymous threats or not,* she told herself for the umpteenth time. Her son had found his niche.

They drove home after the game, she fixed hot chocolate and they sat and talked for a few minutes before Danny went upstairs to bed, Footers following at his heels.

"Good night, Mom. See you in the morning."

"I'll be along to tuck you in," she called after him. She locked up, made sure the downstairs was secure and then went upstairs to her own bedroom where she got ready for bed. After tucking him in, and ignoring that Footers was again lying at the bottom of the bed, Jessie went back to her room, looking forward to snuggling under her quilt.

Jessie got under the covers, thinking she'd fall asleep immediately, and was mistaken. She was wide awake, her eyes on the sky above the strait beyond her windows.

All of her concerns and worries had suddenly surfaced, robbing her of needed rest.

Tossing and turning, Jessie tried in vain to get comfortable. It was no use. Just relax, she told herself. If you can't sleep you can at least doze. But she found herself worrying about everything, including her date with Hank, what she'd wear, whether or not she should leave Danny. The whirlpool of her thoughts didn't allow her mind any reprieve.

Flinging the covers back, Jessie went down to the kitchen and microwaved a mug of water. Then she grabbed a bag of herbal tea and headed back up to her room. As her tea steeped, she settled back under the covers. Again her mind went to tomorrow and Hank. She pondered his situation, why he had taken the job on a remote island. Was it really because of his son? And why had his son joined a commune—a cult? Were the Sweers people really as harmless as they appeared on the surface?

Sipping tea, Jessie stared at the sky of moving clouds and listened to the moans and occasional howls of the wind, glad she was in the shelter of her house. Again her thoughts went to Hank and his former wife. What kind of a woman had she been? she wondered. I respect Hank, she thought. He was a take-charge man, and she believed him to be honest, someone to trust. She hated to think that he might be naïve about his son.

She finished her tea and sank deeper into her bed, eyes still on the moving sky. And then she remembered no more.

Jessie awoke at dawn, realized she had too much on her mind to linger in bed where she'd only dwell on her worries, so she got up and went down to the kitchen to make coffee. The newspaper she'd bought the night before lay unread on the counter, and she anticipated reading it with her coffee in the peaceful silence of the early morning.

As the coffee dripped, she went around the house, to rooms they scarcely used, and opened the drapes, realizing that she needed to dust and vacuum, or hire a cleaning lady to help her out.

"Jeez," she said aloud, grinning. She'd come to the island to better their lives, and now she was considering a cleaning lady as well as having hired a babysitter, electrician and locksmith. She hoped she wasn't so impressed by how her inheritance would benefit Danny's future that she'd become complacent about their finances.

Going back to the kitchen she poured herself a cup of fresh coffee, then grabbed the paper and sat down at the kitchen table. A glance at the clock told her it was almost seven, even though it wasn't light yet. The northern part of Washington was closer to Alaska than San Francisco; and it got dark earlier and light later at this time of year.

She opened the paper, and then stared at a small article at the bottom of the front page.

CARTOONIST'S WIFE ALMOST KILLED

The text went on to explain how she'd been run off the road, and that the late-term pregnant Lynda came through unscathed, but shaken. Then the reporter went into the history of her husband's controversial campaign against a United States senator. There were no suspects listed although Ben's cartoon campaign against the national politician was detailed. It ended with Ben's barely veiled accusation that the senator could be behind his wife's hit-and-run accident.

Jessie sat back, digesting the newspaper account. She wondered what the article would mean to the island. Would it bring reporters? She hadn't heard of any so far.

Getting up, she poured herself more coffee, then went back to contemplate what she'd read about the Thrashers. She was still sitting there with her second cup of coffee when Danny and Footers came into the kitchen.

"I thought I heard you get up, Mom." Danny went to the door and let his dog onto the patio. Then he faced Jessie. "I think Footers has been too cooped up and I'd like to take him for a walk on the beach this morning."

"I'll go with you, Danny." Jessie grinned. "I've been cooped up too and could use the fresh air." She didn't add that she wasn't about to let her son go down on that beach alone after what had happened. This time she'd have her weapon in her pocket.

They waited another hour, until it was full daylight, and then locked the door and headed for the beach path. The way down didn't seem as dangerous as the last time; it was safe if they were careful.

Once on the beach Jessie could see that the tide was coming in, that there wouldn't be much of a beach for long. There was only about twenty feet of gravel and sand from cliff to water.

But it was enough for Footers to get some exercise, she thought, watching as Danny threw driftwood for his dog to retrieve.

The tide came in fast and within a half hour they headed for the cliff path again. Once on top, she hesitated. "In the summer the beach will be like a football field, and you and Footers can play for hours before the tide sends you to the path."

"I know, Mom. Steve told me about how opposite the tides are, low in summer during daylight and low in winter during the night."

They went on to the house, Jessie to make breakfast, Danny to wipe Footers down with a towel so that he didn't shake salt water all over the kitchen. Outwardly calm, Jessie was suddenly stricken with a new concern. It was only a few hours until she would be picked up for her date with Hank.

"Hey Footers!" Danny cried after glancing at her in the doorway. "Our mom is a hottie!"

"For goodness sake, Danny. I'm your mother not a—a hottie. Why on earth would you even think that?"

He shrugged. "The way you look, Mom. What I said was a compliment."

She hesitated, at a momentary loss for words. Finally she thanked him and went back to the kitchen to make sure his supper with Max and Signe was all set. She'd made a chicken veggie casserole that was ready to heat and a green salad ready to toss. Both were in the refrigerator.

She felt antsy, uncertain about how she'd dressed—because her own son had called her a hottie. She glanced down at herself: her scooped neck, long-sleeved green top that was tucked into her hip-riding slacks with a wide leather belt. And her high-heeled boots that kept the hem of her trousers off the ground. She was right in style for a date to a basketball game, and perhaps dinner before or after.

"Mom?"

She turned to face her son who'd come into the kitchen.

"I didn't mean to make you feel bad," he said shuffling his feet. "That is, I just thought you looked so great that I was proud that you're my mom."

His praise was unexpected—and welcome. She needed all the moral support she could get. Smiling, she pulled Danny into her arms and gave him a hug. "I know that, Son. It's not you, it's me. As you know, I don't often date and I'm just unsure I guess."

"My mom, unsure? You gotta be kidding."

She shook her head. "Even mothers have their moments."

"But the police chief is a nice guy."

"I know." She ruffled his hair. "I'm being silly."

"Yeah," he agreed, then took Footers outside before Max and Signe arrived. While he was gone Jessie went into the hall where there was a mirror, and checked herself out. Maybe I shouldn't have left my hair long even if part of it is clipped back, she thought. And maybe I put on too much eye shadow and rouge. She turned away. One thing was certain; with her hair free, her eyes highlighted with mascara on her long lashes, she looked just like the painting above the fireplace.

You can't help how you look, she reminded herself. Just because you seem different from your work persona—her everyday look, she admitted to herself—doesn't mean you shouldn't look your best if you're on a date. She was out of practice.

Then it was too late. Max and Signe arrived at the back door with Danny. In minutes she'd given them the whole rundown of the place, her cell phone number and the fact that they'd be on the last ferry back to the island.

During all of her instructions Hank came in the back door, greeting Max and Signe as he stepped into the kitchen. His gaze shifted to Jessie, and for a moment he just stood there, staring, as if she were a stranger. Suddenly feeling awkward, she stepped forward, grinning.

"I'm ready to go, Chief."

He nodded, smiling, but his eyes were suddenly hooded. "Good. Let's go then."

She kissed Danny, patted Footers and grinned back at her two beaming babysitters, and then followed Hank out to his car, where she stopped short, staring.

"A BMW sport convertible? I'm surprised, chief."

He raised his eyebrow, but suppressed a grin. "Why so? The top is up."

She shook her head, grinning, unable to tell him that he'd just blown his image of a speed-conscious police-man. "I guess I expected you to drive a four-door Ford or Chevy."

He clucked his tongue. "Shame on you Jessie. Didn't they teach you in police training that you should never stereotype anyone?"

"Yeah, they did. Sorry."

He held the door open and she slid onto the passenger seat. "It's okay. I'm guilty of the same thing so we're even."

And with that ambiguous statement, he climbed behind the wheel and they were off down the driveway.

She wondered what he meant.

CHAPTER FORTY-TWO

"So how did you come to drive a sports car?" Jessie asked as they waited their turn in line to board the ferry.

"I've always owned a convertible." He shot her a humorous glance. "Is there a law that says a cop can't have a convertible?"

"Not that I know of," she replied. "I just wondered about you."

He glanced again, this time holding her gaze for long seconds. "About what?"

"About your choice of a personal vehicle," she said, and managed not to sound disconcerted. He'd surprised her, that was for sure. He'd already been an attractive man, but she'd had questions; now he was next to an enigma, a man who didn't quite fit the mold of a police chief.

But what was that? she asked herself. A cookie-cutter cop? And what was that—someone who fit her personal profile of who a law enforcement officer should be? She recognized her own ignorance. He was a normal professional with a penchant for sports cars, nothing more, nothing less.

Once on the ferry they got out of the BMW and went upstairs from the vehicle level to the restaurant. "Coffee? Wine?" he asked.

"White wine."

He grinned and left her at a window table to get their drinks. She sat on the low stool that was anchored to the floor, as was the table in front of her, and waited for his return.

What the hell, she thought. Wine to relax was what she needed; not coffee to hype her up.

"Here we are," he said, and placed two plastic containers of white wine down on the table, then took the stool opposite her.

Once seated, he picked up his glass as if in a toast. "To a good time tonight and—to us."

She lifted her glass. "I love basketball," she said inanely. "To a good time."

They both sipped wine, neither acknowledging that she'd skipped the "to us" part.

They kept the conversation to island problems, their own history of law enforcement, hers in San Francisco, his in Seattle, and the miles melted away as they left the ferry and drove south on I-5 into Seattle. It was with surprise that she realized that they were at the turnoff to the Seattle arena where the game would be held.

They pulled into the parking garage across the street from the old Seattle fairgrounds where the Key Arena was located, and then crossed to the entrance to the basketball court.

She had a great time rooting for the Sonics, shouting and cheering louder than Hank. Near the end of the game she glanced at him, saw how amused he was by her enthusiasm, and subsided on the bench.

"I played basketball in high school," she told him. "Sorry if I got carried away."

"Hey, I think it's great to root for the home team, everyone else is."

She grinned and he grinned back. After it was over they moved with the crowd to the entrance door, then across the street to the garage where they found Hank's car. Once inside they wound their way to the exit, but on the street again, Hank turned left instead of right to the freeway. Jessie raised her eyebrow in a question.

"It's only nine-thirty, takes less than an hour to drive north and catch the eleven-forty ferry, so I figure we have almost an hour to grab something to eat," he told her.

"That would be nice, Hank, as long as we don't miss the ferry."

"We won't. Believe me, I've got the time down pat," He grinned. "Remember, I have season tickets and make this trip when I can get away."

Hank turned into a driveway beside a little place at the foot of Queen Anne Hill that looked more like a house than a restaurant and parked behind it. Shutting off the engine, he faced her. "This place has the best food in Seattle and serves it quickly."

It had once been a cottage, built in the 1920s, and they were seated in what had been the living room near the fireplace. It was cozy, dimly lit by firelight and candles, and she wondered how many young men had proposed to their future wives at this very table. He helped her out of her leather jacket and hung it over the back of her chair before sitting down himself.

"Well, what do you think?" The candle flame seemed reflected in his pale blue eyes. "Nice? Even romantic?"

"Both," she admitted. "It's a lovely place."

They were immediately waited on, and ordered the salmon dinner and a glass of wine, which was brought immediately.

As the waiter left, Hank lifted his glass. "Another toast?"

"Why not." Jessie held up her wine. "You first."

He gave a nod, his gaze lingering on her face, and for long seconds he seemed to be considering. "To Fate, that brought events full circle, and Jessie back to the island."

"And to Hank, who belongs there more than he realizes," she added.

Slowly they sipped, their eyes locked by something that couldn't be explained. For a moment it was as though the world around them had gone still. And then the waiter came with their salmon.

They discussed the game as they ate and realized that they both enjoyed sport events: basketball, baseball and football.

As they finished eating, she managed to change the subject back to their work on the island. "So what is your take on the Thrasher situation?"

He glanced, and shook his head.

"You don't have an opinion?"

"Of course I do, Jessie." He drained his glass and motioned for the waiter to get their check. "I'm afraid there's no time for coffee or desert." He smiled. "The ferry awaits us."

The waiter came back with the check, Hank glanced at it, and then placed three twenties on the tray. Then they got up, put on their jackets and headed for the entrance. Back in the car again, he started the engine, drove out to the street and turned toward the freeway. Once they'd reached I-5, Jessie went back to her question that he hadn't answered earlier.

"So just what is your take on the Thrashers, Hank?"

He glanced, his eyes questioning.

"Minutes ago you said that you had a take on that situation but you didn't say what," Jessie said.

"I didn't elaborate because I'd hoped to take you away from all that drama for a few hours. The what-ifs of the island can be all-consuming and stressful."

"Stressful to whom?—me?"

He nodded. "You've had your own incidents since moving to the island, some of which seem similar to what's happened to Lynda Thrasher."

"You mean the notes and Danny's accidents?"

He nodded again.

"You think those incidents are connected?"

A silence went by.

"At the moment I'm trying to figure everything out. I'm not sure." A pause. "The last thing I want is for Danny to be in danger and"—he paused again—"my assistant chief."

"Me, too." A pause. "But I was wondering about the senator. The latest newspaper article is saying that Ben Thrasher is still on the attack and is now hinting that the politician might be behind Lynda being run off the road and the notes."

"I know and I'm about to run a national check on the senator through the F.B.I. computers and the other tracking systems." He hesitated. "I've already done that with any other likely suspect on the island."

"The commune members?"

"Yeah, they were all clean."

"When did you do that, Hank? After the incidents involving Danny, me and Lynda?"

"It was before you came to the island, Jessie." Another pause as he steered into a passing lane to avoid slower vehicles. "But nothing has changed as far as they're concerned. They're harmless, if radical."

They rode in silence for several miles. Was Hank discounting that they could also be supremacists, were fanatics when it came to believing that women were subservient to men, that they could in fact be upset about her position of assistant chief? Was he giving them leeway because his son was a member?

He glanced again, as though sensing her questions. "Tell me, Jessie. Do you believe the incidents involving the Thrashers and you and Danny are connected?"

"Oh, God, how could they be?" She looked at him and for a moment was caught by his eyes. Then he turned his gaze back to the traffic. "There are no similarities in our lifestyles, apart from the fact that they, like me, are newcomers to the island."

"They've owned the property for quite a while, but didn't move here until after their house was built." Hank paused. "So you're the only newcomer, but you are also connected to property, your ancestral home."

"That brings us back to square one."

"Maybe, maybe not. Although we didn't find fingerprints on the letters and notes, I'm hoping the crime lab can determine who produced the paper and what stores sell it. It's a long shot but we'll see what we come up with."

"Good going, Hank. I hope something."

"And I should have an updated list of white vehicles registered to island residents on Monday, including people who own recreational property here." He hesitated. "And, as you know, the ferry crews have been alerted to watch for white cars or vans headed to or from Cliff Island."

"Something ought to break on this. It's not that big an island."

"But there are lots of places to hide," he replied, dryly.

Another silence settled around them. They arrived at the ferry landing just as the cars were beginning to load onto the ship.

"We timed that just right," she said with a laugh.

"And that's all that counts."

They followed the line and were soon parked with the other commuters. He switched off the engine, set the brake and then turned to her. "How about having an after-dinner coffee now?

She nodded and they went up to the cafeteria where they decided on another glass of wine instead. After that they spent the rest of the voyage drinking coffee and sharing their view on everything from kids to cops. Talk is good, Jessie decided. It was a way to get to know someone better.

They returned to the car deck ten minutes ahead of docking. Hank held open the passenger door for her, but as she was about to get in, he took hold of her upper arms and turned her to him. And then he kissed her.

When he lifted his head, her eyes fluttered open to be caught by his gaze only inches away. "That was my goodnight kiss," he whispered. "In case I don't have a chance later."

She gave a slight nod. "Is it my turn now?"

His pale eyes gleamed in the dim light. "I'd like that."

She moved closer and put her arms around him, pulling his face down to hers, until their lips met. And then she kissed him. But her kiss didn't end as his had; instead it went on and on until they were wound so tightly together that they fell backward onto the passenger seat of his BMW.

The ferry whistle blew, announcing the ship's arrival, and Hank stepped back to close the door once Jessie was completely inside the car. Then he came round to the driver's side and climbed behind the wheel where he faced her.

"Thanks for a great evening," he said in a low tone. "That was the best goodnight kiss I've ever had."

Jessie managed a nod.

By the time he turned down her driveway some time later, she realized what a nice time she'd had with Hank. Overall he was a great guy.

Hank saw her inside, acknowledged Signe and Max who'd been on call but reported no incidents. Two of their volunteers had been patrolling the island. After Hank left, the couple got their things together, explained that Danny had been asleep for several hours, that all had been quiet.

"But I understand what you mean about the cellar door, Jessie," Max said.

"You mean the basement door in the kitchen?"

"Uh-huh. I heard a creaking sound behind it, like someone could be standing on the top step."

"And you'll never guess what he did," Signe piped up, looking indignant. "He opened the door, switched on the light and went down there."

A chill touched Jessie's spine. "And what did you find, Max?"

"Nothin', not a damned thing, even after I looked in the secret room." He grinned. "What else could a cop do? I had to have a look and I'm glad I did. I figure the sounds are probably normal to this old house."

"That's been my conclusion, too, Max. But it is a little unnerving."

"Yep, but you can rest easy tonight. There are no monsters in the basement."

She thanked and hugged them both, then watched as they went out to their car. Before they were gone she closed and locked the door, again reassured about the basement. But she made her usual safety check throughout the house before she went upstairs herself. After looking in on Danny, she went to her room.

And then Jessie forgot her moment of apprehension as she climbed into bed. She'd enjoyed her date with Hank. She hoped he'd ask her out again. Soon.

CHAPTER FORTY-THREE

"YA KNOW, MOM, I'VE BEEN THINKING ABOUT FOOTERS, that he's always cooped up in the house while we're gone." Danny came into the kitchen the next morning, ready to ferry across Puget Sound to the outlet mall near Mount Vernon off I-5. "Do you think there's some way he could be left outside instead?

"I've been considering that, too." Jessie smiled. "How about we get bids on a big kennel, one that has a dog house? I could look into it tomorrow."

"That'd be cool."

"In for a penny, in for a pound."

"What does that mean?"

"Nothing, it's just one of my literature misquotes."

She glanced at her watch, noting that their ferry would leave in forty-five minutes. "We need to get going in ten minutes."

Driving the Saturn down the driveway, Jessie realized how much smaller her car was compared to her cruiser. She turned toward town and drove to the ferry landing where they got in line. Several vehicles pulled in behind her.

There were a few dozen cars in line, more than usual for a Sunday morning. Most of the weekenders left later in the day or on the first Monday morning ferry. Then she saw the white minivan in her rearview mirror—and three vehicles behind it was a small white car.

Oh my God, she thought, but managed to restrain her reaction in front of Danny. Instead she went over ways to get the plate numbers once they were all on the ferry.

"Why don't you go up and get in line at the cafeteria," she suggested after boarding. "I need to check in with headquarters on my cell phone."

It was a flimsy reason, but Danny only nodded. "I'm ordering a burger with fries, what do you want, Mom?"

"Black coffee." She grinned. "We only had breakfast a few hours ago. I'm not a growing boy."

He laughed. "See you up there."

"Ten-four," she replied.

Danny got out and wove his way through the other cars to the stairway and disappeared. Once he was gone Jessie got out, too. She waited until the ferry was underway and most of the people had left their vehicles and gone to the upper decks. Then she pulled her pad from her handbag and wrote down the plate numbers on the white SUV and car. The drivers had already gone and she hadn't seen them. She went up to join her son.

"Hey, Mom, I'm over here," Danny called.

She joined him at a table near a window. "I have a number," he told her. "They'll call us when our order is ready."

They sat down, chatted about the proposed kennel for Footers, and then about their reason for going to the outlet mall: his winter jacket and warm clothes. His California garments had proven too thin for the northern reaches of the San Juan Islands of Washington State.

The ferry stopped at two other islands on its way to Anacortes. Once on the mainland Jessie headed toward I-5, made the turnoff to the freeway and drove north for several more miles, before taking the off ramp to the discount mall.

For the next several hours they went from one high-end discount store to the next, looking for trousers, T-shirts and jackets, and finally ended up with a restored wardrobe for Danny that represented the northwest climate, not California.

"So, are you satisfied with your new stuff?" Jessie asked.

"Yeah, I'm cool. Thanks Mom."

They were on their way back to the Saturn when Jessie saw the discount cosmetic shop. Danny waited outside. "Remember, Mom, we have to leave soon to catch the ferry."

"Hey, you're the person who loves Bruce Shepherd's work, I remember you," a woman said at her elbow once she was browsing.

Jessie turned to face the female voice. Then she nodded, recognizing the woman, but not where they'd met.

"You loved his carvings, just as I did." The woman smiled. "Remember? The arts and crafts store on Cliff Island."

Jessie stared for long seconds at the overweight forty-something woman, and then smiled. "Yes, I think I do remember. You bought something while I just admired."

"Yeah, that's true."

"So what are you doing at the outlet mall?" Jessie dropped into momentary small talk to get rid of the woman who seemed slightly strange.

The woman, her large nose and small eyes highlighted by makeup, smiled. "Just shopping, Chief."

"Chief?"

"Uh-huh. Aren't you the police chief of Cliff Island?"

"Of course not. I'm his assistant."

The woman shrugged, smiling. "Please forgive. I believed you were the chief of police. But then I'm not abreast of local politics."

"Lots of people aren't," Jessie said edging toward the door, having determined that the store didn't carry her line of makeup.

"I'm Sarah," the woman said, prolonging the conversation. "I have a small place on the west side of the island." She shook her head slowly. "I run my business by computer, out of the rat race so I can raise my family."

"You have children?'

"I will have soon." She patted her large stomach. "In only a few months."

Jessie didn't ask about her husband, because she sensed that there was a problem on that level.

"And what is your business?"

"Stocks and bonds. I keep track of the stock market for my clients."

"I see." Jessie nodded, not quite sure of what Sarah's words meant, but didn't care.

And then Jessie made it to the door, and after a brief goodbye they separated, Sarah to disappear into the mall, Jessie to meet Danny outside the store. In minutes they were on their way back to catch the ferry. Jessie wondered if Sarah was also on the road to make the same schedule.

"Mom, we lucked out again. The ferry is about to load," Danny said as they reached the terminal.

"I know, son," she said. "We're meeting every schedule we're supposed to today."

Once home, they let Footers outside, and later still they all went to bed early.

But Jessie had things to check in the morning: the two plate numbers for starters. Exhausted from hardly any sleep on Saturday night, and from rising early on Sunday to head to the outlet stores, Jessie went right to sleep.

And slept until morning.

CHAPTER FORTY-FOUR

BY MONDAY NOON JESSIE FELT AS THOUGH SHE'D ALMOST accomplished a day's work, and her shift wouldn't be over for another six hours. She'd dropped Danny off at school, made the arrangements with a local carpenter to construct a kennel and dog house, and after arriving at work had prepared a probable cause to run the commune, God's Love Enterprises, Patrick Sweers and the list of members, including Bruce Shepherd, through the national computer tracking systems. Hank had been off for the morning so she'd gone ahead with the search without consulting him.

She tried not to think about her personal feelings for Hank. When it came to work responsibilities she had to stay objective—even though her thoughts returned many times over the last two days to how she'd felt in his arms.

I am the assistant chief, she reminded herself. And it was imperative that a security run be made again. She sensed that Hank might let it slide, believing that they were still okay.

But were they? It was her son who could have been killed by the white van—that turned out to belong to Bruce. And what about the Lynda Thrasher incident? Although she admired Bruce's work and liked him at their first meeting, she wasn't about to let personal feelings get in the way. Hank and Bruce were estranged. Was it possible that Bruce could be getting back at his dad by making problems for the new assistant chief? She didn't know enough of their dynamics to even take a guess. Hence her decision to check them all out.

Jessie took a sip of coffee, realized it had gone cold while she worked, and pushed it aside. She'd get a fresh cup at Starbucks when she started her afternoon patrol. In the meantime, she tidied her desk, and wondered if Hank had gotten the results of his check on the senator. But it made no sense that the senator, if he was behind the incidents directed at Lynda, would be connected to her and Danny. And she wondered if he could even have become a senator if he had something in his past that could turn up on a police scan. The whole thing wasn't logical.

Feeling she was on a roll, she grabbed her jacket. She'd even been tempted to submit Nita's name. But she'd realized that would be futile, too. The old woman had probably not left the island for decades, maybe wasn't even listed under Social Security or with the IRS. Besides, there were other ways to find out about Nita. She intended to do that this afternoon.

Her one annoyance had been in losing the pad in which she'd jotted down the plate numbers of the white SUV and compact car, the vehicles she'd seen on the ferry. It hadn't been in her purse or car. If she'd found the numbers she would have run them, too.

By the time she was driving away from the station, Hank still had not appeared. He'll soon know what I've done, she reminded herself. And he probably won't like it.

The thought made her stomach swim.

* * *

Jessie monitored the ferry traffic as it moved onto the road, and then she made a swoop around the island, through town, past the schools and then back to town again. She pulled up in front of Starbucks and went to buy a black coffee. She needed a caffeine boost.

"Hey, Officer Cline. How you doing?"

She was on the sidewalk almost back to her car, and turned to face Tommy of the arts and crafts shop. "Hi, Tommy. I'm doing just fine."

"Heard your boy was almost hit when he was riding his bike home. Is he doing okay?"

"Yeah, thank goodness."

"I'm glad to know that Danny wasn't hurt. Hit-and-run incidents never happen here. If this wasn't a first, then I've never heard of another case."

"Thanks, Tommy." Jessie realized that he must not have heard about Lynda Thrasher. "We hope there is never another case."

"You got that right." He hesitated, as though he had something else to say. "So, how is your mother doing?"

"Still in Mendocino, Tommy, painting canvases with wonderful scenes."

"I hope she'll come in to see me when she visits. I'd love to have some of her work on consignment." He gave a laugh. "I'd really love it if she moved back to the island and used my shop as her showcase."

"I'd love her to move back, too. I'm working on it."

He shrugged. "According to our newspaper editor, she lived here for a time after her marriage to your father, and didn't move away until after he died."

"That's true," she said. "She took me and left."

"And you were only a toddler."

A silence fell between them. When she didn't respond

he went on. "Your mother is really good, Jessie. I think her being up here would blend right into her vision of what she paints."

"And what's that?"

"The mood of her paintings—the message portrayed."

Jessie smiled. "You're saying that she's good."

"Yeah, and as yet undiscovered."

"Thanks, Tommy. "I'll tell her what you said." A pause. "I use everything I can to get her up here. And I'll let you know when she plans to visit so we can both try to influence her to move north."

He nodded.

"Let me ask you a question, Tommy?"

"Sure. Whatever."

"It's about the island newspaper."

"Okay?"

"The current paper only puts out an issue once a month."

"That's right, but that hasn't always been so."

"What do you mean?"

"It used to be a weekly, but expenses reduced its viability and now it's only monthly." He shrugged. "We're lucky to still have a newspaper at all. The owner is semiretired now and only keeps the business going to stay active."

"How long has this newspaper been going?"

"About fifty years."

She was taken aback. "Certainly not the same owner."

"Oh yeah, father and son."

"Explain?"

"The father started the paper—the information is all in our little historic museum—and the son took over and is the man who is semiretired now, but keeps the paper going monthly."

"Does the newspaper have archives?"

"Of course. Arthur Bing is a confirmed bachelor who is an Internet junkie. He's in the process of putting all the back issues since 1947, when his father started the paper, onto microfiche."

"That's wonderful, Tommy. Then he should have any reported stories about my family available to read."

Tommy nodded. "I'm sure."

"Thanks for the information, Tommy. I expect my mother to come up at Thanksgiving, and if not then, the Christmas holiday for sure." She grinned. "Believe me, Danny and I are lobbying for her to move up. We're the only relatives she has."

"Good luck, Officer Cline."

She stepped forward. "Tommy, please call me Jessie. All my friends do."

His smile widened. "Jessie it is. And good luck with your mom, uh, Jessie."

"Thanks."

She walked back to her cruiser which she started and moved a block down the street, to the front of the newspaper office. She just hoped it was open.

"You're Arthur Bing?" She stepped into the tiny, dusty office and addressed the heavy man behind the desk who was working on his computer.

"Yep, I am." His words puffed out of him like the sound of an invisible stalker breathing heavily in a sci-fi flick. "And you're Jessica Cline, our new assistant police chief."

She nodded.

"What can I do for you, Jessie?" His round face broke into a grin, his chin folding down on itself into the fat of his neck. The man was obese.

"Do you have the past articles that were written about my family?—from the beginning of your publication?"

"Certainly, they're on microfiche."

"Could I look at them sometime, so I can get a sense of my ancestry?"

He smiled, as though he had been waiting for her request. "Of course, Jessie. I have everything my newspaper has ever written about your family." He cocked his head and she could see that he was proud to be able to supply her with the requested information.

"Thanks Mr. Bing. I appreciate your vision of saving island history."

"My pleasure."

"When can I view your microfiche?"

"When are you free to do so?"

"Saturday afternoon?"

"Done. I'll be here. Say about one?"

"That's good for me."

He came around his desk and extended his hand. "I think you'll find it interesting, Jessie."

She left, knowing she'd met yet another good person who'd lived their entire life on the island. As she went back to her car Jessie felt like she was about to have a learning experience—one that would be vital to her and Danny.

And as she headed back out on patrol, her sense of place was strong; her mom may not want to tell her everything, but the newspaper articles might, including how Nita fit in.

She was headed along Island Highway when the call crackled over her radio.

"Officer Cline. A shooting at the Ben Thrasher house." The dispatcher gave the time and location.

"Copy that," Jessie said. "I'm on my way."

She slammed on the brakes, wheeled the car into a U-turn, and then punched on the roof and wigwag lights, and the siren. Jessie floor-boarded the gas pedal and headed for the Thrasher residence.

Please God, she prayed. Let Lynda be okay. She was only an innocent victim of—of whom? Her husband Ben?

The thought came unbidden, but Jessie pressed harder on the gas.

Could Ben be behind everything? She vowed to find out.

CHAPTER FORTY-FIVE

JESSIE TURNED INTO THE THRASHER ESTATE AND STOPPED just behind Hank's police cruiser. She switched off the engine, siren and lights, and with her pistol drawn, moved cautiously toward the house. She noticed that the garage doors were wide open and one of the vehicles was missing. The front door was also open.

"Come on in, Officer Cline," Hank said from the entry. His cool blue glance took in her drawn gun. "We're secure, for the moment."

She got the message and put her weapon back into its holster. "What happened here?"

A middle-aged woman stepped forward. "Lynda, that is Mrs. Thrasher, and I were discussing furniture polish in the living room when suddenly there was a loud ping and the sound of breaking glass." She sucked in a ragged breath. "We didn't know what had happened at first, until we saw the cracked window and the broken vase on the table in front of it."

A frightened and very pregnant Lynda stood in the living room doorway, as though afraid to step into the open where she could become a target. "Alma is only here once a week to clean when our regular housekeeper is off, and I feel terrible that she's involved in this." She glanced furtively toward the shattered front window, then back to the chief. "Do you suppose it was a hunter's stray bullet?"

He shook his head. "It's against the law to hunt on the island." Hank turned to Jessie and inclined his head toward the front door, indicating that it should be closed.

She did so at once, feeling a chill. Did he think the shooter could still be out there, drawing a bead on one of them? Although she knew it was unlikely, it was also possible.

No sooner had the door closed when it burst back open and Ben stood framed in the doorway. "What in the name of hell is going on here?" he demanded. "I get off the ferry to this?"

Hank and Jessie turned as one, but before they could react, Lynda rushed forward, as fast as her pregnancy would allow.

"Oh Ben, I'm so glad you're back! I was so scared!"

He folded Lynda in his arms, as though to protect her from the others in the room. His words to her were low and soothing but inaudible to Jessie and Hank.

"For God's sake, tell me what's happened?" His rude demand was directed to Hank.

An insensitive bastard, Jessie thought. His wife was terrified, barely under control, close to delivering their baby, and he was taking a demanding position. A glance at Hank told her he was thinking similar thoughts.

"We got a call that there was a shooting," Hank said calmly, his demeanor nonetheless superior to Ben's. "I got here in five minutes because I was close." He tilted his head in Jessie's direction. "Officer Cline arrived several minutes later. Someone shot into your house."

Alma stepped forward and put her arm around Lynda. "You need to sit down, dear. I'll explain to your husband."

Lynda allowed herself to be led to a chair, one she chose that was not in a direct line to a window. And then Alma turned to Ben and told him what she'd just said to Hank and Jessie. It was obvious that neither woman knew anything more than what they'd already said.

"I see," Ben said. "So we really don't know what happened. It could have been a bird hitting the window."

"Not likely, Mr. Thrasher," Hank said, sharply. "A bird doesn't fly though a window, shattering the glass and only leaving a small hole." He tucked his handheld radio under his arm as he took a pad and pen from his pocket. "I've already located the bullet embedded in the wall opposite the window."

"Son of a bitch!" Ben's expression changed from annoyance to shock. "Where?—I don't see a hole."

Hank pointed to the place on the gold embossed wallpaper above the wainscoting. "I've already called Central Communications for a forensics expert. The person will be on the last ferry tonight." He hesitated, and although Hank's expression hadn't changed, Jessie saw his dislike of Ben. "Until then, your living room is a crime scene and off limits."

"What in the hell do you mean by that?" Ben asked. "That we can't go into our own living room?"

"Exactly." Hank said. "A man from our volunteer patrol will be assigned here to make sure the scene stays secure until the crime lab technician arrives and clears the site. Our island man is on his way and should arrive momentarily."

"But this is my house."

"Of course it's your house. But it's also a crime scene. Someone shot into your house, and it appears to be intentional. Until we know differently, and until the crime lab examines the scene and extracts the bullet from the wall, it will remain off limits to you and your family." Hank spread his hands. "Sorry, that's the law."

Jessie watched the changing expressions on Ben's face, knowing he was upset by the fact that he wasn't in control. And as she examined his face, she wondered if his upset was about something more than what had happened—*if he knew why it had happened.*

A thought out of left field, she told herself, because she was biased against believing Ben's sincerity. But was her bias that believable under the circumstances? She didn't know. And then she didn't have to. Hank took over once again. "You'll have to adhere to police procedure," he told Ben. "And that correct process must apply here."

The volunteer officer arrived, and after Jessie and Hank secured the room with yellow crime scene tape and gave final instructions to the man, they were able to leave.

"I want to talk to you, Cline," Hank said once they were outside and out of earshot of the others.

"Is something wrong?" She knew there was; he'd called her Cline.

Hank's eyes were direct. "Let's just say we need to chat about a few things, Jessie, okay? Tomorrow morning." Gone was the warm way he'd looked at her on their date.

She nodded, feeling disturbed, and then got into her car and followed him out of the Thrashers driveway. Jessie couldn't imagine what he meant, aside from what had happened at the Thrashers. That was probably it; he wanted to discuss how to handle the situation.

But remembering the stern set of his features, she realized it was more than that and suddenly knew why he seemed so upset.

They'd left the Thrasher property and were headed back to the main road when she realized she couldn't wait for tomorrow morning to know what was bothering him. It would worry her and she'd never be able to sleep tonight. Following him she switched on her wigwag lights, indicating that she needed him to stop, avoiding the radio which anyone could listen in on. He pulled over to the side of the road, got out of his cruiser and walked back to her car.

"What's up, Cline?"

"Cline?"

Their eyes met, steely blue and brilliant green. A moment of anger flashed through her. Surely he hadn't prejudged her action about the commune. Running a check on the group that many people on the island described as a cult was what any good police officer would have done under the circumstances. But she was the first to lower her gaze, admitting to herself that he might be miffed by her not telling him first.

"Yeah, Assistant Chief Cline."

She was taken aback by his cool attitude. "What's this all about, uh—Chief?"

He leaned against her car, his eyes unwavering, looking more like a television series actor. "Can't you guess? Surely you had a procedure protocol even in San Francisco. Did you think it didn't apply at such a small police station?"

"Of course not, Hank." She hesitated. "You're referring to my submitting God's Love Enterprises to the national computer tracking systems?"

"Uh-huh, that's right. Since I'm the chief it was suppose to be cleared by me."

"I'm sorry, Hank." She paused again. "Because I respect you so much I have to be honest. I felt you'd rely on your old check and I couldn't, since it was my son who was run off the road."

"Uh-huh, so you figured I might be protecting my son?"

"No, I know you're too much of a professional for that, Hank." A pause. "But if you're like me you'd probably be inclined to refer to the older computer check." She reached to briefly touch his hand on the lowered window ledge. "I feel protective of my son too, Hank, which is why I requested updated information."

"The report is on your desk, Jessie."

"And?"

"It's basically the same as the earlier one. The group is peaceful, and they lack a murderous intent."

"Thank God!"

He straightened. "You're relieved?"

"Of course I am, Hank. I don't know Bruce very well but I see that he's a very sensitive and highly talented young man. I don't particularly agree with his decision to be a part of the Sweers clan, but I think he's sincere. I'm happy that he's cleared, that the van that hit Danny was stolen and not lent to someone."

"In all honesty, Jessie, I know he wasn't the driver because he really was over on the mainland, but I wasn't positive that he hadn't lent his van and was covering up for someone." A pause. "I'm still not positive."

"But now you feel better about his honesty?"

He nodded.

"Then my computer run on the commune turned out to be a good thing for both of us, right?"

A silence went by.

"You're certainly not a passive police officer are you, Cline?"

"I've never been accused of that, *Chief*."

"Yeah, I guess I read about that in your references when you applied for the job."

She raised her eyebrow, waiting for him to continue.

"It's all in your personnel file." He hesitated. "I think we've cleared the air, but I hope that you'll consult me in the future. I understand that this hit us both on an emotional level—your son and my son."

"I believe we have, too." She smiled. "At least I can sleep tonight knowing I'm not losing my job."

"Sorry, Jessie. You've explained now, but for a while it looked like you went over my head." His gaze intensified. "From here on out we need to be completely honest with each other, let the chips fall where they will, and ultimately work together."

"Agreed. I appreciate your being candid."

He reached and grabbed her hand. "Done." And then he gave a salute and started back to his car, abruptly swinging around to face her. "One last thing, Jessie, just so you know. I also ran a check on Ben Thrasher through the national tracking system. We should have the report tomorrow."

She nodded, and then watched him get into his car and pull away from her. She moved forward slowly. What would that check reveal? How long would it go back? A decade or more of newspaper accounts?

Jessie continued down the road, headed for Max's house to pick up Danny. She wondered if she'd have a sleepless night after all.

Along with everything else, Hank no longer seemed interested in her as a woman.

CHAPTER FORTY-SIX

JESSIE SAW THE REPORT ON BEN THE NEXT MORNING AND was not surprised that he didn't have a police record and had never even been arrested, although he did have a lot of controversy surrounding his national prominence as a political cartoonist. He hid his extracurricular activities extremely well, Jessie thought when Hank reported the results of the search.

"At least he's pretty much eliminated as a suspect," Hank said dryly.

She glanced beyond him to the window overlooking the parking lot and the beginning of the woods. Lines of rain ran down the pane, blurring the view so that the sky seemed to begin at treetop level. Abruptly, her gaze was direct.

"Not necessarily," she replied, finally. "I feel that Ben Thrasher may not be all that his media hype portrays, that he may not be a person who has never broken the law, only someone who hasn't been caught."

Hank got up from the chair behind his desk where he'd been sitting to hand Jessie the report on Ben. "Why is it, Jessie, that you speak with such knowledge about this guy." His steely gaze was suddenly penetrating. "What do you know that you're not sharing here?"

She hesitated, wondering how much she should reveal.

"I really have no proof of anything. But I think I told you that I took a class from him back when I was at Berkeley. He was a womanizer then, and later I observed him on the Internet art forums." She hesitated, uncertain of how to continue. "He's seduced a number of women on the Internet and arranged meetings. He's not loyal to Lynda, or to any other woman on the planet."

"Can you prove that, Jessie?"

She shook her head. "Even though I know it's true, I can't."

"So we're back to square one with Ben Thrasher."

"I don't think so."

"How so?"

"Because I'm on to him. He may not be the person trying to shoot his wife but he might have a clue as to who is."

"The senator, or someone hired by the senator?"

"Maybe, maybe not."

"Then who?"

"We haven't taken into consideration all the women Ben has spurned."

"You've got to be kidding, Jessie. There's no evidence that Ben has other women."

"There's my word."

A silence went by.

"We need proof."

She got up to face him. "I know." She stared at him. "Anything else, Chief Shepherd? I'm overdue for patrol."

He moved around the desk until he was right in front of her. "Nothing else, Jessie." A pause. "Until you're ready to tell me why you're so suspicious of Ben Thrasher."

He held her gaze.

She nodded. "I'll remember that, Chief." And then she

left him and headed out to her car to start her patrol. But she felt unsettled, uncertain of what she should or shouldn't tell him. Leave it for now, she told herself. You don't have proof of anything. All you'll do is appear to be a whiner about the past.

Unacceptable.

She would wait. Until she had something viable.

The department was prepared to act at once, and the volunteer patrol had been alerted to several extra runs an hour past the Thrasher property. But the next few days passed uneventfully. Everything was quiet; there were no new threats. By Saturday Jessie wondered if the shooter had made a statement and would now disappear for good.

That afternoon she dropped Danny off at his friend Steve's house. The two boys were doing a science class project together and Jessie was leaving him there for two to three hours while she was at the newspaper office.

"Thanks, Mr. Bing," she said entering the old newspaper office. "I appreciate your being here when I realize this is your time off."

"Hey, I'm honored. And as I told you before, call me Arthur."

"Sorry, Arthur."

He nodded, grinning. "I've accessed the articles myself, and I think they're all in chronological order."

"But, Arthur. That was a lot of work. I didn't expect you to do my work for me."

He led her to the computer screen. "No problem. Believe me, in my semiretirement I enjoyed having a real project."

She nodded and sat down, ready to begin.

"As I told you," Arthur said, "I collected all the articles onto a disk, then fed them back onto the hard drive as a document so all you have to do is click on that document and you'll read everything we've ever written about your family." And with those words he left her to read the old articles on the computer screen.

But as she read the old reports—her father's death out on the boat with his cousin, when he accidentally fell overboard in a storm, to years later when her uncle also drowned, leaving her grandmother's brother, her great-uncle and the last of the family line, except her—she was sad.

Jessie sat back in the chair. What had she really learned: that she and Danny were the last of a lineage? that many of the descendants had died in accidents? that there was nothing else to investigate?

And there was only a mention of Nita, that she was a second cousin of Jessie's grandmother, that she was the last of her family, her only child having died many years ago in childhood.

Jessie got up from the chair. It was a skimpy history. But one thing was for sure; if there'd been questions about anyone's death it would have been recorded in the newspaper.

Wouldn't it? Jessie wondered, and after thanking Arthur, went to pick up Danny. But what had she expected? Small town newspapers didn't have investigative reporters. Many just wrote up the events as they were told after the fact. They didn't assume anything was wrong. On the contrary, they assumed everything was as it was suppose to be.

So what if I didn't learn more about the family today, she thought. There are other ways to check, including the Internet. She'd do that when she had time.

And then she picked up Danny and drove home.

When they went to bed several hours later Jessie expected to sleep until morning.

And she did.

Monday started the week out great: the dog house was about completed, Danny was top scorer on the basketball team and Jessie felt that maybe the person who had targeted Lynda and Danny and her had given up their reign of terror.

Because she had to work later than usual, Signe had volunteered to drive Danny home once Jessie was in the house and called her. It was almost dark when Jessie finished up at a rural house that had reported a theft in their tool shed. The call was routine and Jessie even wondered about the couple who'd called in, because they were both unemployed but had homeowner insurance that covered theft. But she checked out the scene, took down their statement and was finally on her way back to the station.

The area was the most uninhabited part of the island and the side road was like a thirty-foot-wide line through the forest. When the window shattered next to her Jessie was so startled that she almost veered into the trees. Swerving and fighting for control of the wheel she finally brought the police cruiser to a stop.

And then she realized that someone had shot at her.

The opposite window was also shattered with a hole in the middle. The bullet had entered through the driver's window, whizzed past her face, and exited out through the passenger window.

Oh God. She'd almost been killed.

Someone had shot at her and there was no time to get out and investigate. She was isolated and would be a prime target if she did.

Of its own volition, her foot floor-boarded the gas pedal, her hands clutched the steering wheel and she sped off with a hail of gravel behind her. She squinted as shards of glass flew past her face. Once she reached the main road she radioed for help. By the time she reached the edge of town Hank had already swung in behind her.

She brought the cruiser to a stop. He was there immediately and yanked open the door. But momentarily she was unable to get out of the car. She needed a minute to pull herself together.

"For God's sake, Jessie. What in the hell happened?"

She could only shake her head, gathering her strength. "Someone shot at me," she said finally.

"What? Where?"

She managed to explain what had happened.

"How would anyone even know you were out there?" he asked sharply. "Did you tell anyone where you were going?"

She shook her head. "No one. I got the call when my shift was almost over. I did call Signe about Danny, but she didn't know where I was going."

Hank helped her out of her car and into his, momentarily holding her close, as if he, too, had been shaken. And then he took her to the clinic. "The doc needs to check you over, Jessie. You have a few cuts from the flying glass."

She could only nod, glad someone else was taking over. She needed to think about what was happening. First someone shot at Lynda, now her. Why? What was the connection?

She was too tired to figure it out now. After she regained her strength would be time enough.

CHAPTER FORTY-SEVEN

ONCE SHE WAS RELEASED FROM THE CLINIC, WITH A DIAGNOSIS of superficial cuts to the face that would heal without scars, Hank drove her home, explaining that Signe would bring Danny after his school events were over.

"Your car has been towed to our only island garage that replaces car windows," he told her. "It'll be out of commission tomorrow, and you'll be off patrol until it's fixed. I'll pick you and Danny up in the morning, take him to school, you to the office, and Max will take your patrol for the next couple of days. I'll drive you home and Max or Signe will bring Danny home."

"Sounds like you have everything worked out, Hank."

"Uh-huh, everything that's important." His pale eyes were suddenly unreadable.

"But Max can't do double duty. He already has his own hours," she protested.

"Which are part-time." His eyelids lowered. "He'll take over for now. And don't forget, we have our certified volunteers to fill in so someone is always on duty."

She could only nod, her mind too filled with questions about the person who had tried to shoot her, and who had narrowly missed achieving that objective. When they finally reached her house he saw her inside where Footers was wild to go outside.

"Hey," he said, retrieving a note on the door, "the fence guy says the kennel fence and gate are complete." He handed it to her with the attached bill. "Your dog now has an enclosed area while you're gone."

"I guess I'll put Footers out there," she said, trying to seem normal even though she was still shaky. "I don't want Danny's dog vanishing next."

"Agreed," he said, and opened the back door for Footers. As he followed the dog outside he glanced back. "Get the coffee on. We could both use a cup."

Jessie figured she could use more than caffeine and took a bottle of scotch from the cupboard, a stash of a few bottles of liquor that had been there since before she arrived. Her grandmother's? her uncle's? Whatever. What mattered at that moment was that it was there.

When Hank came back she'd already taken two short glasses from the shelf. He glanced with raised eyebrows.

"I need something to slow me down, not hype me up," she explained. "I figured scotch was better than coffee."

"You may be right," he said, and took a chair at the kitchen table. Although I can't drink when I'm on duty, as you know."

"Are you?" she asked.

He shook his head. "But I'm here to see that you and Danny are safe."

"For the moment," she replied, and poured some of the amber liquor into their glasses. She added water and ice cubes and then sat down. "You don't have to drink it but I do." And then she lifted her glass as if in a toast. "To catching the Cliff Island predator."

As her glass stayed in the air between them, he picked up his own. "Okay, Jessie, I'll drink to that."

And then she drank and he sipped.

"Footers is locked in the kennel," he said, making small talk. "It's so big he loves it."

"That's great," Jessie replied, knowing she was gulping the scotch, because it was already spinning through her veins, making her feel safer. She was relaxing, and the big reason was because Hank was there. She felt protected even if she got drunk and the shooter was now outside her house waiting for a second chance at her. Hank would make sure that didn't happen.

She sipped more scotch, and realized that she was getting drunk fast. And then she heard Hank locking the back door and saw him crossing the kitchen to her. Vaguely, she knew that he took the glass from her and set it down on the table. And then his hands were on her arms, helping her out of the chair. She tried to shake him off.

"I can manage," she said tartly.

But she couldn't. Her knees folded as she tried to stand up. Her mind said she hadn't drunk that much, but her common sense reminded her that she rarely drank at all and hadn't eaten all day.

Oh shit! She was drunk on only a couple of ounces of scotch. She needed to regain control of herself.

"Hey, it's okay," Hank said softly, his breath warm on her ear. "You're safe, sweetheart."

Sweetheart? Had she heard right?

Her mind told her again to get control of herself but her limbs wouldn't respond. She found herself leaning on Hank as he led her to the hall and up the stairs to the second floor.

"Which way?" he said as they reached the top.

"Left, the door at the end of the hallway," she said, and her words sounded strange.

Her mind seemed to work better than her speech or limbs; she needed to get to her bedroom and then she could manage for herself. She needed sleep.

"We're here," Hank said. "Are you able to get into bed by yourself?"

"But I can't go to bed!" she cried, and was able to straighten up. "I forgot Danny! I need to make sure he's home safe."

"I'll see to it," he told her softly. "You just get into bed, okay?"

"But he's not home yet."

"He'll be here soon. I'll stay until then, all right?"

She nodded but her limbs failed to respond to her mental commands. Oh God! She was so drunk. How had she been so stupid as to drink that much so fast, scared or not?

Again Hank was there, helping her undress to her bra and panties, casting her clothing aside, pulling down her covers and slipping her under them.

Her eyes fluttered open to meet those pale blue eyes that were usually so cool and emotionally removed from personal feelings. This time the eyes that met hers flared with fire, although it was immediately banked down.

"Go to sleep sweetheart," he said softly, and she wondered if she'd dreamed the words as her eyelids drooped. She was suddenly too tired to worry about nuances—or the fact that he'd undressed her, seen her almost naked body.

Then she felt his mouth on hers, lightly at first, then more demanding. She responded, her lips opening under his, her body aroused by his touch, even as her senses were dulled by alcohol. Abruptly, his presence was gone, and his voice sounded above her.

"Not now, Jessie. I want you fully aware, as needing of me as I am of you."

She could only nod. Oh God. I swear off alcohol forever, she promised silently.

But as she sank into sleep she wondered what was real and what wasn't. She'd been shot at, that was real. She'd had a couple of shots of scotch and gotten drunk, that also was real. But had Hank kissed her, wanted to make love to her? Had she imagined that?

Whatever? It was a beautiful thought to go to sleep on, she told herself groggily. And then she did just that, went to sleep, feeling that someone was holding her hand, making her feel safe.

Hank?

CHAPTER FORTY-EIGHT

"I JUST HAD A CALL FROM BEN THRASHER," HANK SAID THE next day.

Jessie glanced up to see her boss in the doorway. She hadn't heard his approach, and wondered how long he'd been standing there watching her work. "What's up with him?" She managed a normal tone. "Something more they remembered about the shooting?"

"Nope." He moved into her office, and placing his hands flat on her desk, leaned forward, his silvery eyes direct. "Lynda had a threatening phone call."

"Oh shit!"

"My reaction, although I put it in more professional terms with Mr. Thrasher." He hesitated. "I'm just on my way out there and thought you might like to ride along."

She got up. "Definitely."

"Good. I'll fill you in on the way."

Jessie grabbed her jacket and followed him out to his patrol car. Her own cruiser was due to be ready for her by tomorrow morning. The local garage had ordered the window glass from the dealer on the mainland and it had come over on the first ferry that morning. Hank had picked her and Danny up for school and work, Signe would see to Danny after school until Hank took them both home around six.

Jessie got into the car and he took the wheel, always the professional, like this morning. She'd been relieved that although he'd been concerned about her well-being, he hadn't mentioned her shaken and upset state the night before, when she'd gulped too much scotch and imagined him kissing her. This morning, when he'd seemed caring but official, she'd been relieved. The combination of almost being shot, and the double shot of scotch, had put her out of reality. She could have been imagining things—because she was attracted to him?

Don't go there, she instructed herself. Whatever is true the real truth is that she worked for the man, needed her job and didn't need problems.

He drove out of the lot, turned onto the main road and then headed for the Thrasher estate.

"So, what's the background, Hank?"

He glanced, his gaze piercing. "The same old crap with a different scenario."

"You mean a phone call instead of an anonymous letter?"

"Yeah. Someone called and told her she wouldn't be alive to raise her child."

"Oh my God! That poor woman. Was the caller a man or woman?"

"I asked Ben that. He said she thought it was a man, but that the voice sounded hollow."

"A voice synthesizer?"

"That was my first guess." He glanced again. "So I think we need to operate under the assumption that it could be either male or female."

"Agreed."

He slowed for the Thrasher turnoff and a few minutes later they were moving up their driveway and came to a stop in front of the entry. Hank turned off the engine, grabbed his handheld radio and stepped out of the car. She followed, getting out before he was around to the passenger side to help her. She wasn't an invalid, even if she had almost been killed and then gotten drunk the night before.

"Cline?" He stood before her, blocking her way. "You need to get into the habit of letting someone help you."

"Someone?" She looked him straight in the eye.

He nodded, slowly. Then abruptly he turned and led the way up to the front door and rang the bell.

She followed. Maybe he was right. Maybe.

Hank and Jessie waited to listen to the tape of the phone call as Ben pushed the button on his phone system; it seemed that all of the Thrasher calls were taped, legal or not. But although Hank mentioned that the tape might not be admissible in court, he also said it could be helpful to their investigation.

Ben nodded, his dark eyes narrowed with—with what? Concern? Apprehension? Or something else? Jessie couldn't tell.

The words on the tape, spoken by a voice that could be either female or male, were sudden in the silence of the room. "Lynda. I am the person in the hammock, not you. The inheritor of the intellect belongs to me." A pause. "You will die."

There was a dial tone.

Ben turned the answering machine off, and then turned to Hank. "You see, this is a crank caller."

"Crank caller?" Hank asked sharply. "I'm not convinced of that by any means. This is not a typical call by a random caller; it's more like a direct threat." He hesitated, his gaze narrowed on Ben. "Why would you think otherwise?"

"But how can it be a threat?" Ben bristled. "There's no one I can think of who would say such a thing."

"How many people know your wife is pregnant?"

Ben, his lean face creased with stress, seemed oblivious of accountability. "Everyone we know. My coworkers, the newspapers that print my cartoons, the people who've interviewed me for national publications, the interviews on live TV programs."

Hank shrugged, as though withdrawing the question. It was true that the man and his family were topics for the national media, that it was almost impossible to trace the many people who might be opposed to Ben's agenda.

But someone out there had their own agenda that included Lynda. And it was serious. Someone wanted her to die, of that Jessie was convinced.

Her next thought was even more sobering. The threatening events that had happened to Lynda had also happened to her and Danny. That connection was baffling. There was no one on the island who knew she'd once known Ben. And even if there was, wasn't it obvious that he didn't remember her from so long ago?

Left field thinking, she reminded herself. She and Ben were so obviously a thing of the past; he didn't even recognize her from that adoring student over twelve years ago. He'd traveled many miles, and probably many women, since then.

Hank took the tape of the voice and then they stood to go. As the two men talked, Jessie spoke to Lynda who'd seemed subdued during the whole process.

"If anything else should happen, and you're here alone, please call me," Jessie said, handing her card to the woman. "I don't live too far away and I'll be here quickly."

"Thank you, Officer Cline. I appreciate that." She glanced away. "I confess to getting scared a few times."

Hank concluded his conversation with Ben and he and Jessie went back out to the patrol car.

"Strange situation between those two," Hank said, glancing at her as he negotiated the driveway to the road. "I don't know that I believe a damned word the guy says."

"Amen."

Jessie felt his glance but kept her own straight ahead of her. He didn't comment, and went to pick up Danny so that he could take them both home. She was grateful; she didn't want to get into a discussion about Ben. He was a bastard.

But was he even worse than that? She didn't know.

By the time Hank brought her and Danny home it was dark and the automatic exterior lights had all come on. He saw them into the house and waited as Danny brought Footers in from the new kennel.

"I know you're off duty now, Hank, and you've been so helpful today. Danny and I are grateful, so how about letting us do something for you?"

He cocked his brow. "Uh-huh, I'm listening."

"I'm about to put a chicken casserole in the oven, which we'll have with rolls and a salad." She hesitated. "Danny and I would love you to stay for supper."

He considered, his expression serious. "Is the casserole homemade?"

"Of course. I make our soups and casseroles on my days off and freeze them, so that supper is almost ready when we get home and are hungry."

"A woman after my heart," he said, still serious. "And my stomach too."

"So, what do you think?" She was suddenly uncertain.

He grinned. "My God, Jessie. How could I refuse a home-cooked meal? Of course I'll stay."

She laughed, relieved, and realized he'd been teasing her. "Great." She took the casserole and a half-dozen

French rolls from the freezer. She popped the main dish into the oven, already preheated to 400 degrees, and then wrapped the rolls in foil, to be heated a little later. Then she grabbed a bottle of Chardonnay from the frig, took the corkscrew from a drawer and two wine goblets from the cupboard.

"You can be the bartender while I cut up the salad," she told him.

He nodded, looking amused. "You're quite the woman, Officer Cline."

She glanced. "Jessie, remember?"

"How could I forget?"

She met his gaze and their eyes locked in an electrifying moment. Before either of them could say anything Danny came into the room to set the table, breaking the connection.

"Setting the table is my job," he explained to Hank, unaware that he interrupted anything between the adults. As Danny worked, he jabbered about school and sports and soon he and Hank were talking about the Mariners and Sonics and baseball and basketball in general. When the table setting was finally complete, Danny went back to the family room to check his e-mail.

There was a sudden silence.

"Nice boy. You've done a good job bringing him up, Jessie. I think he'll always be there for you."

For a moment she didn't know how to respond, and suspected he was thinking about his own son, and the fact that they were estranged. "I hope so, Hank. Danny is my whole world. I'd hate to think otherwise."

"Yeah, otherwise as you put it, can be a sad place."

"But not a permanent place, Hank. Things can change."

"So." She grabbed her glass of wine which he'd just poured. "Let's have a toast."

He picked up his glass, waiting.

"To our sons."

He nodded. "Our sons, their success and happiness."

They sipped.

And then Jessie's eyes fell on her phone and she realized that she hadn't checked her messages. As they put down their glasses, she picked up the receiver, punched in her code and listened to the messages, one from her mother and one from a stranger.

She turned, facing Hank who watched from where he sat at the kitchen table. Abruptly, his expression changed. "For God's sake, what's wrong Jessie?"

She motioned him to the phone, then punched in the number to repeat the messages. He took the receiver, hearing her mother say that she'd call again in the morning—and the other one.

"You will die, too."

"It's the same voice," he said in a low tone.

She nodded. "The same voice that threatened Lynda."

For long seconds all they could do was stare at each other. And then he hung up.

CHAPTER FORTY-NINE

WITHIN THE NEXT HOUR HANK HAD AUTHORIZED A PHONE trace on both the Thrasher's phone line and Jessie's phone line. "Hopefully the calls were not made from a phone booth," he told her. "But if so, and if it's on the island, we'll at least dust it for prints, in the hope that they'll match with other evidence in the future."

"Other evidence?" Jessie asked, even as she knew that the M.O. of the person out there indicated that there would be other incidents.

He nodded. "You know as well as I do that the situation is accelerating." He hesitated. "Somehow, the reasons are still unclear, why you, Danny and Lynda Thrasher are the only targets so far."

They were still sipping their first glass of wine, when Jessie got up to check the oven and retrieve the wine bottle from the refrigerator.

"There's still another ten minutes until we eat," she told him. "A refill?"

He nodded, looking grim. "I'm sorry about this, Jessie." A pause. "We'll get this creep, and then we'll throw the book at whoever it turns out to be."

"We have to catch the person," she said, swirling the wine in her glass. "But so far there haven't been many clues, except for the white van stolen from your son." She hesitated. "And—"

"And?"

"And I just don't want a tragedy before we have a clue to the person's identity. There has to be a connection between Lynda and me." She took a gulp of wine. "I told you I once knew Ben, took a class from him. But it's been so long ago he obviously doesn't remember me." A pause. "And Lynda and I have nothing in common. She's from a totally different background, one that is alien to me. There doesn't seem to be any connection at all— social, professional or educational, not to mention that I'm many years older than she is."

"There is one connection," he said softly.

She lifted her eyes meeting the directness of his gaze. "Which is?"

"Ben."

A silence went by.

"Yeah, there's that."

Another silence.

"So? What does that add to the equation now?"

Jessie shrugged. "Nothing. No one on this island, aside from you, knows that I ever knew him. I can't see a connection here."

"You can't. But could someone else?"

"For God's sake, who?"

"Who in the hell knows? But we can't discount that factor, Jessie. We're cops, remember?"

She nodded slowly. The oven timer went off and she jumped up. "Guess we'll have to put the whole issue on hold because supper is ready."

"Okay." He stood up. "I'll get Danny, if I can pry him away from the computer." He walked to the family room doorway and then faced her again. "But we need to discuss this further, Jessie, maybe tomorrow morning."

"You're right Hank. We'll talk later." But as she dished up supper she was glad for the reprieve. Despite knowing that she must reveal anything she knew, she needed more time to prepare herself.

One thing was for sure. She would be honest to the best of her ability.

The next morning she had a call from Hank to confirm the time for picking up her and Danny. When she offered to drive them herself in the Saturn, his response was "Nope."

"By the way, Jessie, I've already had a call from Lynda Thrasher who reported finding a note on her front doorstep this morning. You didn't have one, did you?"

"My God, Hank, I hardly ever open the front door so I haven't checked this morning."

"I'll wait. You go make sure. If there isn't one then maybe you and Lynda aren't as connected with this predator as we think."

"Okay. Just a minute then."

She put down the phone and headed out of the kitchen to the hall and front entry. Unlocking the door, she swung it open. A folded sheet of paper fluttered to the doorstep in front of her. Horrified, she stood motionless for several seconds, her glance darting beyond the driveway to the shadowy woods, looking for movement. As reason reasserted itself, she toed the paper into the house, then slammed and locked the door.

Careful of smudging fingerprints, she ran to the kitchen and picked up the phone. "There is one, Hank!" she cried. "Hang on. I'll be right back."

And then she grabbed a baggy from the cupboard and a tweezer from the bathroom and ran back to the front door, pinching up the paper and dropping it into the baggy.

Once back at the kitchen phone again she told Hank what she'd done.

"What did the note say?"

"Oh my God," she told him, "it says, 'The one who sells apples on the street corner will win, not you.'"

Hank's whistle came over the line. "Son of a bitch. The word win again, like in Lynda's note. Whoever this bastard is, they talk in riddles. And I'm willing to bet there won't be any prints."

"I suspect you're right. But we can also have the paper and the type of ink tested by the crime lab, as you did before without results. Also hairs and fibers. Maybe they can narrow the evidence. Sometimes paper isn't as mass market as it seems."

"Listen, Jessie, I'm on my way to pick up you and Danny. Don't tell him about this, it will only scare him."

"I won't."

"And don't let him take Footers out to the kennel yet. Make any excuse you need to until I get there, okay?"

The bottom dropped out of her stomach. "Do you think someone is still out there, Hank?"

"Probably not, but I don't want to take chances." His voice lowered. "I don't want anything happening to my assistant chief or to her son."

"We'll wait in the kitchen, Hank. I'm ready and Danny is just getting his backpack together in the family room."

"Good. I'm five minutes away."

And then he disconnected and she went to the connecting room to make sure that Danny stayed there. She needn't have worried. He'd checked his e-mail; his grandmother had caught him on-line and now they were instant-mailing back and forth.

"Grandma can't come for Thanksgiving," he said as he typed a response. "But she's planning on Christmas to stay over New Year."

"Tell her that's perfect. We'll plan on it."

He typed her words. "She says she'll call on the weekend."

"Tell her I'll look forward to that, that the arts and crafts shop people want to talk to her while she's here."

"She's looking forward to everything," Danny said. And then he logged off, stood up and called to Footers. "Sorry my pal, but it's the kennel, which is better than being cooped up in here all day."

About to stop him, Jessie was saved by the tapping at the back door. "It's Hank!" Danny cried and headed for the back door.

He let the chief in and then went to get his cell phone which he'd left upstairs. Hank took Footers to the kennel, and by the time they'd left, Jessie felt secure that the house was locked up, Footers was safe and the lights would come on at dark.

The talk was centered on sports and island events as Hank drove Danny to school. Once he'd been dropped off and seen safely into the building, Hank headed for the police station, his bearing suddenly somber. She was scheduled to get her car back today and was glad for that. Her own vehicle allowed her to be more independent.

Yet, she'd miss Hank's presence when she and Danny were so threatened by some phantom predator. She also worried about Lynda. What kind of a crazy person would threaten an innocent young woman who was expecting her first child? A lunatic, she thought. But who would that be? No one seemed to have any idea, any more than why she and Danny had also been targeted.

Her thoughts lingered on the phone messages and the

notes as she and Hank rode in silence. Something about the recorded words, written or said, bothered her. What was there about them that triggered something in her memory? The reference to the hammock on Lynda's phone message, and the allusion to selling apples on the street corner rang a bell in her mind, but she couldn't make the connection.

As they drove into the parking lot she suddenly did remember where she might have seen it. Jessie scarcely noted when they parked and Hank got out of the cruiser.

"Hey, Jessie, we're here," Hank said after coming around the car and opening her door.

"Oh, yeah, I see that." She managed a smile. "Sorry, my mind was somewhere else."

"I guess. So it appears." His eyebrows shot up. "You looked like you were having an epiphany."

She got out of the car and followed him toward the station. "I'm just thinking about the phone and note messages. Something is familiar, but I don't know what."

He held the door open for her. "Can you explain?"

She shook her head. "I need to think more about it and when I figure anything out you'll be the first to know."

He looked down into her face for a moment longer, and she felt his need to make her explain. But then he stepped back. "Okay Jessie. Just be sure you keep me in the loop."

"Without a doubt, Hank. Like I said, I'll let you know as soon as I know."

And then they went into the station to start their day.

In mid-afternoon Jessie got her car back and was able to take her place on patrol, relieving the volunteers. It was still light by the time she checked her own property, made sure Footers was okay in the kennel and then went into the house so that she could access the Internet on her computer. She'd been mulling the threatening messages all day and remembered where she'd seen posts about a hammock and selling apples on the street corner.

It was on the artists forum—a chat room that Ben had frequented in the past, where he'd had interchanges with women, including the terms used in the threatening messages, terms used in a sensuous way, not threatening as they were now. Hopefully, she could bring them up from the archives.

But the archives didn't go back that far and she finally logged off, frustrated. She needed to tell Hank, in case she was right, and in case he could access the forum through their investigation. Ben had obviously moved on a long time ago. The women he'd once seduced with his wit and words were no longer available on the forum.

And maybe she was wrong, Jessie thought, as she headed back to the station for one last check of her office messages before she picked up Danny.

Think about your Thanksgiving dinner, she told herself, because the holiday was only a few days away. She intended to bake a turkey, have a dinner with all the trimmings, wished her mom could be there as well as Christmas, but thought she might ask Max and Signe and Hank to join them. Lost in thought about her possible dinner she went into the station.

"Jeez, Jessie, I'm glad to see you!" Hank ran down the hall toward her.

"What happened?" Her heartbeat went from seventy to hundred beats a minute in seconds. "Is Danny okay?"

"Danny? He's fine. It's Lynda."

"Oh my God! What's happened to Lynda."

"She's gone, disappeared without a trace."

Jessie could only stare, openmouthed.

CHAPTER FIFTY

IT WAS AS IF SHE'D JUST LEFT THE THRASHER ESTATE AND now they were back, and the reason was even worse than the last time. Jessie had followed Hank's cruiser in her own car rather than going together, in case of another emergency on the island.

Hank's stance indicated vigilance as he got out of his car; his gun, although still holstered, was exposed and ready for quick retrieval. Jessie followed suit, unsnapping her holster. And then she followed him up to the porch.

About to knock, the door was flung open and Ben stood framed in the doorway, dressed in stained jeans and a black turtleneck sweater, his hair in disarray and his face creased with deep lines and groves.

Jessie knew he was in his late forties but today he looked sixty. He motioned them inside, puffing erratically on a cigarette. Leading them to the living room, he indicated the overstuffed chairs near the fireplace and both Jessie and Hank sat down, facing each other across an antique coffee table. Ben leaned against the mantel after snuffing out his cigarette in an ashtray; his nervousness apparent in the uncontrollable tic of his blinking eyes.

He's scared, Jessie thought. Or guilty of something?

"Let's start at the beginning, Ben," Hank said, as he

pulled out his notebook and pen. "When did you know she was missing?"

"Shit, I don't know that I can do this?" He sank his head into his hands momentarily, as though stricken with fear, and Jessie glimpsed the Ben she'd known years earlier. Back then, before she knew the real man, she'd naïvely thought of him more tenderly when he'd been uncertain and upset, and had wanted to protect him.

"Take a deep breath," Jessie suggested. "We need every detail to help us find her."

"Are you certain she didn't go for a walk, or out for morning coffee with a friend?" Hank asked.

"No way!" Ben retorted. "She was too pregnant for a walk and she would never leave without letting me know, especially when I'm home. She thought coffee klatches were a waste of time."

Jessie was silent as Hank continued his questioning. But she wondered if it was Lynda or Ben who hated socializing with people on the island—who kept her so isolated. She suspected that he wanted complete devotion from Lynda, even as he left her home alone while he had his flings and affairs.

"Did you have a disagreement?" Hank's gaze was abruptly direct.

"Fuckin' no, Chief. Lynda and I don't argue. We love each other and never disagree."

Hank scribbled quickly on his pad while Jessie pondered his words. Was Lynda too infatuated by her charismatic husband to dispute his wishes?

"So where were you when your wife vanished, Ben?" Hank had glanced up from his pad, a steely look in his pale eyes. She realized again that Hank didn't like the guy, although she was sure that Ben didn't realize that. In fact, Ben was pretty oblivious to everything but himself.

A typical sociopath.

"I'd gone down to the beach to my boat so I could row out and check the crab traps." He shook his head, his eyes darting wildly. "Lynda's parents, her sister and some of my grown kids are flying in tomorrow for Thanksgiving. We wanted to have a crab dinner tomorrow night for them."

"You have a path to the beach?" Hank asked.

"We have a tram." He glanced to Jessie and back to Hank. "It stayed at the bottom of the bluff until I used it to go back up."

"You sure of that?" Hank's question was direct.

"Of course. I only took the rowboat out into the cove. The tram was in sight at all times. I would have seen, even heard its engine, if it had gone back up."

"So you got crabs?" Hank asked, casually. Too casually? Jessie wondered

"Yeah, five of them, enough for our dinner."

"So where are the crabs now?"

Ben's eyes narrowed. "C'mon, Chief, I'll show you."

Ben led them back to the kitchen—a vast high-ceilinged room with hardwood floors, high-end appliances and marble counters, to the sink where the crabs were still intact in a water-filled bucket.

"It's saltwater," he explained. "They need to be cleaned but what's the use if Lynda is gone."

For the first time, Jessie could see that he was upset about his missing wife, beyond his distress in defending himself. She almost felt sorry for him. But only until Hank's questioning brought her back to reality.

"So you came back with your crabs to find Lynda gone?"

He nodded.

"And there wasn't a note, no sign of a conflict, and her car isn't missing? Is that your statement?"

"It is." Ben seemed to vibrate with his nervousness.

"What do you think happened to your wife, Ben?" Hank asked, his voice deceptively soft.

"Jeez, man. If only I knew."

"What do you think *might* have happened, Mr. Thrasher?" Jessie asked, her question falling into a sudden vacuum when neither man spoke. "Was she abducted?"

"Yes, I think that's possible, especially since there have been all of the other threats against her."

"Can you suggest people we should investigate?" she added.

He glanced away. "I can't think of anyone, nor can I imagine a single person who'd have anything against Lynda."

As Hank was again scribbling, Jessie stayed silent, watching both men.

"But there might be one person, Mr. Thrasher?" she asked finally.

He raised his brows, as though puzzled by her question.

"Remember? You suggested that the senator should be asked about your wife's harassment, but were afraid of accusing him directly because of a possible libel suit?" She tilted her head, waiting for his response. "You know, the politician you've been drawing in your syndicated cartoons?"

His gaze seemed to intensify. For long seconds he only stared, as though considering her question. Or was he remembering her? she wondered suddenly. About the moment she thought he might be, he spoke.

"There are many people who are angry with me, Officer—uh—" His gaze dropped to her name badge, "Cline. It's a given in my line of work. But among all of those people it's hard to determine who might be so crazy that they'd seek revenge by hurting my loved ones."

She kept her gaze level, never showing him by even a waver of her eyes that she was someone he'd once known—and forgotten. Yeah, forgotten, she told herself. He truly didn't remember her. How many others? she wondered. How many women had he used, made promises to and promptly forgotten? Another area to investigate, she reminded herself.

She stared at him, seeing his twitching eyes, his thin lips and weak chin now that he no longer sported a beard to cover it. He was a loser—even if he had a young wife and successful career—for now. Of course he was a man with enemies. He didn't play by any rule other than his own: how he could manipulate others to get ahead.

Something has come back to haunt him and he knows it.

Jessie's perception was instant, and without proof other than intuition. His past might be catching up to him, she thought. But how? And who?

"Aside from the senator who represents your professional life, what about your personal life? Can you think of past friends who may have a reason to hurt your wife, Mr. Thrasher?" Jessie realized that Hank had stopped scribbling to watch her exchange with Ben.

"Not one fuckin' person, Officer," he retorted, angrily. "I'm not chopped liver, a person someone can screw, so don't try to act like I know what's going on here. Because I don't know. If I did, if I hadn't been scared shitless about my wife and unborn baby, I'd never have called the police in the first place." He stepped closer. "Get it? I don't know what happened to Lynda!"

She held his gaze. "I only needed a yes or no, Mr. Thrasher, not profanity."

Hank quickly took control of the interview. "Okay, Mr. Thrasher, we know you're upset. I have one last question and then we'll get to work and try to find Lynda."

Haughtily, Ben inclined his head, waiting.

"Was anyone else in the house with your wife when you left?"

He shook his head. "In fact she'd slept in, was just getting up. None of the people we employ were here and none were expected for a couple of hours." A pause. "When I left she was making coffee in the kitchen."

Hank put his pad and pen away. "Be assured, Mr. Thrasher. We'll do everything we can to find your wife."

"Please find her." Ben's concern sounded genuine.

After inspecting the house, making sure that there was no sign of a scuffle, and no forced entry anywhere, Jessie and Hank went outside and did a walk around the grounds. Ben watched from the porch and as they returned to the cars, he spoke.

"See? There isn't a clue or indication as to what happened. I tell you, officers, my wife never goes anywhere without looking good, and in the hour I was in the rowboat she wouldn't have had time to straighten up and put on her makeup, too." He gulped air. "And now she's gone without her purse. And that aside from the fact that her car and keys are still here."

"Could someone have picked her up?"

"Who, for God's sake?"

Hank shrugged. "I don't know, that's why I'm asking you?"

Ben spread his hands. "I have no idea."

Jessie followed Hank out to their cars where he hesitated by her door. "We'll put all our resources into place, but I think we might find they did have a fight and she's out there in the woods watching. It's apparent that she's hoping Ben will have a wakeup call and be here for the birth of their child."

"I admit I thought of that, too, Hank. But—"

"But what?"

"What if something terrible has really happened?" she asked. "Lynda wasn't behind the shooting and other threats."

"We're following procedure for abduction, and possibly murder."

"Oh shit." The words whistled out of her and she was reminded of the Laci Peterson case in California. No, don't go there, she told herself. Lynda's story would have a good ending. It had to.

There were no emergency calls so Jessie followed him back to the office. Once inside, Hank put out the APB for Lynda Thrasher, even though she had only gone missing several hours earlier. In light of what had already happened to the woman the early warning was advisable. Then Hank instituted a ferry alert on departing vehicles, requested the names of passengers on small float planes leaving the island and had Max come in for extra duty.

Before Jessie left on patrol Hank stopped her, reminding her to be extra cautious. And then he pulled her into his arms and kissed her. "Stay safe," he whispered. "We have unfinished business when this mess is over."

She could only nod before heading outside to her car.

By the time Jessie and Danny were safely in the house with Footers she'd realized the word was out. The national media was reporting that Ben Thrasher's pregnant wife had disappeared; the five o'clock network news stations already had people on the island to report the latest happenings; and speculation was almost out of control. There was a media frenzy in the making and Jessie could only speculate on what would happen tomorrow. Their one certainty was that more media people would be on the late ferry tonight and on the morning runs.

Oh God, she thought. What did it all mean? She just hoped that Lynda was indeed trying to manipulate her husband and would turn up safe and apologetic, had been hiding in the woods to force Ben into being more sympathetic to her feelings. She tried to discount her own wayward notion that Ben had killed his wife because she'd discovered his extramarital affairs and confronted him.

Oh please no, she thought. Don't let it be that. Let Lynda and her precious baby be safe.

But Hank's call later that night was alarming. "The Associated Press has picked up the story and the phone at the station is ringing off the hook," he told her. "We'll probably have a few hundred messages by eight in the morning at the current rate of calls," he told her. "Be prepared. This may be our last night of sleep for a while."

Disturbed, her house locked for the night, Danny already asleep, Jessie lay awake, not so much worried about tomorrow's media frenzy, but wondering where Lynda was at that moment.

The poor woman. She had to be so scared.

If she was alive.

CHAPTER FIFTY-ONE

NITA WATCHED FROM THE TOP OF THE ROAD ABOVE THE ferry landing, her bike and cart propped by a rock, seeing all the media vans and trucks coming onto the island. She felt sick. The evil had struck and taken the Thrasher woman and her baby.

But the evil one wasn't finished; Nita knew that from her observations of what had been happening in recent weeks, and from her sense of connection to the ancient ones. The evil would strike again, but this time the result would mean total death, not an older life for a new life, and the end result would mean two would die this time, a woman and a boy, maybe more if anyone stood in the way.

She watched the vehicles disappear up the road and into town, and wondered how the local police department would cope, including Jessie, the person who needed to concentrate on protecting her son.

Poor Jessie, she thought. She tried so hard. But there was only so much she could do to protect Danny from a Tsonoqua-type person.

But the evil one was not Tsonoqua, Nita reminded herself. The Spirit of the Wind was not the monster of the forest for her own kind, only for those who sought to destroy. She would protect Danny. But she needed help.

Once again Nita vowed to step into that void.

Tsonoqua was the head of her household, too. She was once the being portrayed on the totem who protected the family. She would protect it now.

Nita skipped her minor errands and began pedaling back to the shed above the beach near her tugboat. She must make plans.

And she must watch for the evil, make sure she was there first to prevent the wickedness. The only heir of the Tsonoqua clan depended on her vigilance.

There was no one else.

CHAPTER FIFTY-TWO

JESSIE DROPPED DANNY OFF AT SCHOOL THE NEXT MORNING, and then drove on toward the police station. She was still a block away when she was stopped by the traffic congestion. Media vehicles were everywhere, and the locals had crowded the sidewalks, trying to learn what was happening. Everyone had heard that Ben Thrasher's wife had vanished.

Jessie turned on her bubble lights and siren, and slowly made her way to the station where Hank was waiting for her. Entering his office, he waved her to the chair in front of his desk and then plunked down in his own behind it. He looked as though he hadn't slept. There were dark circles under his eyes but his gaze was as penetrating as ever. "I'm glad you're here, Jessie. I need your help."

She nodded. "So I see. I hardly made it through the media vehicles blocking traffic."

"Yeah, the first of them arrived on the midnight ferry and they've continued to stream off the two morning ferries today." He sighed. "I'm thinking this is the tip of the iceberg; they will be arriving all day long."

"Son of a gun," she said, controlling her vocabulary. "Ben is truly a celebrity."

"Did you doubt it, Jessie?"

"Uh-huh, I guess I did." Her gaze didn't waver. "As the old saying goes, I knew him back when. It's hard to believe that he's so important."

"You don't think he is?"

She hesitated. "I know he isn't, Hank," she said finally. "He's a fraud, and it's another case of the public buying into a persona." She shook her head. "Shit! I wish I wasn't so jaded."

"But rightly so, Jessie."

"How do you mean?"

He shrugged. "Only that you've been in California law enforcement for years, seen it all, and now you're up here on a remote island. I'm sure that you've found that human nature prevails, California or Cliff Island." He hesitated. "By the way, your opinion of Thrasher is also my personal take on the guy."

She nodded. "Sadly, our analysis of human nature is true, much as I wish it weren't." A pause. "So what do you think happened to Lynda? What's your gut feeling?"

"I don't want to guess yet. What's yours?"

"She's alive."

"You know statistics say she isn't?" Hank's expression was troubled. "There have been Coast Guard boats out there since daylight inspecting our coastline and doing an underwater sonar search. Military helicopters have been called in to scan the surface and divers are going down in the cove below the Thrasher estate to inspect the crab traps, among other targets."

"Oh my God, Hank. The crab traps?"

He nodded. "There was a murder case in Alaska some years ago where the body was put into a four-by-four crab trap. The flesh was cleaned away by sea life and the bones, except for the skull, floated away because the trap door was left open." He hesitated. "It was almost a perfect crime. But if Lynda was placed in the water the tides and currents would carry her away, never to be recovered, unless she happened to wash ashore."

Jessie was silent as she considered his horrifying words. She knew he was only trying to prepare her for the worst.

"We also have a local group, sponsored by the county sheriff's department, who are about to search the woods near the Thrasher estate. The sheriff is bringing in a search dog who will hopefully settle the questions of whether Lynda went off into the woods, or was led to the beach tram, or departed from the driveway, which would mean a vehicle of some sort."

Jessie only nodded a response. "So," she said after the pause. "What's our current status?"

"It's a fuckin' circus," he said. "The story is on cable news, with momentary updates by the people who represent Ben and the opposing force that represents the senator's office. Senator Pearsen, Ben's nemesis, is calling for an investigation into Ben's background. The words are thinly veiled insinuations that Ben is behind Lynda's disappearance, that his wife's impending pregnancy infringed on his lifestyle, that he already had grown kids by earlier marriages and didn't want another child."

"What're you saying, Hank?"

"I'm only repeating a media commentator who alleges that Hank has been involved in affairs, didn't want more kids or a wife who demanded a traditional life, and hence made the situation go away." He spread his hands. "At this point I have no way of knowing what is true here and what isn't."

"Me either."

"All I know is that we're under siege by the national

news media. Our investigation—because the person involved is Ben Thrasher who is a celebrity—will be under a microscope." He got to his feet. "Jessie, we've got a huge problem."

"I understand that, Hank." She stood, still facing him. "But Ben Thrasher has a bigger one. He's the asshole, not us, the person with a past that's about to surface. We're only the investigators who are trying to help."

"I know that, Jessie. But I also know that when he gets on the hot seat he'll try to defer suspicion from himself to the next practical place, and that means law enforcement, his enemies, or anywhere else he can think of to place blame."

"Are you saying that you think he's guilty of his wife's disappearance?"

A silence went by while his gaze was unwavering.

"I think he knows something, whether or not he's directly responsible."

"Is that a hunch or something more substantial?"

"Don't know, Jessie. Maybe just intuition."

"Understood. I have the same feeling."

And then they each went about their own business of the morning, knowing they needed to keep up on island problems, as well as the national media situation of Lynda Thrasher outside their door.

The Thrashers would not be allowed to take over the island.

The ferries continued to be overloaded with the media and within twenty-four hours the Thrasher estate was crowded with reporters and their satellite connections to their stations. It was a madhouse: all of the island police volunteers were either on duty or on standby and Max had gone to full-time until the Thrasher situation was re-

solved. In addition to the county sheriff's office having assigned a unit, state and federal help had also descended
upon the island.

The bottom line: Lynda had not been found. No one,
not the police, the volunteers nor the tracking dogs
who'd scoured the woods had uncovered a clue as to
what had happened. It was still as much of a mystery as it
had been in the beginning.

Again, Jessie was thankful that Danny was safe; she'd
made arrangements with Signe that Danny and Footers
stay overnight with them, and they'd play it by ear the
next night—whether or not she needed to be on call all
night. Her first priority was to keep her son safe.

"We have no leads," Hank told her the next morning.
"We're working around the clock, we've got law enforcement resources from everywhere, and still there are no
fuckin' clues."

"Yeah, I know. It's pretty upsetting." A pause. "I want
your okay to pursue another line of investigation."

"Please explain."

She nodded. "This may take a while, so please bear
with me. Remember that talk we were going to have
about my connection to Ben?"

He inclined his head. "Go on. I'm interested in anything at this point."

Jessie took a minute to gather her thoughts on how to
present her reasons for action that wouldn't give away
her own past—that had nothing to do with what was
happening now. Finally she began.

"You know that I knew Ben a long time ago, right?"

He nodded.

"The years following were interesting in that I followed some of his antics on the Internet, after stumbling
onto him on an artists forum."

"But why would he have used his real name?" Hank asked, leaning forward.

"I asked myself that and came up with two reasons. He wasn't famous back then, and outside of the artistic community no one had ever heard of him."

"You said two reasons."

She nodded. "The second was ego. He was the celebrity on a forum of wannabe artists who seemed like misfits and emotional cripples who only talked art and had never done anything significant in the field. Therefore Ben became their on-line guru."

"Sounds sick."

"It got sicker."

He tilted his head in a question.

"He got involved with several of the women, and the on-line exchanges accelerated to the point of suggestions to meet." She glanced away. "After that the messages obviously went to private e-mail. But over time, several of the women seemed compelled to report, without naming names, that they were the chosen ones of the forum celebrity, i.e., Ben Thrasher."

She paused.

"Go on, Jessie. Your story is fascinating—and I'm wondering why you recognized what was happening."

"Yeah, I'm sure you do." She met his eyes. "Let it suffice to say that I know this guy's M.O., that he hadn't changed at all once he graduated to the Internet. It was just another way for him to meet someone, have sex and then throw the woman aside when he moved on."

A silence ensued.

"So what is it that you need, Jessie?"

"This is going to sound like I'm out in left field."

"Okay." He spread his hands. "I'm ready for that."

"I want to check out all new residents on the island, even tourists on extended vacations."

"You think someone moved here, or came to visit because of Ben?—someone who might have been one of those Internet conquests?"

She ignored his incredulous expression. "I think it's possible."

"We can't spare the manpower right now."

"I know. I'm willing to do this on my off time. But I need your okay."

He looked thoughtful—and cautious. "Do you think the threats to you and Danny might be connected to Ben's Internet conquests—and Lynda's disappearance?"

"Possibly."

"Okay, you have my go-ahead, on police time."

She was silent for long seconds. "Thanks, Hank. I might just find the break we need. You won't be sorry for this permission."

"I know. I have faith in your, uh, female intuition." He came around his desk. "I'll also authorize a court order if you need to access the member list of that artists forum, so you can match the tags to the real persons." And then he folded her into his arms, holding her against him for long seconds. "Just be safe, Jessie."

She nodded, grateful that he'd respected her feelings and not asked personal questions. Stepping back, she went to her own office to begin her work. She suspected it would not be in vain. She now had the tools to track Ben Thrasher. She just hoped the results wouldn't come in too late.

Lynda and her baby must be saved. If they were still alive.

CHAPTER FIFTY-THREE

JESSIE CHECKED THE WEEKLY NEWSPAPER OFFICE FIRST. Arthur Bing, the owner she'd talked to when she was researching her own family history, gave her a list of new subscribers in the past year.

She glanced at it. "Not very many names here—maybe ten."

"Unfortunately, that's true. It's the old timers on the island who keep the paper afloat." He grinned at her. "And please, Jessie. Let's not let it be known that I gave you the list. I might be violating our subscribers' right to privacy."

"Mum's the word."

She was smiling as she headed up the street to Tommy's arts and crafts shop. Going inside she was glad to see the owner at the cash register. He glanced up as she approached.

"Hey there, Jessie Cline. I'm surprised to see you in my store when the whole island is crawling with media trucks and reporters."

Jessie nodded. "Yeah, it's a circus. We've got every man available on the job." She hesitated. "Which brings me to my reason for being here."

His gaze intensified. "Shoot."

"As you know, Lynda Thrasher vanished from her home, the reason for all of the media attention."

"Uh-huh. And?"

"And it's imperative that we find her as soon as possible." Another pause. "We're following every possible lead, however remote it seems." She spread her hands. "I needed to ask you to name any newcomers to the island that you can think of in the past six months to a year."

For long seconds he was thoughtful. "Personally, I know very few," he said finally. "Maybe four or five families and several single people."

"Would you write them down for me, Tommy? And also anyone who might have extended a vacation into a longer time period on the island, or new converts to God's Love Enterprises who may have moved to the commune."

"Of course." He pulled a tablet and pen in front of him and then listed the new residents he knew about. Finishing, he glanced up. "I don't know anyone who has extended their vacation, nor do I have any information about the comings and goings at the commune. I suggest you check the bed-and-breakfasts and the Marina Hotel that caters to boaters."

"I know, and I intend to do that."

He handed her the sheet. "Probably not much help, Jessie."

She thanked him, left his store and headed for the post office to talk to Val Howard. Hopefully he would also accommodate her with a list of new residents.

Her luck held. Again the list was surprisingly small, although twice as long as the newspaper subscriptions. Several names turned up on all three lists and she felt it was a good start. Later, after Danny was in bed she intended to access the artists forum, see if any of the people matched the name of someone on the island. She'd decided that even if nothing clicked she'd tell Hank that they needed the court order for the real names behind the tags.

But for now she needed to finish her shift, check into the station and then pick up Danny.

The house was quiet, Danny had gone upstairs to bed over an hour ago, and Jessie sat staring at the computer screen. After seeing to her e-mail, especially several worried posts from her mother who'd heard about Lynda Thrasher's disappearance on television news, she'd looked in on the artists forum.

One of the names, a Sarah Rawls, whose tag was simply SarahRawls2, was a frequent poster, and although there were no direct messages between her and Ben, she contributed to threads about Ben's work. And she insinuated in some of the on-line conversations that she knew Ben.

Jessie sat back in her chair. The name Sarah Rawls appeared on all three of the lists: Tommy's, the post office's and the newspaper's. The woman was worth questioning.

A left-field lead that might not go anywhere, Jessie reminded herself. The name could be a coincidence. She wished it wasn't almost eleven or she'd call Hank with her information, but tomorrow morning was soon enough. Hank had been putting in long days and needed his sleep.

Once she'd turned off the computer, and made sure the house was secure for the night, Jessie retraced her steps to the kitchen and put the tea kettle on the burner to heat. She loved to sit up in bed against the pillows and sip her final cup of herbal tea of the day while she stared out into the night. It was her way to unwind when life seemed complicated—as it did now.

Now, as she waited for the water to boil, she leaned over the sink and gazed out the window. The wind was rising, as the weatherman had predicted, and she knew rain would soon follow. A typical fall storm was blowing south out of the Gulf of Alaska.

The sudden whistling of the tea kettle interrupted her musing and she quickly turned off the burner and poured the water into a mug. Then two things happened at once. A gust of wind rippled over the window, immediately followed by a faint sound of movement behind her.

She whirled around to face the empty room—and the basement door.

A glance told her it was still locked. Had the sound really come from that direction? Or was it only another noise from outside?—like a loose gutter rubbing against the shakes?

Rationalization didn't help. Her body was at full alert, and instead of picking up her mug, she grabbed her holstered weapon from the counter. Lately she'd made sure it was handy, a precaution that came in handy now.

Quickly Jessie removed the pistol and tiptoed to the basement door. Pressing her ear against the panel she listened intently. Nothing.

But again she had a sense of a presence, someone on the steps who also strained to hear. And again her impulse was to fling the door open to satisfy her own sense of safety.

Don't be stupid, she told herself. You've done that before and found nothing. The bolt is still in place. No one could be down there.

Backing away, Jessie moved across the kitchen to the counter and picked up her tea mug. She decided against turning out all of the downstairs lights and left one on in the kitchen and another in the hall. Then she went upstairs to her bedroom and placed the mug on the nightstand. Still unsettled, her weapon within reach as she put on her nightgown and brushed her teeth, she took it along when she checked on Danny.

Silently, she slipped through the shadowy hall to his room, peeked inside and saw that he was asleep, Footers on the floor beside the bed.

Still uneasy, Jessie glided back down the hall toward her room, careful not to make a sound. Just as she passed the stairs there was another faint sound that seemed to come from the lower landing where a flight of steps to the kitchen intersected the main stairway.

She froze, listening. A cold chill touched her spine.

The storm had intensified outside, but again everything was peaceful inside.

What had she heard? Fingers of wind that had snaked under the eves to find an entry into the walls? An upstairs window left open a crack? Or only the boards and timbers of the house cooling under the onslaught of bad weather?

She waited, wondering if she'd really heard something or not. Paranoid, that's what you are, she thought. Just because bad things were happening on the island she'd become quick to jump to scary conclusions.

But it's better to err on the side of safety, she reminded herself, because someone out there was a serious threat to her and Danny. She meant to keep them safe.

Back in her room she sat against her pillows, sipped her tea, watched the rain pummeling her windows and knew that her practice to unwind and process the day's events would never work tonight. She was there for the long haul.

The faint sounds behind the walls of Wind House had stolen her peace. The place needed a sentry for the night. And she was it.

CHAPTER FIFTY-FOUR

THE NEXT MORNING JESSIE GRABBED HER UNIFORM JACKET from the hall closet. About to close the door, she hesitated, her eyes on the coat she'd worn the day she and Danny had gone to the outlet mall.

The day she'd written down the plate numbers of two white vehicles on the ferry.

She stepped back into the closet and spread the hangers to separate the coat from other garments. Then she plunged her hand into one of the pockets—and came up with the pad with the plate numbers.

Son of a bitch, she thought. Why didn't I think to look in my coat pocket?

Danny secured Footers in the kennel, after making sure he had food and water for the day. Then they got in her cruiser and headed for town. After dropping him off at school and making sure he was safely inside the building, Jessie headed for the station and started her day.

"Hey, Hank," she said from his doorway. "I have two license plates to run through the computers, one a white SUV and the other a Honda compact."

He raised his brows. "Why so?"

"They were on the ferry when I took Danny to the outlet mall. I wrote the plates down, knowing I should check on white vehicles leaving the island and then I misplaced my writing pad." She hesitated. "It was in my coat pocket and I just discovered it this morning."

He held out his hand and she gave him the pad with the numbers. "I'll run it though the state registration system right away and we'll hear back almost immediately."

She nodded and watched as he punched the information into his desktop computer. After a few seconds he looked up.

"The state stats reveal that the SUV belongs to a Jerome Blackstone who lives in Seattle but has owned property on the island for the past seven years, and the Honda belongs to a Sarah Rawls who relocated from California last year but only recently bought Washington car plates." He opened a folder and thumbed through the pages. "That's why she wasn't on my updated car registration list." He glanced up. "She is now."

"Oh shit." She handed over the three lists she'd collected yesterday that all included Sarah's name. Then she updated him on what she'd found out on the artists forum last night.

"But you don't know that the Internet woman and the Sarah who lives on the island are the same person."

"No, I don't. But the circumstantial evidence is growing." She hesitated. "So I need to go to her house and question her."

He stood up. "I agree she needs to be questioned, but I think I should be the one to do it."

"I disagree."

His whole posture went still. "Please explain, Jessie."

Oh God, she thought. How could she make him understand her gut feeling, her female instinct that told her this Sarah was somehow connected to Ben, whether or not she had anything to do with Lynda's disappearance.

"I want to face this woman, Hank, because as I've told you, I understand her attraction to Ben. What I don't know is if they'd had a relationship, if she couldn't let go, why she'd move to his island if she didn't have an ulterior motive, or if he'd wanted her to move here."

There was a silence.

"I'll run check on Sarah Rawls through the national police and FBI computers and see if anything comes up on her, okay?"

She nodded.

"And we'll look into her background and personal history, as far as what is available."

"Good. I don't know what you'll find but in the meantime I want to go out and question her."

"I think you should do that."

"Thanks," she said. "I knew you'd agree." About to turn away, his next words brought her gaze back to his.

"I'm going with you."

"I can do this on my own, Hank."

"I know that, Jessie. I trust your decision."

"But not enough for me to question her alone?"

"You're right in a way. I trust your investigation, but I don't trust the person you're investigating."

"Sarah Rawls?"

"Uh-huh. We've got an abduction of a pregnant woman here, and we need to move forward in a precise manner in the event that this Sarah Rawls might be involved in the case."

"You're right," she said finally. "So how do we go about it? Bring her in here? Go out to where she lives?"

Hank was thoughtful. "I want to wait for the computer readout on her before we decide, so we have more of an idea of what we may be up against. She's probably totally innocent, but if not, there's a lot at stake here."

He came around his desk, hesitated, gave her a silent hug, and then led her to the media room where they communicated with Central Communications for the county. "We'll get a readout within a few minutes and then go from there on how to progress with this Sarah person," he told her, before sending his request for information.

"I understand," she said. As he finished, another office worker came into the room and asked him a question about a phone request. Jessie saw that he would be involved for a few minutes, and after gesturing that she'd be in her office, left the room.

Involved in her paperwork, she didn't hear Hank's approach a few minutes later until he spoke.

"We need to question Sarah Rawls, Jessie," he said from her doorway. "She's past forty, never married, lives on a small inheritance, and is addicted to computer forums. There's no apparent reason for her moving to this island." He stepped into the room. "Except maybe her infatuation with Ben Thrasher."

She'd just finished a report and stood up at his words. "I'll go out to her place and question her right away." She hesitated. "I'll have to get her location."

"I've got it." He held out a printout.

"Good. I'll go now."

"No."

"No? I thought you said—"

He cut her off. "I said she needed to be questioned. But you're not going out there alone, as I said before."

She stared at him but before she could speak he did.

"We'll go together, treat it as a routine check of vehicles since she owns a white Honda."

Within five minutes, after he'd given instructions for Max and the voluntary force who were coping with the media presence at the Thrasher estate, they were headed out to his car.

Their destination: Sarah Rawls.

The moment Sarah opened the door Jessie recognized her as the woman who'd admired Bruce's carvings at the arts and crafts store, and the person who had spoken to her at the outlet mall. That meant she'd not only been on the same ferry, she'd also happened to shop at the same town on the mainland, the same mall and the same store.

Coincidence?

"Well, hello again." Jessie smiled and pretended surprise. "So this is where you live? Nice place and a terrific view."

Sarah nodded, managed to smile back but her expression was puzzled. "How can I help you, Officer Cline?" Her gaze shifted to Hank.

"Chief Shepherd," Hank said, his tone noncommittal but pleasant. "We're making the rounds of the island and since you're on our list, we needed to ask you a few questions. This is just a routine call."

"Goodness, about what? I assure you I haven't broken the law, even if I did wish I could own *more* of your son's art." She paused. "You have an extremely talented son, Chief."

Hank acknowledged the compliment with a nod. "More?"

"Uh-huh. "I bought several of his carvings and have my eye on a couple more." She stepped back to hold the door open wider. "Please come in and I'll show you."

They stepped inside and Sarah closed the door behind them. "Just follow me," she said, as she led them across the tiny entry to a large living area that opened into the

dining area, beyond which a bar separated it from the
modern kitchen.

"Lovely house," Jessie said. "I like the Northwest rustic feeling of cedar walls, high ceilings and all that glass
facing the water."

"Me, too," Sarah agreed, moving slowly toward the
huge stone fireplace, her pregnancy obvious. "I've loved
that combination since I was a child and spent several
summers on this island."

"You lived here as a child?" Hank quickly hid his surprise.

"Not really. My grandparents rented a vacation cabin
and I got to spend a few weeks with them for two summers. But that was enough time for me to fall in love with
the island." Sarah indicated two carvings on the mantel.
"See, as I said, here are the art pieces created by your
son," she told Hank. "They have a place of honor in my
home."

"So I see." He strode across the room for a closer look.
"I hadn't seen these before."

There was a silence.

Abruptly, Sarah faced them. "I'm afraid I'm doing all
the talking and you came here for a reason." She spread
her hands, palms up in a gesture of waiting for them to
begin.

"Like I said, this is routine because you happen to
drive a white car," Hank said, and then went on to
explain that all white vehicles on the island were being
checked out due to two hit-and-run accidents.

"And the culprit drove a white car?"

"Yeah," Jessie told her. "Although it may have been an
SUV."

"How awful." Sarah looked shocked. "And I thought
this island was practically crime free, but then I rarely

"Luckily no," Hank said, watching Sarah closely. "Mrs. Thrasher, although shaken up, was unharmed, as was her unborn baby." He didn't mention Danny, whose incident had already been traced to Bruce's stolen vehicle.

"Mrs. Thrasher? Not Lynda Thrasher who vanished, whose disappearance is all over the newspapers and television?"

"I'm afraid so," Hank replied.

"Oh my dear God!" Sarah's horrified words matched her expression. "And you think the hit-and-run accident is connected to what's happened to her?"

"We don't know that at all," Jessie said. "We were checking white vehicles before Mrs. Thrasher's disappearance."

"The poor woman. Think how she must be feeling, fearful for her baby." Tears welled in Sarah's eyes. "I know how I'd feel in that position. Terrified."

"And your baby's father as well, I would guess." Jessie glanced to the windows that framed the water view, schooling herself to sound casual, and then looked back at Sarah. "I know Mr. Thrasher seems distraught."

"Uh, of course, although I'm estranged from my significant other." Sarah's tone hardened. "He went back to California."

"I've obviously upset you and I'm sorry." Jessie pushed back a strand of hair and tucked it behind her ear. "Have you ever met the Thrashers?"

Sarah shook her head. "But of course I've heard about Ben Thrasher, I think everyone has. He's quite famous."

"Yeah, that's true." Hank stepped forward and ended the conversation. "Would you mind if we had a look at your car."

"Help yourself," she replied, and walked them back

to the front door. "It's parked right outside. I'm sure you saw it when you drove in."

"Thanks," Hank said, nodding. "We appreciate your help."

"No problem."

She watched from the doorway as they looked over the Honda, and then waved as they drove away. Once back on the road Jessie was the first to speak.

"No scratches or dents on the Honda, but then it was Bruce's van that connected with Danny's bike, and Lynda's vehicle wasn't hit at all." She paused. "So what'd you think about Sarah?"

Hank kept his gaze on the road in front of them. "She might be a little odd but she seems sincere enough about not knowing the Thrashers." He glanced at her. "The one thing I did forget to ask was about her work—what she did for a living."

"I know that."

He glanced again. "Did I miss something?"

"No, she told me before that she has her own business and works from home helping her clients with their stock portfolios, the reason she could move to the island." She went on to relate how she'd met Sarah at the outlet mall and their earlier brief conversation. "Remember, that's where I got her car plate numbers—on the ferry."

"Interesting coincidence."

"Uh-huh, that's what I thought."

"Okay, Cline," he said using her last name again. She'd come to realize that he did that when he processed information, when his thoughts moved into professional mode. "We'll keep her on the list and probe a little deeper into her background. On the surface she seems legit."

"Yeah, we need to make sure its not a façade and I know where to start."

"Okay, let me in on it, too."

"The Internet artists forum. I'd like to find out who the real person is behind SarahRawls2. I can retrieve old posts written by this tag, but I believe we'll need a court order to allow the server to give up private information."

"I'll get it authorized."

They continued on into town and he dropped her off at her car, explaining that he wanted to check on progress at the Thrasher estate. "They're still using divers and the volunteers are combing the woods in a broader area."

"And still nothing?"

"So far."

"Have the owners of the private boats in the marina been questioned yet? She could have been taken off the island that way."

"The Feds are doing that, in the event of that possibility and our proximity to Canada."

She nodded.

"You hold down the fort for our regular island calls," he told her through his open window. "I'll keep you updated on our crisis." And then he headed back the way they'd come and she got into her cruiser.

But all during the balance of her shift her thoughts returned again and again to Sarah Rawls. Something about the woman didn't seem right. It was almost as though Sarah had cleverly backgrounded herself before the questions could even be asked. She was either completely innocent or a damn good actress.

The information from the artists forum should tell the tale.

By the time she'd picked up Danny and they'd gone home, fixed supper and cleaned up afterwards, the exhaustion of a long day following a sleepless night was catching up on Jessie. After she'd seen to her e-mail, and knew Danny was asleep for the night, she headed for her own bed.

There'd been no more strange sounds in the walls or beyond doors and she was too tired to stay up, straining her ears, to make sure. Once she'd slipped under the covers and relaxed, her gaze on the changing pattern of a turbulent sky, she was gone, sinking into the welcoming arms of sweet oblivion.

At first the scream sounded far away, but as she slowly awakened, Jessie realized it was Danny, his cries backgrounded by the dog barking.

"Mom! Mom! Help! Come quick!"

Jessie leaped out of bed, grabbed her pistol from the nightstand and ran to his room. She flipped on the light to see Danny cowering in the corner.

"What happened?"

"I saw a dark shape beside my bed." His teeth chattered as he spoke. "I screamed and Footers barked."

First she made sure that no one was there and then she calmed him, realizing that he'd probably had a nightmare. To make him feel better, they went through the house together, she with her pistol, and he with his cell phone. When they reached the kitchen she heated two mugs of water in the microwave for herbal tea. "It'll calm our nerves," she told him with a grin, "and then we'll have a slumber party in my room."

And they did.

CHAPTER FIFTY-FIVE

"Mom, I'm sorry about last night," Danny said the next morning. "I must have dreamt seeing a black shape, and then I scared Footers." He shuddered. "I just don't want to think about it again."

"You don't have to, Danny." She smiled. "Besides, you have other things to think about—like basketball practice today, right?"

He brightened, his thoughts diverted by her comment. "Can you believe that the coach told me that the team was depending on me?"

"Of course. They know how lucky they are that you moved up here from California. You're their secret weapon in reaching tournament status."

"Aw, Mom, you're biased."

She ruffled his hair. "And I'm also right." She stepped back, smiling. "How many times have I lied to you?"

He shrugged. "I can't remember a time."

"So believe me now. Everything happens for a reason and the ultimate outcome will be good. Soon the frightening things that have happened will be a thing of the past. The police chief and I will make sure of that."

He grinned. "I know that. Sorry for being such a jerk."

Danny was laughing as he went to put his dog in the kennel. Jessie closed the door behind them, and then went up to her bedroom to get her briefcase and holster; she'd carried her pistol with her under her clothing where Danny couldn't see it. For all of her encouraging words she was as uncertain as her son, especially when her thoughts flashed on the inexplicable sounds in the walls and behind the basement door. Or the unsettling feeling of an unseen presence in the house.

Going down the front staircase, Jessie made sure the entry door was still bolted before going back to the kitchen. She went through her safety routine: the coffee pot was off, the heat was turned down, and the answering machine was on. All seemed secure.

She went out to her police cruiser, expecting to see Danny. He was nowhere in sight. Retracing her steps, she veered off to the dog kennel, saw that Footers was safely behind the chain-link fence, but there was no Danny.

Her breath caught in her throat. She spun around, her gaze darting everywhere, but she couldn't see her son.

Where was he? It was impossible—but he was gone.

She called his name, and then ran over the grounds, searching for him, and finally headed for the cliff path to the boat house, still calling his name.

There was no answer.

Realizing that he wouldn't hear her above the sound of the waves if he had gone to the beach, she started down, moving as fast as she could.

At the bottom of the cliff she saw that he hadn't come that way; the sand at the base of the steps was untouched from the last tide that had swept it smooth.

She whirled around and started climbing back to the top, breathless when she reached it. Panting, she had to pause to catch her breath. And then she was running again, passing Footers in his kennel on her way to the kitchen entrance. The door was still locked, just as she'd left it.

Danny was nowhere in sight. He'd vanished.

She ran to her car and grabbed her purse, fumbling for her cell phone. She was about to punch in Hank's number when it rang in her hand.

"Jessie?" a woman whispered in her ear.

"Yes?"

"Danny is safe."

"What? Who is this?" She didn't recognize the voice.

"Danny is in danger and he must be kept safe." The words sounded far away.

"Where is my son? What have you done with him?" Jessie's voice was on the edge of hysteria. "Who are you?"

"Never mind that. Danny will speak to you."

There was a brief silence.

"Mom?"

"Danny is that you?"

"Yup, it's me, Hummy."

"Hummy?" Their old code name to use when he was safe? Jessie was stunned. He'd never had to use it back in their California days. But he was now.

"I'm okay, Mom. Do as she says. She won't hurt me."

"Who—who has taken you, Danny? Tell me now."

"Jessie?" The woman's voice was back.

"Let me talk to my son!" Jessie screamed, even as her whole body shook with fear.

"He's safe. Trust me, Jessie. I was your grandmother's friend."

The connection went dead.

Her grandmother's friend? Nita? But the voice didn't sound like the old lady.

Jessie's knees buckled. Someone had taken her son. Just as someone had taken Lynda.

Oh, dear God! What was happening? Why had Danny

used their code name? Was he really safe—even though his abduction spelled danger? She couldn't think straight.

Controlling her terror, she managed to punch in Hank's number, listening to the rings, waiting for him to pick up.

She was hardly able to contain herself. But she had to. Her son's life was at stake.

Hank was on Island Highway headed for town when he got Jessie's call. He listened as Jessie explained and then interrupted.

"Where are you now, Jessie?"

"Standing next to my car in the driveway."

"Get in the house immediately—and stay there until I arrive!" he shouted in her ear. "For God's sake, run like hell. You're a sitting duck out there in the open!"

She broke the connection and ran back into the house. He was right; she wouldn't help Danny by getting shot. Once behind the locked door, she radioed Central Communication on her handheld radio and started to give the information to the dispatcher.

"Chief Shepherd just called in that information, Officer Cline. The ferry system will be alerted and we're ready to put out an Amber Alert for your son if necessary. We're waiting for further instructions. You copy?"

"Affirmative."

A minute later Jessie watched through the window as Hank pulled up behind her cruiser. Pistol in hand, he headed to the door, his gaze darting between the buildings and the woods.

Jessie opened the door as he approached and Hank stepped into the kitchen. She strived for control, to keep her professional persona and not break down.

"It's okay, Jessie," he said, as he holstered his gun. "We'll find him." He pulled her into his arms, holding her against him, trying to calm her, and she knew he was identifying with her and sensing how he'd feel in her place. "I need to hear every detail," he told her softly, and his breath was warm against her cheek. And then he stepped back so he could look into her face. For long seconds he held her gaze before leading her to a kitchen chair. He sat down next to her, still holding her hands. He inclined his head, indicating that she could begin when she was ready.

"I think it started last night, maybe the night before."

He frowned. "Please explain."

"I'll sound paranoid because there are no facts to back up my perceptions—except Danny being gone."

"It's okay, sweetheart," he said softly. "Just do the best you can."

Her lips trembled and he waited until she composed herself. "Night before last I didn't sleep after hearing strange sounds, and I felt so apprehensive that I left the lights on and kept checking the house all night." She gulped a breath. "Then last night Danny woke up screaming that someone was in his room." She lowered her eyes. "I'd gone to sleep because I was so tired from not having slept the night before."

"Not to mention a heavy workday," he added dryly.

She managed a brief smile. "There was no sign of anyone having been in the house. I checked out every nook and cranny. Everything was as I'd left it." She paused. "But I hardly slept for the rest of the night."

He nodded. "Can you go back to the beginning and describe both nights?"

"Yeah, they're imprinted on my brain."

"Go ahead."

There was a silence.

Jessie took deep breaths and then began describing what had happened. "I was stupid, remiss," she said, concluding her narrative. "I didn't credit the seriousness of the situation, and I should have. We've been threatened. Danny was almost run down and I've received ominous letters." She swallowed a sob. "My son is gone and it's my fault."

"No way, Cline," he said, reverting to his professional manner. "Get a grip. You need to stay focused so we can figure this out." He paused. "In the meantime, we need to begin the search.

She nodded, and after relocking the house, followed him out to his police car. Leaving hers parked, they left the house behind. Once on the road, Hank again radioed Central Communications.

"I need Max to search Nita's tugboat—he'll know what I mean. And send someone to the school to question Danny's friends, see if anyone knows anything about why, or who might be involved in his abduction. Officer Cline and I will be following all leads to locations on the island. We'll be in touch."

"Affirmative, Chief Shepherd." A pause. "More outside law enforcement agencies are moving in on the Thrasher case, Chief. Agents from the FBI and state investigators."

"Any new developments?"

"None, Chief."

"Okay, copy that."

And then they searched the island, heard back from Max who'd inspected Nita's tugboat, the volunteers who'd gone to the school, the gym, the home of Danny's friends and anywhere else he might have been. Jessie and Hank trolled the side roads but several hours later the combined result was the same. No one turned up anything, or even a clue to what had happened to Danny.

He was nowhere to be found. Jessie tried not to let the terrible thought sink her for good—that her son was gone forever.

CHAPTER FIFTY-SIX

HANK DROVE HER BACK TO HER HOUSE AT THE END OF THE day. There'd been no news about Lynda Thrasher or Danny. Hank had ordered an Amber Alert, the newest tracking system for abducted children, forwarding all the stats that Jessie had given him about her son.

She checked on the house. Everything seemed as she'd left it: doors locked, her vehicles undisturbed, her answering machine without messages.

But once they were in the kitchen, Hank, gun drawn, ordered her to stay put and then moved through all the rooms in the house. When he returned, his gun holstered, she was trying to control the anxiety that kept her heart fluttering. *Oh God, take them away,* she prayed. *I need to stay strong for my son.*

But nothing could take away reality. Her child was gone. She went to the shelf and took down the old bottle of scotch that she'd used that other night when she'd been upset. Taking two glasses from the shelf, she hesitated, glancing at Hank.

He nodded.

She poured the liquor into both glasses, then handed one to him. He picked up the glass.

She raised hers. "To staying calm, cool and collected," she said, "because I need to get the bastard who took my son."

He raised his glass. And then Hank, his eyes never leaving Jessie's, took a large swallow, acknowledging her toast.

They both put down their glasses and then there was a silence.

"I need to tell you some old history, Hank. Because it might be important to finding my son."

He tilted his head, waiting.

Instead of talking, Jessie refilled their glasses. Then she sat back down and faced him, trying to gather her courage. What she was about to say she'd never intended to reveal.

"As you know, I once knew Ben Thrasher when he was my teacher." She took another gulp. "What you don't know is that I had a brief affair with him."

He met her eyes. "You don't have to tell me this, Cline."

"Yes, I do. I'll tell anything and everything to save my son."

Their gazes locked.

"Okay," he said finally. "Go on. All I can say is that I'll try to understand."

"Thanks, Hank."

"So, continue. I'm listening."

She stared at the liquid in her glass, and then she began.

"I was so naïve back then, and married to a man, another struggling artist, who was immature and unable to support us. I was stressed out, trying to make ends meet with a minimum wage job painting artistic images onto windows to advertise company products, when my mom suggested I take the course from Ben Thrasher, an artist she respected highly. I did, because my mom, worried about me, paid for the course. And when Ben took a special interest in me, told me my artistic talent was awesome, that he was attracted to me as a woman, I thought I was in love with him. Even though he was married, which I didn't know at first, I succumbed to his attention. Later he told me that he was trapped in a bad marriage—and I believed him. And consequently, we had an affair."

"And you became pregnant?"

"As it turned out, I was already pregnant, before my brief encounter with Ben." She hesitated, unable to meet Hank's eyes. "But my husband found out, decided our baby didn't belong to him, and filed for divorce."

"That happens, Jessie," Hank said. "You can't blame yourself."

She lifted her eyes, meeting his. "I didn't, Hank, but the local news did, and then someone posted on the Internet art forum naming me as Ben's other woman who was pregnant with his child." She paused. "For a short time the story was local front page news, because Ben was well known in the community, and it was even mentioned in one of the tabloids. I can't tell you how awful it was."

Hank was silent.

"Danny is not Ben's son, Hank. He's the son of the man I was married to, an immature artist who wanted a way out of responsibilities." She sipped the whiskey. "Ever since I've tried to make things secure for my son, without financial support from his father, and I never wanted Danny to be involved in a controversy involving his birthright. In the final analysis I can prove he belongs to the man I was married to, and not Ben Thrasher."

"Why didn't you put things right back then, Jessie?" Hank asked softly.

"Because I was afraid it meant more tabloid coverage."

"And you couldn't face that?"

She stared him straight in the eyes. "No, I couldn't, because tabloids want a continuation of a sensational story, a way to make the truth sound like another excuse. My only way of stopping that was not to respond, to disappear, until they moved on to the next sensational case."

"I see."

But she wondered if he did, if he could understand how a woman with no means couldn't fight back without financial backing. She'd done the only thing she could: remove herself, and her child, from the situation—and the media.

And now it was back and she couldn't hide.

"Jessie, please, I understand." Hank placed his hand over hers. "Before my wife died of cancer she was obsessed by a fanatical religious cult. Bruce was just a boy but her lasting impression on him resulted in his altered view of the world. I've had regrets ever since."

Another silence passed.

"Thanks, Hank. I appreciate your support."

"I'm just sorry that you may have been struggling alone when you should have had the support of the person who loved you."

She glanced away. "There are worse scenarios, Hank. I always figured I could explain everything to my son after he reached college age. Now, I don't know." She hesitated. "I just pray that the media doesn't pick up on old news now that Danny has disappeared, too."

"I'll try to head that off."

"There's only so much you can do, Hank. But I thank you for that."

A long silence went by and then Hank reached to tilt her chin upwards, so that she had no option but to face him. "Do you think someone out there believes Danny is Ben's son, just as Lynda's baby is Ben's child?"

"Believe me, Hank, I thought of that, crazy as it seems."

"So if we give this possibility credence, that there is someone out there who has been tracking Ben for years, then we might believe that both children, Danny and Lynda's unborn baby, are targets of an unhinged person with a hidden agenda?"

Jessie nodded. "That's occurred to me."

"So that might mean that Ben is not responsible for his wife's disappearance—or Danny's—as the senator, law enforcement and the media are suggesting."

"True."

Another long silence stretched between them.

Finally, Hank stood up. "Get your things together, Jessie. We need to get going."

"Get going? I'm already home."

He nodded. "But you aren't staying here alone tonight."

"But I have to. Danny could come home. And there's Footers."

"Your dog is fine in the kennel. He has food, water and shelter in his doghouse."

"But—"

"You can't stay here," he repeated, interrupting. "Not until we know what's going on. You aren't safe."

"But—" she said again.

"No buts, Jessie. You need to be here to find Danny. Danny would never want to be the bait to get you."

"Oh my God, Hank. Do you know what you're say-ing?"

He shook his head. "I'm only guessing at this point. But until we know you aren't staying."

"I have nowhere else to go."

"Yes, you do."

"Where?"

"My place."

And then he led her out to the cars, she got into hers and he got into his. Hank led the way, and as she followed she knew he was right. She needed to be around to find her son.

And that meant staying alive. Her guess was right. Someone was out to get her. She just hoped that person had not already gotten her son.

CHAPTER FIFTY-SEVEN

"THANKS, HANK," JESSIE SAID AS HE SHOWED HER INTO HIS bedroom after they'd arrived at his place. "But I'll be fine on the sofa."

"No way. My apartment isn't Wind House but my cleaning lady changes the sheets once a week and they're clean and crisp today."

"But Hank, I'm the guest here. And I'm not used to special treatment, Wind House or not."

"Hey, I'm gonna be insulted if you don't take the bedroom. I know a bachelor's pad isn't all that great but I want you to have a good sleep, if you can."

She hesitated, fighting tears. "I'll never sleep, Hank. My son is missing."

He was suddenly close, folding her in his arms. "Jessie, Jessie," he crooned into her ear. "You must, so you can fight the battle tomorrow. Your son needs you to be strong."

She subsided against his chest, momentarily taking strength from his presence. Finally she raised her head and looked up at him. His eyes were hooded, but intense.

"Alright, and thanks, Hank."

His nod was slow, but decisive. And then he pulled her closer, lowering his face so that his lips claimed hers, kissing her in a way she'd never experienced before, as though she belonged to him and he to her.

She wanted to resist and somehow she couldn't, until he suddenly released her, holding her at arm's length, gazing into her eyes.

"You need to sleep, sweetheart."

"But—"

His smile was tender. "Shhh, now is not the time for us. We'll talk tomorrow, or sometime soon. After we're past all of the current fears. In the meantime, you need to sleep." He went to a chest of drawers, opened one and pulled out a T-shirt and tossed it to her. "A nightshirt," he said, grinning. "And there's toothpaste, towels and wash-cloths in the bathroom."

And then he left her alone, leaving Jessie with a lingering thought.

He'd wanted to stay.

It only took until noon the next day before the press made the connection between Lynda's disappearance and Danny having vanished from his own yard. By then Hank had received confirmation of the name behind the SarahRawls2 tag on the Internet artists forum. It *was* Sarah Rawls who resided on Cliff Island.

"She was involved with Ben, maybe still is," Jessie said, staring back at Hank who'd just come to her office and given her the news. She jumped up. "She has Danny."

"We don't know that, Jessie. She may be a victim of Ben Thrasher, too." He spread his hands, as though in a plea for her to be patient, until they had the facts. "In any case, we need to proceed with caution. If she has Lynda and Danny we can't let her know we're on to her or she—"

"She could harm them," Jessie said, finishing his statement, fear tying her stomach into a knot.

"Yeah, Cline. We have to be practical here, and not rush in and tip our hand." He hesitated. "We want our hostages back alive and well."

"Tip our hand? Are you a poker player, Chief?"

His gaze was level, penetrating. "Only when I have to be, Cline."

"Like now?

"Uh-huh. I understand your need to arrest her, make her talk." A pause. "But what if she didn't?—and we couldn't hold her. She'd be free to go—and cover up her tracks. We need to develop probable cause into enough evidence so we can get a search warrant as quickly as possible."

Jessie took in a deep shuddering breath. She managed a nod, knowing he was right. Everything that could be was being done to find Danny. Dear Father, she prayed, let me stay strong. I mustn't panic, for Danny's sake.

But her mind lingered on Sarah Rawls. Why would a pregnant woman hurt another pregnant woman? It didn't make sense. But Jessie knew, sense or not, she couldn't just sit back and wait for things to get better. Danny was her priority and she had to find him. After that she'd decide whether or not they could stay on the island.

Nita was the connection—and maybe the old woman had Danny. Jessie needed to get her to tell what she knew. But first she had to find her. Max had checked the tugboat out several times since his first search, and reported back that it didn't look like Nita had been there since Danny's disappearance.

"You're in no shape to resume your duties, Jessie,"

Hank said, bringing her thoughts back to their conversation. "I want you somewhere safe and that means my apartment. You aren't going home unless someone goes with you." He'd grabbed his jacket as he'd spoken. "I can't do that right now as we have another mess out at the Thrasher estate. The county sheriff's office issued a search warrant and they're searching Ben's house right now."

"What's happened now?"

"I guess you have to hear this, Jessie. The media is on another feeding frenzy since Danny's disappearance and his alleged connection to Ben Thrasher hit the wire service. We're just lucky that we're on an island and have a time lag before they get here on the ferry."

"Oh, shit!" She jumped up. "Say it hasn't been on television, Hank."

"I can't say that, Jessie, because I don't know."

"I have to call my mother, before she hears what's happened to Danny on TV." She wiped a hand over her forehead. "Why didn't I know that this could happen? Why was I so stupid?"

"Hey, call your mom. You aren't stupid, just a frightened mom yourself."

She nodded. "But I need to stay on the job. I can't just hang out somewhere and wait to hear what's happening." She gulped a breath. "I have to keep trying to find him."

He shook his head. "God, I'm sorry to tell you this, but Rose has been fielding calls with questions about you since she came to work this morning." He hesitated. "It'll be best all the way around that you stay out of sight—for your safety and to avoid a media crunch here at the station."

"They know about my old scandal?"

"I'm afraid so." He pursed his lips, as though considering his answer. "It seems that the good senator, the one Ben was so ruthlessly trashing, is the person who paid a private investigator to dredge up Ben's past indiscretions, and the guy came up with you. He's even insinuated that you'd moved to this island to be close to the father of your son, that Ben might be behind Lynda's disappearance."

"That bastard!"

"My thought completely. Evidently the senator is going balls out to destroy Ben after this opportunity fell into his lap. He suggested to the media that the crab traps needed to be inspected."

"That's already been done."

Hank nodded. "But since other law enforcement agencies are involved now, they pulled the traps out of the water completely this morning. A forensic team will examine them for whatever trace evidence might have been left behind. Strangely, the door on one of the cages was open."

"But that could have happened accidentally when the traps were examined before."

"Yeah, could have. But they're under pressure to make sure."

"So I've become a part of the problem?"

"God, no, Jessie. It's only that we need to do what's expedient until things settle down."

She lowered her lashes so that he couldn't see her feelings in her eyes. She realized that she had to leave the police station, that she needed to be off the case, but she wasn't about to sit in Hank's apartment, wringing her hands, waiting for someone to do things for her.

As always, no one could protect her son better than she could.

"Okay, Chief." She met his eyes, her emotions under control. "What is it you want me to do?"

He handed her a key. "It's to my apartment. I want you to stay there for now."

"So the reporters can't find me?"

"Son of a bitch, Jessie. You know better than that. I don't want you disappearing next."

She managed a smile. "Thanks Hank." She went to him and took the key. "I'll be there if you need me, okay?"

He peered into her face, as though he were trying to decide if she was sincere. Finally he grinned. "I'll check on you every couple of hours, keep you updated." A pause. "You can call your mom from my place."

"Thanks, Hank. I'll pay you for the charges."

She grabbed her things and they went out of the station together, he to his car and she to hers. Jessie followed him out of the lot and he turned to the right, the street that led to Island Highway and north to the Thrasher estate, while she went left in the direction of his apartment. Once he was out of sight, Jessie braked, and then made a U-turn and headed toward her own place. She needed to check on Footers, her voice mail and the security of her house. She was a trained policewoman and could protect herself. She'd call her mom from her own phone, if the reporters hadn't found out where she lived.

Besides, the trail that led to her son started there, and she meant to follow it—police rules be damned.

The phone was ringing as she went into the house. She ran to grab it from the kitchen counter.

"Hello?"

"Jessie, thank God!"

"Mom, is that you?"

"Yes, it's me. Where have you been? I've been trying

to get a hold of you since last night. I've been worried sick. I couldn't even get through to your police station." Her words came in a rush, the sentences running into each other in her upset. "Have you found Danny?"

"You heard." Jessie's voice wobbled but she managed to keep from crying. "I'm sorry, Mom. I was just going to call you."

"I heard it on the national news." Clarice sounded devastated. "Have you found Danny yet?" she repeated.

"No. But I'm—"

"That son of a bitching bastard Ben. First his wife is missing, then Danny. I can't tell you how much I regret influencing you to take his art class way back then," Clarice said.

"That's in the past, Mom. I have to stick with the current facts and not go off on a tangent." She drew in a shaky breath. "There is one thread that I'm hanging onto that maybe Danny is okay, as the woman on the phone said."

"Woman? Phone? What are you talking about, Jessie?"

She explained the call after Danny disappeared.

"So this woman said Danny was safe, that she was a friend of your grandmother's?"

"Yeah, that's what she said. And then Danny got on the phone, using his nickname, Hummy."

"Which should mean that he's telling you he's safe?"

"Maybe. I'm not sure."

A long silence went by.

"Mom, are you still there?"

"Uh-huh." Another pause. "It's Nita."

"What?"

"Nita, who was your grandmother's friend. She is also a shirttail relative to your father's family. And Danny

is the last male descendant to their once powerful clan."
A hesitation. "If she believed him to be jeopardy she is
fully capable of abducting him to a safe place."

"What are you saying, mother?"

"Only that what you've said has given me hope. I
can't even begin to guess what's going on in Ben
Thrasher's life, but I can in your and Danny's situation."
A loudspeaker voice suddenly overpowered Clarice's
words. When it was over, Jessie was the first to speak.

"My God! What was that? It sounded like you're in an
airport."

"I am, in the San Francisco airport. I have to go
because my flight is boarding."

"To where?"

"Seattle."

"But—"

"But nothing. I'll arrive in time to rent a car and make
the last ferry to the island."

"Oh, I'll meet the ferry."

"No way. Believe me, I know the route to Wind
House. I'll see you ten minutes after docking." Clarice's
voice had gained volume. "In the meantime, don't do
anything foolish, Jessie."

"Like what?"

"Like facing Ben's demons. His plight might not
include you, whatever the media have to say otherwise."

Then, after a quick "I love you," Clarice disconnected.

Jessie sat back in the quiet room, digesting her
mother's words. And then she noticed the flashing red
light on her phone: she had messages.

She punched the button, and a long series of beeps
from hang-ups filled the room. But then a woman's voice
came on, bringing Jessie forward on her chair.

"Hummy is safe. Trust me. He will not be harmed."

Then there was a beep and another series of hang-up calls, probably from media reporters. But somehow, after her conversation with her mother, and the use of her son's nickname, one he would never have given to anyone he didn't trust, her hope for her son's safety soared. Maybe he was safe as the female voice said. Nita?

She didn't know. But she had been forming a plan. She was basically off the case. That meant she must act on her own. And she meant to do just that. Lynda was still out there. She needed help.

CHAPTER FIFTY-EIGHT

JESSIE TOOK HER MOM'S SUITCASE AND COAT, SO GLAD SHE'D arrived that she didn't dare voice her relief for fear that she'd break into sobs, a thing she'd managed to control until seeing her mother.

She'd watched for the car headlights in the driveway, having timed the ferry arrival with the minutes it took to drive to Wind House. Once the car had come up the lane, and she'd determined it wasn't yet another reporter about to knock on her door with demands of a statement, she'd flown out to her mother. They'd hugged until they were both in tears, and then Jessie had led Clarice into the kitchen where Footers awaited them.

Clarice dropped her purse next to her suitcase and then faced Jessie, her question suddenly direct. "Any word?"

Jessie shook her head. "Just another message on my answering machine."

"Did you save it?"

"Yeah." Jessie moved to the phone and punched in the replay. "Here are all the messages, Mom. I've saved them."

And then the messages spilled out into the quiet room, the woman's and Danny's. The most recent one of only a few hours ago when no one was in the house said:

"I'm safe, Mom. I'll be home soon and explain everything. Nita is protecting me. She's our friend." And then there was the dial tone.

There was a silence, and then Clarice broke it.

"Nita is making sure that no one can zero in on her location, Jessie, and that's why they hang up so fast."

"Are you sticking up for her?"

"I guess so."

"Please explain, Mom."

Clarice took hold of Jessie's hands, looking straight into her eyes. "Nita has stepped in before, Jessie, when events had gone from upsetting to life-threatening." A pause. "She did that for me when I needed to protect you."

"You'll need to explain, Mom," Jessie said again.

"I know, and I will, as best I can." She hesitated, gathering her thoughts. "Please bear with me, Jessie, and I'll pray you won't judge me for removing you from your birthright."

"Wind House?"

She nodded. After another long pause she began to explain. "Nita once helped me, and you, Jessie, after your dad drowned—under suspicious circumstances." Again Clarice hesitated. "She helped me leave the island with you, Jessie, because we both knew you and I were in danger. Your father was the heir to this house and the family heritage. His cousin, the son of the uncle who left you this house, had taken your dad fishing. Your dad only went because he thought it was a chance to repair the rift in the family. He was wrong. Your dad didn't come back and his cousin claimed that he'd gone overboard in a sudden squall and hadn't come up."

"Are you saying he was murdered?"

Clarice looked away. "There was never any proof of foul play, but I knew that your father going overboard was not accidental. But I couldn't prove it. And that meant your grandmother's nephew, the son of her brother, would inherit the house and property in accordance with family tradition."

"And you felt we were in danger?" Jessie asked.

"Yeah, I knew we were because I was too vocal with my questions of what had happened. I soon felt that I could lose a lot more: my own life, and yours."

"So you fled."

Clarice got up and poured herself more hot water for her tea. "That's right. I wasn't as fearful for myself as I was for you, Jessie. I wasn't your father's child, you were, and I knew your great-uncle and his son feared that your grandmother could change the will despite family tradition."

"So you fled."

Clarice lifted her gaze, meeting her daughter's. "I did. You were more important to me than any amount of worth in the world. I only wanted you to grow up and to be safe."

"And now I'm not."

A long silence went by.

"Maybe not," Clarice said finally. "Your father's cousin, and then his uncle, both died, and then you were in line to inherit again. I can't tell you how horrified I was when I heard the news. I never wanted you on Cliff Island again, and then you were going, taking my grandson with you."

Jessie got up from her place across the table and moved to enfold her mother in her arms. "I'm so sorry, Mom. You sacrificed so much for me, and I understand your feelings—now that I have Danny, whom I'd do the same to protect." She patted her mom's shoulders. "I love you, Mom. I understand your decisions for me. I just hope I can live up to your expectations."

"You already have, Jessie."

"But my boy is missing, and I'm not there to protect him."

"But Nita is, just as she did those years ago for me."

"Mom, Nita is perceived as being odd, if not outright crazy."

"Believe me, Jessie, Nita is not a modern woman, she marches to her own drummer, but she's not crazy. She knows exactly what she's doing, according to the old ways."

"Old ways?"

"Uh-huh. Your heritage."

"And that means protecting Danny?"

"That's what I think she's doing, although I don't know why." Clarice frowned, considering. "There's more to this problem that is still obscure, but maybe not to Nita. Nita knows everything that happens to her family. She must have feared for Danny's life. I'd bet my own life on that."

"So she took him from his home to protect his life?"

"That's my guess."

"You think the same person who abducted Lynda didn't take Danny?"

"I believe Nita may have prevented that. I think there's more to this whole situation than we realize, except that it all revolves around Ben Thrasher." A pause. "He's evil."

"So, you think Danny and I are still in danger?"

"I have no way of knowing, Jessie. But from an outside perspective, I would think that's possible."

Jessie had no response, but her thoughts whirled with all of the evidence that she knew. When her mind slowed and she considered her mother's opinion, she had to agree. She could be in danger. She just hoped Danny was safe with Nita, as her mother had suggested. If not, he was in terrible jeopardy. She was glad her mom was there for support. But she needed to stay focused.

She couldn't drop the ball. Danny's life was at stake. And so was Lynda's—and her unborn baby.

Jessie knew what she had to do. And she'd do it at first light—before it was too late.

CHAPTER FIFTY-NINE

HER MOTHER KNEW THE HOUSE AND JESSIE LET HER PICK which guestroom she wanted. Clarice chose the one across the hall from Jessie's, where the windows looked out upon the front driveway and the totem of Tsonoqua that was illuminated by Jessie's newly installed exterior lights.

Clarice stood at the windows, momentarily silent. "Once that totem terrified me," she said, finally. "I think I was so frightened after your father's death that I actually believed the mythical spirit depicted on that cedar pole had the power to control the wind, to steal my child."

For long seconds Jessie resisted an impulse to admit that she'd had those very feelings since living in Wind House. Then, tears welling in her eyes, she strode across the room and hugged her mother. "Thanks for coming. I can't tell you how much it means to have you here." A pause. "I'm so sorry you heard about what happened on the news and not from me, Mom."

"I understand, Jessie. You were trying to protect me, and didn't realize how fast the case would go national."

"Yeah, but I should have known. I underestimated Ben's position as a national celebrity, that what happens to him makes the network news, not to mention the cables."

It was after midnight and Jessie saw the fatigue on her mother's face. She quickly checked the guest room's connecting bathroom for fresh towels, soap and toothpaste and then turned to go. After kissing her mom goodnight, Jessie left her to unpack and get ready for bed. "See you in the morning," she said softly and then closed the door behind her.

Jessie did her nightly survey of the house and locks, and then headed for her room with Footers, where she hoped to catch a few hours sleep before she headed out at dawn. She was jittery, unsettled and frustrated that she had nowhere else to look for Danny. She'd just climbed into bed, praying that her mind could accept her mother's story about Nita's credibility so she could sleep, when her cell phone rang on her nightstand. She grabbed it.

"Jessie?"

"Yeah, it's me, Hank. What's up?"

"As I told you when I believed you were going to my apartment, I'd check on you every few hours." A pause. "So how are you doing?"

"Okay." She gathered her thoughts. He'd realized soon after they'd left the station early in the afternoon that she'd gone home. At first he'd sounded angry, but she'd explained that she had to make sure their dog was okay, check her answering machine for messages and talk to her mother. She'd also explained that her mother was already on her way to the island and she needed to be there when her mom arrived. He'd finally accepted her reasons for changing their plans.

"Have you heard anything more from Danny?"

"Just the last message I told you about, that he claimed to be fine, that he was with Nita."

"We haven't been able to locate Nita," he said. "I don't know what to make of her presence in all of this."

She hesitated, considering what to tell him. Then she decided to come clean with everything she knew and explained her conversation with her mother, that Clarice believed that Nita was protecting Danny before he became a victim like Lynda.

"That's a strange theory, Jessie. I hope it's true but we can't let down our guard." He hesitated. "Old Nita is eccentric to say the least, and Danny is also connected to Ben Thrasher, at least as far as the media believes. So I suppose it's possible that she interjected herself into the mystery for reasons known only to her that have to do with her own Native American family history."

"I know. That's my hope at this point. At least Danny might be okay if that were the case."

A long silence went by.

"I've questioned everyone involved with Ben's household: the maids, cook and the gardener."

"And what did they know? Anything?"

"Nothing. They said Lynda usually took a short daily walk around the grounds but no one was there to see her go. They all assume that she did."

"Poor woman. I pray she's okay."

"Yeah, we're all praying for that, Jessie. A $25,000 reward fund has been set up for Lynda's safe return."

"And the searchers and dogs haven't found anything?"

"Not yet, and the search has been expanded to other places on the island, including Deep Lake, an abandoned warehouse and the wetlands on the southwest corner where a creek empties into the strait."

"Dear God, poor Lynda. She must be scared to death because no one has found her." She paused. "Has anyone checked out Sarah Rawls' house, made sure Lynda isn't there?"

"We don't think she's there. It's too obvious. But we're watching Sarah's place, waiting for a break. We don't have any proof that this woman is involved, even if she knew Ben from the Internet."

"Get real, Hank. The woman is involved. We just don't know how deeply she's into this situation." She gulped a breath. "My gut says she into it up to her ears."

His sucked in breath came over the airwaves. "Jessie?"

"Yes?"

"Just promise me that you'll go slow. Don't take this into your own hands and rush into the lion's den."

"Are you suggesting that Sarah's place is the lion's den?"

"I'm saying I don't know. I just don't want you to rush into a trap."

"I won't do that."

"Promise?"

She hesitated. "I promise." She wasn't lying. The trap she was planning to set was of her own making. And she wasn't about to be the one caught. Nor could she stand back and wait for what was to happen. That could result in deaths: Lynda's, her unborn baby—and, God forbid, Danny.

The whole ugly mess needed to be stopped now, while it was still possible.

Jessie only catnapped until shortly before dawn. Silently, aware that her mother probably wasn't sleeping well either, she slipped into black sweats and a hooded jacket. Carrying her running shoes with her, she tiptoed downstairs to the kitchen, a silent Footers padding behind her. She left the note she'd written in the night on the kitchen table, telling her mother that she'd been called to work and would call later. Then she went out into the misty stillness of the predawn.

"Sorry, Footers, but you have to go into the kennel until I get back." She kissed the top of his nose, then sent him inside and closed the pen. "I can't have you giving a bark at the wrong moment."

And then she headed for her Saturn which she'd removed from the garage before her mother's arrival, anticipating her need to stay silent when she drove off. She unlocked and opened the driver's side and slid onto the seat. Starting the engine, Jessie didn't close the door or accelerate until she was well down the driveway where the sound wouldn't awaken her mom. She hoped that her mission would be finished before her mother woke up.

Once on the main road, Jessie headed for the southwest side of the island, directly opposite the Thrasher estate where searchers had concentrated most of their work. She wanted to observe her suspect without any fanfare, so that the person believed she was safe. Jessie would play her subsequent course of action by ear once she was on site. Her suspect's action would motivate hers.

There was no traffic and she drove along without meeting any cars, for which she was grateful. Almost to the turnoff, she slowed and pulled into a dirt lane that ended in the woods, exactly where she wanted to park her car out of sight of the road. Getting out, she adjusted her sweatshirt hood over her hair, made sure her pistol was on her hip under her jacket and her cell phone in her pocket. Then she started out, picking her way through the woods to the next driveway, which she followed to the house. One light was on in the kitchen. Jessie smiled wryly. Her subject was afraid of the dark, even as the person terrorized the innocents.

And then Jessie struck it lucky.

She saw movement in the kitchen, then the back door

opened and a dark shape stepped outside. Jessie crept closer, not wanting to lose the person in the darkness among the trees. The figure, dressed in black as Jessie was, darted into the woods. It was hard to see if it was a man or a woman.

Jessie moved forward, following. But before she felt secure enough to leave the shelter of the trees and underbrush, another figure separated from the shadows to follow the first one.

Jessie dropped back, breathing hard. She'd almost blown her cover. "Thank you, God," she whispered under her breath. "You just saved me."

She kept the second figure in sight, knowing that person was tracking the same one Jessie had targeted. She wondered what was going on. It was a twist. Was it Hank?—following the same leads she'd developed?

No, she told herself. The dark shape, obviously a man, was not quite as tall as Hank. It was someone else.

She continued to follow, careful of where she placed her feet so that she didn't make a sound, secure that she'd programmed her phone to call Hank with one key punch.

And then she could see a clearing up ahead, and the person from the house headed for the door of a tiny cabin, opened it and disappeared inside. She quickly ducked behind a bush, knowing someone in front of her was probably doing the same. And then she waited, watchful.

Several minutes passed.

And then the person ahead of her separated from the shadows and moved forward.

Jessie waited, watching for what would happen next. The shape, also in black, moved to the door of the cabin, stopped as though listening to what was going on inside the place. Abruptly, the person opened the door, stepped inside and disappeared into whatever was happening behind the walls of the cabin.

And then there was silence. Jessie hesitated, wondering what she should do next, knowing that a police officer should call for backup—if she was in jeopardy.

But was this really a backup situation?

Especially if this was not what she thought and only an assignation between a man and a woman who wanted to be isolated from the eyes of propriety.

Her decision was instant. She pulled out her cell phone and called Hank. He wasn't there but she left her message, just in case.

"I went to Sarah Rawls' place, and then followed someone, maybe Sarah, although it didn't look like a pregnant woman, into the woods for approximately a quarter mile." And then she gave the time. "Someone else was hiding in the woods, and thank God I saw him before he saw me. I'm going in Hank, as soon as I see what's happening. They're both in this cabin right now." She paused. "I have my pistol but I need backup. This could be the bottom line to our investigation.

"Signing off now. You know where I am. I hope you check messages within minutes as I do. Hank, I'm counting on the fact that you do."

And then she left her protection of foliage and moved forward to the cabin, and it's only window. She had a ringside view of what was happening inside.

Her first look inside took the strength from her legs and her knees buckled. Lynda was there. And she appeared terrified.

Jessie sank back, fearful of being seen. It was a crisis. Lynda was about to die.

CHAPTER SIXTY

JESSIE SLIPPED BACK INTO THE DARKNESS, AWAY FROM THE cabin to the shelter of the trees. Then she called Hank again on her cell phone, and left another message about what she'd seen, wishing she had her police radio. But an incoming call could have given her away, so she'd left it in her car.

"I have to act, Hank. I can't identify the two people in black because they were out of my line of vision, but the situation isn't good. Something is about to happen. I need backup, now!"

She returned the phone to her pocket and inched back to the cabin, careful to stay in the shadows. Once under the window again, Jessie peeked, seeing that Lynda was still tied up on the cot in the corner, her mouth gagged and her eyes darting wildly. About to pull her pistol, it was suddenly yanked out of its holster by someone who'd come up behind her.

"You're a problem that never seems to go away, aren't you, Jessie?"

She recognized Ben's voice, even though he spoke in a harsh whisper. "So you did remember me, Ben," she said, facing him.

"How could I have forgotten, bitch? Let's say our last meeting, although years ago, was memorable, every detail noted in the media—like now." He twisted Jessie's arm, forcing her to the door and inside the cabin. She was aware of the gun in her back.

The one low-watt light bulb hanging from the ceiling did little to illuminate the shadowy corners of the tiny room. But she could see the hopelessness in Lynda's eyes.

Jessie tried to twist free and his grip tightened painfully. "Your wife needs help, Ben. Let me take care of her."

"Leave her alone, bitch." He gave her a push that landed her on the floor next to Lynda's cot.

Slowly, she got to her feet. "What about the baby?"

She met his eyes, and recognized his utter insensitivity for what it was. He was a cold and calculating sociopath who would manipulate the situation to his own benefit. The bottom seemed to drop out of her stomach. A glance told her that whatever had brought them all to this moment, Ben Thrasher meant to be the only survivor. Sarah Rawls, who'd hung back in the corner, suddenly sprang forward, unaware that she, too, had become extra baggage.

"I want the baby, Ben." Sarah's voice sounded manic. "Your child belongs to me!"

"You doomed the baby along with its mother when you took Lynda."

"What are you saying? Everyone thinks I'm pregnant. I've been planning for this baby for several months. No one will know that it's not mine."

"I'll know, you dumb piece of shit." He scowled at her. "It's not gonna happen. You're outta luck, in more ways than you realize. You should have known better than to try to trap me."

"What do you mean?" She moved toward him. "I love you, Ben. I've been there for you for years. I knew who

Jessie was when she first set foot on the island." She jabbed a finger in Jessie's direction. "I knew she'd come because you were here. I'd researched her background, knew her son belonged to you."

"That's bullshit!" Jessie said. "Danny is the son of my ex-husband."

"That's not what the newspapers said!" Sarah turned on her. "I was making sure that my baby was Ben's only child." She stepped closer. "I'll see to it that your precious son follows you after you die, pig! You and he can be together in hell."

Jessie stared at the woman, unable to credit such malevolence. "In any case, SarahRawls2, you aren't expecting a baby, Lynda is. Lynda's baby belongs to Lynda, got that?"

"She moved closer. "So you checked the forum."

"Uh-huh. I know a lot about you, Sarah. It would behoove you to let Lynda go."

"Is that a threat?"

"It's a fact."

"No, you bitch, it's not." Sarah lunged forward, her hand ready to hit Jessie, when Ben took two steps and hit Sarah with the butt of Jessie's gun, knocking her to the floor.

"Oh my God!" Jessie stooped to help Sarah, who lay stunned. "You've hurt her bad. Her jaw might be broken."

"Get away from her, Jessie, or you're next."

She stood, facing him. "You need to take your wife home, Ben. She's gone through more than any woman in her condition should."

His laugh was harsh. "No one is going home tonight, Jessie. I'm wiping my slate clean, starting over."

"What does that mean?"

"You aren't stupid, Jessie. Figure it out."

She stared at him, unbelieving that he could be so inhumane. Although she controlled her reaction, she knew exactly what he meant. He intended them all to die, including his unborn child, in a way he orchestrated so that he would be blameless.

"What about the media, Ben. Aren't they camped out at your place. Didn't they see you leave?"

"On the contrary, Jessie."

"How is that possible?"

His dark eyes glinted in the light from the bulb. "Because I left by a back door, headed into the woods for a half mile, and then went down a path to the beach where I'd hidden a motor boat." His grin was more like a grimace. "I came by boat and that's how I'll get back. The house staff will all swear I was working late in my study where they never disturb me. A perfect alibi."

"An alibi for what, Ben?" she asked, innocently, because she wanted the other women to hear.

"For the demise of all of you." He grinned. "Don't you know, Jessie, that you came upon Sarah, who had a fixation on a famous person, me, and this Sarah, who is psychotic, pretended to be pregnant so that she could have Lynda's baby, after which she intended to kill Lynda and keep the child. But you intervened and were overpowered, hence Sarah pushed the pregnant Lynda off the cliff, both you and Sarah went over, too, still struggling against each other to survive?" His grin broadened and Jessie realized how disturbed he was, how mentally ill, but how motivated he was to survive at any cost—the lives of three women and his own child.

"Help her up." He pointed with the gun, indicating that Jessie get Sarah to her feet. "And then cut Lynda loose so she can stand as well."

Jessie kept her eyes lowered, doing as he said, grateful he hadn't realized that she'd called for backup with her cell phone—that she even had a cell phone on her. He'd been focused on her gun.

Please, Hank, check messages. If you don't we'll all be dead, she prayed silently.

They stood in a row, Sarah still reeling from her blow to the face, Lynda crying under her gag and unsteady on her feet, and Jessie who pretended weakness although she was mentally calculating her chances of rushing the bastard.

He ushered them outside and then turned on a flashlight so that they could follow the path to the cliff. As high as her house was on the other end of the island, the cliffs on the southwest side were even more sheer and higher.

He means to have us fall, just as he'd said, she realized again. And then he would take the boat back to his hidden moorage, climb up a path to the woods, and get back into the house and have the best alibi in history.

It's up to me, Jessie thought. Hank knew where Sarah lived but he might never find the cabin in the woods, until it was too late.

Ben marched them forward along a path. As they walked, Jessie tried to formulate a plan to save them. But Ben had placed her between the other woman, both of whom were hurt or inhibited by their physical state. Abruptly, the woods opened into a clearing, beyond which she could see the strait several hundred feet below.

Oh my God, Jessie thought. I have to do something. But she knew that the other two didn't have a chance if she was shot, and by her own gun. The three women would go over the cliff along with the pistol. And Ben would never be a suspect.

She mulled her options, and knew she had to make a move even if she was shot. She just needed to gauge the best time to act.

They all paused in the small clearing. Then Ben stepped forward, the gun level and pointed at Jessie. But no one expected the sudden move by Sarah who rushed forward, begging Ben to reconsider, that she'd sacrificed everything for him, that—and then the shot rang out and Sarah staggered backward, grabbing at Lynda who ducked to avoid her. Sarah teetered on the edge of the precipice, then fell and disappeared. Her scream followed her to the bottom.

The sudden silence seemed deafening.

Jessie put her arm around the still gagged Lynda, feeling her trembling, knowing she was terrified. Her husband, the man she loved, was about to kill her and her baby, so that he could continue his career and not be exposed, so that he would come up the innocent, not the perpetrator. Lynda was replaceable in his mind; he wasn't.

He didn't want the world to know that he'd been involved with Sarah Rawls who wouldn't let go, who had been willing to kill Ben's wife for her baby.

He raised the gun again and when the shot rang out Jessie thought Lynda must have been hit because *she* wasn't. It was Ben who fell.

And then Hank burst out of the woods, his pistol ready to fire again. Behind him was . . . Nita.

Everything seemed to happen at once after that. Backup units were on the scene minutes behind Hank, officers from the county sheriff's office. Then Lynda was placed on a stretcher, as was Ben who was only wounded, and they were taken away separately by ambulance. A yellow crime scene ribbon was strung around the clearing.

Hank was at her side the whole way back to his car. She noticed the crime scene tape around the cabin as they passed it, but felt so shaky that she didn't want to ask any questions . . . yet.

"You're safe, Jessie," Hank whispered. "I got your messages and then Nita appeared to show me the way to the cabin. It was Nita who saved you and Lynda."

She nodded against his chest. He would tell her everything . . . later.

Over the next several days the island subsided into a normal routine, the last of the national media people and their vehicles having taken the ferry to the mainland. Sarah had been found on the rocks below the cliff and pronounced dead on the spot. Ben, who'd been shot in the right shoulder, was still recovering under police guard at Harborview Hospital in Seattle. Lynda had been released to her relatives, and although she was still at her home on the island, Jessie knew she'd soon be headed back to California where she intended to have her baby.

Jessie had gone to the Thrasher house at Lynda's request and they'd talked, Jessie about her past with Ben and Lynda about her marriage to a man she'd begun to distrust long before the threats began.

"Yes, I was in a bad marriage," Jessie admitted. "And I did have a brief encounter with Ben who was my art teacher, but my son is not Ben's son. He is the biological offspring of the man I was married to at the time," Jessie told her. She didn't add that a DNA test was in progress to confirm that once and for all.

"So this Sarah was wrong about that. She'd bought the tabloid speculation." Lynda shook her head. "In a way I'm sorry, Jessie. I would have liked our children to be related."

And then the two women cried together.

They parted with a promise to stay in touch. Jessie went home to Danny and her mother, who both sang the praises of Nita. Tonight Nita would also join them for supper and fill in all the gaps, from the past and from the current threat.

Jessie had asked Hank to join them.

The old woman seemed awkward in their group, unused to dinner parties, even though Clarice and Jessie had kept it simple, setting the kitchen table, not placing them in the formal dining room. Hank arrived dressed casually in jeans and a blue turtleneck sweater, as Jessie had advised, because the supper was designed to be low key for Nita's sake.

"Hey," he said, coming into the house. "Good to see you, Danny." He gave Danny a loose hug, then acknowledged Clarice, whom he'd already gotten to know over the past few days, then turned to Nita, an old woman who was dressed in loose pants and parka, whose dark eyes in her wrinkled face were alert and penetrating. "And you, too, Nita. You not only saved your family, you saved the credibility of our island law enforcement."

The old woman nodded, her whole countenance serious, accepting the compliment—because she knew it to be true. But Jessie sensed that she was pleased, that she approved of Hank.

Clarice moved next to Nita and dropped her arm around the slender shoulders. "Nita has been saving this family for many years. She's the reason that I'm still here, that Jessie and Danny live in this house now, after all that happened in the past." She stooped to kiss the old woman's cheek. "Thank you, Nita. We're all here because of you and your dedication to our family and the old ways of honesty and loyalty."

"We'll have a toast," Jessie said, and poured a splash of wine into all their glasses.

"I don't drink spirits," Nita said.

"And I've never had alcohol," Danny piped up.

"It's a special occasion. A sip won't hurt you, Danny," Jessie told him.

"What's the toast? Hank asked.

"Nita." Jessie said. "Without Nita we wouldn't all be here now."

They ate in silence, with only small talk. Finally Clarice cleared their plates, smiled and said dessert would be served after the coffee was made.

And then Nita looked up, glanced at each one, and began to talk.

"I know you're all waiting to hear what happened, why I took Danny."

Each one acknowledged her statement.

She pushed back her chair so she had a better view of everyone. "I knew Sarah Rawls had been watching the Thrasher place since she arrived on the island. But I didn't know why. When Jessie and Danny came, she altered her route to include Wind House. And then I made it a point to find out why. Danny had to be protected. He is the last male in the family lineage."

"But how could you do that, Nita?" Jessie asked.

The old woman smiled. "I know I seem like an ancient, but I'm not illiterate. I went to our local newspaper office and went through the archives. I made the connection with Ben Thrasher and Jessie, and then I wondered about Sarah. I couldn't find her in any published work so I turned to the Internet—because a few years ago I'd hired Arthur Bing at the newspaper office to teach me about computers."

"You use a computer?" This time it was Clarice who was surprised.

The old woman grinned, relaxing her dour expression. "I use Arthur's from time to time. How do you think I kept up with some things in your life, Clarice?—and in Jessie's? Surely you didn't believe I would see you safely off the island and then forget about you? I've tracked you over the years, never intending to interfere with your lives. In later years the Internet helped me do that."

"So you knew who Ben was?" Jessie asked softly.

"Yes, I knew. I cross-referenced his name with Sarah Rawls and came up with a match, even though it was an innocent seeming communication on Internet forums. I followed the threads backward and realized there'd been more. He was seducing women."

"Son of a gun," Hank said. "So you already knew about his earlier connection to Jessie, and saw a similar pattern?"

She nodded. "I realized this woman, Sarah, was unhinged when she suddenly pretended to be pregnant. I knew she was a threat to Lynda Thrasher because of her fixation on Ben, and then I understood that she believed Jessie and Danny were also in her way. So I had to take action."

"So you used the old tunnel?" Clarice suggested.

Nita nodded. "I had to, and the passage into the house."

"What?" Jessie cried.

"I'll show you, Jessie," Nita said. "You were never in danger in this house, at least not after you changed the locks and the key she had no longer worked. Sarah had looked at this house when your uncle thought he could sell it, and she knew about the secret room in the basement, but not about the tunnel. The secret places were once well known to the family. Your grandmother and I used the tunnel to the beach every day back then, before there was a cliff path with steps. Anything you might have heard was me, protecting you, or Tsonoqua trying to warn you."

Jessie exhaled a long breath. "But I was scared to death, Nita. Was it you that last night when Danny had a nightmare?"

She nodded again. "I wanted him to come with me then. The woman was outside in the woods and I didn't know what she was up to." She hesitated. "Now that you know the secret places you will never be frightened again."

"Did it ever occur to you to tell me what was happening?" Jessie asked.

Nita's gaze was direct. "Would you have believed me?"

Jessie held her eyes, but was the first to look away.

"Enough said," Clarice interrupted. "Explain the old tunnel—and the passageway I didn't know about."

"The tunnel goes from behind the secret room down to the beach. The passage starts at the top of the tunnel, a staircase to a second floor closet."

Jessie gasped. "There's a secret passage behind the secret room?"

Hank put down his glass. "Surely you didn't access the house when Jessie and Danny were in it?"

"Yes, I did, that last night. But I frightened Danny and he thought I was a scary black figure."

Jessie pushed back her chair. "My God, Nita. Why would you terrify us like that?"

"Because you were in danger and I wanted to make you safe." For the first time she lowered her eyes. "I was wrong. I didn't mean to terrify you, I only intended to protect you. Then I had no option but to remove Danny— because I believed Sarah would harm him. But I had no proof so I acted to be on the safe side."

A stunned silence went by.

"Justice has been done," Hank said finally. "We'll all get past this, and go on with our lives."

Jessie nodded, as did the others. And then they had dessert and coffee.

They were free to go on with their lives. Jessie's emotional baggage had been extricated. Several days later the DNA test proved that Danny was not Ben's son. She decided that she liked the island and her ancient roots, that Tsonoqua was benign, at least to her favored family. She smiled to herself, knowing the thought was silly, even as it was comforting.

"The island was a good place to raise a son," Hank assured her. She agreed. Even her mother finally agreed to that, reinforced by the calming presence of Nita. Her mom agreed to spend half of the year on Cliff Island, the other half in Mendocino.

The past was finally in the past and Jessie was free to think about another relationship. With Hank? she wondered.

It was a possibility that intrigued her—and she suspected it did him as well. But she would just have to see what the future held in store for them. That was good enough for now.

Only time could tell.